Raindrops and Sycamores

Mary Jane Butler

First published 2021

Publishing partner: Paragon Publishing, Rothersthorpe

ISBN 978-1-78222-857-8

Book design, layout and production management by Into Print
www.intoprint.net
01604 832149

Part One

I GET CONFUSED sometimes from looking at the world from so many perspectives. My responses to people and situations become so diffused that I'm often accused of not listening, or indeed not caring. It must be the manifestation of the way I listen that annoys people. I consider myself a good listener overall, but I'm not good at small talk. Funny how I'm in trouble now for saying too much; my girlfriend is giving me the silent treatment; I guess it's her way of punishing me.

We first met at a book launch in Triskel Arts; she was talking to Diarmuid Ó Buachalla as I came in. I was immediately struck at how attractive she was. Diarmuid was making her laugh. I watched as she gathered her beautiful red hair into a tossed pile only to fall around her again when she laughed. Making my way over eventually, Diarmuid was saying something about the moon, and something about a goddess.

"Ah, Piers, there you are…thought you were never coming," he smirked. I knew then he'd spotted me observing them; he never misses a trick. "Have you met Catriona?" he asked, knowing full well I hadn't.

"I've been hearing all about you," she said with a wide smile.

"I hope he's telling you good things about me."

"Ah, mostly," she said mischievously, raising her eyebrows.

"Watch yourself, Cantwell, she's a Taurus!" Diarmuid said. "Piers is a Cancer… soft and temperamental… a moon person don't you know." Getting no reaction, he added "But then again, sure aren't we *all* soft and temperamental?" Diarmuid's dabbling in astrology amuses me because he gets so many things wrong; it doesn't seem to matter because his eccentric and embracing personality usually wins people over. "Catriona is a musician, Piers. I had the great pleasure of hearing her play recently… we had a great night, didn't we, Catriona?"

"We did, we did… you weren't bad yourself," she said. I knew she was being gracious, having heard his tin-whistle playing more times than I care to remember.

As if reading my mind Diarmuid said, "I love the music you know, but it wouldn't be my forte, Catriona."

"Where was that?" I enquired.

"The Art Hive in MacCurtain Street," she answered.

"Tigh Filí they're calling it now, Catriona, it's hard to keep up," Diarmuid laughed.

Ó Buachalla once told me it was the process of doing something which was important. He liked to paint, liked to play music, liked to write, but he just happened to be a good poet. Creativity, he said was often strangled by our endeavours for perfection; humility and openness were the secret!

He surprised me then by singing my praises, saying I was a fine poet, a unique individual. "But he has a long way to go before he comes up to my standard though!" He added.

"You're very modest," Catriona said nudging him playfully and looked at me to see how I was taking it. I didn't react. Ó Buachalla never bothers me: he's erudite but never elitist, in fact, he has helped me out many times. She seemed a bit thrown when neither of us said anything and I thought I should say something friendly but Diarmuid beat me to it.

"How's that sister of yours, the fiddle player? Maura, isn't it?"

"Moira! Ah, she's great altogether … playing away."

"And a fine singer too, by all accounts."

"Yes, Moira is the real talent in the family."

Diarmuid enquired about a certain tune he'd heard her sister play and from then on it was all about tunes and instruments. She became quite animated talking about the music and I was strangely drawn. I suddenly felt uncomfortable realising I'd been staring intently at her, and more importantly that she was fully aware of it. I was glad to excuse myself when Claire Riley arrived.

"Where the hell were you, Thursday?" Claire complained but I had no idea what she was talking about. "The Spailpín! The Yarn Spinners…you said you'd come down."

"Oh, that! I only said I might!"

"Yeah, but I wouldn't't have gone if I knew you weren't coming… it's not my kind of thing."

"I take it you didn't enjoy it then."

"Ah, 'twas alright I suppose," she conceded.

"How did you get on with the magazine," I asked to lift the mood.

"Who's yer wan," Claire said, looking over my shoulder.

"Who?"

"The redhead! As if ya didn't' know. Will ya look at Ó Buachalla fawning on her. God, he could be her grandfather!"

"He's just being friendly, Claire… anyway, it's none of our business."

"Oh, I don't know about that, pet, she seems very interested in you…the poor girl can't take her eyes off you." She laughed at me when I refused to be baited. "Yeah, the magazine… they took four… and I gave them, Wolf, as well."

"What! After all you said."

"Well, they saw it and they liked it… sure maybe I wanted it out there," she admitted. The poem was about an escaped wolf which sadly ended up being shot. (We are both interested in the wolf in Irish folklore and how Cromwell did his best to get rid of them.) Claire thought her poem was over emotional and not in her usual style. I advised her to write another poem but she never did.

I couldn't help looking over when I heard Catriona and Diarmuid laughing. Claire had no time to tease me however, because a guy in a long black coat suddenly seized her arm, his loud voice attracting attention. She stuck out her tongue and turned her eyes in jest as he hauled her away. Even though I'd learnt to keep out of Claire's affairs, I thought I should go after them just in case, but at that very moment Catriona Lynch moved across the room exorcising any other concerns.

"Mesmerising isn't she?" Diarmuid said sneaking up on me. I turned round to his grinning mug. The bastard reads me like a book.

"Christ, what is she doing with him?" I exclaimed when I saw Healy.

"Sure, she's always with the divine cultured one…he needs the stunner don't you know… reminiscent of the Pre-Raphaelites, I suppose." He was joking, but I couldn't help thinking that she'd suit Healy's image alright; she'd certainly compensate for his constipated personality. "This vino is toilet cleaner, Piers… get me another for the love of god before it's all gone," Diarmuid chortled to divert me.

In the Corner House a few weeks later, I was flicking through a tabloid from the bar when Catriona Lynch tapped me on the shoulder and congratulated me on winning a poetry prize. I was about to ask where she'd heard about it but asked instead if she'd join me for a drink.

"Yes, I'd love to… I'll just get my bag," she said. It was only then I saw Ger Healy and Chris Donovan. Donovan was smirking down at me as I handed the paper back to the barman. Healy was all smiles talking to Catriona but his face turned to stone as she walked away.

I suggested we sit over by the fireplace because I wanted to talk to her away from the bar. Catriona is a music student so naturally we talked about music. Beethoven, Haydn and Mozart were high on her list of composers; she loved Irish music, both traditional and contemporary; two uncles on her mother's side were traditional fiddlers. She played guitar and wrote songs, mainly on the piano. "But I'm not as good as Tori Amos, though," she said laughing. "She plays two pianos on stage… can you imagine." I had no idea then who Tori Amos was!

I took the opportunity to talk about Wagner, about how he had been much maligned and misunderstood, how he had wonderfully merged poetry and music and about how much I admired him for taking risks. "But wasn't he very against the Jews, though!" She remarked.

I went on a rant then saying it wasn't Wagner's fault that Die Meistersinger was Hitler's favourite opera or that people thought the portrayal of Mime and Alberich was anti-Semitic. I told her I believed it was his wife Cosima, who was the anti-Semite. I added that if Wagner really disliked Jews, why would Isaac de Camondo, of the famous Jewish banking family in Paris, go to meet him with Delibes in 1876, the year the Bayreuth Opera house was inaugurated and why would de Camondo go back six years later to hear, Parsifal. Throughout,

Catriona smiled with sensuous lips and soft eyes, but I could tell she wasn't a Wagnerite. Realising my intensity, I tried to lighten the mood by telling her that Woody Allen said he couldn't listen to any more Wagner because he was getting the urge to conquer Poland. She didn't laugh. I didn't tell it very well. I should never tell jokes!

Catriona sighed at the mention of her studies and complained of the fate of the students, exiled from their true home on Union Quay, having to endure Moore's Hotel and other scattered locations. She decried the fact that she will nearly be finished by the time the new school is up and running. "But sure 'twill be great for the new students, anyway," she said brightening again.

This simple remark penetrated my defences. I became keenly aware of her lively eyes, her endearing throaty voice. All the while, I had an urge to brush an errant strand of hair from her engaging face. I imagined my fingers on her white neck; I imagined kissing her inviting kissable mouth. All at once her mannerisms seemed familiar and it became evident that I had been observing this woman for some time, but in that moment too, came the awareness that she was very young.

* * *

I had arranged to meet Catriona in a new bar on MacCurtain Street. I was running late and only had time for a sandwich before jumping in the shower. I hate rushing, it makes my heart race, so I don't know why then I allowed myself to be distracted by a poem. My poems are like fledglings never quite ready to leave the nest but this one, about my father, was going further and further from the spark thoughts that inspired it. I picked it up for a quick read over, but things jumped out immediately.

Hot and out of breath, I entered a very noisy pub and pushed my way through the crowd. Catriona, at the bar with Joe Collins, spotted me and came and kissed me. I expected her to be annoyed that I was late. "We're over here," she said leading me to a table where a big bulk of a guy was about to sit down. Catriona, thinking it enough of a claim to have thrown her jacket there earlier, argued her case. I was relieved but slightly amused at how easily the lad capitulated.

At the bar, I checked my phone to see if Ó Buachalla left a message but also to avoid Collins, who always just happens to be around. I wasn't going to make it any easier for him.

Back with the drinks, I noticed Catriona throwing looks in Joe's direction and fearing she was going to call him down, I launched an explanation as to why I was late.

"Sure, you weren't too late," she said. "I think ye writers are away in another world most of the time anyway." I was being compared to Donovan and Healy no doubt.

"Sure, aren't musicians the same," I said for the sake of equilibrium, "I suppose it's a necessary thing…we have to create a new world to overcome the misery of this one." When I saw the hitherto carefree expression fade from her face, I knew I'd gone too far.

"You should have waited for the next bus," she said good-naturedly.

"If I'd waited for the next bus, I'd have been too late …can't keep a lovely lady waiting!" Catriona laughed heartily saying it sounded like something from Jane Austen. It did sound archaic but at least she was smiling again. She began telling me then about a play she'd seen with Donovan up in Firkin. I had to strain my ears over the increasing cacophony which didn't seem to bother her in the least. If I hadn't been so tired, I would have suggested going up to the Cork Arms. The play I was familiar with, apart from the fact that it was Donovan she went with, I had little interest. Her voice became a distant drone as words and measures inundated my brain: something new was formulating, something I couldn't believe I'd missed.

"You're not listening, Piers," Catriona said cannily and took off up to the bar which quickly brought me back from the ether. Collins! The fucker was making her laugh! The bottle-green velvet top she was wearing emphasised her breasts. She doesn't even have to try to be alluring. Mentally I began to undress her, imagining her fair skin, her nakedness, her ultimate surrender. My friend, Barry Stack, thinks the strip is more exciting than seeing a woman naked. He came to that conclusion from life drawing classes. I'm not so sure about that though, given my experience with Catriona.

Coming back finally, she placed my pint down awkwardly, spilling creamy froth on my hand. "I'm sorry, pet...I don't know what's wrong with me," she said with an edgy laugh.

"No harm done," I said wiping my fingers. I expected her to say something but she just sat there without a word or touching her drink. "A penny for them," I asked.

"Hmmm," she said, as if waking from a dream.

"Is there something wrong?"

"No! I was just thinking...ah, it's nothing...just something Joe mentioned about Moira." She waved her hand in agitation, dismissing whatever it was. "Where were we," she said and resumed her account of the play.

She could talk to Collins about whatever it was, yet not to me, and now I had to listen about the bloody play again. There was just too much useless detail. I just snapped. "Ah fuck the play, Catriona, it's a piece of crap!" I blurted. She looked at me expressionless for a second, then scrunched up her face so tight it made her look like an old woman. I reached for her hand, saying I was sorry but she recoiled as if I were a leper.

"I'm going to the loo," she said, standing up suddenly and taking her jacket from the back of the chair. She returned quickly enough but with the jacket on, zipped up like armour against me. "I'm going home!" She announced so forcefully I was taken aback. She battled her way to the door, unaware of Collins calling and waving like a schoolboy. Collins! I could just imagine the grapevine!

I should never have spoken to her like that. I should have explained that I thought the play banal and clichéd. Better still, I should have kept my mouth shut. The big mistake, of course, was not going after her.

* * *

I work in a medical supplies company - three-day long shifts rather than a full week because it gives me time for other things. I turn up on time, maintain the strict hygiene code and do the job as best I can. Sorting tiny objects under a screen all day isn't the most fulfilling work. I appreciate that these devices help prolong people's lives, but I can't get excited about it. I try not to get bored by concentrating on what's in my head: inspiration often comes between batches of stents and tiny balloons. The money of course is the primary objective which enables me to support my daughter and to keep a roof over my head.

I met her mother, Helen Kearns, when I was teaching in a secondary school in Blackrock; she worked in advertising, still does. It was Helen who pursued me, as I recall, but I must admit, it gratified me at the time. I was drinking with Toby Holland in Jury's when I spotted her. She was lively and good looking. Toby, sick of me eyeing her, urged me to make a move. Making a move as he called it, was something he was expert at. He flirted with the nearest females, just to prove a point. He found out from the woman he was chatting up that they were all off to a party in Ardfoyle Crescent, near Parc Uí Chaoimh, but she didn't know the exact address.

Toby got a supply of beer from the Hotel Manager, whom he knew through the bank, and we left straight away so we'd get there before the others. In the taxi, I said that if we had any sense, we'd be going down the other side of the Lee to his place: Toby lives on the Lower Glanmire Road near the railway line.

We loitered like spies under scented trees trying to guess which house; we both picked the one most brightly lit and so it was. When the petite blonde and her entourage arrived, we trailed behind them through redbrick pillars up to an oval stained-glass door. To this day, Helen doesn't know we gate-crashed that party.

We were only going out a few months when Helen got pregnant. I was stunned! I thought she'd taken care of that side of things. I thought it strange how calmly she dealt with the situation considering how much her job meant to her. The problem for me, however, was that Helen believed marriage to be the logical follow up. No laissez faire then! No way was I getting married! After much compromise, we rented a house in South View Terrace, not far from St. Finbarr's Hospital, which was ideally situated for both our workplaces. It was a bargain rent wise and had a rear garden. I especially liked that I could walk into town in about twenty minutes or less. I liked Mr. Cotter too, an elderly man who was delighted to have us because he was afraid the house would be broken into and used for drugs when it was unoccupied.

Helen wasn't as happy: the house was small and if the truth be told, not fashionable enough. Her passion for furniture and fabrics had to be put on hold. I think the only reason she agreed to move in was because she saw it as a steppingstone to something better. But overall, she settled in reasonably well and worked right up to the last three weeks of the pregnancy.

Our baby girl was born across in St. Finbarr's on the 25th of June. When I first held her, I was terrified. She was christened Rose Kearns after Helen's paternal grandmother; I had assumed she'd be Cantwell but Helen made it quite clear that would be the case only if we were married.

Helen and I stayed together for a little over three years, our relationship never developing into anything beyond what we initially had, which was not enough. We argued a lot, sometimes over silly things, like the time she ordered a suite of furniture that was simply too big. Luckily, I had the sense to check it out before it was delivered. I suggested we buy a smaller sofa or two side chairs instead but that was knocked on the head. Later she said the sensible thing would be to buy a place of our own, seeing that we were both working. I suspected that the whole furniture thing was to drive home how small the house was. Alarm bells rang in my head: I could see myself in some suburban estate shackled by debt and custom; I could be stuck teaching teenagers until I was an old man.

I barely looked at the brochures Helen put in front of me; she accused me of being selfish, of not thinking of Rose's future. To be honest, the only future I worried about was my own, and being pushed in a direction where I unequivocally did not want to go, caused me to panic. I felt I was being devoured by someone else's reality and all my dreams were vaporising around me. However, in a bizarre way, it acted as a catalyst because the more pressure put upon me, the more I retreated into a world of my own. I wrote quite a lot, read books, listened to music. I began to look at the world more from my own perspective. I started to call my daughter Rosie, which had at least two syllables. Whenever Helen talked about moving, I changed the subject.

My first collection of poetry was published by Wasserman Books shortly after Rosie's second birthday. One established poet had the grace to comment: 'Among the standing army of Irish poets, Piers Cantwell is a unique voice. His work is texturally clean with an abundance of newly minted images and metaphors. I look forward to the appearance of his next collection.' Helen was happy for me initially, but it wasn't long before she realised there was little money in poetry and I was spending less and less time with her. That was unintentional on my part, it was just the way things went. Occasionally, I accompanied her to work functions which often involved clients. I enjoyed the food and wine but didn't find the people as interesting as she did. I had to listen to a lot of corporate talk: aspirations to have property in Dubai; the killings to be made in Poland and Croatia; how Beijing was the place to invest. Invitations to these events ceased when it was clear I wouldn't provide the degree of feigned enthusiasm that Helen required of me. In comparison, I took her to book launches that offered plonk, if you were lucky, no food, and people she wasn't too enamoured of.

The last play we saw together was in the Half Moon; admittedly it wasn't great, but all that concerned Helen was the place itself; she swore she'd never set foot in that "stuffy claustrophobic hole ever again."

Helen didn't like Claire Riley and was often rude, which was a problem for me. She maintained Claire had designs on me. I genuinely tried to reassure her on that score! She didn't like Ó Buachalla either, saying he was an attention seeker and that the way he dressed was a disgrace. I often think Diarmuid is on a different plane to the rest of us; he only cares about his painting and his writing. Helen stopped coming to literary events and I suspect it was a relief not only to me.

The final straw for Helen was when I decided to quit teaching. I was sick and tired of trying to relate to hormonal buzzing teenagers, I needed a less stressful job, one I could leave behind at the end of the day. True, the long holidays enabled me to look after Rosie, but I couldn't let that single benefit chain me. Naively, I thought Helen would understand!

* * *

Besides my daughter I love my grandmother more than anyone. It was she who instilled the love of poetry in me. Nan can recite Gray's Elegy, which is impressive, well most of it, what's a few verses here and there – there must be nearly thirty. I've no great retention myself. Jeanette Winterson described herself as a walking poetry book: she learns a new poem every two weeks and is never stuck for anything to read on a train because it's all in her head.

Claire thinks poems should be allowed permeate the subconscious in the way songs do. She believes songwriters to be the real poets: "They're freer and more honest than those up-your-arse academics anyway!" (Claire has a hang up about not having gone to university.) Her father told her that listening to Bob Dylan was like tripping on words and images. He admitted he didn't always understand the lyrics but songs like, *Visions of Johanna*, *Tambourine Man*, and *Tangled up in Blue* for example, sounded bloody good to him. Claire thinks there is too much dissecting and analysing of poetry in schools, and once suggested it shouldn't be taught in schools at all. We disagreed on that one. I conceded that the approach could be better but I for one, was glad poetry was on the curriculum.

I'm free until Tuesday so I'm taking Rosie to see Nan. Haven't seen much of Rosie recently because Helen has been out with her mother a lot. I'm meeting them in Scoozi's which is a bit odd – we usually only go there on Saturdays or bank holidays.

I'm relieved to find them already seated in the section they prefer. I was to be early for that very reason. Rosie, busy colouring, scrambles off her chair when she sees me. I scoop her up and her arms fly around my neck; we have our bear hug; she giggles when I tickle her under the arm.

"Don't excite her, Piers," Helen implores. Rosie pushes me away when I try to help her up on her chair.

"Sorry I'm late… I had to park down Penrose Quay," I explain. Helen smiles, knowing I will do anything to avoid indoor car parks.

"We came on the bus… I just couldn't face the Friday traffic…"

"You, on a bus!"

"Number eight" Rosie interjects, drawing an imaginary figure eight in the air. "I liked the bus, Daddy."

"Did you, pet?… do you remember the last time you were on a bus?"

"She wouldn't remember that… she was only three."

"I do remember, Mummy!" Rosie attests making Helen smile. "Look Daddy!" She says upending the contents of a Winnie-the-Pooh bag. "Granny gave me them." Rosie then presents each item for inspection: a toy phone; a pink comb; a box with gold and silver glitter and a multicoloured purse.

"They're lovely, Rosie…Granny is very good to…"

"And this," she adds, opening the purse and taking out a ten euro note.

"My, we are rich… you'll be able to buy me a pint." I say and Rosie beams. I know it's a silly thing to have said, but the way Helen is looking at me is uncalled for.

Helen smiles at my predictability when I order the chilli burger and remind the waiter to bring the condiments.

Coming out of Winthrop Street on to Patrick Street, my heart leaps when I see Catriona looking over at us from the Savoy. Before I can wave, she looks away and hastens her step. She could have acknowledged me, at least! Helen is saying something handing me Rosie's bag, but her words evaporate as my eyes follow Catriona down Patrick Street.

Rosie bombards me with questions on the drive out of town. She's excited that we're going to stop in Youghal for a paddle in the sea. "And then we'll go to Nana's."

"No, Nana's tomorrow."

"Why can't I sleep in Nana's?"

"Because we're going to Granny's for our tea and she'd be disappointed if we didn't stay." Rosie accepts the situation and holds her doll, Angie, up to the window.

I don't know when the precedent of staying in my mother's house, when I have Rosie with me, was set but my mother expects it now. I'd much rather stay with my grandmother. My Life seems to be full of bloody compromises.

Rosie falls asleep outside Killagh and now I don't know what to do. Nan says never wake a sleeping child if you don't have to. I pull in for a while but she's dead to the world. Nothing for it now but to keep going which means getting to my mother's earlier than planned.

* * *

Although nothing has ever been said, I feel I'm a disappointment to my mother. Refusing to marry the mother of my child, a transgression indeed, but worse, I turned my back on teaching after her sacrifices to send me to university. If people ask, she tells them I am writing a book. Poetry is never mentioned or that I'm no longer teaching. Evelyn is a nurse in Waterford, so there's no problem talking about her. My brother, Ivor, left home after his Leaving Cert and went to England and there has been no contact since. If people ask about him, she says he's working in London. Evelyn and I never talk about Ivor to our mother because she gets her back up. She's probably riddled with guilt for having been so hard on him.

When my father died of a heart attack, my mother acted as if it were a personal betrayal. I resented her crying at the graveside as if everything were about her. I was so upset I couldn't even go to the hotel with the family afterwards. I wandered around the town feeling like an orphan, putting my head down whenever I saw anyone I knew until exhaustion and the cold drove me home.

Looking out at the trees from my bedroom window, I couldn't stop thinking of my dad down in that muddy hole in the ground. He was dead, yet I couldn't fully grasp that I would never see him again. I felt more anger than sorrow at that moment and turning from the window I ran amok scattering everything before me and fell on the bed sobbing.

I was roused from my anguish by a knock on the door and my mother calling me. I didn't answer her! She opened the door anyway and looked around at the state of the room. From the doorway, her consoling words were that life throws difficult situations at us sometimes, but that we had to be strong; she would be depending on me now because I was the eldest. I was fourteen! My world had just fallen apart!

It seemed to me that my mother never reacted to anything in a normal manner, it was either completely over the top or subdued indifference. My father had been a buffer between us but after he died there were constant rows.

Even though I was reared a catholic, I got a hard time when I first attended secondary school by those who knew my father was Church of Ireland. I was a 'Fucking Prod' and other more ridiculous names. Any excuse to bully the first years I suppose, but I took it all to heart at the time. There was a lot of psychological stripping at that school; I guess I was spared to some degree because of my father's position in Waterford Glass and the fact that Doctor Kelly was a friend of the family. It upset me, however, when my friend Paul was constantly picked on. Paul never had the materials he needed. I was forever giving him my compass and protractor in maths class, and paper and pens in English. I remember buying him battered sausages and chips when some of us sneaked downtown at lunch time. We got caught once, but it was Paul who got flak for weeks because he was deemed the ringleader.

That first year, I got a bad school report. My mother took it badly, slamming and banging things. "Do you want to be stuck in this godforsaken hole for the rest of your life," she roared, bursting into tears. I was used to her outbursts, but what puzzled me was why she hated Dungarvan so much.

My father was handed the report before he had time to take off his coat. He read it over and folded it into his pocket without saying a word. "Is that it?" My mother cried, "No wonder he's the way he is. That boy can do no wrong at all in your eyes! All his teachers comment on how lazy he is." I was affronted, I may have seemed indifferent, but I never saw myself as lazy.

"Let's have our dinner in peace, Mary...I'll talk to him later," he said. My mother mumbled something and was turning away when my father put his arms around her waist and kissed the back of her neck. I was confused, I thought she was annoying him. I remember this vividly because outward affection was rare in our house.

Later, I got the lecture: I was an intelligent boy, it was my future which was at stake; how did I manage to get such a poor report? Was I going out of my way to be difficult? I wanted to tell him then how unhappy I was at that school, but he looked so tired, all I felt was shame for letting him down. He died a year and a half later and it was some consolation that my efforts to improve had pleased him.

* * *

Sometimes, I wonder if my mother is all there. When I think of that day – I was about eight or nine - I came home from school with the neck of my jumper torn and blood on my shirt. She seemed okay at first when I told her I was in a fight. "You shouldn't be fighting, Piers," is all she said but when I told her with whom I was fighting, her face hardened. I stood there amazed at the sudden change. In hindsight, I think she took this for defiance because next thing she pulled me by the scruff of the neck into the kitchen. I still remember the whacks of the wooden spoon and her shouting, "how many times have I told you to keep away from people like that!" The strange thing was, I had no memory of her ever telling me any such thing!

Only for Nan coming I think she'd have killed me. But then there was a new agony: when Nan saw the red marks on my legs, she lost her temper. They began arguing and shouting but the thing I remember most was my mother accusing Nan of mollycoddling me and Nan saying she wouldn't have to mollycoddle anyone if she treated her children like any normal person. I'd never seen Nan so angry. Getting my mother into trouble upset me more than the hiding and I ran outside crying and sat on the stairs with my hands over my ears. That was how my father found me when he opened the hall door.

My father never once looked at my mother during dinner. Evelyn wasn't there for some reason. Ivor was the only one to speak and neither paid him any attention and that unnerved me so much, I couldn't swallow my food. I escaped upstairs as soon as I could. As I lay on my pillow my heart was thumping in my ear and I thought, what if my heart stopped, would she be sorry then?

When Ivor wandered in later, all fresh and powdery in his pyjamas, I told him to fuck off! He climbed up on the bed regardless and rolled his truck over the ridges of the bedspread. Suddenly, I was gripped by a new fear: what if he repeated the word; she'd know it was me!

Ivor vroomed his truck over me until he got tired; he fell asleep beside me and the warmth of his body was a comfort. When I woke in the night, I was under the covers. Ivor was in his own bed.

* * *

My father's office was on the third floor. I liked looking out the window. I remember the smell of the leather chair and the light shining through the blue glass paperweight on his desk. It was always a Saturday morning that we went there and we never stayed long.

Our outdoor adventures were the best of all, wandering through woods, along riverbanks and beaches. By the age of seven, I could identify most trees: ash; elm; sycamore; beech and oak. I also knew hawthorn, elderberry, and blackthorn. In first class, I won a prize (six purple-and-gold-wrapped chocolate sweets) for naming all the leaves on the nature table and knowing that hurleys were made from the ash tree. When I was twelve, I was amazed to discover that our neighbour, Jack Penrose, made wine from elderberries and sloes and even from the petals of furze and dandelions.

Strange how an event, one thought unpleasant at the time, has become a cherished memory: my father and I, caught in a sudden downpour, dashed for shelter under large sycamores. The heavy rain eventually penetrated our green canopy, with large droplets plopping onto my face and neck. The rain stopped as suddenly as it began but to my great annoyance my father remained under the trees. Impatient for our destination, I pulled on his arm to come away; what that destination was I can't remember now. "Trees are so beautiful after rain, don't you think," Dad said absently and smiled when he saw me shrug my shoulders. "When you're older…if you're ever unhappy, just come to a place like this…you'll be amazed how troubles fade away."

The incident has metamorphosed into an adult's retrospective view: my father drawing me close, his left arm across my chest, his right hand resting on my shoulder; the sound of the rain beating on the leaves; birds flitting overhead; wet verdant odours; the serenity of his breathing and the feeling of protection from the whole world as I leaned against him.

I cherish the memories of times spent with my father: Ardmore strand – the sun, a giant orange-red ball hanging low, almost playful with its reflection on the water and my father standing serenely until its farewell peep on the horizon. Dad laughed when Evelyn asked if the sun went to sleep in the seabed; he said the sun never sleeps and that when we are in bed at night, the sun is waking people up at the other side of the world.

I remember my first sunrise: it seemed like the middle of the night; Evelyn and I had our jackets and hats on; the grass was wet even though it hadn't rained; we were to be very quiet because the birds were about to wake up and this was their special time. We heard little twitters at first, then loud caws from the big trees beyond the houses. I thought the crows were funny but I had to stop myself from laughing. Birdsong increased as light spread across the sky. I kept my eyes peeled on a valley of golden light between the hills and was getting quite impatient until Evelyn pointed to the bayoneting gold from a patch of broken cloud far to the left. "Don't stare at it…you'll go blind!" She warned. I closed my eyes fearing it was already too late.

Dad told us ancient peoples worshiped the sun and that he could understand why. He believed light was a manifestation of god. It all sounded wondrously strange to a little boy, who didn't quite understand but loved to hear such things all the same.

After Ivor was born, we were taken out more often. I still remember my mother's moods: she cried a lot and wouldn't answer when we spoke to her. The outings were probably Dad's way of protecting us. I've often wondered since how he coped. The only time I remember him being stressed was coming up to budget time; he was chief accountant. I think his pressure vessel was music; he'd shut himself up in our sitting room listening to his favourite pieces. Under no circumstances were we to bother him.

We usually stayed in the kitchen which ran the full back length of the house. The range was kept lighting winter and summer, so it was always nice and cosy. The TV was there too. Our dining room was rarely used, except at Christmas or special occasions. My mother used it for her sewing and would sometimes go in there to read when she wanted to get away from us.

I often sneaked into my father when no one was around. Sometimes he'd hardly even notice me, other times he'd hold a finger to his lips; it might be Mozart or Schubert or Evelyn Rothwell playing Haydn or Pergolesi concertos: the oboe was his favourite instrument. According to my mother, Dad loved Evelyn Rothwell's playing so much he called his daughter after her! (Rothwell now known as Barbirolli since her husband's death in 1970). He liked sopranos, like Joan Sutherland and Elizabeth Schwarzkopf, but most of all, he loved Maria Callas and agreed with Tullio Serafin who said, "This woman can sing anything written for the female voice." He loved Tenors too, Jussi Bjorling, John McCormack, Caruso and many more; I particularly remember Joseph Schmidt singing, 'Tiritomba'; seemingly I used to do 'my special dance' to it around the room but thankfully I have no memory of that. I think it was from my time spent in there with him that I learnt to be silent.

Sunday mornings were different, then it was Bach's fugues or Beethoven's Ninth. I knew instinctively to keep my distance. My mother has often claimed since that his solemn Sunday music was a substitute for religion.

I was however, allowed in one Sunday. I'd been in bed for over a week. Doctor Kelly had been and put a cold stethoscope on my chest. Dad came up with a drink for me and was delighted that I wanted to get up. I have no idea where the rest of the family were. He took me downstairs, propped me up with cushions and tucked a blanket around me. I felt cock of the walk, all snug with a warm drink and better still, I had Dad all to myself and music to boot.

The lowest bass note in the introduction to Bach's Toccata and Fugue in D minor is indelible in my soul: the excitement of the deep resonance that seemed to vibrate right inside my ribcage. No wonder then that Bach's fugues have become a ritual in my own life: I inherited the records and am taken to new heights every time by the deft fingers and feet of Lionel Rogg.

Wagner stated that the true spirit of English musical culture was bound up with the spirit of English Protestantism, that the oratorio attracted the public more than opera and that listening to an oratorio was almost as good as going to church. I wonder did my father ever listen to Wagner. There was no Wagner in his collection.

* * *

I'm delighted to see Evelyn's car in the driveway, it's been a while since I saw her. I no sooner have the engine turned off when my mother appears and says, "Ah, she's asleep. Don't leave her in the car!" I feel under regulation straight away. Rosie wakes on being moved and insists on getting out herself. A wisp of hair clings to her flushed moist cheek as she stands precariously on the gravel. I ignore my mother's fussing and take Rosie's hand and head inside to the bathroom. Rosie sits up on the toilet bowl to pee. She looks so small with her little stockinged legs dangling. Then she washes her hands and smells the soap, which is in the shape of an oyster shell. I know from experience not to rush her. She strains even further on her tiptoes to turn off the tap and looks at me with childish triumph. I turn the tap back on, moisten a flannel and wash her face to freshen her up.

Evelyn kisses me on the cheek. Her thick black hair is cut in a bob which doesn't really suit her. Rosie comes to life with Evelyn's attentions and is thrilled to get a swing around the room. Mother looks on poker faced. I guess she'd prefer if Evelyn took this activity outside but then there's a hint of a smile. Evelyn falls back on the sofa laughing and Rosie sits beside her.

"Have you any kiss for Gran," Mam asks, and Rosie reluctantly approaches. I'm a little wounded by the awkwardness, it's never like this with Granny Kearns. Rosie knows her better, of course. Yet, I don't think that's the reason, I believe Rosie knows Granny Cantwell is not a happy person, and more insightfully, that she disapproves of her daddy.

Rosie returns and sits on my lap and is a bit clingy until she spots the cat, whereby she frees herself impatiently from my arms.

"Be careful, Rosie, he's not too friendly," my mother warns.

Rosie pats Smuts' head and reaches in further to stroke his fur. I'm nervous now! When Smuts is under a chair it's like, Do Not Disturb! He's quite passive, however, and I take a sigh of relief.

"Look Daddy!" Rosie says when Smuts yawns, "He only has some teeth." When Smuts suddenly spreads his claws, Rosie retreats skittishly into my arms. She gets further excited when he comes out, humps his back, stretches his back leg with a shiver and struts off towards the kitchen. My mother follows eager to facilitate his every whim.

"I didn't expect you to be here, Evelyn." I say sitting back on the sofa.

"I finished early … glad I came now!" she says getting up and opening the window. "How've you been? How's the writing going?"

"Okay…haven't been doing that much lately…many distractions!" I can't tell her what the distractions are because Rosie is all ears.

"I called to Nan earlier…she was all talk about ye coming. You're the whitehaired boy alright," Evelyn grins. Rosie is looking puzzled because I have dark hair. Evelyn jumps to mock attention when my mother calls us in for tea, saluting and marching forward with Rosie following behind.

The table is laden with brown bread, salads, and cold meats. The crystal cake stand with an array of cakes is a magnet for Rosie; Mam has had it for years but I think this is the first time Rosie has seen it. Rosie makes no protest when my mother helps her up on the chair.

Mam pours reddish gold tea from a large aluminium teapot and asks me if Rosie would like tea. Why can't she ask Rosie? For a quiet life, I ask Rosie if she wants tea. Not surprisingly she shakes her head and looks at me as if I should know better. I wink at her and she grins.

Mam gives Rosie orange juice; I'm surprised she has any. When Ivor wanted juice to take to school onetime, she gave him oranges. You can imagine what they were used for at lunch time.

My mother notices the food left on Rosie's plate and tells her to eat up. Rosie puts her hand on her tummy saying she has enough. "Have you room for a cake," Mam asks, thinking that's what she's after but Rosie shakes her head.

"She had a big lunch, Mam..."

"In Scoozi's," confirms Rosie, dragging the vowels.

"You might have one later," Mam says, forcing a smile, but I can tell she's annoyed. Evelyn, catching my eye, looks up to heaven.

"Thanks Mam...that was a lovely," I say and she brightens a little.

"Yes, very nice!" Evelyn concurs but is ignored.

My mother doesn't have a dishwasher, (bad for the environment she says). I offer to wash up but she won't hear of it. Evelyn never offers! Her excuse is that she'd never meet our mother's standards. There's a certain amount of truth in that, but Evelyn is generally impervious to my mother's criticisms.

My mother mutters under her breath when she sees the window open in the sitting room. "I opened it, Mam... it got a bit warm," Evelyn owns.

"Yes, but it will get cold! This house loses heat... and I had the attic insulated..."

"It's probably the walls...the solid blocks," I find myself saying but I really haven't a clue; I probably heard Uncle Tommy saying something to that effect. Mam nods, happy that someone is sympathetic to her problem. Mam turns on the TV for the news. News was like a sacrament in our old house, like they expected the outbreak of world war three any minute. I avoid news, if that's possible, in this media saturated world.

Rosie is thrilled when I suggest going for a walk and runs to the bedroom for her jacket. She beams with satisfaction when Evelyn admires the little ponies on the jacket pockets. She even lets Evelyn help zip her up and they both dash out the door in front of me.

High white clouds soar across a bright blue sky and the grass on the green is shivering silver in the light. Evelyn and Rosie are way ahead. I take my time, glad to have a minute to myself. Why didn't she wave back? Maybe she doesn't want to see me anymore. But if that were the case, she'd have no hesitation in saying so! But how can I know, I haven't seen her? I should have gone across to her, so what if Helen asked questions, it was a golden opportunity and I blew it!

"Daddy, come on," Rosie calls and I hasten my step. Evelyn and I give Rosie ups-a-daisies and she's thrilled to be jumping over actual daisies, even though their little heads are closed. It's all great fun until she spots a seagull ahead and takes off running.

"How are things Evelyn…anything exciting?"

"Don't know if you'd consider what I get up to exciting, Piers," Evelyn smirks.

"And how's Brian? Busy as ever on the farm I suppose."

"I haven't seen Brian in ages! Well, I've seen him, but we're just friends now," she says looking away. Rosie calls excitedly for us to see the seagull. "Well come on, daddy, what's keeping you," Evelyn laughs. The gull flies off at our approach causing Rosie to puff and raise her hands supinely.

"That child, where did ya get her?" Evelyn laughs.

"Lift me up, Evelyn," Rosie demands. Evelyn sits her up on a wall and we look out at the sea. I exhale deeply into the breeze. *Why is she torturing me?*

"You okay Piers?" Evelyn asks.

"Yeah, fine! Just thinking of something."

Rosie wants to walk along the wall. Evelyn is worried about the sheer drop on the other side, but I keep a tight hold of her as she walks fearlessly along. The wall gets higher as the path slopes downwards and I begin to worry too with my arm fully stretched but thankfully the wall soon meets a pillar. Rosie wants to walk back again but I flatly refuse, whereby she leaps trustingly into my arms without warning, raising the heart inside me.

Rosie gets more ups-a-daisies on the way back, after which she runs off wanting me to chase her. She giggles when I scoop her up but is impatient to be put down again. Before I do, I make her promise that she won't run off again; she does run off, but this time in the direction of home.

"How do you keep up with her?" Evelyn asks.

"I have to," I laugh. "She's a good kid really…just full of energy."

"But exhausting!"

"You'll get a taste of it when you have your own."

"I don't think that's likely to happen …"

"Sure, women all say that."

"Is that so?" Evelyn says, raising her eyebrows.

* * *

Evelyn and Rosie are talking and laughing in the bedroom. I should have prepared Evelyn for the bedtime ritual: Rosie will exact her full measure and more, and then Angie will be presented for her quota.

"She's a gas ticket," Evelyn says, finally coming out. "The odd things she comes out with…you'd never think she was only four."

I'm suddenly uneasy as to what those odd things might be. I'm rather relieved when Mam asks Evelyn if she is staying the night.

"I can't." Evelyn says, "In fact, I'd better be going… I'm on early tomorrow."

"Sure, it's early yet…we don't often see you," I interject.

"No, I'd better go before I get too tired," she says, gathering her belongings and kissing my mother goodbye. "I'll see you soon, Piers" she says and ruffles my hair as she passes out.

"I wonder what brought her," Mam says pensively, staring into the flames. "You never know what's going on with her!" The revving of Evelyn's engine draws Mam to the window. "Go out and help her, Piers, before she does damage," she pleads.

Such a fuss, there's enough room for a bus. I reverse my car out on to the road anyway. Evelyn backs out and gives a double beep. When she's out of sight I suddenly feel alone. I wish she could have stayed.

Rosie little head pops up when I look in on her. "When are we going to Nana's?"

"Straight after breakfast," I tell her and she turns in content.

"Is she settled?" Mam enquires.

"Yes…she'll soon be asleep."

"I find the sea air knocks them out. She's grown since we last saw her… mind you, she's on the small side, but thank goodness there's nothing frail about her."

"Helen is on the small side too, Mam."

"Yeah…that's true. She's obviously taking after the other side of the family…no look of the Cantwells at all …or the Powers either." I don't know why her saying this should annoy me. Mam then starts talking about my cousins: they have all put their education to good use. "Audrey is starting a new job…more money I believe. It's the children I feel sorry for…all morning in that crèche. It's the one of the Stanton's…do you remember her?"

"No!"

"Ah you do…the tall thin one with the curly hair… making a mint she is. Only that Joan picks them up at lunchtime, they'd be there all day. Tommy's not a bit happy, he thinks it's too much for Joan… and he says the children are dragged from their beds at an unearthly hour. They're hardly ever in their own house, by the looks of it. And there's no need for it…Danny has a good job." Mam looks at me for a response. "And you know Audrey doesn't give Joan a penny."

"Well, that's her own fault…"

"What is?"

"Not taking money."

"I suppose. Don't get me wrong…it's not always about the money, but Joan feeds them and she's always taking them places and buying them things."

"Some people have to work, Mam… not everyone's as well off." I check myself from saying anything further not wanting the litany of how she had to work when our father died; how else could she keep us in college on a widow's pension? No doubt, it was hard for her. But, I know, from Nan, that my uncles helped with our education, especially Frank who is a building contractor in England and he still sends money, according to Nan. My father didn't leave her too badly off either, by all accounts, but you'll never hear any of that!

I get a break when she receives a call from a friend and head to the bedroom to read my book for a while. When I return to the sitting room, my mother is in a better mood and quite talkative. All I need to do is sit and listen. I stick it out for as long as I can before feigning tiredness.

Getting back to my book, I find I'm reading the same sentences over and over thinking about her: why did she rush away? why so standoffish? I go to check if she left any messages but I left my phone in the sitting room. Tiptoeing past my mother's bedroom, I hear the radio on down low. I try not to make noise but the sounds seem to amplify in the quietness. No messages! I send a text: miss you dreadfully. PC. Since I once signed a card, PC, Catriona gets a kick out of calling me Mr. Politically Correct or Personal Computer.

Lying in the dark, I indulge in the delectable details of how we got together: I popped into The Corner House one Friday evening to see if Barry Stack was around but there was no sign of him. I was just leaving when Catriona Lynch came through the door. She seemed disappointed that I was going. "Sure, you have time for one drink," she said invitingly. Naturally, I stayed.

She was quite exuberant and I guessed she had been drinking elsewhere. I decided to go after the second drink but not wanting to leave her there, half cut, I suggested she leave too.

"Are you telling me what to do now?" She retorted saucily with her chin in the air. All I could do was laugh. When she saw me putting on my jacket, she said, "Wait! I'll come with you."

We walked together down Bridge Street. I assumed she was heading to the taxi rank at the top of Patrick Street. "You might have to wait," I said. "Fridays are usually busy."

"Wait for what," she asked, knitting her brows.

"Don't you want a taxi?"

"Why would I want a taxi," she laughed "I only live up the road!" I was puzzled, where did she think we were going? Seeing that she lived close by,

I offered to walk her home. She was fine going down MacCurtain Street but on Summer Hill she had difficulty walking in high heeled boots and kept stopping and talking. Eventually we turned in to Clifton Terrace where she lived. When we reached the house, she seemed to find a second wind and sprightly climbed the steps to the hall door where she rummaged in her bag for the keys. I helped her up the stairs to the first floor and stifled a laugh when she searched again for the keys because I'd taken them out of the door below. The flat door opened onto a tiny hallway off which were three doors. Catriona dashed to the right which turned out to be the bathroom. There was a door facing me and another to the left. When she came out, her coat was off and the front of her blouse was wet. I reckoned she was trying to sober up. She hung up her coat in the hall and then smiling up at me, asked if I'd like some music, a hilarious suggestion given the circumstances. She passed into the room on the left and spoke out from the darkness. There was a sudden crash, which sounded like a stack of CDs falling and then I heard her muttering something about a damn lightbulb.

"Catriona, I should go!" I called in.

"So soon," she said coming out.

"Well, it's quite late…you must be tired." I said, hoping she'd be oblivious to the time.

"I suppose you're right," she said, ignoring the keys in my outstretched hand and proceeded to open the middle door which turned out to be the bedroom. This time a light came on and I could see her sitting on the bed. "Piers…are you there?" she called. "Come in can't you…you're not in that much of a hurry, are you?" I drew her attention to me putting the keys on the bedside locker. She frowned, probably wondering what I was doing with them. "This cursed thing!" she complained as she struggled with one of her boots. I went to help and began opening the laces of her boot. "No," she laughed, "they're only for show…there's a zip at the side." It amused me the way she said zip, it sounded more like zuppe. It took me some minutes to free the zipper and I pulled off both boots. She stood up then and took off her blouse and skirt. I tried to steer her into bed but she resisted me, raising her hands behind her head. I had no idea what she was doing until her hair tumbled down and she was holding two hairgrips. I was unprepared! Her curvaceous body and beautiful red hair were enough to drive any man wild. She got into bed while I stood her boots beside the locker. "Would you like to stay, Piers?" She asked in almost a whisper. I didn't answer but went to the other side of the bed and lay down beside her, outside the covers. She nestled her head in the crook of my arm and I heard all about her evening: Chris Donovan and a Joe Collins were mentioned several times. Thinking her asleep, I eased her head off my shoulder, but as I did, she lifted her hand to my face and said, "You know I really like you, Piers Cantwell."

"I like you too, Catriona Lynch," I said, kissing her forehead. When I was sure she was asleep, I went around to switch off the lamp. I didn't do so immediately, however, but stood gazing down on her as she slept.

Saturday afternoon a week later, I spotted her sauntering along Paul Street and stepped back into the recess of Waterstones. "Well, if it isn't Miss Lynch," I called, as she passed. I pretended not to notice how flustered she was. I was on my way to the Crawford for another look at the James Barry exhibition and asked if she'd like to come along.

Catriona didn't know that Cymbeline was a Shakespeare play. Barry's picture shows Iachimo voyeuristically staring at Imogen's beauty as she sleeps. Over coffee, I recounted how Iachimo was a sly devious character who got into Imogen's bedroom by hiding in a chest; how he discovered a mole on her left breast and how he had used that knowledge to discredit her to the man she loved: who but a lover would know such a thing?

"The bastard!" She exclaimed, inviting disparaging looks from the sedate customers in the Gallery Café. I couldn't help laughing but as I looked into her lovely hazel eyes, I had a sudden prick of conscience.

"About last Friday!" She said after a while. "I must have been in some state… I was in bits Saturday morning. Did I ask you to bring me home?"

"No! I offered …I was only too glad to," I said and she seemed relieved.

"There was a birthday drink for one of the lads after classes. I should have gone home then for something to eat but I promised to meet Chris over in the Lavit for an opening. I drank a fair bit of wine there. I definitely shouldn't have gone to the pub."

"You were funny though," I smiled.

"Yeah right," she muttered.

"You asked me to stay with you ...do you remember?"

"Oh god!" She exclaimed, hiding her face with her hands, obviously not wanting to be reminded.

"I'd love to stay with you another time, though," I ventured and it had the desired effect. She lifted her face and smiled, but then, like a fool, I blurted, "Especially now since I've seen your beautiful body, how could I resist?" Blushing deeply, she averted her eyes; she looked so vulnerable, so young. I felt such a bloody eejit! I gave her hand a squeeze but she continued to look away. "Catriona...look at me. The other night, you said you really liked me... is that true, or was it the drink talking?"

She sat back and held my eyes as if she were seeing right through me. "No, Piers, it wasn't the drink talking. I thought you'd know that by now! I only went to the Corner House in the hope you'd be there."

A warm glow spread to my toes. Catriona Lynch didn't think I was too old for her. I began to babble about how we should get together soon.

"We're together now," she laughed.

"You know what I mean!"

"I do," she smiled, "We could meet tonight!"

"How about right now?" I dared and couldn't believe my luck when she said okay.

There were no curtains on the two large sash windows; the wooden shutters were painted and looked like they hadn't been opened in years. A rose on the ceiling wasn't properly affixed and there was no bulb in the bare fitting hanging down. She saw me looking and said, "I'm waiting for the landlord to fix that." There were no pictures or posters on the walls, potted plants being the only lively feature. There was a small fireplace, incongruous to the scale of the room; I imagined there must have been a finer original. A guitar stood on its stand in the top corner by the window and beside that a keyboard. At the bottom of the room was a table against the wall and on top of that a mini sound system and a stack of CDs and next to that a small fridge just inside the door. Opposite the windows there was a small, much-worn kitchen unit with a lamp on the countertop near the cooker. I knew the bedroom was on the other side of that wall.

She opened a window to air the room and hurried off, to tidy up I supposed. As I looked out on the panoramic view of the city, picking out familiar landmarks, I could clearly hear the train announcements over in Kent Station.

"That whole area over there by the river is earmarked for development," Catriona said, putting her hand on my shoulder. "Cork is changing fast, Piers. Just like the rest of the world I suppose. Don't get me wrong, I'm not against change, I just think we've lost the run of ourselves. We don't seem to understand what matters anymore. What do you think?"

I didn't want to think! I didn't want to talk! All I wanted at that moment was her. "Yes, we do seem to be losing our way," I found myself answering. "All this crazy construction. God knows where it's going to end."

"We'd better get used to it," she said glumly. I knew then I had to change the mood fast. I drew her to me and kissed her for the first time, the reality of which was more than I could have imagined; I had to stop kissing her like a diver coming up for air.

In the bedroom, she stood before me assuredly, her wavy red hair offsetting her pale cream skin; she could have just stepped out of a Caravaggio painting. She lay on the bed with her legs crossed up behind and watched me undress. No other woman had ever given me such scrutiny and I felt vulnerable as I moved towards her. She rolled on her back and gathered me in a warm embrace. I kissed her sensuous mouth and felt her warm breasts against my chest.

"Do you like me, Piers?" She asked, pushing me up by the shoulders.

"I do like you," I said pushing down with my weight.

"Ah but really."

"Really, really," I said, ending her questions with kisses.; she was sweet and inviting. Every cell in my body responded. I sank my face in her neck inhaling her scent and got pleasurably completely lost in skin and breath and hair.

* * *

I hear Rosie coming and pretend to be asleep. "Daddy...get up," she orders, pulling down the covers. She lifts my eyelids with her tiny fingers and I roar laughing.

"Go and see what Granny has for us. Tell her I'm getting up."

"Hurry Daddy!"

"Okay bossy boots."

My mother hums as she clears off the table. Rosie has eaten a good breakfast and it seemed to please her. Rosie watches my mother pouring milk on to a saucer for Smuts and asks if she can give it to him. She spills a little milk onto the floor and looks up nervously but my mother only smiles. "Why has he not have a bowl," Rosie asks gaining confidence and her sentence construction amuses me.

"He'd be very confused if I gave him a bowl now," Mam laughs. "A saucer was always good enough for him. Isn't that right Smuts?" Smuts laps up the milk and Rosie watches with glee.

"Milk is bad for cats!" Rosie says and looks to me for confirmation.

"Smuts likes milk... It's never done him any harm," Mam says, glaring at me.

"We read that in the pet book, Mam," I say to alleviate any suspicion of criticism.

"Oh, pet books! And vets! How did we ever manage?"

I take Rosie up to get dressed and she is cooperative and eager to be off. By the time I've gathered my things, she's already belted up in her seat with Angie on her lap and her Winnie-the-pooh bag beside her. "That's a lovely bag Rosie," Mam remarks, closing the door. Rosie smiles and holds Angie's arm to the window to wave goodbye. Before I go, Mam asks me to make lunch for Nan, saying it will give her a chance to get a few things done. My mother is good to Nan, calling every day, sometimes twice a day. Nan, I think, takes her for granted.

Nan's front door is wide open, despite all the warnings - she likes to keep an open house, believing that if you're good and kind, evil will have no place to lodge itself. If she can be of help to someone, she will do her utmost. "Nan! We're here," I shout from the hall.

"That's a fact," Nan says, coming to greet us. "Come here to me," she says grabbing my arm and I bend down for my kiss. "And you lady, how are you?" Nan turns in to the sitting room and Rosie follows eagerly. When Nan is settled in her fireside chair, Rosie pulls out her 'special' stool. "There's a sweet little lady named Rosie O'Grady, I wish I could call her my own," Nan sings. God knows if this is an actual song: Nan often makes up words to well-known tunes. Within minutes, Rosie is laughing and chatting and telling Nan about going to the big school in September when she's five.

"Yes, it's your birthday soon…ah… the 25th of June," Nan says. "You didn't think I'd forget that did you? Oh, hello Winnie…"

"It's a bag!" Rosie explains and takes out the treasures. She puts glitter on Nan's eyelids – 'to make her beautiful.'

Later I overhear Rosie telling Nan that Granny Kearns is sick and will be going into hospital. This is news to me! Sometimes I learn more about what's going on in Rosie's life from her talks with my grandmother; Nan has a way of drawing her out without quizzing or nosing. She never formally asks Rosie for a kiss but steals one occasionally when she is drawing, daydreaming, or wildly excited about something.

Nan's face has a youthful look despite her age. Only her neck betrays, wrinkled and leathery like a tortoise, and her hands are dotted with liver spots, none of which seems to bother Rosie. I was afraid of old people when I was young. Miss Sheehan in the grocery had wild wiry hair and sat behind a low counter with a canvas bag over her lap. I used to think something was wrong with her legs, if indeed she had legs. She wore strange gloves with the tops cut off and when she gave me change, her cold fingers sent shivers down my spine. I was also afraid of my grand-uncle, Pat Organ, whose hands were dark and wrinkled with fingers like fried sausages; thick hairs grew out of his ears and nose; when he put his peaked cap on my head, I thought I would instantly get old. Pat was Nan's eldest brother and lived alone somewhere up the side of a mountain.

I laughed when Nan told me her maiden name was Organ. Dungarvan, she said was full of Organs and had I not heard of the most famous one of all, Little Nellie of Holy God. I've been hearing about Little Nellie ever since.

Her photograph is on the mantelpiece: a frail little thing in a communion dress propped up in a chair. Nan never misses an opportunity to talk about her: Nellie was only four and a half years old when she died but had already been confirmed and was receiving the Sacraments. Pius X declared that Nellie was his justification for the decree, Quam Singulari, recommending the early and frequent Communion of children. Nan boasts that Nellie's Father, William, was a Dungarvan man. I usually close my ears when she goes on about religious things. I know more about Little Nellie of Holy God than I care to. For my part, I'm more interested in how the child ended up with severe injuries when seemingly she was okay before she was taken into care.

My grandfather, Billy Power, was a fisherman. Nan tells everyone he died young: he died of pneumonia when he was seventy-five; he wouldn't stay in bed as ordered but insisted on going down to meet the trawlers for his fish supply and to see what was going on in general. Nan claims the east wind killed him. His picture is beside Nellie's. Whenever Nan hears bad news, she looks up and says, "go bfóire dia orainn, Billy, it's as well you're not here to witness this."

When I mention lunch, Nan tells me there's leek and potato soup in the cupboard. "You need something more substantial than that," I say heading to the kitchen. There's nothing interesting in the fridge and the only bread is anaemic sliced pan so I call Rosie to come with me to the shops.

"I want to stay with Nana," she insists.

Knowing I'm reluctant to leave her, Nan says, "Put up the fireguard there... she'll be alright till you get back. You won't be too long, will you?"

I buy a cooked chicken, salad ingredients and a nice loaf. On the way back, I bump into Liam Connors. Liam is now married to Angela, the once love of my life. I ask after Angela, more out of politeness than interest.

"Not a bother on her...I'll tell her I met you...she'll be delighted."

"Rosie is above with Nan, Liam, I better run!"

"I'll talk to ya again, Piers," he says waving me on.

Everything is fine! Rosie is in her element. I apportion the chicken and salad and cut slices of bread. I make the bloody soup: not much making – add cold water and stir, bring to the boil and simmer. Monosodium glutamate wafts out and Nan says, "Something smells good!" I place the hot concoction in front of her. "Ah lovely," she says rubbing her hands together. Rosie wants the same, so I ladle out another serving on condition she eat her chicken. Helen would lose her life if she knew. Rosie says the soup is lovely too! Nan smiles at me like a conspirator.

After lunch, Nan gives Rosie the okay to watch TV. Nan rarely watches TV she prefers the radio. "What's troubling Evelyn," she asks unexpectedly. "Is it something to do with the boyfriend?"

"I didn't notice anything…she seemed fine to me."

"Wonder of wonders," Nan says.

"But she's not going out with Brian anymore … hasn't been for ages, apparently."

"Oh! Really! Hmm…there's something bothering her, but she'll tell you nothing… just like your mother." When Rosie is sufficiently occupied, I tell Nan that I've met someone. She's impressed that Catriona is a musician. Nan's maternal grandfather, Mat Cody, was a well-known tenor and Billy's two brothers were fine fiddlers; Billy didn't play an instrument but as Nan says, he had a voice.

"Have you said anything to Helen," Nan asks.

"No, there's nothing to tell yet…anyway, things are a bit uncertain."

"Uncertain," Nan quizzes. When I tell her why, she says, "Oh Piers, you were always such an óinseach … your head is always somewhere else! Take my advice, pay attention when a woman is talking to you."

"There's another problem, Nan… she's much younger than me."

"You'd swear you were ancient! How much younger?"

"Fifteen years."

"If ye're suited, it shouldn't matter much… look at your father and mother."

"That's hardly a consoling comparison," I joke but she remains serious.

Rosie, having lost interest in the TV, is looking for paper to do a picture of Smuts for Nan. Nan tunes in to her straight away. While I have the chance, I head up to my room.

My mother arrives around three with magazines for Nan and a paper for me which is nice of her. She knows I like to read the local newspapers when I can. "What's that on your face, Mam? It's all sparkles," Mam says, putting the magazines behind Nan's cushion.

"Oh... that's my new make-up," Nan says, winking at Rosie.

My mother goes down to tidy Nan's bedroom. (Nan is sleeping downstairs since her fall). When my mother comes back, I get the feeling she wants us out of the way for a while, so I tell Rosie we're going for a walk.

"Wrap the child up well!" Nan roars after me. "May is a treacherous month!"

I drive over Devonshire bridge and park in the square. We walk down Davitt's Quay towards the library but Rosie changes her mind and wants to see the boats instead. I tell her we can pop into the library, later, if she wants.

Past the castle, I worry that Rosie has walked too far so when we get to the Moresby memorial, I pretend I'm tired. There's a bitter wind but Rosie keeps pulling her hood down. I consider calling to Tommy and Joan across the way in Park Terrace but I remember what Mam said. Saturday is probably the only day Joan gets to herself.

I'm turning back with the intention of taking Rosie to the library where it's warm, when I hear someone shouting my name. "Up here ya gombeen!" Paul Ellis is waving at us from further up. Rosie is delighted when Paul makes a big fuss of her, introducing her to his mates and answering her questions. "Here, take these," Paul says, packing fish into a plastic bag. "Sure, give them to someone if you don't want them," he says closing the van door. I gratefully accept the fish even though it means going back to the house. Rosie vigorously waves goodbye to them all.

Rosie runs past my mother and straight over to Nan. "Nana, I'm going in a big boat in the summer with daddy's friend," she reports breathlessly.

"Really! That's wonderful!" Nan says.

"My God, where did you get these," Mam asks when she see the fish.

"From Paul Ellis."

"Paul Ellis...I don't think I know him," she says. If she paid more attention when I was growing up, she'd know who he is.

"Yes... in the summer," Rosie says and I can see she's puzzled.

"Paul means when the weather is warmer, Rosie." She nods as if she knew that all along.

"There's a mighty amount here," my mother exclaims. "I'll help you clean them…they'll last in the fridge and you can freeze them when you get home."

"I won't take any…I'd have to go straight home… Rosie might want to go to a playground or something. You can freeze them, can't you?"

"I'll give Tommy some… he loves the bit a fish." Mam spreads newspapers on the kitchen table and we set to cleaning the fish. Ivor, Evelyn, and I had to clean fish many times when we were growing up. Mam is expertly chopping off heads, cleaning, and filleting; mind you, she has the best knife. My grandfather had a special knife and a metal glove; I wonder where they went. Rosie puts her nose in out of curiosity but makes a hasty retreat.

"Will I leave out a bit of fish for your tea, Mam? Tommy can cook it for you later," my mother calls out to Nan.

"No, I'll have a slice of apple tart later…I had a big lunch," Nan replies.

Mam puts some of the fish into Nan's little freezer compartment and the rest into two plastic containers, one for Tommy and one for herself.

"It's a pity I cooked a chicken casserole for your dinner," Mam says and wonders why we're laughing.

"We had chicken for lunch," Nan explains.

"And soup," Rosie adds.

"Sure, we'll have fish so…the casserole will keep."

My mother looks a lot younger when she smiles.

* * *

Things have gone reasonably well this visit and it was a plus to see Evelyn, so I don't understand the sinking feeling now as I drive along. I guess it's because there's always the fear that everything will fragment, that I will be undermined in some unexpected way. Such is the effect my mother has on me.

"Daddy, we never went for our paddle," Rosie exclaims. I'd forgotten about it, but I should have known she wouldn't be cheated. How she remembered surprises me because I took the bypass.

"I think it's going to rain, pet…do you really want to?

"You said we could, Daddy!"

"I did, but that was Friday." I realise I'm wasting my time explaining. I drive back towards Youghal and park at the back of The Tides Restaurant. We take our towels and cut across rough ground to the beach. At least it's warmer than yesterday.

Rosie takes off her shoes and tucks her skirt into the legs of her knickers and dashes off. I roll up my trousers and follow. My body stiffens to the cold shock of the water. It doesn't seem to bother Rosie who is splashing and laughing.

"This isn't swimming, Rosie...we don't have swimsuits...we don't want to..." She's not listening, screaming in wild abandonment with each wave. Her enthusiasm is contagious and I can feel my spirits lifting. The beach is deserted – no one even in the distance. Thunderous clouds loom over the water creating a surreal expanse of metallic grey, broken only by the breaking surf and the silver flash of a seagull.

Littoral smells invade my nostrils as I walk across the sand. Those smells, which I had always associated with the sea, are not out on the water; out there are completely different sensations of wind and salt and sounds. The seaboard is such a strange in-between world, my world as a child: crabs, barnacles, lugworms, bladder wrack, shells, sand, and rocks. All that it sustains is here now for Rosie.

Thankfully, this is not a fishing area. I remember the rotting fish on the strand, unwanted fish thrown from the boats, and flies walking over dead staring eyes. Ironically, some of that 'unwanted fish' is valued today. Granddad would be astounded! I was with him once when they were burying a male blue shark: the ugliness and clinging stench was my first lesson on death. I wouldn't like Rosie to see anything like that.

"Look Daddy!" Rosie says tottering purposefully over the sand ridges and stones with various shells cradled in her skirt, which she holds out like a creel. Her skirt now has two shades of red, the wet parts a deep crimson. I wipe the sand from her hands and legs and dry her off. The shells are her only concern, so I put them in the wet towel and wrap the dry towel around her. We scramble up on to the road and down into the rough ground again. It seems longer on the way back. I should have driven closer to the beach! Rosie is shivering by the time we reach the car. I pull out dry underwear and a track suit but she wants to wear a dress. Helen has a lot to answer for! Once the track suit is on however, she's happy and warm. Unfortunately, I don't have a spare pants.

Rosie examines her shells as we drive along. I sing along to Jeff Buckley's 'Hallelujah' on the radio. Rosie joins in too and we hallelujah our way through Killeagh. The heavens suddenly open and I thank my lucky stars that we escaped this at the beach.

After tea we have fun with Rosie's shells. I'm not sure what the game is, but I must place mine in a circle. Rosie taps the sand from each of her shells and scoops it into little mounds; this magically enhances the game, somehow. I'm surprised at how much sand she gathers.

Helen arrives after seven and is a little subdued. I don't ask after Josie because I wouldn't like her to think I was quizzing Rosie. I explain about the wet clothes in the separate bag, but I don't think she's listening. Helen lifts Rosie on to her lap and asks if she's had a good time. Rosie just nods.

"She's tired, Helen…we stopped in Youghal on the way…"

"Oh, you're very tired, sweetheart!" Helen says drawing Rosie close.

I offer Helen a tea but she declines saying she's got to go. Rosie just about manages a farewell hug and I get a kiss on the cheek from Helen which is a surprise.

There is always a strange vacancy when Rosie leaves. A too sudden gear shift! I didn't understand the feeling in the beginning, but I now know it's because of having to be so focused when I have her. She has a powerful effect for such a small individual!

To unwind, I put on, Richter plays Schubert. Sviatoslav Richter is renowned for his refusal to allow his own personality to intrude upon the music. Schubert wasn't well known in his day and made little money from his work. Thanks to George Grove and Arthur Sullivan's discovery of his hidden masterpieces, we have his music today. Liszt described Shubert as the most poetic musician who ever lived.

Feeling more relaxed, I try Catriona again. My heart jumps when she answers. "Hi, how are you? I've been trying to get hold of you."

"I'm fine! Got your texts."

"I missed you! Sorry for snapping at you in the pub. I was very tired and I had a lot on my mind."

"Like what?"

"Work."

"Oh Piers, you can be so funny," she says.

"When can I see you?"

"Ah… could meet you Tuesday."

"Tuesday! I was hoping we could meet sooner…like tonight."

"Can't, I'm going out."

"Where are you going?"

"To Jimmy Manning's …it's kind of a dinner. I'm going with Chris."

"Who's Jimmy Manning?"

"A friend…well a friend of Chris's…I know him from the school."

"I've never heard you mention him."

"Maybe that's because you never listen."

"I could meet you after."

"No!" she says emphatically.

"I'm off tomorrow!"

"I'm busy tomorrow, classes and that… and I have plans for later. I'll see you Tuesday, I have to go now." Why is she shutting me out? Is it because she saw me with Helen? And who the fuck is Jimmy Manning?

* * *

Toby and I lead quite different lives but we can connect easily, even after long intervals. He thinks I'm way too serious, but I tend to lighten up when I'm with him. He's an Events Manager in a bank; I'm not too sure what that is exactly because he never talks about work. It amazes me that he works in a bank at all because he's the most unconventional guy I know. I asked him once how he could work for banks, being the epitome of capitalism, in my opinion. He said it was no different from any other job, that going to the supermarket, using computer software from Israel or Korea, purchasing cheap goods from the Philippines, all bought into capitalism; did I expect him to change the world single-handedly?

Toby has a funny side: when we were drinking one time, he stated that from then on, he was going to tell women he was a poet, when I asked why, he said: "You know well why, Cantwell, you bloody poets rake in the women."

"Where did you get that idea?" I laughed.

"That fellow Shelley started all that…he couldn't run away with just one woman…no… he had to have two."

"Byron was the real lady slayer, though."

"Oh yeah…he loved them and crushed them… on tables and under tables; well everywhere he could, really." Toby's eyes twinkled at the scenarios. "And ye bastards are doing a good job of it ever since."

"Gee, I hope not! Byron was a toff, after all, Toby. Lord being the operative word. He left a trail of destruction… even his own daughter was a casualty! I suppose he got a lot of attention because he was a lord."

"Fuck it Piers, don't go all analytical," Toby interrupted. You used to love The Romantics," he said getting annoyed. "You've been reading the critics…they're like those revisionist historians, putting contemporary moral interpretations on past events. Things were as they were… of their time. If we listened to them, we'd be judging all revolutionaries as terrorists."

"Now whose getting analytical… and digressing into politics," I said, ostensibly serious but really winding him up. "I'm not suggesting for a minute he wasn't a good poet, Toby. I like many of Byron's poems. I prefer Shelley, as a person, I mean. I believe he cared about people and I like how he tried to free himself from religion. He gave us a lot to think about."

"But he shouldn't have tried to persuade Irish Catholics to stop drinking though! Big mistake!" Toby laughed. "And telling them one religion was as good as another…now you have to find that funny." His eyes then strayed to a female who had just come in and that was the end of that conversation. I rarely talk to Toby about poetry anyway, apart from the poets he studied in college, I don't think he's that interested.

Toby and I are an odd combination, both being anachronistic of our age: I grew up listening to classical music mostly, but I never divulged that to my friends when I was a teenager, with them I listened to what was in vogue.

Toby has eclectic tastes; a free spirit in his approach to most things; he doesn't give a damn about trends. He has an amazing vinyl collection: lots of Chess Label records he got from his uncle Tobias who had spent a lot of time in America. Toby knows all about the Chess Brothers, Phil & Leonard who were Polish Emigrants. He especially likes, The Blues, Leadbelly being his hero. His party pieces are, Rock Island Line and Goodnight Irene, the original version, before it was sanitized for white American singers. I once made the mistake of talking about an article I'd read on John and Alan Lomax, suggesting that Leadbelly was dragged around like a show piece and put up in cheap hotels and was expected to be grateful. The article also said Leadbelly was depicted as a captured savage in striped prison uniform on posters.

"What gobshite wrote that," Toby demanded, "I probably would never have heard of Leadbelly only for them," he declared. "They put Irish singers and musicians on the world stage too. As far as I can see, anyone who does anything good gets a load of flack. Blacks were not allowed in many hotels. Did you ever think of that? You should listen to, 'It's a Bourgeois Town' – Me and my wife we were standing upstairs/We heard the white man say/I don't want no niggers up there. Leadbelly sums it up, doesn't he?"

"I'm just telling you what I read," I said.

"Ah, but even talking about the article you're endorsing it," he accused. I'm more careful now what I say to him.

The first time Toby came back to my flat on the Western Road, I played Telemann's Suite in D Major for Hunting Horns & Orchestra for him. It's a piece I often play to cheer myself up, even the record sleeve makes me laugh: three guys on horseback with big, looped, hunting horns and a little beagle between the horses. I will never forget the look on Toby's face. "Cantwell," he said, "you are some mad bastard! Is this a wind up?"

"No. Telemann was an important composer in his day...even considered superior to Bach." He looked at me in disbelief. "Really, Telemann was a most prolific composer, he wrote more than Bach and Handel put together. At least that's what it says on the sleeve notes!" I laughed. Whenever Toby comes to my place now, Telemann is a special request, and he listens to the whole album.

The only classical composer Toby talks about is Stravinsky; he calls him the Rock 'n Roller. I think he was impressed that the first performance of the 'The Rite of Spring' caused riots in Paris and that Stravinsky knew Genet. It's interesting really what becomes popular. Stravinsky endures because towards the end of his life, he committed most of his major works to record, under his own conductorship. He was an Internationalist who embraced many genres, so I guess that's why Toby likes him! I must admit, I haven't listened enough to Stravinsky.

I wonder about all the talented composers, and poets, who got lost in the sands of time. We probably would never have heard of Vivaldi, for instance, only for scholars, like Marc Pincherle, and of course musicians like Nigel Kennedy. How could Telemann have faded into the background, when he was the main man of his time?

Toby got me interested in old films, which I now love. At a party, one time, he did his take on Tex Ritter's song from High Noon. He had everyone in stitches as he swaggered around with imaginary guns and holsters, singing, "I can't be leaving till I shoot Frank Miller dead." Another time I brought Toby to a colleague's birthday party for company; the minute we got there he began chatting up a young woman, telling her she looked like Jane Russell. Not surprisingly, she had never heard of Jane Russell. "Jane Russell, the actress… have you never seen The Outlaw? She was great as Rio!" Toby enthused.

"And you're Billy the Kid, I suppose!" Announced a grey-haired man suddenly appearing at her side.

"Hello Doc!" Toby grinned, lifting his hands to his imaginary holsters. "Shall we pull on the fourth cuckoo?" The man, who turned out to be her father, burst out laughing.

"Can I get you a drink son," he asked. Toby went out with Jane Russell for months until she got a nursing job in Australia.

I got used to Toby's eccentric ways over the years. I'll never forget the day he stopped outside a furniture shop on North Main Street where a bed was displayed. Toby said, "That's a beautiful bed! Stay out of it…keep walking!" Then he started talking about spiders working together and something about smoke. I had no idea what he was on about. Sometimes he'd fill you in, other times not. It was only when he lent me the film, 'Farewell my Lovely,' based on a Raymond Chandler story, starring Dick Powell, that I understood. I laughed my head off remembering the bed in the window.

I hammer the brass knocker down a little too forcibly on the green-peeling-worse-for-wear door. Toby takes his time, no doubt to chastise me. He opens with a grin and turns on his heels without a word. I follow him down the hallway into the sitting room where a fire is struggling for life in a cast-iron fireplace. I fall into a large armchair and immediately feel at home.

"What would you like to listen to," he asks. I tell him to surprise me. He stoops down to a little cupboard and produces a bottle of white rum. "This is good stuff! I brought it back from Cuba," he says, pouring two measures. He puts on Sarah Vaughan, an old 78 in perfect condition. No one dare touch Toby's vinyl collection. I'm careful with my records too, but he's very intense about his. Unfortunately, I can't say the same of his treatment of books: he never uses a bookmark but turns down the pages which drives me crazy.

We sip our rum listening to Sassy Sarah. It's nice when someone chooses something you wouldn't normally listen to but absolutely enjoy – 'I'd like to try something I never had…oh lover man where can you be.' Black Coffee, my favourite, comes on – 'I'll never know a Sunday in this weekday room.' Sarah's unique phrasing takes you somewhere special – 'I'm hanging out on Monday my Sunday dreams to dry.'

"You sounded wound up earlier. What's wrong," Toby asks when the record ends.

"Did I? A bit restless I suppose…just back from Dungarvan…"

"Your mother?"

"No! She was okay! I just needed to get out."

Toby, I know from experience, will not leave it there. I bring him up to date generally and in turn, he tells me about his trip to Cuba, how he never made it to Guantanamo because of Hella, the Norwegian he met in Santa Clara. He goes into such detail about the lovely Hella, it's bordering on the pornographic. Nothing about Che Guevara.

"Anything exciting with you?"

"No, nothing exciting," I say, resisting the urge to spill my guts.

Unfortunately, after a few more dollops of the sugar-cane juice, I'm telling Toby Holland more than I should.

* * *

The rumbling of a train wakes me and for a minute I don't know where I am. I struggle out of bed and into my crumpled clothes. My head feels twice the size as I make my way down the narrow stairs. The glasses from last night are rinsed out on the draining board. There's no sign of any breakfast things, Toby must be bad too! I fill a glass with water and gulp it down over my sandpaper tongue. Some of the water misses my mouth and trickles down my neck and even that is welcome.

Glaring sunlight assaults my eyes as I step onto the street. An articulated truck whizzes past and its after current leaves my heart pounding. Why do people drive so fast down this street? It's not a motorway! Opposite the railway station, I look up the stone steps that lead to Clifton Terrace and consider trying the flat, but right now, it would be like climbing Everest. She's probably at the school anyway. Besides, she made it clear she was busy today.

In town, everything seems to be coming at me; everything sounds too loud. I go into a café for breakfast but I'm kept waiting so long, I get up and leave. Maybe it's just as well - don't know if I could have kept it down. I buy a bottle of water instead and take the bus home.

Revived somewhat after a shower and shave, I eat a little breakfast but I'm not as good as I thought and I take to the bed for a while. Closing my eyes is helping my headache but my mind is on overdrive. I force myself up after an hour and turn on my computer. I open a few files but I know straight away it's a waste of time, besides, I need some air.

I fight off my hangover and walk into town. I buy two books in Waterstones. People tell me it's cheaper to buy online, but I enjoy browsing in bookshops. I planned to go to Vibes and Scribes, but now I'm feeling rather hot. As I walk down Lavitts Quay, a Lee impregnated breeze blows through my hair and open jacket. I breathe in deeply and convince myself that I'm feeling better. Passing by the Mercy Hospital, I decide to continue out to Fitzgerald Park. I like these free days to amble about, you never know what interesting things you might come across. Sometimes I wander around public buildings or churches but today is not a day for any of that.

Children in the park playground remind me of Rosie. I could easily have taken her for the extra day. Helen, no doubt, would say I was interrupting the routine. Not being married puts me at a disadvantage. I suppose I'm to be grateful, that I get to see my daughter at all. I let a lot of things slide simply because I know Helen tries to be reasonable. My mother, of course, would say that I have only myself to blame.

I set to reading the introduction to one of the books until my eyes ache. I turn my face to the sun and mull over what I've read, but Catriona Lynch is all too pervasive. Maybe it's because I didn't go after her that has her so miffed - what a fuss over such a minor thing. Why do women go over the top about everything? Well, if the woman thinks I'm going to run ragged every time there's a hiccup, she has another thing coming.

I turn my mind to what I'm going to write for Barry's catalogue and start jotting down sentences on the paper bag from the books. I remember a printed poem in my pocket and use the back of that also. I'm pleased that it's all coming together nicely. Admittedly, I have been formulating it in my head for weeks. Catriona hijacks my thoughts again: did she mention that Manning fellow just to annoy me? I'm not sure I like the power she has over me.

On the way home, I stop at Frank O'Conner House in Douglas Street. A few interesting events coming up, but they are on Tuesdays and Thursdays, not the best days for me. By the time I reach Langford Row my legs are packing in. I force an extra spring in my step knowing I'm on the last lap.

I call Rosie the minute I get in. Helen doesn't like me calling too late. Rosie's still on about her shells: "I gave two to Granny and one to Mummy." Then I hear all about a new shell game.

"What's this I hear about going on a boat," Helen asks coming back on the phone. "She's telling everyone!" I explain about meeting Paul. "She seems to have had a great time... shells, boats, Nana Power... she didn't mention Granny Cantwell. How is she?"

"The same!" I laugh. "Talking of Grans, how's Josie?"

"I've been meaning to talk to you, Piers," Helen says lowering her voice almost to a whisper, Josie's not well…can't talk now. I'll tell you when I see you."

I go upstairs to write up Barry's article, at least the bones of it, while it's fresh in my mind. He'll be surprised that he won't have to hound me for it.

My stomach is giving odd growls but I don't want another takeaway. I need to shop anyway and it will take my mind off things for a while.

Too exhausted when I get home, I make a whopper of a sandwich and settle in front of the television. Flicking through the channels, I find a programme on natural disasters: the unpredictability of Yellowstone Natural Park engages me until tiredness gets the better of me. I dive into my never-so-inviting bed and switch off the light and even though Catriona is on my mind, I manage to fall asleep.

I wake to the alarm ringing but I'm confused because it's only half past twelve. I hear ringing again and realise it's the doorbell. Worried, I grab my dressing gown and dash down in my bare feet but when I open the door, Catriona Lynch is standing there.

"Hi!" She says bright and cheery. "Oh, you were in bed. Sorry, I know it's a bit late …"

"Ah, that's okay…come in. How did you find the house?"

"The taximan knew the house."

"They know bloody everything," I grumble and she laughs. It's only then it sinks in that Catriona Lynch is actually in my house. But why so late? If she had called me, we could have met. She moves closer to me and I find the sense to embrace her. A subtle waft of perfume - something new, and her breath smells of alcohol.

"Am I forgiven?" I ask.

"Oh, forget that now," she says nestling into me.

"Are you planning on staying," I tentatively ask.

"If that's okay," she answers a little unsure. I take her hand and lead her upstairs. On the landing, she kisses me and playfully cups my balls. "I missed you!" she says. I'm thinking, if you missed me so much why didn't you take my calls, but the physical distractions make me mute.

Catriona responds so sweetly I feel everything is okay again and I want to pleasure every inch of her; it's an added turn on that she's in my bed. Spent and happy, I curl her hair around my fingers and let my tensions ebb in an aura of quietude.

"You don't mind me coming to the house," Catriona asks after a while.

"No, of course not... why would I mind?" My earlier observations begin to surface and nag: she was very dressed up; and that perfume? "What were you up to this evening," I ask, trying to sound casual.

"We went for a meal... and then on to the pub," she says candidly.

"We?"

"Me and Moira... and Joe Collins... it was for my birthday."

I'm completely stunned. She's saying something else but I'm not listening as the name Joe Collins imbeds itself in the core of my jealousy; that she celebrated her birthday with him hurtles me to blind anger.

"I didn't know it was your birthday," I utter, feeling my jaw tighten.

"How were you to know," she says.

"Well, perhaps if you'd told me ..."

"Sure, I haven't seen you. I didn't know what was happening. Anyway, I was annoyed with you."

"I see! So, you let Joe Collins take you out for your birthday instead."

"No!" She laughs. "It wasn't like that... Moira booked it as a surprise. I'd planned to meet Chris and Ger for a drink but I couldn't when I found out what Moira organised."

My god, they even knew it was her birthday! "What about Collins?"

"It was sheer coincidence we bumped into Joe."

"I suppose it was a coincidence too that he went to the restaurant!"

"Look, Piers, he's Moira's friend... she invited him! I didn't even think he'd come." *Not half! The fucker is like a moth to a flame.* "Why are you being so quiet," she asks, drawing my face towards hers.

"What about afterwards," I ask, turning my face away.

"Afterwards? What do you mean?"

"Did he see you home?"

"I'm not at home, Piers," she laughs, moving her hand across my chest. "You're being silly."

Jealousy is new for me and I make the mistake of pushing her hand away, as scenarios play out in my head. I know I shouldn't be acting this way, not after the last time but when I come to my senses, Catriona is rolling away from me and getting out of bed. "WHAT ARE YOU DOING?" I exclaim, seizing her arm.

"Let me go!" She shouts, struggling to free herself from my grip. I manage to pull her back onto the bed but she moves her face from side to side as I try to kiss her. I persist until I pin her lips. Slowly she yields and our tongues touch and it's taking all my strength to curb my renewed excitement.

"You're right, I am being silly. Not seeing you has made me crazy. I can't help it if I'm jealous."

"For god's sake, Piers, what have you to be jealous about?"

"I don't know." I reply, still wondering who gave her the perfume.

"That's your problem, Piers, you're never sure of anything. It's as simple as this, do you want to be with me or not?"

"You know I want to be with you."

"Well then!"

"You should know me by now, Catriona…I was wrong, but you shouldn't have tortured me. That was unfair!"

"We'll forget that now," she says shaking my shoulders.

"We're making a commitment here! Right?"

"I guess we are," she says kissing my cheek.

"You guess?"

"We *are* making a commitment."

Strangely elated, I relax into her arms and wish her a happy birthday, though technically a day late. I'm settling in to sleep when the question comes, "Was that Rosie's mother, the other day?"

"Yes…Helen."

"She's very good looking!"

"She's not bad," I tease. "I better get some sleep, love…I've to be up at six."

"Oh, I didn't realise it was so late," she says releasing me.

Catriona stirs when the alarm goes off. I drag myself reluctantly from her warm body. Before I leave, I go back up to say goodbye. I lift the tousled mane from her face and kiss her cheek. "I'm off now, love…see you later," I whisper and she looks up bleary-eyed.

"Okay, see ya later, pet," she croaks.

I'm already missing her! For once I don't mind the red lights. It gives me time to recall last night's details. Euphoria takes hold: I don't care how much power she has over me.

* * *

Catriona is eager to meet one of my friends. I reminded her that she already knows one of my friends. "I know," she said. "I just want to meet someone your own age." I was conscious then of our age difference. Claire is a few years younger than me, but she was out of town. I didn't want to annoy Barry and the only other person I could think of was Toby but I wondered if meeting him was a good idea at this stage. But when would be a good time?

"Toby's a bit of charmer! He'll probably come on to you," I say as we head into town. She looks at me oddly, probably thinking I'm being possessive. Toby lives a bit too close for comfort for my liking.

Toby beckons us to a table in the corner of a jointed Counihan's. "Catriona, meet my friend and great tormentor, Toby Holland."

"Lovely to meet you," he says shaking hands "Piers couldn't stop talking about you," he says grinning at me, "I feel I know you already!" I don't remember telling him that much about her!

"Have we met before," Catriona asks with a quizzical expression.

"No! I don't think so!" Toby answers.

"You look very familiar," Catriona says weighing him up.

"I wouldn't forget meeting someone like you," Toby smiles and then asks us what we'd like to drink.

"I'd imagine he's a bit of a charmer alright!" Catriona concedes when he's out of earshot. Knowing something, however, is not always a defence! Sure enough, they begin chatting away about this and that and he's making her laugh. I envy him that ability: I have no capacity to make anyone laugh. The talk now is about poor Fidel Castro and what Cuba will be like when he's gone. He's telling her how he met Castro's grandnephew and how lovely the

Cuban people are. Not a word about the lovely Norwegian!

Joe Collins puts his head in the door like a scout and when he catches my eye, I beckon him to join us, endeavouring to impress upon her how magnanimous I can be. Toby engages with Collins out of politeness but homes in on Catriona at the first opportunity. Collins, of course, is taking everything in. Joe doesn't stay long, however, because he wants to hear Hot Guitars in The *Crúiscín Lán*.

Coming up to closing time, I decide it would be best to ditch Toby. I don't want him walking home with us. It will have to be swift, or otherwise he'll ask questions. Outside the pub, I tell him I'm taking Catriona home. "I'll give you a ring during the week," I say already walking away.

"Why are we going this way," Catriona asks as we walk down Pembroke Street.

"To shake off Toby! He'd only want to hang on to us," I explain. "And right now, I want you all to myself." I smile to myself imagining Toby staring after us. 'Friendship is constant in all other things safe the office and affairs of love.' At the end of the street, I pull Catriona into the doorway of the Old Cork Library and there between two pillars and two sentinel owls, kiss her honey mouth and hold her close.

* * *

Rosie's fifth Birthday has come and gone. It was the first birthday Josie missed and Helen was upset about that. God knows what Rosie was thinking. Despite everything it went off well and Helen was fantastic with all the children. Not long after I arrived, a guy called with a gift for Rosie and seemed quite familiar with her. Helen introduced him as Tim Arnold. He stayed only a few minutes and Helen saw him out. I observed him from the window as they were talking. He was thin, average looking, with light brown hair. He kissed Helen on the cheek before getting into an expensive looking car. Strange how Rosie never said anything about him.

Helen brought the subject up herself the following week: she's been seeing Arnold for some time; she meant to tell me before now but Josie's illness had put everything on hold. I felt duplicitous not having told her about Catriona and resolved to do so when the time was right.

It came as a shock when Helen informed me some weeks later that they were planning on getting married. I was happy for her but all I could think about was how it would affect Rosie and me. I kept my concerns to myself however, because she is under enough strain: Josie has refused further treatment and things are not looking good.

* * *

Storm force winds and torrential rain outside. I'm glad I'm tucked up in a warm bed. I wonder what all the little animals do in this weather; where do the birds shelter when the trees are bare? And the homeless, what do they do? I stop myself from thinking of these things and start reciting poems in my head. I start with, The Sloth, and Child on Top of a Greenhouse, by Theodore Roethke. I think then of Jeanette Winterson: I should learn off more poems too.

My heart skips a beat when my phone rings. "What's up? Is Rosie all right?" I ask without even saying hello.

"Rose is fine! It's Mum, Piers…she's gone," Helen says with a break in her voice.

"I'm sorry Helen."

"I wasn't long gone. I was tired… and the weather…I was worried about driving home. I should have stayed," she says sighing heavily.

"You weren't to know."

"June was there, thank god! She said Mum never opened her eyes after. God Piers, I can't believe it." Her voice trails off into muffled sobs.

"No one is ever prepared for these things, Helen."

"We'll have to wait for Sean! Oh god, I can't think straight…"

"Look, get some sleep…you sound exhausted. I'll take Rosie tomorrow."

"No, that's okay. No point in taking too many days off. But she'll have to be told!"

"We could tell her together."

"Yes! I'd appreciate that!"

"I'll call over tomorrow after work."

"Okay!"

Helen's house is in darkness and her phone is off. I wait a half hour before returning home, not knowing what else to do. She calls an hour later to tell me there was a rosary for the family and that she forgot about me. I'm flabbergasted when she asks if I'd mind going for a drink.

Her directions to June's place in Wilton are spot on; I beep the horn and she comes out straight away and we drive to the Wilton pub and Helen fills me in. The funeral is on Friday and that Sean and his son Steven are flying in tomorrow. "I haven't said anything to Rose yet... "June is holding off telling the boys. I'm putting pressure on her, I think." Helen puts her hand to her forehead as if trying to figure out some great puzzle. She looks very pale. Mind you, she always looks pale, but there is an added exhaustion. Being here with her like this feels rather strange, it's like our years apart have no great measure. I want to put my arm around her and comfort her but convention does not allow me.

"Oh, Piers, I never thought Mum would go so fast." Helen holds her fingers to her forehead as if going to salute. "We were told to expect the worst. I thought...I don't know...I thought we'd have more time..."

"It's a mercy in a way...that she didn't linger in agony, I mean."

"Yes, she was in great pain." I give her hand a reassuring squeeze which she reciprocates but then, meeting my eyes, withdraws her hand abruptly. "Get me another drink, will you, Piers," she asks, after an awkward moment. Did she suddenly remember Tim? Why is he not with her?

"Where's Tim tonight," I ask, sitting down beside here with the drink.

"I told him to go home. He was beginning to annoy me. Ah no, he was good in fairness... but Piers, he didn't even know Mum really," she says, looking to me as if needing approval.

"He'll understand. It's a difficult time for everyone." Helen nods in agreement.

I noticed they were still serving food when I was up at the bar. "I'm getting something to eat...do you want something?" Helen shakes her head. "Another drink maybe?"

"God no...I've loads here," she says, drowning the already drowned whisky. She smiles when I come back with a sandwich and another coffee "You didn't have any dinner, did you?"

"No! I didn't have much at lunch either."

"Mum liked you, Piers! She said you were honest. Mind you, she thought you were a right bastard in the beginning for not marrying me. Imagine if we had got married, we'd have driven each other crazy. We'd have been bad parents too, bickering all the time."

I can't believe my ears! "I suppose you're right," I eventually say.

"You're a good dad! Rose loves you… and I'm fond of you too."

"I'm sorry for the way things went, Helen. You're right, it wouldn't have worked…but I could have handled things better."

"Yes, indeed you could," she says, heaving a sigh, "You never gave me much credit for thinking. I may not have known much about literature, but I wasn't stupid."

"Helen! I never suggested you were stupid!"

"No, but you certainly considered me lightweight. You never talked to me about anything real…like the way you talked to Claire Riley." I'm about to protest, to tell her I never thought of her in that way, when she says, "Ah Piers, I'm sorry, I'm not myself right now, that's all in the past."

Driving Helen home, my thoughts are on Rosie, trying to work the best approach to take. I want no padding - no talk of heaven or god. Well, that would be my way anyway, Helen might have other ideas. The one thing that bothers me is that I have to talk to Rosie in June's house but there's nothing I can do about it.

"What about Rose," Helens asks out of the blue.

"I told you, I'll be over in the morning!"

"Sorry…I mean about the funeral … I don't think she should go, Piers."

"You have a day to think about that, Helen. And anyway, I can take her."

"No Piers, I'd like you to be there! June will probably organise something for the children." I'm rather touched that she wants me there. "Thanks for understanding," Helen says then.

"Understanding?"

"Yes, about earlier…about the Rosary."

"That couldn't be helped… you had a lot on your mind."

"Well thanks," she says, patting my arm.

A white car shoots out across our path and I brake so suddenly we are thrown forward. I issue a string of expletives as the car speeds down the other side of the road.

"My god! They could have been killed!" Helen declares, equally shook.

"What do you mean *they*, we could have been killed! I bet it's a stolen car!"

"It looked a bit of a wreck though…did you see the smoke coming out of it?"

"No! …"

"Well thank goodness no one was hurt."

I pull up outside her house, still not the better of it and take deep breaths to calm down.

"I'll be over early. Try and get some sleep."

"I'll do my best," she smiles.

My throat tightens as I watch her open the door and step inside. I feel bad that she's alone. If only I could comfort her. Why does everything have to be so complicated? Why does guilt have to be a factor.

I arrive too early next morning and remain in the car listening to the news: an American helicopter has been shot down in Iraq; the bombing campaign is continuing in Afghanistan. Funny how we don't hear much about what's happening there: the same old shots of remote desert areas. Catriona was upset when a whole wedding party had been killed because they discharged weapons into the air after the ceremony, a tradition there seemingly.

Helen opens the door and comes to the car, her eyes glazed and puffy. "Why didn't you knock…were you here long?"

"Not long… I was listening to the radio. You look tired…did you get any sleep?"

"Yes, I slept okay," she assures me but I don't believe her.

As we sit drinking coffee, Helen runs her fingers, like teeth of a comb, through her thick fair hair, lifting it from her forehead in a series of rills; it falls over her face again when she removes her hand.

"I could have stayed you know," I say aimlessly but when I see the alarm in her eyes, I quickly add, "I mean I could have stayed in the house."

"I was fine, Piers," she says. "Really," she adds to convince me. "My god! I'd better jump in the shower…look at the time."

Helping myself to more coffee, I look around for something to read but all I find are cookery books. I don't take the liberty of looking elsewhere which drives home how wide the gap is between us now, only for Rosie this house has nothing to do with me. I wash out the coffee pot and mugs and turn off the kettle switch.

"Piers," Helen calls from the hall. "Will you put that in the car for me," she asks pointing to a large bag.

"Christ! What have you in here?" I exclaim when I go to lift it.

"Clothes," she smiles "and shoes for me and Rose." Helen follows with a suit draped over her arm which she hangs up in the back. "I'll just make sure everything is off," she says. I assure her that everything is off but she goes inside anyway. This was one of the things that used to annoy me when we lived together.

* * *

June forces a smile; she makes no bones about disliking me. Their brother Sean didn't like me either. I'm determined to stay calm and go with the flow in the coming days for Helen's sake.

June places a mug of tea before me without asking if I wanted any and points to the sugar and the milk on the table. Rosie comes in still in her pyjamas. She doesn't engage with me at all and goes straight to Helen. Maybe the boys were teasing her or something. However, when they come in, she seems quite at ease with them. June finishes her tea and ushers the boys out to get dressed. "Have you been a good girl for Auntie June," Helen asks lifting Rosie onto her lap. Rosie nods.

"We have something to tell you, Rosie…something sad …"

"I know! Mummy is sad," Rosie replies, almost looking though me. Helen's eyes mist up and Rosie kisses her.

"Mummy is sad because Granny Kearns won't be coming home from hospital," I begin. "Gran's gone to heaven…she won't have any more pain in heaven." I say betraying myself. In truth, I'm not equipped to explain death to a small child.

"I know!" Rosie states matter-of-factly.

"You do…did Joseph tell you?" I ask.

"Joseph doesn't know!"

Helen frowns at me but I don't dwell on how Rosie knows, I'm more interested in how she feels. "We're all sad about Gran not coming home…"

"It's alright Daddy…she's in a nice place."

"Yes Rose, Gran's in heaven now," Helen confirms.

Rosie snuggles into Helen like a baby. The matter has been dealt with in less than five minutes. I'm left wondering who was really conducting affairs.

* * *

I skipped the removal because I needed to see Catriona. I had hoped to talk to her about Rosie, something I had been meaning to do for some time, but when I arrived, she was busy working on a song and afterwards, she began telling me about her day. I didn't think it was the right time anyway, and besides, we were both rather tired. I expected her to say something about the amount of time I spent with Helen, but she didn't, which I appreciated. We had an early night and it was nice to fall asleep beside her.

A whipping easterly wind blows as we follow Josie's coffin. Helen is wearing a large wrap over her suit, so hopefully, she won't be too cold. Sean Kearns and June's husband Owen are the only bearers I know. Then someone mentions that the tall lad is Sean's son, Stephen.

The children are staying with Helen's cousin, Sandra, who lives on Model Farm Road. Rosie seemed happy enough to go, so one less worry for me. Still, I wonder what she is thinking right now.

Helen, composed, holds Tim's hand at the graveside: she was never one for public displays of emotion. June, also composed, links a tearful Owen. Owen Wills could do no wrong in Josie's book. Helen, too, speaks endearingly of him.

When the coffin is lowered, June and Helen throw roses. Standing well behind, I say my own prayer: *Goodbye Josie, you were easy to like, salt of the earth.*

Thank you for being such a good Grandmother to Rosie, she will miss you greatly. I don't know if I believe in an afterlife, or god, or whatever. You knew that about me, I could always be honest with you. Yet here I am talking to you. I'm full of contradictions, Josie.

* * *

Tim Arnold has moved in with Helen! No mention yet of the wedding. Helen is looking better; the painful strain is gone from her face. Rosie has adjusted, better than expected. Her focus now is on Christmas. I'm not one for Christmas much but I was delighted when Helen invited me for Christmas morning. Catriona was none too pleased for various reasons but mainly because she wanted me to come to Tower. I tried to impress upon her the importance of Rosie seeing me at Christmas. However, when she heard it was only for the morning, I was roped into going to Tower afterwards. I tried to wriggle out of it saying that Christmas wasn't the best time to meet her family but it turned out that it was her mother's idea to invite me.

Sunshine streams through the windows and birds are chirping in the garden, one could be forgiven for thinking it was spring. I smile to myself at the idea of going to someone's house for breakfast. I gather up the respective gifts: Martel Brandy for Tim, his favourite tipple seemingly; Rosie's fairy outfit and a voucher for a fashion outlet for Helen. I bought chocolates and whisky for Tower.

The traffic is light and I find I'm driving too fast and slow down. It will be a different story in an hour or so. Driving past houses, I begin to imagine the people inside – excited children with their toys and excited animals. At least the weather is nice for people to get out and about. There is another side of Christmas though, hangovers; rows; disappointed and frightened children; elderly and lonely people; loneliness made palpable by the seeming happy season.

Tim greets me at the door wearing an apron. "Happy Christmas," he says and I follow him into the kitchen. "Helen will be down in a sec," he says getting back to the cooking. "Is there anything you don't like…mushrooms, pudding," he asks as he lifts sausages from the pan on to a plate.

"No! I'll have whatever is going."

"Grand!" he says.

Rosie comes rushing down the stairs, Helen behind her. "She heard you...I didn't even have time to fix her hair," Helen laughs. Rosie and I have our bear hug, the excitement of which brings on a cough. She soon recovers and shows me her new black patent leather shoes which I duly admire.

"Well, what did Santa bring you?"

"A buggy!" Rosie says pulling me by the hand to the sitting room. Angie is propped up in the buggy with a soother wedged between her close-knit plastic fingers.

"And a new baby doll," Helen prompts, pointing to the abandoned beauty under the tree.

"Breakfast's up," Tim calls.

"Tim loves his fry up. It's not exactly Christmassy. Do you remember the champagne breakfast we had one year...and the mouldy strawberries?"

"I do! They looked fresh when I bought them!"

"You never let go of anything, Piers," she laughs. "You were so serious over the bloody strawberries! Sure, we were fine with the champagne?"

"You mean you were!" I retort and she laughs again. Reminiscing is the last thing I would have expected.

The dining room table is all decorated. Helen loves this kind of thing. I'm nicely hungry and breakfast goes down well with two mugs of Helen's delicious coffee. "What's the weather like out...is it very cold," Helen asks a little concerned.

"A nip in the air but it's nice enough."

"Don't worry love, she'll be fine. We'll wrap her up nice and warm. Won't we Rose," Tim says patting Rosie's head. Rosie smiles up at him. *Fuck you! She's my daughter and her name is Rosie.* Tim talks and smiles and I wear my poker friendly face. Helen rises to clear the table, but Tim insists on doing it.

"Let's go into the sitting room, Piers," Helen suggests. "Are you sure you don't want any help, love?" she calls after Tim.

"No pet, I'll be with you in a tick."

Pet! Love! Helen and Tim; Helen Tim and Rosie. I better get used to it. This is how it's going to be. I wonder now if it was such a good idea coming here at all. Rosie pulls me over to the tree to show me the angels she made at school. "They are the nicest angels I've ever seen!" I tell her and her sweet face placates the jealous beast in me.

Helen gives me the nod when Tim joins us and I fetch the presents. Rosie's eyes light up when she sees the fairy dress with wings. She is further excited when she finds the magic wand underneath. Helen tries to dissuade her from putting the dress on but capitulates when she sees Rosie's disappointment.

"Thanks for the brandy, Piers, I'll enjoy tucking into that! The office is closed for the week... thank god for Christmas. How about you? Have you much time off?"

"Not a whole week...but it's nice to get any kind of break." No doubt. Helen told him of my teaching days.

"Indeed...if this weather holds up, we'll be able to get out and about. A bit of fresh air would do Rose good," Tim says but this time I let it flow over me.

Rosie rushes in and dances around in sparkling pink and lilac, waving her magic wand; we are all put under a spell, including Angie and the angels. The new baby doll is not included. Helen sits on the arm of Tim's chair, sharing in his enjoyment of Rosie's antics. I feel guilty now seeing them so relaxed. Deep down, I do want them to be happy!

When Helen has difficulty getting Rosie back upstairs to change, I tell Rosie that it's a special dress for parties but she looks unconvinced and goes off none too happy. Rosie, not one to sulk for long, returns with a big grin and carrying a present for me. I open it slowly to prolong her excited anticipation.

"Oh, thank you Rosie...this is lovely..."

"Put it on, Daddy," she insists. I take off my jumper and put on the Christmas one. Tim and Helen are trying to keep a straight face.

"This must be Rudolf," I say picking out the reindeer with the red nose.

"Press his nose," she says all excited. Rudolf's nose lights up and she roars laughing and sits on my knee and starts pressing too.

Tim has given Rosie a storybook, beautifully illustrated with fairies of all shapes and sizes, little woodland animals, and a princess of course. Turning over the pages with her, I'm nostalgically reminded of, The Snowman, by Raymond Briggs that my mother gave me one Christmas.

Towards noon, not wanting to outstay my welcome, I tell Helen that I should get going.

"Stay a bit longer, if you're not in a hurry," Helen encourages. "We don't need to be in Glanmire till three. Everything's ready... we have only to put on our coats," she assures me.

"I'm in no great hurry," I reply, happy to have the extra time with Rosie.

Rosie now has a ribbon in her hair and is wearing a new blue coat. I think the coat makes her look too grown up, too prim. Helen belts Rosie in and puts Angie beside her while Tim puts the doll's buggy in the boot. Rosie, clutching a present for Mrs. Arnold, waves me goodbye. When the car is out of sight, I take off Rudolf and put my own jumper on. No doubt, I'll be wearing Rudolf again soon enough.

Traffic has increased. I keep to the slow lane because I don't want to get to Tower too early. Halfway down, I pull in. Leaning on an old iron gate, I'm immediately captivated by the pale golden light descending in shafts on the fields. It reminds me of my poem, Light Descending. On the right edge of the near field, three horses are grazing, their chestnut coats gleaming in the sun. The light shafts dissipate when clouds drift across the sun. The landscape changes spectacularly with the movement of clouds across the sky. Every season has its treasures but I especially like the fragile silver light through the bare trees in December and January.

Catriona and I have already exchanged presents which I'm glad about now. We had planned on going for a drink after shopping but the pubs were too packed. We had a lovely time at home anyway. We lit a fire and lots of candles and Catriona put Christmas lights on her rubber plant. Our bodies cast giant shadows on the walls and the Christmas lights flashed on and off. We fooled around on the keyboard playing as many Christmas songs we could remember; Catriona could have gone on for hours, but my amorous advances put paid to that!

Of all the times I dropped Catriona home, I never met her parents. It would have been easier if I had before now. There are lots of cars outside the house so it takes me a while to find somewhere to park. The front door is ajar but I press on the bell anyway. Catriona's mother, a tall woman with faded red hair, welcomes me. She thanks me for the whisky and chocolates but tells me there was no need. "They're all in here," she says, ushering me into a room and closing the door behind me and I'm left standing there with umpteen pairs of eyes on me. Catriona waves from the piano with a big smile. Her brother Jack, whom I've met once before, brings a chair and shyly says hello. Catriona's sister, Moira starts to sing, 'Some Day My Heart Will Awake.' She has an incredible voice; Catriona certainly didn't exaggerate. Catriona joins me at the earliest opportunity and kisses me full on the mouth right in front of everybody. She looks stunning in a dark blue velvet dress and she's wearing the sapphire pendant I gave her.

"What would you like? We have Champagne!"

"I'll have a beer, if it's handy," I say, thinking it the safer option.

"A boring old beer," she mutters, but goes to get one.

Catriona introduces me to her uncle Peter; he strikes me as a very gentle sort of person; the red hair is obviously a Hennessey trait. Jack comes over (he has brown hair) with a tray of canapés and I take a slice of brown bread and salmon, out of politeness.

"He's a lovely lad," the elderly man beside me says. "He gets a right teasing you know with the name," he smiles. "Jack Lynch, the Real Taoiseach," he qualifies as if I didn't know.

A woman on the other side of him whispers, "He's the boyfriend!"

Catriona's father, Harry holds court like a king. "Happy Christmas to you...we meet at last," he says vigorously shaking my hand. "Do you play an instrument at all?" He enquires in a broad west Cork accent.

"No, sorry..."

"He used to play piano," Catriona says grinning and I stare wide eyed at her.

"Let him settle in...he might play for us later. How about you Eileen," he asks, moving on. "Any chance of a song?" Eileen is only too willing and sings, 'The Contender' and everyone joins in the chorus.

Catriona's mother, now in the room, is chatting to people when Harry suddenly bursts into, 'Dein Ist Mein Ganzes Herz' and I notice her disquieting look in his direction. Moira hastens to the piano but makes no attempt to play.

Catriona tugs my sleeve, "This won't last long," she giggles, and sure enough Harry stops dead in his tracks. "He does the same with La Donna É Mobile… he only knows a few words." Catriona laughs heartily and Moira glares over at her. Moira then plays the intro to, 'With a Song in my Heart' and Harry finds his feet with this. During the applause, Mrs. Lynch whispers something in Harry's ear and pats his shoulder. He looks contrite for a moment but then looks up at her adoringly. Mrs. Lynch bends down and kisses his cheek. I must say, The Lynches are an extrovert bunch!

Mrs Lynch then goes over and talks to Peter who subsequently fetches his fiddle from the sideboard. Taking a few minutes to tune up, he smiles at his sister and starts to play. 'Mná na hEireann' gets everyone's attention. The haunting slow air permeates my consciousness, soothing and drawing forth memory: the Comeraghs and Monavullaghs in winter and in summer mode, where the secret voice of Eriú resounds over rock and river; my father holds my hand as we tread paths of laurel, ferns and brambles, paths that sometimes lead to fulgent mountain streams.

The last notes are sounded. Peter holds the bow aloft and everyone remains quite still. Mrs Lynch breaks the gossamer silence. "That was beautiful, Peter, thank you."

"Anything for you, Mae!" He says endearingly.

Harry, much affected, wipes a tear from his eye. Peter's wife, Geraldine, breaks the spell by bursting into a humorous song and everyone is laughing including me.

People begin to leave around four o'clock and I assume the session is over but I'm taken by surprise when Harry calls for my party piece.

"I'm sorry, I don't have a party piece…besides there's far better talent in the room."

"Talent! Forget talent… let yourself go, man, it's Christmas," Harry says.

Catriona pulls at my arm, saying, "We'll do, 'It Came Upon the Midnight Clear,' it'll round things off nicely."

"Catriona, I'm not playing the piano!" I whisper to her but she continues pulling my arm. I played the base part of the duet in the flat the other night for fun but if she thinks I'm doing it now, she must be mad.

"Oh, you're such a stuff-shirt stick-in-the mud," she berates. I hold tough, however. "Oh alright! Read a poem so!" She says too audibly and a little derisively for my liking.

"A poem would be lovely!" Geraldine says amiably. An embarrassed silence ensues as I throw dagger looks at Catriona.

"Catriona! Don't press people," her mother says, coming to my rescue.

"Yes, leave the man alone, if he doesn't want to!" Harry says in agreement.

Catriona shoulders me playfully but I don't look at her. "Don't tell me you're going to sulk now, Cantwell," she says, again too audibly.

"You shouldn't have put me on the spot!"

"I only asked you to play the piano, for god's sake," she says pouting. Is it my imagination, but has she been acting the little girl ever since I arrived? Is this what she's like on her home turf?

Finally, Catriona and I are left alone but I don't get time to talk to her because Moira marches over and practically orders her to the kitchen. I get no acknowledgement at all. "I'll be there in a sec," Catriona says and Moira goes off looking pleased with herself. This is a revelation! Usually, Catriona doesn't take kindly to being ordered about. She stands up then and looks at me oddly.

"Is something the matter," I ask.

"No!" She replies but then pulls my head back roughly by the hair and kisses me hard on the mouth and leaves me sitting there confused.

Over dinner, I'm told that the Christmas session has become a tradition of sorts in the area. I missed great music earlier: the brothers, Paddy and Mike McHugh had called and beat out a medley of tunes on the box and tin whistle and having accepted a drop or two set off to another designated rendezvous. Peter had played his heart out all morning, with Paddy and Mike, on his own, and with Cian O'Driscoll on guitar.

"That Cian can play with the best of um!" Harry declares. "He's only seventeen…he plays note for note…not just chords mind. Pity he had to go so early. But sure 'twas great to have him at all! A great lad altogether!" Peter says little, about the music or anything else, giving me the impression that he is a modest individual.

Mrs. Lynch says it's different every year, you wouldn't't know who'd call and that was the exciting part. Harry expresses his disappointment that Maureen Casey couldn't come this year. "She has great songs but the poor soul hasn't a note in her head," Harry laughs.

Moira, I notice, hangs on his every word; she glances at me from time to time but I don't know whether she's being friendly or challenging. What is it with bloody sisters?

Harry is none too pleased when Jack scoffs his dinner and leaves the table. Mrs. Lynch smiles when he's gone and says to me, "Poor Jack, he's been waiting all day to escape."

"He has every other day of the year to go to Keith's…one day won't kill him. It's not every day we have such fine musicians in the house!" Harry says in a tone that suggests she is too soft on him. "And he hardly ate anything."

"He won't go hungry up at Mahon's…"

"True! Anyway, if I know him, he'll be raiding the fridge when we're in bed…or trying to set the house on fire frying his concoctions."

Geraldine and Peter, who have no children, seem to be enjoying Harry's accounts of Jack's antics. All this talk of family makes me feel like a real outsider. Mrs. Lynch talks then about how much Tower has changed, how the new people haven't much interest in music or the community in general.

"All they care about are their big jeeps and big houses," Catriona grumbles, "they'd roll over you as quick as look at you!"

Harry chuckles as he forks a lump of ham. "Too much pressure on people nowadays, love… no one has the time. They want the big house, but don't have time to live in it. They tell us we have one of the richest economies in the world…can you credit that," he says laughing. "A small island on the edge of Europe!"

"And people believe it…they can't see it's a trap," I say without thinking.

"They'll see soon enough…money won't lead them anywhere!" Peter says expressing an opinion for the first time. Geraldine nods in agreement.

"On the road to nowhere," I say then.

"Oh, Talking Heads sang that!" Moira comments and I feel the ice is breaking a little.

"Yes, I believe they did, but I was thinking of Luis Buñuel," I explain but she looks away as if I've insulted her.

"Who is he, Piers?" Catriona asks, addressing me for the first time.

"He was a film director…"

"I never heard of him!" Catriona says, "Is he French?"

"Spanish…well Spanish Mexican…he took…"

"I've heard of him," Mrs. Lynch interjects, "The Discreet Charm of the Bourgeoisie… wasn't that one of his films. Mind you I've never seen it," she laughs. "He was before your time, dear." Is she deliberately making a point about our age difference?

"How did you come to know about him?" Catriona asks, genuinely interested.

"Oh, through my interest in Lorca… he and Lorca were friends."

"Oh right!" She says nodding her head.

The conversation turns again to music, to my relief; Harry is all praise for the McHugh brothers, saying they'd still be playing their hearts out somewhere.

"I don't think those two are human!" Catriona says and they all laugh.

"And the drink never affects them," Peter adds to more laughter.

"I hope you weren't expecting plum pudding, Piers," Mrs. Lynch says, "no one here ever eats it."

"I like plum pudding, Mae," Harry asserts.

Mrs. Lynch smiles at him. "You like the idea of it, Harry. Your mother used to make lovely ones and you remember her setting the pudding alight with the whisky…it's a nostalgic thing. But be honest, you never eat it now."

"I suppose you're right, Mae," he says looking wistful suddenly.

"We don't have trifle either!" Catriona shoots at me. "Piers loves trifle!"

"Ah, you should have told me! We could have made one," her mother says. "I'm afraid it's pear and almond tart or fruit salad, Piers."

"Be warned, young man, the fruit salad is spiked!" Harry says smiling at Moira.

"I only added a little drop of vodka!" Moira says defensively.

"We know your idea of a drop," Harry laughs and Moira manages a smile.

I enjoyed the dinner: turkey portions on a little bed of stuffing on thick slices of ham, served with broccoli, potato, sweet potato puree and a nice sauce. No Brussels sprouts, no roast potatoes, and no monstrous bird on the table. When Moira brings in the deserts, I'm offered a portion of each and both are delicious. I detect only the merest hint of vodka in the fruit.

After dinner they retire to the sitting room but to my surprise, it's not the room from earlier. I can't believe my eyes when I see another piano, admittedly a smaller modern one. What house has two pianos? This room is equally large but cosy and more intimate with a Christmas tree and a TV.

Mrs. Lynch pours a brandy for herself and offers me one which I accept. "A Hennessy for a Hennessy eh!" Harry jokes as he settles into the big-cushioned armchair. I bet he's burnt her ears with that umpteen times! Moira brings Harry a whisky. He didn't drink wine at dinner. I guess he's more of a pint and a drop man. Peter helps himself to the chocolates I brought and is drinking lemonade. There is also an unopened box of Roses and a tin of biscuits on the table. Geraldine and Moira are drinking Chinese black tea that Peter brought back from Hong Kong.

Everything now is slow and relaxed, candlelight and Christmas lights, the only illumination. I like their tree! Sparsely decorated with thin strips of tinsel, and a few clip-on birds. The bell-shaped fairy lights with nursery rhymes look quite old; some of the rhymes are worn away. A silver star on top looks old too.

The smell of the pine needles evokes pleasant memories of our old house, of a time that is now a universe away. Christmas means nothing to me anymore, well apart from Rosie's enjoyment of course and people's seasonal expectations. For me, everything has been stripped away inch by inch: Santa, the baby Jesus, the spin on the birth in Bethlehem; well, the whole thing really of supplanting the old pagan festival. At least, in this house, I got something real with the people and the music.

Harry's laughter eclipses my thoughts. Moira is grinning from ear to ear, but the joke is not shared. Catriona starts humming a tune. "I can't get that out of my head," she says humming a little louder. "Peter, what's that tune?"

"I don't know! Sing it again."

Catriona does one better by playing a sketchy melody on the piano. Moira, suddenly interested, goes over and pushes Catriona aside rather rudely. No one bats an eye, least of all Catriona. I can't believe what I'm seeing.

"Cian played it this morning," Moira says and plays the tune.

"Yeah! That's it exactly!" Catriona exclaims, content to have put a shape to it.

"I don't remember him playing that at all," Peter says.

"You were in the kitchen with Mammy," Moira informs him.

"What's the name of it?"

"I don't know!" Moira answers, starting to play something else.

Catriona sits on the side of my armchair and leans against me, discreetly stroking the back of my neck. I still can't get my head around her behaviour earlier.

"We've had enough music for today, dear," Mrs. Lynch states calmly and Moira closes the piano and returns to Harry's side.

"Did she just remember that tune from this morning?" I ask Catriona.

"I suppose. Ah…she probably heard it before somewhere."

I sip my brandy and think of Rosie - she'd be asleep now. I hope the day's excitement wasn't too much for her. She did look a little flushed. The fairy dress was a success anyhow. I smile to myself remembering the rejected baby under the tree. Helen probably thought she'd be delighted with a new doll. Catriona's sighs draw my attention. "Everything okay?" I whisper.

"Yeah," she says but the sighs continue. I know those sighs. "Would you like to go for a walk, Piers. I don't think it's too cold out."

"A walk would be great," I reply, genuinely eager to escape. I was going to suggest it myself but I didn't want to rock the boat in anyway.

"Come on so," she says attempting to pull me up.

"Let him finish his drink first," her mother says half laughing. Catriona lets go of my arm and sits on the floor like a crumpled puppet.

"I'll have it later," I say smiling across at Mrs. Lynch and Catriona is animated with invisible strings.

Catriona is delighted to see the roofs frosted up, saying it's more like Christmas.

"We had Spring this Morning, Autumn in the afternoon and now it's Winter," I say laughing. "That's why we're so temperamental, I suppose," I add, hinting at her behaviour earlier.

Catriona links my arm and we make our way down the Kerry Road, walking on the footpath until it runs out. It is such a relief to be finally alone: it was difficult relating to her with everyone's eyes on me. Perhaps, it was a strain on her too, it would explain the odd behaviour.

We huddle in off the road when a car passes and it leads to a kiss. Her nose is cold; her smell is familiar; she feels mine again. I unbutton her coat and let my hands wander over her velvet covered curves. "Do you want me to stop?" I tease.

"I certainly do," she says with mock indignation, buttoning up her coat and pulling me back onto the road. She links my arm again cheerfully and we head to the village at a steady pace.

The village is eerily quiet - not a person to be seen in any direction. People are always out and about in Cork no matter what time of year it is. In my teaching days, I was considered a countryman, but I'm a townie really. Dungarvan is a big enough town.

We sit on a low stone wall near the Huntsman pub for a breather. "It wasn't so bad, was it," Catriona asks, looking at me earnestly.

"I like walking!"

"Not the walk, silly, Christmas with my family?"

"It was very nice...*is* very nice." She nestles into me and sighs and I'm hoping these are contented ones.

A partial moon, amid twinkling stars, plays hide and seek behind naked trees and our breaths cloud ghostly in front of us as we make our way back. Halfway up we stop and kiss: two lone figures on the Kerry Road on Christmas night under a propitious sky.

In the hallway, we hear Moira playing her violin upstairs and low conversational tones from the sitting room. I feel awkward now, like an intruder, wishing I were somewhere else. Catriona opens the door and I meekly follow.

"Where's Dad," Catriona enquires.

"Gone to bed," her mother replies. "He was exhausted." Catriona glances at me raising her eyebrows.

"It's real Christmassy out, Mam…the frost is like snow on the roofs."

Peter, a little concerned, asks what the roads are like and Catriona assures him that the roads are fine but he goes outside to check for himself.

"We didn't expect this drop in temperature," Geraldine says looking equally concerned. Peter returns and tells Geraldine that they should go now in case it gets any worse.

"If you're worried Peter, stay the night. Jack can sleep on the sofa," Mrs. Lynch says.

"We'll head away now, Mae, thanks anyway." Mrs. Lynch helps Geraldine carry their stuff to the car. Peter, I notice, only carries his fiddle.

"I'm so glad we went out! I was getting claustrophobic," Catriona says handing me the brandy from earlier. I don't want to talk about earlier, at least not here, not now!

"You can finally relax with your drink, I see," Mrs. Lynch says returning. "Would you like a fresh one?"

"No thanks! This is fine…more than enough!" Catriona laughs at me but her mother takes no heed.

"I read some of your poems recently, Piers," she says. "Mind you, there were a few I didn't quite understand. Raindrops and Sycamores is lovely… it brought back memories of my walks along the River Sullane with my grandmother. It's about your father, I believe. You obviously loved him very much. You must miss him."

I'm a little taken aback, not expecting this conversation. "I do…he died when I was fourteen."

"That must have been difficult, for your mother," she says.

"Why didn't you read a poem for us, earlier," she asks, tilting her head attractively to one side.

"Because he's too much of a snob!" Catriona interjects. "The atmosphere wasn't conducive to poetry."

"That's not true… I never said that." Catriona grimaces accusingly as much to say, you may not have said it, but that's what you were thinking. *Why is she confronting me like this? It's my first time meeting her family, she should be making it easier for me if anything.* "I just thought people were happier with the music,

– 69 –

Mrs. Lynch."

"Oh, please call me Mae, no one calls me Mrs. Lynch," she smiles. "You were probably right…Christmas can be a boisterous time."

"Is that what you think of our music, Mam?"

"No, love…I just mean there's a lot of drinking at Christmas."

"I'm only joking, Mam," Catriona says sounding again like a little girl which I find disconcerting. Maybe it's because I don't usually see her in the context of family.

"You might read for us another time."

"Yes, I'd like that very much." I think Mae would be an interesting woman to know. Some say daughters turn into their mothers. Not bad in this case! Mae must have been some looker in her day.

"Catriona, call Moira and we'll clear up before we get too tired."

I get up offering to help too but Catriona pushes me forcibly off my feet back on to the armchair and I roar at her calling her a bitch, quite forgetting myself.

"For goodness' sake, Catriona," Mae chides, at her daughter's rough physicality, but then she catches my eye and smiles. "You're a guest, Piers! Relax there for a while. We're only going to load the washer… and put away a few things. Help yourself to whatever you want," she says pointing to the drinks cabinet.

Earlier, I did notice the dishes piled up on the countertop and pots in the sink. My mother would not be happy with that, neither would Helen, come to think of it. Here, they are all very relaxed, no mad rushing and scurrying - and things get done just the same.

I root through the magazine rack and pick out the Holly Bough: funny, with all my years in Cork, I have never read it. The historical pieces interest me and I like the old photographs. There's a strange kind of quiz with numbers and letters. I decipher a few but it would be rude to fill them in. Bursts of laughter break from the kitchen; all goes quiet for a while and then more laughter.

Mae comes in to say goodnight and tells me Catriona is making up the bed for me. I thank her and wish her good night.

Catriona appears wearing a sweater and tracksuit bottoms and I'm disappointed, I rather liked the luring smoothness of her velvet dress and the sheerness of her stockings. "You'll be glad to know, we have the place to ourselves," she grins. "Jack is staying in Mahon's and Mam's gone to bed."

"I know, she just said goodnight to me. But what about Moira? She might want to watch TV or something."

"No, she'll stay upstairs…Moira does her own thing."

"I hope I'm not cramping her style…"

"You're not! As I said, she likes to do her own thing."

"What was all the laughing about earlier?"

She thinks for a minute, "Oh, nothing really…only Moira doing her impressions."

"Her impressions?"

"Moira studies people's mannerisms…she's a right mimic…it's amazing what she picks up on."

"Did she pick up on any of mine?"

"So what if she did! She does it with everybody," she says a little tetchy.

"You looked lovely today, by the way… your dress was beautiful."

"Thanks! It was Mammy's present."

"You should have left it on."

"I didn't want to get it dirty cleaning up. Anyway, I feel more comfortable in this. Oh! I forgot! I have the very thing," she says going over to the TV. "I recorded, 'It's a Wonderful Life' for you." It was nice of her to record it for me. She goes to the kitchen for 'goodies' as she says and returns with a plate of turkey and ham and a bowl of olives and cheese. She goes off again and brings in bread and a bottle of champagne. "I hid this earlier," she grins, handing me the bottle to open. "And I know where there's a few more," she laughs. I mute the pop with a cloth as she tilts the glasses ready, giggling at her little conspiracy. She bites off an olive from a cocktail stick and tries to pass it into my mouth but I pull away. "Ah you're no fun, at all, Cantwell," she complains.

Surprisingly, we polish off the food and the champagne. Catriona, succumbing to drowsiness, rests her head on my lap and falls asleep while I wait devotedly until Clarence gets his wings.

Catriona shows me to the room where I'm sleeping. The bare floorboards are spattered here and there with daubs of white paint and there are old picture frames standing against the wall. A lampshade and shoes are piled the corner. I put my clothes on the windowsill and get into the sturdy enough fold-up-bed. The quality bedlinen is a far cry from what I'm used to.

I'm mulling over the day's events when the door opens and Catriona sneaks in beside me and puts her hand over my mouth. When I chuckle, she threatens to pull out the hairs of my chest if I don't stay quiet. Her attempts to muffle me only succeed in giving me an erection. I roll on top of her and putting my hand over her mouth, tell her she's making more noise than I am.

Next morning Harry is the only one up. "I see you're an early riser like myself," he smiles. "There's a fresh pot of tea made. There's ham here...but cut more if you want," he says. "You have to help yourself around here in the mornings."

"I always wake early, so I may as well get up."

"I'm not one for the *leaba*, either... morning is the best time, anyhow," he says looking out the kitchen window at the fields beyond. He seems quite different from yesterday. He enquires about the work I do in the medical company. When I tell him I'm not that interested, other than the money, he laughs and says, "sure isn't that why we all work!"

"I guess it is," I say laughing too.

"The sky is good...I think it'll be fine," he says. "Have you any interest in the horses? There should be mighty craic later," he says. Mae enters the kitchen and bids us both good morning and proceeds to make a fresh pot of tea. She seems rather low-key, even with Harry. Perhaps she's not a morning person. I finish my breakfast and make myself scarce.

The front sitting room is full of empty bottles, a few here and there still have drink in them. I consider collecting them up but it would mean going back to the kitchen to get sacks. I'm not sure what the story is with Mae. I wonder did she hear our antics last night - manoeuvring in that bed wasn't easy! Besides, they might be offended if I start clearing up.

I relax in the other sitting room reading the historical articles in the Holly

Bough. After some time, I get bit restless because the morning is slipping away and there's no sign of Catriona. I leave it for a while longer before calling her. "Hello…who's that!" she croaks.

"Who do you think …"

"God! What time is it?"

"It's gone eleven …nearly twelve."

"Is that all!"

"I've been up a good while. Are you getting up?"

"You could have had a lie in, Piers… for once in your life," she complains. Catriona comes down eventually but still in her dressing gown; I was hoping we could go out for a while. She kisses my cheek rather perfunctorily and says, "You should relax more, Cantwell!" Her manner is different somehow which makes me think that I'm not quite fitting in here.

"I'm perfectly relaxed! Just wanted to see you before I go. Must get back… things to do."

"Okay!" She says without hesitation and I wonder if her mother said something. Maybe she feels awkward with me here now

When I say goodbye to Harry and Mae, Harry seems genuinely surprised I'm not staying but Mae just says it was lovely to have met me finally.

Catriona puts her arms around my neck and kisses me, more meaningfully this time. I wish she were coming with me but I understand how it is. Stephens Day is a big deal here seemingly; she was saying something about a Point to Point but I wasn't really listening. When I'm leaving, she asks what we're doing for New Year's Eve. I tell her I don't mind what we do, so long as we're together and she seems pleased.

* * *

Gusting winds shake the car in the exposed sections of the road. There is a strange piece of music on the radio. No time for reflection, however, because I need to concentrate on the driving. Normally, I wouldn't drive down in weather like this, but Nan has been ill with a chest infection and is still quite frail, according to my mother.

My grandmother's house is like my true home now since my mother moved.

Frank and Paddy added an extension with a proper kitchen and a downstairs toilet and shower. The old kitchen was a tiny area with a cooker and a press, when I was young. Nan's cosy little sitting room was a dining area. Nan sleeps downstairs now in the old sitting room, a room that was rarely used as far as I can remember. I don't like my mother's bungalow; I don't think she likes it herself, but it's closer to town and less expensive to run. Last summer, I went by our old house; it still had the old windows, but there was a new door and a fancy wrought-iron gate which made the place look more private. Mam's rose bush was still there - planted when Evelyn was born. I presume her herb garden is still out the back.

Nan is up and dressed and happy to see me. My mother mustn't be long gone. When Nan is settled by the cheerful fire, I pour some whisky into two nice glasses - Waterford Crystal - what else!

"Sorry I didn't get down at Christmas…but I had a great time elsewhere."

"Cheeky!"

"How was your Christmas?"

"Oh grand! My god, the amount of food, I never saw the like. Your mother enjoyed herself. She went back down after she brought me home. They had a great time, I believe. Your mother sang a song…I'm sorry I missed that. Paddy said she still has a grand voice. Anyway, tell me…what news have you?"

I tell Nan about the lovely morning I had with Rosie. She says it was good of Helen to invite me. "Come on …don't keep me in suspense!" Nan says, eager to hear about the rest of the day.

"The Lynches are an extrovert bunch, Nan… not a bit like us," I laugh. "The mother was sizing me up big time…and the sister…well let's say she wasn't too friendly." I tell her about the session that they host every year.

"That's lovely… there was always music in the house at Christmas when I was young. It's nice to know some people still hold the tradition…it's a rare thing now," she says, looking a little sad.

"Oh, I don't know…there's a lot of music in Dungarvan… I bet there were lots of sessions at Christmas."

"I suppose. It's just that I'm getting old…I don't get to hear it."

I talk about the Lynch's two sitting rooms and two pianos and she seems interested, but then she changes the subject suddenly asking about Rosie and Helen.

"Helen is still sad after poor Josie, but she's looking better."

"Good! Good! And Rosie?"

"She had a bad cold before Christmas but she's okay now."

"No! I mean how is she after Josie?

"Oh fine…kids are resilient."

"She's a strange little one all right. Isn't she?" Nan persists.

Give me a fucking break! Well, I won't give in to her!

"Rosie knew Josie was going to die, you know," she says, her eyes boring into me. "She told me Josie would be going to heaven soon."

"Someone must have told her…maybe Josies herself," I say to fob her off.

"No! You see I asked her that." *Is there anything I can do to circumvent her penchant for the mysterious?* "And do you know what else? She asked me why I was staying so long in the world. Can you credit that?" Nan says shaking her head.

"Ah you know kids."

"I do know kids! I reared my own and haven't I grandchildren and great grandchildren. You think I'm a superstitious old woman, don't you? But I can tell you I've never met a child quite like Rosie… it's like she sees through everything and that's strange for a five-year old!" Nan says, gazing into the flames. "Maybe it's some kind of gift… they say the Lord sends the gifted among us."

Loud voices outside the window distract me momentarily and I don't catch her elided words - something about Little Nellie. *I'm sick to the teeth of Little Nellie and I'm sick of her omniscient lord in the sky.* "Who, in the name of god would be out in this weather?" Nan asks.

"Just youngsters larking about," I say, pulling the curtain back. "They're oblivious to the elements." Nan smiles, she is very tolerant of young people. "I'm getting hungry, Nan. Are you hungry?"

"I could eat something, alright…your mother brought soup. Tommy put stuff in the fridge…I couldn't tell you what."

I'm about to heat up the soup when I discover there's only sliced pan and

I use it as an excuse to escape. "You don't have to go out in that... sure we have plenty in," Nan says a little peeved.

"I need a few things...and I'll get bread."

"Humph!" she says, looking up to heaven.

Rain ricochets off the ground and rivulets race along the channel below the kerb. It reminds me of when Paul and I used to make boats out of matchboxes. I lived vicariously through Paul's adventures: he had a gang and had a camp out near the sandpit; they had running battles with Sean Boyd's gang. Sean was a year ahead of us in school. My life in comparison was so boring, I felt deprived.

Rain pricks my skin like a myriad steel pins, chilling me to the bone. Paul would surely call me a wimp! I know it was crazy coming out! Nan is back there knowing exactly why I came out, and that's what's bugging me.

The herbal aroma of the vegetable soup with chicken stock, wafts through the kitchen. My mother has liquidized it; I hope Nan appreciates the efforts she makes. I search through Nan's crockery and find lovely floral-patterned bowls. Nan seems pleased to see them. "They were a gift from Paddy's wife," she informs me.

Nan's cheeks look hollow without her teeth. False teeth were more as a cosmetic thing in her day, according to my mother. Mam has been trying to get her to the dentist for a new set. Thinking of teeth reminds of a story Toby told me about a woman who went to Russia with a Trade Union delegation: the Russians were appalled by her teeth and offered to fix them – extractions and implants. The woman was so neglectful of her new teeth, it became a running joke among her friends that even her false teeth went bad.

Nan is more sloppy than usual and doing a new thing, breaking bread into the soup. I remind myself that she is ninety-six after all! I clear away the bowls and wipe the table and make a joke of cleaning Nan off as well but she is not amused! She seems to need a lot more humouring lately, I notice.

I pile on the last of the coal and head outside for more. "Close the bloody doors," Nan shouts and I rush back to close them. "Good man," she says when I fill up the scuttle. "Is there no let up at all to this weather. It'll be the death of me. I can't even move the fingers."

"Spring won't be long now…once January is over it'll get a lot better."

"January is a long month…it even sounds long, doesn't it?"

"February sounds equally as long," I laugh. "They're the only two with four syllables."

Nan starts to go through the months. "February is shorter than January… January still feels the longest month."

"I was only saying that February sounded as long…"

"Oh, all right! You love to argue… always nit-picking."

"Nan, you're the one who's arguing …I was just…"

"Enough!" She says crossly and I stop talking.

Nan dozes off and I put a blanket around her knees. I fetch my book, Alfred and Emily, by Doris Lessing. It's clever the way it's written - fiction and nonfiction. I find Lessing's relationship with her mother interesting: I wish I had the strength to live my life apart from family. Claire gave it to me, it's not a book I'd have picked up myself but I'm enjoying it.

"You want to tell me about that woman of yours, don't you?" Nan says, as if continuing a conversation from a minute ago. Does she even know she was asleep?

"Would you like another drop, Nan," I ask, giving her time to recover.

"Ah, I won't! I'm not as tough as I used to be," she says with none of her old banter.

"I'll make tea so…"

"Yes, that'd be good!"

Nan drinks her tea and I have another whisky.

"I think I'm in love, Nan."

"I see a change in you, alright. She's beautiful, you say."

"She is, but not just looks; I fell for looks before and look where that got me."

Nan and Helen never really hit it off. Helen is a suburban woman who doesn't understand the dynamics of living in a town, not to mind the country. "Catriona understands me, she knows I need time to myself sometimes. She's like that herself."

"And Rosie… does she like her?"

"Rosie doesn't really know her. They've met briefly once or twice but I try to keep them separate."

"Now why would you do that," Nan says shaking her head. "Keeping things in compartments…that's a real male thing," she adds accusingly.

"It's not like that! You know I don't get enough time with Rosie as it is. Besides, I couldn't give Catriona much attention if Rosie were around."

"And she'd fade away from lack of attention, I suppose."

"It's early days, I don't want to mess it up. I think she is the one for me."

"Well, I'd better meet her so! God knows I could be taken any day." *This is a new thing – Nan never talks of her demise.* "That reminds me, Piers…do you know what else Rosie said to me… she said Billy was in a different world now! Bedad! What do you make of that?"

When I bring Nan some tea and toast next morning, she tells me not to leave it so long the next time. I kiss her cheek and I promise to come down soon. I make an excuse of being in a hurry for not calling on Mam.

"If you wait a few more minutes, she'll be along." Nan says.

"No, I better get going."

"Okay, I'll make some excuse," she says with a wily grin.

The rain has stopped but an ominous sky looms low over a shrouded landscape which I find oppressive. The traffic has slowed to a snail's pace because of flooding. I feel claustrophobic being stuck behind a long line of vehicles.

* * *

Helen is planning her wedding, a small affair she maintains, but I wonder. The plus side is I'm spending more time with Rosie. I can't believe she'll be six in June. She is doing well in school, according to her teacher. She's doing the solar system with the children at present and they are delighted. Rosie is drawing lots of pictures of planets, bright yellow suns, and lots of stars.

I showed Rosie photographs I took of the moon and was surprised that she knew the moon is a satellite of the Earth. She was intrigued that Jupiter had many moons and wanted to know how many. I told her I didn't know exactly but named the Galilean ones for her but I didn't expect her to remember them. However, the next picture was of Jupiter with a red blob for the Great Red Spot, circled by four silver moons, outside of which were smaller white ones in the available space. We had lots of fun putting the pictures up. Rosie was delighted to show them off to Mr. Cotter. When he thanked her for the art exhibition, she beamed in appreciation.

* * *

Cloud shadows drift over patchwork fields under the clear majestic mountains. "I never knew the Waterford landscape was so beautiful!" Catriona exclaims, gazing out the car window.

"Yeah, it takes my breath away every time. It's pure heaven when the sun shines. I'll show you some of my favourite places when the exams are over."

"I look forward to that," she says, squeezing my thigh.

Uncle Tommy is the first member of my family Catriona meets. I leave them talking and head to Nan's room but she's already coming out. "Your mother is on her way over," she says and laughs at my reaction.

Tommy seems to have taken a shine to Catriona. He's bantering about Cork always stopping Waterford from getting out of Munster in the hurling. "We're going to do it this year!" He declares.

"Up the rebels!" Catriona throws back at him. I smile because she has no interest in hurling whatsoever. The slogan, Up the rebels, amuses me - clever how the GAA filched the Rebel Cork thing from historical context.

"It's lovely to finally meet you," Catriona says, shaking Nan's hand. "Piers has been trying to get me to come down for ages."

"She's a busy woman, Nan," I say in her defence.

"In that case, it's very good of you to come and visit." Nan asks about her studies and about what music she likes. They seem to be hitting it off okay.

My mother is surprised by our presence. "You have a full house this morning, Mam." she says, wide eyed.

"I do indeed...a lovely surprise." *Nan is such a good liar!*

"Are you a Cork woman," My mother asks as they shake hands.

"She's a Cork woman all right, Mary," Tommy shouts from the kitchen.

"I'm from Tower, near Blarney, but I'm living in town..."

"That would be Cork, Mary," Tommy confirms from the doorway. "Dungarvan is town here Catriona… Waterford is the big smoke."

"We have a talented lady here, Mary," Nan says, extolling Catriona's achievements.

"My sister is the real talent in the family," Catriona says modestly.

My mother is taking everything in. Tommy calls her to the kitchen and I'm glad as it gives Nan and Catriona more time to talk.

Tommy shakes Catriona's hand for the second time, saying it was lovely to meet her. "Up the Deisce!" He shouts back. I'll explain to her later what the Deisce is.

I leave them talking and go up to get a notebook I left the last time. It's not where I left it. My mother must have been tidying - wish she'd leave things where they are. I find it eventually under a stack of books. When I come down, the three of them are laughing and despite my enquiring looks, no one gives anything away.

Catriona thanks my mother for the invitation to lunch and apologises for being in such a rush.

"Maybe another time," Mam says.

"Yes, I'll look forward to that," Catriona says all smiles.

Nan takes Catriona's hand in both of hers and is slow to let go which is bit embarrassing, but Catriona doesn't seem to mind.

A few miles up the road, Catriona puts on a CD which I find quite irritating but I say nothing as she seems to be enjoying it. I'm happy that she has met Nan at last! Nan liked her too, I could tell. Catriona stops the CD and looks out at the landscape. Neither of us say much lost in our own thoughts. We're almost home when Catriona turns to me and says, "Your mother is really nice!" *Why the emphasis on my mother? I brought her to meet Nan after all.*

* * *

Joe Collins is the proverbial man about town with a finger on the pulse of what's happening: who's playing where, what plays are coming, who's doing what in general. He owns a leather shop near the Coal Quay and cuts a fine dash himself in leather waistcoats, hats, and belts. I've accepted that Joe is part of the package with Catriona. He seems genuine enough, but it's difficult to have any meaningful conversation with him. Collins let slip one time that Ger Healy was bad mouthing me. I made light of it, saying I'd be worried if Healy were saying anything good about me. He inadvertently revealed a more significant piece of information on another occasion: Ger Healy dislikes me more now because I'm going out with Catriona.

Healy is a good poet, admittedly, but he's so far up his own arse, he's hard to take; he's rude and condescending and downright hurtful at times. I once witnessed him tearing a young lad's work to shreds when he knew he had a raw recruit. Instead of offering encouragement he stroked his own ego, showing how knowledgeable he was. He preens like a peacock when it comes to young pretty women, and of course their work is fine. He gives the impression he loves women, but from what I've observed, I suspect he may be a closet misogynist.

Catriona and I were having coffee one morning when Joe joined us. He was a bit too upbeat for the sombre discussion we were having on Iraq. Having listened a few minutes, he said, "For god's sake lads, what's with all the gloom and doom." Catriona, visibly irritated, threw me sideways glances. At that moment I was more interested in his use of the term, lads, which to some Corkonians includes any females present. Try explaining that one! The black community are just getting used to, 'Boy' which is an affectionate term in Cork. When Joe, trying to get in on things, declared that at least the people in Iraq had democracy now, I held my breath.

"What! A broken country is what they have, Joe. People are getting killed there every day. Did you hear the news today…total carnage!" Joe, attempted to speak but he couldn't get a word in. "And for what, democracy? No Joe, there's no democracy!"

"I suppose it's all about oil," he said capitulating.

"God knows what agenda the Americans have. You think what's happening in Iraq is all removed from you, Joe… well it's not…we're all responsible! We're all complicit in this war!"

"How do you make that out?"

"Well, American war planes refuelling in Shannon for one thing."

"Sure, the ordinary people have no say in that…that's the Government's fault." Joe defended.

"The sooner the Irish wake up and do something about it, the better! The Americans think they own Shannon! The way people are treated there…in our own bloody country."

"Yeah, I heard a few musicians had trouble going through there, right enough," Joe admitted. Catriona fell silent then and I thought that was the end of the discussion.

"You can bet your life the government knew all about those so-called Rendition flights," Catriona began again. "Rendition! What kind of a term is that anyway? I always thought that was a performance of a piece of music." She sipped her coffee which by now had gone cold and stuck out her tongue in disgust. I was about to say rendition had other meanings, but I thought better of it.

"I'm going in for more coffee…Joe, how about you," I asked to break away from the politics.

"No thanks, Piers, I better make a move."

Joe, however, was still there when I came out and I heard him say, "Ah come off it, Catriona, you have to admit, that was a bit extreme. It's the Irish taxpayers who have to foot the bill for that plane."

"It's not noticeably out of your pocket, is it," she challenged. "Funny how it always comes down to money. You know, at the time, I thought Mary Kelly was extreme too, but given what's happening now, I think she was right… I wish I had smashed that plane!"

I roared laughing, spilling the coffees on the wobbly metal table; the thought of Catriona smashing a plane was hilarious. "There's nothing funny about it," she said, thumping my arm with the side of her fist. Visibly angry, she mopped up the coffee from her saucer and refused to look at me but when I squeezed her thigh under the table, an unwitting smile softened her features. "Well, you know what I mean…one feels helpless," she said sighing.

It may be unfair, but I see Collins as a remnant of the old princes of Cork, well-heeled and protected. If Joe found himself in trouble in the morning, he need only call to some relation down the Mall. Does he even notice the down-and-outs around town? I have come to like the guy, but I don't think he has the capacity to walk in another's shoes.

* * *

If I were granted one wish, it would be to hold on to the way I feel now. Catriona and I have grown so close that sometimes I can anticipate what she's going to say. We spent as much time together as possible this summer, swimming in the sea and trips into the countryside. On one of the outings, I discovered that Catriona had a strong fear of death: we were pottering around an old graveyard in Inchigeela when she saw skulls and other bones sticking out from under a broken vault. She got so upset we had to leave. Wandering around old churches and ruins is something I like to do but I made a mental note not to bring her to these places in future. I wondered then if something happened to her when she was young to make her so afraid. To cheer her up, we went and sat on the bank of the river Lee a little further out.

I was relaxing in the sun listening to the flowing water and looking at a profusion of daisies, buttercups, and dandelions. "Look," Catriona said pointing to a bumble bee. "He can't take off…he's overloaded." We watched the bee, willing him to take off and were glad when he did eventually.

"Evelyn and I used to catch them in jam jars…we put holes in the lids for air. Evelyn rescued one from a trough one time… with a twig and a leaf. He flew off when he dried out."

"That's so cruel," she said.

"For saving a bumble bee!" I exclaimed.

"For catching them!"

"Didn't you ever do anything like that when you were young?"

"No…what would I want to catch them for?"

"Just to look at them… close up," I said.

"You can see them just fine…it's cruel putting them in jars."

"We're not all as perfect as you," I said grimacing. "Anyway, we always let them go…it didn't do them any harm."

"How do you know…how do you know they weren't scared to death?" She sat in silence looking into the river, then turned to me with a frown. "I broke the wings of a butterfly once," she admitted. "I was only looking at the colours but the wings just disintegrated in my fingers!"

"Poor baby!" I said, attempting to hug her but she pulled away. I guess I wasn't doing a very good job in cheering her up.

"The butterflies love that weed," she said some minutes later.

"Yeah, ragwort…buachalán we call it in Waterford. We used to catch them too."

"Butterflies?"

"No! Caterpillars. Did you never do that?"

"No!"

"I thought all kids did that!"

"You're showing your age, Cantwell," she said shutting me up.

We left the sunny banks and headed for Gougane Barra. I'd never been there and was eager to see the place. On the way, Catriona told me it was her mother's favourite place.

I had expected lots of tourists but there was no one about and I was glad. Catriona showed me a little stream that was a cure for something, but I can't remember what for! What interested me was that the River Lee rises in the hills beyond the park and flows into Gougane lake.

Tired from walking around, we rested at the lake's edge, our quiet intimacy mirrored in the still and silent environs. Gourgane Barra was an important pilgrimage site in the past (probably still is for some). I imagined my Dad among the throng on the hill waiting for the sun to rise and the bonfires and rituals in celebration. I could have stayed forever in that peaceful solitude but Catriona reminded me of my promise to take her to Slievereagh, the place where her father's people had come from.

Catriona had a fair idea of how to get there, but we stopped and asked for directions anyway. A vibrant profusion of fuchsia lined each side of the rocky road as we climbed. I had always thought fuchsia was one of our native plants but Barry told me it was introduced here from South America in the seventeenth century.

Catriona was immediately familiar with the place and delighted to be able to show me the spot where her great-grandparents' house had stood. Of their five children, her grandfather was the only one to remain in Ireland, the rest, three sisters and a brother emigrated to America. Two of the sisters ended up as domestics in big houses in Boston, the youngest was tragically killed by a tram in San Francisco.

"What happened to the brother?" I enquired.

"I don't know... must ask Daddy. It was always the grand-aunts that were talked about."

"Maybe because they wrote the letters home," I suggested, thinking of Ivor suddenly.

"I suppose," she answered distractedly and suddenly took off ahead of me. When I caught up with her, she was gazing out over the rugged boggy fields of reeds. She looked beautiful and solitary, her hair filigreed like a halo in the evening sun.

* * *

Showing Catriona around my own county was an enhancing experience for me. I took a photograph of her standing on Dromana Bridge on the Blackwater. She was charmed by the romance of Villiers Stuart building a bridge to welcome his bride, a replica of one she liked in England. When I was young, I believed he built it for his Indian bride, so she wouldn't be homesick. I believed it because the bridge looks Indian.

"Can you imagine Villiers Stuart marrying an Indian woman– even if she were a princess," I laughed but I don't know if Catriona got what I was implying.

Nan, hearing we'd been to Dromana, began telling Catriona stories about the place, some tinged with local hyperbole but some of historical record, like Katherine FitzGerald: Katherine was born at Dromana Castle and became known as the "Old Countess of Desmond" because she lived to be 140 years; some even claim she lived to 162, but I think that's pushing it! Catriona burst out laughing when Nan told her Katherine died after falling from a cherry tree. One could only wonder what a 140-year-old was doing up a cherry tree. Nan of course was in her element.

On our way home that day, we stopped for a swim in Red Barn near Youghal.

It was the first time Catriona was at a beach in east of Cork. The water was freezing and she was reluctant to go in. She was yelling and resisting when I pulled her in. We came out laughing and shivering but totally invigorated.

We lay on our towels looking at the cloud shapes sailing by in a blue sky. I leaned over and kissed her sea fresh mouth and ran my fingers through the salt drops on her goose-pimpled thighs. At that moment I felt that time stood still just for us. Images and words inundated my mind. I wanted to capture the experience for ever. She got up then to dry herself and suddenly she appeared so young to me in her navy swimsuit. A wave of insecurity enveloped me. The age difference had never bothered me before. When she was dressed, I put my arms around her and held her like I never wanted to let her go.

For Mid-Summer, we went to see The Tempest in Fitzgerald's Park. Ariel ran by our feet; blue-lit spirits moved stealthily among the trees. There was much splashing in and out of the pond and the water sprays reflected the burning torches and surrounding lights. Midges and moths, captured in the light, added to the magic. Catriona huddled close when it got cold. I didn't want the play to end.

The only sour note was that her parents wanted her to give up the flat and commute the following term. I have a suspicion it was her mother's idea and that it wasn't all about money! I guess Catriona must have been persuasive, though, because it was agreed to hold on to the flat for another while. She is now working part-time in the Opera House to contribute to the rent. I had a hard time convincing her to take money from me. She laughed when I told her she could throw me out anytime but I got the feeling she was glad I made that clear.

* * *

Helen has invited me to her wedding at the end of August. Unfortunately, Catriona will be in London with Moira. Why she is constantly dragged into her sister's affairs, I'll never understand. She wouldn't have come in any case. She said it was inconsiderate of me to expect her to attend my ex-girlfriend's wedding. I found her attitude immature.

Helen and Tim are going to Majorca for their honeymoon. I assumed

I would have Rosie and put in for holidays. When I told Helen this she said, "Oh, Piers, you can be so daft sometimes…Rose is coming with us." Seeing my disappointment, she added, "But it was considerate of you all the same." Considerate didn't enter the equation, I wanted to spend time with my daughter!

* * *

Helen did mean a small affair, and to my surprise it was not a church wedding. I thought Rosie would be adorned in satin and frills, but she wore a simple frock. Her white shoes had blue butterflies which she showed to everyone. Helen looked lovely in a pale blue dress and a spray of white flowers in her hair. Tim looked smart in a light brown suit. They will be staying in a villa in the mountains near Sóller; friends of Mrs. Arnold's nephew live close by; they have young children so Rosie will have plenty of amusement. Who would question Mrs Arnold's arrangements?

I felt an irrational twinge of jealousy when Tim kissed Helen after the legalities but on reflection, I realised that it was more fear than jealousy: our three-way paradigm was about to change.

Mrs. Arnold's garden was like something out of an American film with a huge marquee and a stage for the band later in the evening. Champagne was flowing and there was lovely background music. Rosie ran about with other children at the end of the garden between a large eucalyptus and a lantern tree. Rosie told me that's what Mrs Arnold calls it.

The photographs over with, we were ushered into the marquee to take our places for the meal. The food was fantastic. The speeches were brief and Trevor, the best man, was very funny.

The next time I saw Helen she was wearing a more casual yellow and beige linen dress and sandals. The sandals made her look even smaller. Helen was so relaxed you'd never think it was her wedding day. Perhaps I'd never seen her truly happy before.

I drank lots of champagne and danced with Helen more than once. Tim didn't seem to mind. I can't say the same for June, though. I hugged Helen just to spite her.

Before I ordered my taxi, I said goodnight to a very sleepy Rosie, who was wrapped around Helen like a monkey; she could hardly keep her eyes open. The blue butterflies were covered in a reddish dust and her dress was crumpled and damp.

"Goodnight Daddy," she said barely audible when I kissed her hot cheek.

"Goodnight, sleep tight, don't let the bugs bite," I said but there was no response.

The band was still playing for the diehards as I walked to the end of the garden to grab a moment to myself. A light breeze rustled the eucalyptus leaves; birds were still on the wing; Venus and Mars were visible in the darkening blue sky. I mentally recited lines from 'He wishes for the Cloths of Heaven by Yeats. I remained there almost hypnotised by the gentle swishing of the poplars in the next-door garden.

I sought Helen out to say goodnight and foolishly suggested going to the airport to wave them off on Sunday.

"You're being ridiculous again!" She laughed.

"Am I? I must be drunk!"

"It's allowed! Come on, your taxi's here," she said pulling me by the arm.

"I wish you all the happiness in the world, Helen... you do know that."

"Thank you, Piers," she said shoving me into the taxi.

* * *

Catriona rings Sunday evening. Moira's interview with the Royal College of Music went well; She tells me they will be back on Tuesday. I lose count of the things they plan to do. I nearly get vertigo listening about the London eye. I have this surreal image of a giant eye looking down on the city.

"How was the wedding?"

"Great! It would have been better if you were there!"

"Did Rosie enjoy it?"

"Yeah, she had a great time! She loved dancing around standing on my feet...thought that was hilariously funny. I'm not good today...drank too much... can't do anything...except think of you, of course."

"You're such a charmer," she laughs. "I'd make you forget your hangover, if I were there."

"Promises, promises."

"You know I would," she whispers seductively. My god, that woman can excite me even when she's miles away.

"I might be able to get some work done now!" I joke and she pretends to be offended. "Do you want me to collect you, Tuesday?"

"Dad's collecting us...thanks all the same." *More to do with Moira I'd imagine.*

I'm cold from sitting too long; my workroom doesn't get much sun. I've been writing for hours and am happy with the results. I completed, Crying Landscape, about Peter Hennessy's fiddle playing and I don't foresee any changes.

Out on the landing, I'm met with a welcome blast of heat and in my bedroom, a stream of sunlight creates a distorted parallelogram on the bed. I remember lines from one of my poems: 'And the low liquid evening sun/ shines upon her mane a Midas touch.' I sink down into the golden warmth and drift into a sun-spell sleep dreaming of a woman with hair of fire.

* * *

Catriona is coming over and I'm looking forward to seeing her. I'm finally going to play the flamenco guitarist, Mario Escudero for her; it's on vinyl and she doesn't have a record player. But more importantly, I want to talk to her about how things stand with us; nothing has been said since the night of her birthday. I have said I loved her many times in the throes of sex but that's not the same. I want to say the words without those distractions. I want to hear her say the words!

I'm running late so I opt for a takeaway from Lennox's. Outside the chipper, I stop out of reverence, to read the commemorative pavement stone that marks the birthplace of James Joyce's grandfather: James A. Joyce 1827-1866. Sadly, every time the premises is renovated under new management, it seems worse for wear; the timber shop front is now encroaching onto the stone. I think it would have been better on the wall. Could they still do that, I wonder? The guy behind the counter is looking out with suspicion. I go in and order my fish and chips and tell him what I was doing outside.

"I never even knew it was there," he says. "Glad you told me…I'll have a look on my break."

I come away, happy that someone is interested. Funny how sometimes we don't see the things that are right under our nose.

Catriona arrives right on time. We give each other a hungry kiss in the doorway. Absence does make the heart grow fonder! I admire her long flowing multicoloured skirt, saying she could be in a Klimt painting.

"It's silk," she says running her hands over the soft fabric like a preening bird, "I bought it in London…in a sale… for half nothing." I'm amused at how women justify their purchases by proclaiming them to be bargains. "I missed you!" she says.

"Really…with all the London distractions."

"You smell nice," she says putting her arms around me.

"Just out of the shower."

"That reminds me…this is for you," she says, pulling a gift-wrapped box from her equally colourful bag. I rattle it curiously and she laughs. "It's only soap…don't bother opening it now."

I pour a glass of chilled Sauvignon Blanc, the New Zealand one she likes. I refrain myself, for fear it might make me sleepy. Catriona slips off her sandals and curls up on the armchair, her feet peeping from under a sea of colour.

"Put on Escudero," she says impatient and I'm just about to when the phone rings.

"I'll take this, love, if you don't mind." Barry needs a favour. When I tell him Catriona is here, he says something very suggestive making me laugh. Catriona looks up curiously, her bare legs now dangling over the side of the armchair. "That was Barry…he wants me to call down," I say trying to keep a straight face.

I put on the record and settle down on a cushion on the floor beside her and she runs her fingers through my damp hair. Soon we are transported to Moorish Spain by the rapid gypsy rhythms of Mario Escudero, Alberto Velez and Anita Ramos.

I'm waiting for her response to the third track that introduces El Pili. I can hardly express what El Pili means to me: his pure, guttural, emotionally wrenching singing is like a prayer. Catriona gives voice to a sigh as she swings her legs down and gets up to put on the other side. I know exactly how she feels. When we have listened to the other side, I refill her glass and this time I pour myself one.

"You know I never really listened to Flamenco before," she says. "Imagine playing the guitar like that! You'd need twenty fingers."

"Most Flamenco isn't written down at all... I suppose it's a bit like Irish Traditional music in that respect."

"What a wonderful legacy for Spain...all the different elements... Moorish, Byzantine, Gypsy," she enthuses

"The Moors ruled a long time... until the fifteenth century."

"I don't know much about Spain...I mean that far back."

"Andalusia is where the Moors left their deepest imprint seemingly. We might go there sometime," I suggest, testing the waters, but she's too busy with the sleeve notes.

"It says here, Mario and Alberto could well be playing Bach or Scarlatti. It's very complex all right! You know, it helps me understand Scarlatti a bit better...the Spanish influences I mean...I'll certainly be listening to his harpsichord sonatas with new ears."

"He must have spent a lot of time in Spain."

"He went to live there. God let me get this right...when Maria Barbara de Braganca of Portugal married Fernando V1. Gee I hope that's right. They became friends when he was Chapel Master at the court in Lisbon. She had previously been a pupil of his, I think. I can't believe I remembered all that, Piers...it's amazing what pops out of the head."

"You obviously studied him well."

"Where did you get the record? It says here it was released exclusively in Australia."

"I can't rightly remember! It's great though, isn't it?" *Why couldn't I tell her I got it from an ex-girlfriend, who went back to South Africa leaving me a lot of her stuff.*

"We must go to The Long Valley some Friday night - two lads play Spanish guitar."

"Yeah!" I say absently.

"I believe they're very good," she adds.

Already my thoughts are straying, wondering if I should wait for another evening to talk to her, but it will keep nagging at me if I don't.

"It's still bright out, fancy a walk?" I suggest.

"If you want," she says half-heartedly.

The evening is closing in but there is a lingering heat, which is just as well because Catriona has only sandals on. We walk up Bethesda Row but at the top of the road I realise how tired I am. "Would you mind if we went back… it's getting a bit chilly."

"I was quite happy where I was, Piers… it was you who wanted to…"

"Right! Come on so," I say taking her hand and quickening my pace.

"You're acting weird, Piers…is there something wrong?"

"No, there's nothing wrong…just want to get back."

We're not long inside when Catriona says, "There's something wrong, isn't there?"

"No, I told you…just wanted to talk to you about…"

"I knew it! There is something…"

I take her hand and look into to her questioning eyes. "We haven't talked much about things since the night of your birthday. The commitment we made is important to me, Catriona. I just want to know how things stand." An awkward silence ensues. *She could say something!* "I love you, Catriona! I've been wanting to tell you that for some time. This is all new to me… I've never felt like this about any woman before."

She puts her arms around my neck and kisses me. I caress her body through the liquid touch of silk. "I'm glad," she whispers finally, "I thought you were going to say something awful!"

I suppose it's better than a perfunctory, I love you too.

In bed, I experience a side of her I hadn't known before, pushing me away one minute, pulling me to her the next. "Do you really love me, Piers?" She pleads.

"Yes, I do! I'm crazy about you!"

"Oh Piers," she says, digging her nails into my back. "Kiss me," she says, gripping my hair.

Our fervent love making is almost a fusion of wills. A love making that is beyond sex and totally a new experience for me.

Afterwards, my mind is on overdrive: *she hasn't said she loved me. Why are the words so difficult for her?*

Catriona lies serenely beside me with her eyes closed. Words at this moment are redundant. I turn on my side and trace the dewy line on her upper lip and savour the musky fragrance of her skin.

* * *

Saturday morning Helen tells me Rosie has been invited to a birthday party and would I mind picking her up around four instead. My heart sinks. I was ready to go over now. Helen then puts Rosie on.

"Daddy… I'm going to a party. I'm wearing my angel dress," she says excitedly, referring to the fairy dress. I'm surprised it still fits her.

"Oh lovely! Enjoy the party. See you later alligator."

"In a while crocodile," she giggles.

I arrive at Helen's at four on the dot. Rosie looks well and has a slight tan. Helen and I were always careful as Rosie needs a high factor sunscreen. Helen looks good, not much of a tan, but Tim is as brown as a Spaniard. They loved Majorca! They plan to go again next summer. *Who wouldn't with a villa to go to?*

In the car, Rosie tells me that a sea snail tried to bite her. Can snails bite? I hear everything about her new friends and what they got up to. I also hear about Tim this, Tim that; I try not to let it affect me. Rosie soon runs out of steam and goes quiet. My plan was to go and see the American naval ship that came into Cobh yesterday, but I think she's too exhausted to enjoy that now. I take her to the playground instead but she tires of that soon enough.

Rosie watches cartoons for a while before dinner. At bedtime she wants to hear the story of Bertie, the lost fox but I'm a little out of practice and have to think on my feet for his new adventures. It feels so good to be tucking her in again; I missed her more than I realised: my world with Rosie is an ordered world.

* * *

Autumn already and I haven't taken holidays. I'm contemplating a trip to Spain - Granada, Cordoba and Seville - Catriona would like these places. December or early January might suit. I cancelled the last holidays I put in for when Rosie went to Spain, so I need to be sure of the dates now.

I called to the flat full of excitement only to be deflated when Catriona ruled out the idea completely. "We could go somewhere in the summer," she suggested when she saw how disappointed I was.

Catriona called a few days later to say she booked tickets for a production of Beowulf. She said she wanted to do something nice to cheer me up.

Benjamin Bagby's rendition of Beowulf did indeed cheer me up. I was thrilled to hear the sounds and rhythms of Old English. Catriona was more interested in the 6-stringed harp Bagby played throughout the performance. Back at the flat, she read out the leaflet that we got: the harp was made in Germany based on the remains of an instrument excavated from a 7th century nobleman's grave in Oberflacht. A similar harp was unearthed at Sutton Hoo in England. Catriona tried to explain the six tones used in early medieval music and the variant tunings, but it was way too technical for me. However, I was happy to see her so invigorated. Musical instruments are to Catriona what books are to me!

Things are going well between us at present, but the whole couple thing scares me at times, especially when I find myself running things by her mentally: if something appeals to me, I wonder if it would appeal to her too. I even show her work in progress, a thing I've never done before, not even with Claire. I question whether this is a good thing. What's more surprising is that I'm heeding her suggestions. Catriona even persuaded me to write down the stories I tell Rosie at bedtime, a thing I never thought of doing.

* * *

The Lee's gleaming waters flow over the weir like a fulgent glass sheet, and the vigorous grass along its banks, a rippling sea in the evening breeze. Leaves are lively on trees and some flowers are still in bloom. I'm not going to spoil my evening worrying about global warming; that's not to say I don't care about the environment, unlike our Government which has no true commitment.

I could happily walk along this stretch of the river for another hour but I don't want to be late calling to Catriona. We have no definite plans but I told her I'd be over early.

On the way to the car, I see a couple with two children running around having fun. I miss Rosie at times like this, there is never any spur-of-the-moment with us. I feel so removed sometimes, like I'm just looking in on other people's lives. I feel like a mere observer of my own life too at times.

If I'd known Moira was at the flat, I wouldn't have let myself in; she now knows I have a key! Catriona dives on me, barely giving me time to say hello. "Any chance you'd run Moira home, Piers? She has too much stuff for the bus."

"Yeah, no problem! Do you want to go right now?"

"Yes, now would be good," Moira states but adds a thank you when Catriona gives her a look.

Moira does indeed have a lot to carry: a violin, a large bag full of god knows what and a shoulder bag with music sheets peeping out. She carries the violin and shoulder bag and I take the large bag. Catriona follows out with a guitar - it looks like her own guitar. Catriona kisses me quickly on the cheek when everything is in and turns to go.

"You're not coming?" I exclaim, alarmed at the prospect of being alone with Moira.

"No. I'll get in a bit of practice in the meantime. You won't be long anyway; the traffic is light at this hour."

We're in Blackpool before Moira says anything and then only to concur with Catriona that the traffic is light. Thank God, the sooner I get her there the better!

"How's the music going," I ask to make conversation.

"I have no time to practice because of the concert. Catriona is no help! And it was her idea to volunteer in the first place."

"Concert? I didn't hear anything about a concert!"

"It's a benefit for Baby Ella McCarthy… she needs an operation."

"Oh, I see."

"Catriona has her mind on other things," Moira says sighing deeply. "It's her own fault about her results! She's distracted by silly things like love! She's too young for that! She needs to focus on what's important."

At first, I believe it's an unfair attack on her sister but soon realise it's actually an attack on me. My gut reaction is to tell her to fuckoff and mind her own business but I hold my tongue for Catriona's sake. I think on the bright side: imagine her telling Moira she loved me. But then again, she may have just told her what I said. Maybe Moira's jealous; she's two years older and there's no sign of a boyfriend as far as I can make out.

"I thought Catriona did well in the exams," I probe, not willing to let it go.

"She barely passed! It was her lowest mark ever! She's doesn't practice enough!" I'm mulling this over when Moira adds, "She's capable of a lot more…and now she has some fool notion of going on holiday. My parents aren't made of money you know!" I button my lip for the rest of the way and Moira doesn't say anything more.

I haul the bags to the front door. Moira insists on carrying the instruments. "Thank you," she says with an air of finality. I would have expected a modicum of propriety, like an offer of a coffee or something. Why am I bothered? I would have declined anyway.

Rain unexpectedly begins to fall as the evening closes in. Lights refract in the droplets on the windscreen. The rain comes down heavier and the wipers become a metronome for my unsettled emotions.

* * *

Catriona thanks me for my 'good deed' as she puts it and offers me a coffee. "I'd prefer tea," I say a little irked because she should know by now that I hate instant coffee. She looks at me quizzically while handing me the tea. I pretend not to notice.

"What's wrong Piers?" she asks finally.

My first reaction is to say nothing is wrong but there is no use pretending, so I tell her.

"Don't mind Moira! She's up to ninety with the concert. All she had to do was organise a few instruments. She's only playing one piece on the violin… you'd swear she was giving a whole performance."

"She said you barely passed your exams. I was under the impression you did rather well."

"I passed them, didn't I! Moira is a perfectionist. She's a great sight reader and all that, but she couldn't improvise to save her life. I'm not like her, Piers. I like writing songs! You said yourself they were good!"

"They are good! I'm just concerned about you that's all. Moira said it was the lowest mark you got so far."

"Jesus Piers, I get enough of this at home."

"So, it is an issue then?"

"Look out, Cantwell, you're lapsing into your school-teacher mode," she says cynically.

"Moira doesn't approve of me, does she? She was getting a dig at me saying your mind is on silly things like love."

"She told you that!" Catriona says, looking up to heaven.

"Yes, and that you were too young for all that. Maybe what she was really saying is that I'm too old for you!" I say, expecting some feedback.

Catriona is acting now like I've done something wrong and I don't like the way she's tightening her mouth; it reminds me of my mother. To break the tension, I escape to the bathroom but I hear her banging and clattering outside. Another time I'd laugh but now I'm just weary. This is not how I wanted the evening to go.

Catriona is munching biscuits and reading a magazine, or rather pretending to; she makes no attempt at conversation which I think is childish. Maybe Moira is right! Maybe I am too old for her. Catriona sighs audibly but I take no notice now. Eventually, she asks if I'd like to go up to Henchey's for a drink.

"It's raining out...we'd have to walk," I reply, not quite sure if I want to or not.

"It's only up the road. I have an umbrella!"

I keep my hands in my pockets as we huddle under her large, blue-dotted umbrella. It's awkward because I'm much taller. It would be better if I held the umbrella but I say nothing because she's saying nothing.

Catriona is lively as ever in the pub, however, talking and laughing with people from St. Luke's Choir. I drink my pint, divorcing myself from the background mutterings. I'm glad in a way no one is talking to me. One important thing I learned today is that Catriona does not share her problems with me and not just problems either, there was no mention of that concert. What else does she keep from me?

"You're very quiet!" She has the audacity to say on the way home. Only for the few pints I had, I would drive home. All I feel is resentment, with everything playing out in my mind.

Catriona comes to bed and snuggles in beside me as if nothing has happened and brazenly spreads her cold hands on my belly. She only laughs when I roar and push her hands away. The trouble is I'm never able to stay mad at her for long and I do my best to warm her up. My efforts return a dividend of affectionate caresses and I am sweetly swayed.

"Piers!" She says holding me aloft with her hands to my chest. "I've been wanting to tell you this for some time ..." *I don't want to hear it. I don't want her to say it just because she feels she has to!*

* * *

Jack Wasserman is pressurising me for the new collection. Many of my recent poems about Catriona and my father are too personal and others are unfinished. I tell him I'm planning a holiday and hope to get some inspiration. When he hears this, he laughs. "Just send me what you have. And I mean before you go on holiday." External pressure like this is necessary sometimes to get things done, but if someone pressurises me too much, I tend to go in the opposite direction.

Catriona and I have been at cross purposes lately, what with the concert and her job at the Opera House and my time with Rosie. I won't see her this weekend either because I'm off to Kilkenny with Barry: his van is out of action so I'm driving him up to the Butler Gallery with some paintings; he's roped someone else to take the bigger ones. I was only too delighted to be asked because Kilkenny was my father's hometown.

Catriona was in a funny mood when I spoke to her. She has only met Barry once, briefly. She knows I used to go down to his place a lot with Rosie. I couldn't ask her to come because there's no room in the car and Barry has arranged for me to stay with his friend, Bob Campion, in Blackmill Street. But I sensed there was something else on her mind.

Bob Campion is an eccentric character with equally eccentric friends. We had a great time in Delaney's Pub on Patrick Street on Friday night. I can't remember when I laughed so much. Toby would have enjoyed it. Barry and Bob were highly amused at my diversionary tactics when a certain, Irene Meade, took a shine to me. I got a right slagging! Irene was gorgeous! Oh, if life were different!

Left to my own devises for most of Saturday, I walked along the River Nore down by the castle. As I watched a majestic heron standing motionless on a little island, I began to remember my many walks along this stretch of river with my mother and father. My grandfather, the original Piers Cantwell and my grandmother, Myrtle, ran a shop on John Street but they lived out in Loughbouy, hence the walks home by the river. I remember Dad carrying me on his shoulders when I got tired. Myrtle died when I was seven - my memories of her are sketchy: her giving me slices of seed cake on a plate with pheasants on it; the opaque yellow glass in her kitchen door and Evelyn and I helping her in the garden. I remember her floral dress and white leather sandals more than her face.

Barry and I haven't seen as much of each other since I started going out with Catriona; not completely my fault because he has become quite reclusive, or should I say solitary, he's out and about most of the time, so it was great to spend time with him and in Kilkenny too.

Toby and I got to know Barry in college, through playing poker of all things. Barry was studying Law then. Toby was the first to notice that something was up with Barry. He was rather quiet at times, but I saw nothing unusual in that because I can be that way myself, however Toby dug deeper: Barry's father was giving him a hard time, always threatening to throw him out. He was never happy with Barry's results, which we couldn't fathom because Barry always did well in exams. Barry told Toby that no matter what he did, nothing was ever good enough for his father. The only plausible explanation we could come up with was that Barry might not be his biological son but that was knocked on the head when we saw his father at a graduation ceremony.

Barry and I laugh now at what disappointments we turned out to be. His father is resentful to this day of his career choice. Barry, on the other hand, is much happier, painting away and living each day as it comes.

* * *

Cold oppressive days convince me that I need to get away. Going on my own might not be such a bad thing because I have so much to sort out. If I'm to have a future with Catriona, I need to get a better job. Helen hasn't asked for anything extra since she got married. I earn a little extra money writing articles for newspapers and magazines but it would be great if I could get a regular column with a newspaper. O'Buachalla is the man to advise me, if there's money to be earned, he'll surely know how to go about it. I have done some editing and proofreading work for Wasserman's in the past; I could ask Jack if he needs anyone.

* * *

Regina from the office comes on the floor to tell me there's a phone call for me. I'm curious because no one I know would ring the office; they would leave a message on my phone. Regina tells me to leave my protective clothing in the cloakroom. She doesn't engage with me at all on the way. I guess she doesn't approve of people ringing the office.

Her boss, Adam Connelly, is sitting solemnly at his desk and when Regina hands me the receiver, I catch their disapproving exchange out the tail of my eye.

"Piers, it's Tim. There's been an accident, you have to come now…"

"Where are you?"

"CUH! You have to come…Helen and Rose…"

"Helen and Rose what?"

"It's bad, Piers. I must go! Just get here!"

Regina puts a hand on my shoulder saying, "Sit down a minute, Piers, you don't look too well."

"I need to get to the hospital…there's been an accident!"

"I'll drive him," Regina says and Connelly nods gravely without a word.

Trucks, cars, vans, traffic lights. Every minute an eternity. "Nearly there, Piers…nearly there!" Regina assures me. She drops me at A&E and I thank her for driving me. She offers to stay with me but I tell her there's no need.

I make myself known at the desk. A nurse asks me to come with her. I follow her squeaky shoes past cubicles with faded blue floral curtains, into a small room. A large vase of flowers stands before a looming statue of the Sacred Heart.

"Someone will be with you in a moment," she says and leaves me there. *What am I doing here? This place isn't right!* I'm just about to walk out, when the nurse returns with a young Asian man. My god, can this be the doctor?

"You are Rose Arnold's father?"

"Rosie Kearns…yes I'm her father."

"Mr. Kearns…"

"No…my name is Cantwell; her mother is Helen Arnold…her husband told me to come…"

"Oh, I see… I am sorry…"

"He said there was an accident. Is Rosie badly hurt…can I see her?"

He doesn't answer immediately so I try to get past him, but he holds me back with a surprisingly firm grip and says, "Sit please one moment, Mr. Cantwell." *I don't want to sit.* "I regret to inform you… your daughter has died… she was dead on arrival to this hospital."

I think my brain already knew! Yet, it can't be! A sudden gushing in my ears and a palpitating heart forces me to sit. The doctor's voice is fading; both he and the nurse are visually retreating, like I'm looking down the wrong end of binoculars.

"Are you okay now," the nurse asks, having pushed my head between my knees. I manage to nod and she squeezes my arm sympathetically.

The doctor's bleeper goes off but he ignores it; he puts a hand on my shoulder and says, "There is more, Mr. Cantwell, the mother of the child died also a short time ago. We tried everything! Very bad…organs failed… I am sorry! You may see them now if you wish. Take some minutes." His bleeper goes again. He looks pressured. Unexpectedly, he takes my hand and looks into my eyes with empathy, then leaves hurriedly.

Time seems to have stopped. I feel no heartbeat. I am lost in a black expanse. Hearing a voice, I become aware of a woman standing before me. She says her name but it's already lost.

"I'll take it from here, Catherine," she says to the nurse. "Whenever you're ready, Mr Cantwell."

The room is only steps away - large and very bright. I approach the gurney, huge in proportion to her size. Her tiny hand is ice cold and hard as stone; it sends a shock bolt through my whole body. She seems to be smiling, not a care in the world! In my head she is laughing - hiding behind trees - Daddy! Daddy! She's waving her magic wand. We are running with the waves. We are playing the shell game - mounds and mounds of sand.

I hear my name. The woman who brought me here is saying something. I see her merely as an intrusion, someone who has brought me back to a world where my child is dead. *Oh God! Rosie! Rosie! Has there been some gigantic shift in the universe that this is so?* The woman is saying I should come with her now. *No. I can't leave her alone!*

Someone then puts a hand on my shoulder and to my surprise, it's Tim. "Do you want to see Helen before...before they take her down," he asks all choked up.

Down? what does he mean?

June has been waiting outside to see Rosie. Her red, swollen eyes meet mine and for once there is no hint of malice.

At first, I don't recognise Helen and think maybe I'm in the wrong place: an alien distorted face only, visible above the sheet – bloated, purplish blue and patches of yellow. A strange odour offends my nostrils as I touch her arm through the sheet. Her arm does not feel hard. I try to connect with Helen but it's all too strange. The overpowering smell is making me nauseous forcing me to leave.

Outside I begin to shake and tears escape down my face. I wipe them away with my sleeve trying to regain control. Owen Wills comes and takes my hand in both of his and says, "I'm sorry, so sorry...an awful thing! It truly is." Owen sees me looking over at Tim who is standing against the wall like a statue. "Poor man, he hasn't grasped it at all yet," he says.

June comes out and runs into her husband's arms sobbing. When she recovers, Owen suggests we go over to the Wilton pub.

"I'd better stay here!" I tell them.

"I don't think they'll allow you back in now, Piers," Owen says gently.

"Why?"

"Someone is coming to examine Rosie. They're taking her down…"

"Examine her?"

"That's what they told June."

June looks at me with a compassion I would never have expected and says, "Come over to the pub with us, Piers." Strangely I'm relieved to be led away.

Owen manages to find a corner for all of us. I still feel nauseous and the smell of food isn't helping!

"Piers, will I get you a brandy," June asks.

"No. I'd like a coffee, please."

"Well, I need one!" June says.

June takes a sip of brandy and says, "Almost to the year."

"What's that, love?" Owen asks.

"Mother! Her anniversary was two weeks ago! Little did I think," She says, her voice breaking.

Has it really been a year since I was here with Helen?

When they begin talking about funeral arrangements, it dawns on me that no one in my family knows anything. I recall the exchange between Regina and Adam: they must have already known about Rosie!

It was Tim who organised everything when Josie died, now he's sitting there as ineffectual as I am. June is asking where they'll be buried but no one answers straight off. Tim eventually suggests Glanmire. My mind drifts in a sea of confusion. By marrying Helen, has Tim some legal say over Rosie? When I finally look up, however, Tim looks at me and says, "You must decide about Rose, of course, Piers."

I consider my father's grave, but it seems light years away from Rosie's life. He never knew Rosie; she never knew him. An odd sensation goes through my body and my thoughts stray to June's kitchen: Rosie and Helen clinging to each other. Was something being wired in my head that day? Am I mad to think so?

"Rosie should be buried with Helen!" I concede.

"What undertakers do ye want?" Owen asks.

"We could use the same ones we had for Mum," June suggests.

"What about the notice for the paper?" Owen asks.

"The undertakers will do all that," Tim says knowingly and then suggests what to put in and everyone agrees.

I wonder now why I'm so calm, why everyone is so calm. We are talking of putting our loved ones in the ground, after all. Is there some unknown force carrying us along?

June is looking oddly at me as if something is on her mind. I drink down the metallic coffee, wondering what's up with her. Her asides to Owen attract my attention because his expression changes in a gesture of resignation at which June appears deflated. She rallies soon enough, however, and blatantly asks if we would consider burying them with Josie.

How can she ask that after everything has been agreed? I'm waiting for Tim to assert his position but he does the opposite saying he has no objection. The spotlight is now on me. I feel the resurgence of old resentments and am about to launch a vitriol that June rightly deserves, when suddenly Rosie's bright eyes and cheeky face are clearly before me: she's telling Nan about Granny Kearns. Rosie never stopped talking about Granny Kearns. Strangely my anger subsides and I find myself saying that I think Helen would like that very much.

"Right so," Owen says, rising to his feet. "I'll call up in person...that would be better."

Vivienne Arnold breezes in and embraces Tim. They are both crying. She condoles with June and Owen and in turn comes to me. Vivienne takes my hands in hers, looks into my eyes with great sadness but says nothing.

Owen phones June to confirm if Saturday is okay for everyone and tells her he's already been on to Sean. I pull myself together then and go outside to call my mother. I break out in a cold sweat at the thought of giving it words. I tell my mother matter-of-factly, as if in some peculiar way, it has nothing to do with me.

"Merciful god," she cries.

Merciful god! What god? "Can you let people know, Mam ...I..."

"Don't worry, love, I'll let everyone know. Oh my god, I can't believe this," she says starting to cry.

I remember Helen once telling me that she'd hate anyone gawking at her when she was dead. I really should say something. When I go back in, I take Tim aside. His eyes open wide in horror, no doubt visualising Helen's face. "Yes, Piers, you're right...definitely closed coffins. We'll have to contact the undertakers..."

"Don't worry, I'll ring Owen," June interjects, having listened all the while.

* * *

The cause of Rosie's death has yet to be determined so they are not releasing the body. "She was in a car crash...what else is there to know!" I roar at a new face.

The counsellor tries to calm me. "I'm sorry, Mr. Cantwell, but they are doing what is necessary...they need to..." The thought of what they are about to do drives me over the edge and I start fucking and blinding. Vivienne Arnold, of all people, is the one who manages to calm me.

"They have to do their job, Piers. The sooner they do that the better," she says leading me out, Tim following behind. "Come back with us for a bite to eat," she invites.

"Thank you for the offer, Vivienne, but I really need to get home!"

"Okay, Piers, but I'm driving you," she says decisively.

* * *

I am alone! Rosie is dead! Helen is dead! Yet something deep within me refuses to believe it. Averting my eyes from Rosie's pictures, I climb the stairs, take painkillers for my thumping headache and dive fully clothed into bed. Darkness has taken me in the blink of an eye.

Jolted awake by the phone, I answer automatically.

"And where were you, Cantwell? You were supposed to meet me!" Catriona says in that haughty tone of hers. "Did you forget about me?"

"Catriona, love…I need…" My head is pounding again with the strain of having to say it.

"Need what, Piers?" she asks impatiently.

"Something has happened…something awful…"

"Oh what, love…what is it?"

"There was an accident! A car-crash! Rosie is dead."

"Jesus Christ!"

My voice breaks and it takes me a few minutes to recover, "And so is Helen…they're both dead, Catriona!"

"Oh darling, I'm coming over."

"There's no need. I'm in bed. I need to sleep."

"Are you sure? I hate the thought of you being alone."

"It's not that I don't want you to come…I'm just… I'm so…"

"It's alright, Piers. Try and sleep… ring if you need me."

I kick off my shoes, take more pills and pull up the covers.

Catriona is sitting on the bed when I open my eyes. "I let myself in," she says, leaning to kiss my forehead. I sit up and she holds me and I cling to her like a frightened child. Her familiar scent tells me the world still exists. "Oh darling, this is the worst thing ever," she says, rocking me to and fro.

Catriona runs a bath and helps me out of my clothes. I have a flash of concern that I'm losing my dignity, but I really don't care. She wraps a robe around me and leaves me to it.

Hearing her moving around below is a comfort: listening to my mother working downstairs when I was a child, was a comfort. Catriona is talking to someone on the phone but I can't make out a word because the pipes are making such a racket.

A strong aroma of coffee and fried bacon wafts up as I come out of the bathroom. I dry my hair while routinely looking in the mirror. I look the same! Maybe I'm just like my mother, not quite normal.

Catriona tells me it was Evelyn on the phone and that she is on her way. She puts food in front of me, saying I need to keep my strength up. I eat primarily to please her.

* * *

An organ sounds up and is quite hypnotic. Helen and Rosie are side by side at last. The priest's words are a meaningless wind. He is speaking in a holier than thou hushed voice, which is annoying.

The coffins are hoisted: six people carry Helen: Tim and Owen in front and Sean and Tim's brother, John, next. I don't know the other two. Me, Toby, Tommy and Barry for Rosie. Diarmuid kindly offered but wasn't needed. The coffin is light, yet my legs feel like jelly. Walking down the aisle, I think of all the times I carried her on my shoulders.

More meaningless wind at the grave. Helen is lowered first, then Rosie - the mother in the earth receives her child. *Don't worry Rosie, Mummy's with you!*

June throws a flower. I stand back a little, unable to breathe. Catriona and Evelyn step forward to throw their flowers. Catriona's hair is blowing wild like a flame. She should have tied it back, for Christ's sake, she looks like a bloody siren. I shut myself off from her when she stands again beside me. People shake my hand – sorry for your trouble - people from work, from the school, friends, but mostly people I don't know at all.

In the pub, people are talking about Helen, about Rosie. Talk won't bring them back! Catriona wants me to eat something but I'm not hungry. I order a whisky and Barry gets me another one when he comes over. Barry puts his arm around my shoulder in a masculine hug. "I'm off after this," he says finishing his drink. "You know where I am!" After Barry leaves, I accept drink from anyone who offers.

I scan the room to make sure I'm well away from my mother. I spot Evelyn talking to some woman at the far end of the room. Toby is hovering like a bodyguard. I can't hold a conversation with him or anyone else.

I don't want to be cornered by family, so I should really get out of here now. Where will I go? If I go to Toby's Catriona won't be happy.

On Summer Hill, I want to stop at the off Licence, but Toby makes excuses about the traffic.

"More drink is the last thing you need!" Catriona preaches.

"You'd swear neither of you ever took a drink," I say, believing they are in cahoots!

Getting out of the car, I try to steady myself, pretending I'm in control. I make it up the steps to the front door quite respectably, but my legs won't do what they're told on the stairs. Toby grabs my arm and Catriona pushes me from behind. I start laughing, remembering when I had to drag her up these same stairs. I find it even funnier that they haven't a clue about why I'm laughing.

Catriona makes tea. I know she has wine in the fridge. "I'd prefer a drink," I say but they both ignore me. Toby directs all his conversation to Catriona. "Sensible Toby! don't waste any words on me," I say trying to provoke him but he looks at me poker faced. Toby and Catriona are conversing in such a relaxed friendly way, I have a suspicion that this is not the first time he's been here.

"I'll call you tomorrow, Piers…take it easy," Toby says standing before me but I don't look at him. Outside, they're whispering but I can't decipher much, but then, over the echo of Toby's descending footsteps, I hear him say, "Call me…any time…even if it's late."

"Why don't you go and lie down, love, you must be exhausted," Catriona says, with hands on my shoulders.

"Want to get shut of me already, I see. Why don't you call Toby back, he'd be better company?" Catriona sighs and takes the cups to the sink. "Go on… call him back…Toby is a grand…"

"Stop Piers…you're drunk! Go to bed!"

"No, I won't! If you don't want me here, I'll go home." As drunk and all as I am, I see the effect is mighty. Catriona comes over and kneels beside my chair and kisses my brow.

"I don't want you to go anywhere," she whispers, her lips brushing my ear. "You're getting a bit cross from all the whiskey…don't be cross!"

"Am I still your Heathcliff?"

"Yes, you're still my Heathcliff!"

"And are you still my little vixen?"

"Yes."

"I'll go to bed so. But you must come too, foxy."

I wake disoriented and check the time - one twenty. Reality is creeping in like a black monster. I wake Catriona needing to be comforted. The sex is automatic emotionless fucking and afterwards I feel worse if anything. This is the day I put my child in the ground! Is there some moral law by which I should be judged? My child is dead. Tomorrow too she will be dead! The concept grows too enormous for me and I groan. Catriona turns away with stifled sobs, "What's wrong," I ask, lifting the hair from her face.

"This has been the saddest day ever!" She says turning into my arms. This is the first time I've heard Catriona cry!

The room is stuffy with the stale smell of drink; my mouth is dry and furry and my head aches. I go out for a drink of water and the place is freezing. Perhaps, it's fitting that I should be naked and shivering!

Catriona turns over disturbed as I gather up my clothes. I stroke her head until she settles again before stealing away. I tiptoe down the stairs in my stockinged feet and put my shoes on in the hall.

My breath vaporises in the biting night. I pull my collar up around my ears. I couldn't find my scarf and gloves; must have left them in Toby's car. Toby! Oh no! Why did I have to get so drunk?

Eerie laughter echoes from the laneway opposite the old Coliseum. I decipher two shadowy figures jumping about but they stop suddenly. "D'ya want to join us?" A person calls, becoming more visible as he gets nearer to me.

"Join you for what?"

"Isometrics!" The other one says emerging from the darkness.

He's small! I think I could take them if they try anything. "Sorry, wouldn't be able for that, I'm afraid…I've a dreadful hangover."

"A hair of the dog is what you need, boy," the small guy says, going back into the lane. He returns with a bottle of something in a brown paper bag.

"No, really I couldn't! Thanks all the same," I say feeling less threatened but maybe I'm being foolish.

"Afraid you'd catch something," the taller guy shoots cynically.

"I'm not a big drinker usually…but I drank enough yesterday to last me a lifetime."

"Well, you definitely need this more than we do," he says and they both laugh.

I now see the cardboard and blankets in a recess behind them. I know this lane well, it's my route to the train and down to Toby's. "What were ye doing when I came along?"

"Fucken told ya...isometrics," the small guy says, glad seemingly to say the word again.

"Ah don't mind him...we were just try'n to keep warm," the other one says, more friendly. "We didn't want to wander off cos there's a few boyos about. Anyway, wandering around, ya only get hassle."

"Yeah, and the minute yur gone, the fuckers steal yur stuff!"

"Could you not stay in a hostel?"

"They don't let people like us in hostels."

"Why's that?"

"Because we're drunks!" He laughs. "Ah, we steer clear of dem places... ya meet the nastiest people in there, boy. Are ya sure ya won't have a drink?"

"No... even the thought of it is making me sick."

"What made ya drink so much, anyway?" the tall guy asks.

"I was at a funeral."

"Ah, that'll do it every time," he laughs, "Who did you bury?"

"My daughter Rosie...and her mother, Helen." I can't believe I just told two complete strangers such a thing. "She was only six," I hear myself adding.

"God, I'm awful sorry, boy!" He says holding out his hand. "I'm Paul, by the way, and this is Billa." Billa shakes my hand; he's awful sorry too. I thank them and start walking away.

"Take care of yourself," Paul shouts after me.

"All the best, boy!" Billa shouts.

It occurs to me that I should give them some money, but a preservation instinct warns me not to take my wallet out. However, on Brian Boru street, I confront my sense of judgement and walk back. "Have a drink on me lads," I say handing Paul two twenties.

Past Anglesea Fire Station, I feel a wave of nausea and think I'm going to be sick. I struggle on hoping to make it home but I only get as far as Paddy

Farmers pub when I suddenly retch from the deepest pit of my stomach: nothing comes up but a thin watery substance; another empty retch; it's like my insides are trying to come up my oesophagus. Sweat breaks out of every pore, and just as quickly I'm shivering cold.

Home finally, I head straight upstairs where I manage to hang up my coat and kick off my shoes. I dive into the bed and pull the duvet around me.

Sirens fracture the still night. A train screeches to a stop on the tracks by the Coliseum. "Halt!" I'm afraid! Soldiers with British accents pin me roughly against a wall. "Where's your papers, Paddy?" I have nothing to show. I left my wallet in Toby's jeep. "Where are you coming from?" I try to think. Great crowds in a fog, staring into a bottomless pit.

"A funeral," I answer at last but can't remember whose.

"Who did you kill, Paddy?"

"I didn't kill anybody!"

"Liar! Half of Baghdad's dead, mate."

"No! That was the Americans… and your crowd!"

They burst out laughing and the tall soldier says, "He's alright." They walk down a dark lane and put their guns into a large cardboard box. They remove their uniforms – it's Paul and Billa!

"We had to make sure yeh wasn't a spy," Billa says.

"People are always trying to steal things," Paul says leading me through a metal doorway into an amber lit room where a large table is laden with exotic food. Billa pours wine into delicate pottery goblets from a bottle wrapped in a brown paper bag while Paul serves couscous and vegetables from large terracotta bowls.

"Isn't that the Bayeux Tapestry," I enquire, pointing to one of the many tapestries hanging on the walls. They both start laughing.

"That's only a cheap copy. But my grandmother was Norman," Paul says beginning to cry, "became more Irish than the Irish themselves!" Paul wipes his tears away like a jester. "The others are real though," he insists, looking at them appreciatively. "All the way from Persia…they have lovely things there. The people are nearly all dead now, poor things!"

"Yeah, legs and arms blown off the rest of um," Billa says sorrowfully.

They raise their glasses to me saying, "Sorry for your trouble."

Wind howls, tree branches snap, and rockabye-baby cradles fall. Catherine Earnshaw is wandering the moors, her hair blowing furiously. "Heathcliff, Heathcliff," echoes in the night. Catriona Lynch is holding a dead baby in her arms and weeping. "It's not my baby," she avows "it's Jane Eyre's."

The rain is pelting the windowpanes. I've slept in my clothes once again. I undress and put my suit aside for the cleaners and the rest in the laundry basket. I find my coat hanging in the wardrobe and this modicum of decorum reassures me somewhat. As I check the inside pocket for my wallet, fragments filter slowly: reality and dream intertwine; did I really meet a Paul and Billa on the way home?

In the shower I use the lavender soap Catriona gave me. I lather myself well and the stale odours are being washed away. Her traces too are being washed from my body. I watch the foamy swirls going down the plughole, swirls that seem to be taking something of me with them.

There's a stale smell of cigarette smoke in the taxi. Maybe if I'd eaten something, I wouldn't feel so sick. In the breaking morning light, the grey glistening streets remind me of Brel's 'Je Ne Sais Pas'. I imagine myself crying with him in front of the station. The driver, who I believe was saying something, seems palpably annoyed with me now. He sighs audibly to indicate what a bollocks he's picked up. I thank him as I'm paying him but he is indifferent now.

My car looks odd all by itself under the pine trees in the car park. A startled rabbit runs for cover; another one dashes after him, his white scut bobbing. The car park is outside the plant and I could just drive away but I make myself known at the security hut. "Begod, Piers, you're an early bird," Dan says jovially.

"Not working today, Dan, just came for the car."

"Oh right. I noticed her there for a while right enough!"

"Well, she's heading home now," I say, instantly annoyed for giving a gender to an inanimate object.

I fill up at the nearest station and clean the filthy windscreen. The young man looks bleary-eyed behind the glass. I buy a newspaper and instinctively glance at the headlines. Does it really matter to me what's going on in the world? Why did I even buy the fucking thing?

Pylons, trees, dwellings, materialise ghostlike from the foggy landscape. Only for the speedometer I couldn't guess what speed I'm doing. It brightens a little for a while but soon darkens and rains again.

Nan's door is closed. I've had a key to my grandmother's house since I was seventeen, much to my mother's disapproval: much too handy after drinking sessions with the lads. I open the door as quietly as I can but Nan hears me anyway, "Is that you, Mary," she calls out from her bedroom.

"It's me, Nan."

"Och! A stór, tar isteach."

Nan looks as if she's in a cloud in her white nightdress and her white hair against the white pillows. I pull over the chair and lean forward to kiss her. She runs her hand over my head. "We never expected this, did we?"

I sit beside Nan's bed and take her hand; with her, I don't have to talk. I go instead to my safe place under the sycamores with my father: I feel the heat of his body; I smell the rain; I smell the trees; I'm in a sea of green; I want to stay here for ever.

Coming out of my reverie I find Nan has dozed off and I tiptoe away. I rake out the fire and set a new one with paper bird's nests and kindling, the way Nan taught me. Nan thinks firelighters are disgusting things. Tommy wanted to put in gas heating, but Nan refused having read about a mother and daughter in Dublin who died from carbon monoxide poisoning.

I start breakfast but feel uneasy because I know my mother will be along shortly. I bring Nan scrambled egg, buttered bread, and tea. I prop her up with the pillows and settle the tray carefully over her lap. "Be careful with the tea, Nan," I advise.

"I might be in bed, Piers, but I'm not bedridden," she shoots back.

I toast anaemic bread and pile egg on each slice; the eggs become yellow suns, provoking me.

A key in the lock, the weighty push to the door. My mother, surprised to see me, looks pale and drawn. I want to say something kind, but words won't come. I tell her there's fresh tea made and she sits at the table.

"Not a move out of her for two days! Even Kitty couldn't coax her up," My mother says but then checks herself. "Sorry, Piers…I…"

"She's better off in bed with this cold spell."

"Did Evelyn stay with you? I rang her…couldn't get her at all."

"No! She went home I think."

"I don't think she's on duty," she says, her eyes staring passed me. "I'll try to get her up this morning!" She says tuning in again. "You know, she just might, now that you're here."

My mother must have succeeded because I hear Nan complaining, "No, not that one…get me the red one." They come out eventually and Nan says, "Good Man!" when she sees the fire blazing. She stops before the mirror and adjusts the wide white collar of her blouse over her red cardigan. Nan is very particular about her appearance, especially on a Sunday. "It's a shocking day," she says pulling aside the net curtain. "At least it was dry for ye yesterday."

"But it was bitter cold, Mam," my mother says.

"Stop fussing!" Nan gripes when I help her to the armchair. When Mam passes through with the tray, I see Nan hasn't eaten much.

My mother does her usual jobs: making up the bed and tidying the kitchen after which she tactfully says she must call over to Tommy. I stretch my legs out in front of me and stare into the hypnotic flames. Suddenly I think of Catriona and jump up in a panic, alarming my grandmother in the process.

"Hi love… I meant to ring earlier. I couldn't get back to sleep and I didn't want to disturb you."

A silent, loaded interval. "Where are you," she asks.

"Dungarvan!" Another silence. "I came down to see Nan."

"You could have stayed till morning," she says wounded. "You should have woken me."

"I didn't want to disturb you. I was restless… and very hung over."

"I can imagine! You were very cross, by the way…you shouldn't drink whiskey!" She's hitting below the belt; it wasn't exactly a normal day. Suddenly, her words strike like missiles as last night's behaviour flashes before my eyes.

"Are you okay…I didn't hurt you, did I?"

"What? No! When will I see you?"

"Ah, soon! I'm taking two weeks holidays."

"Holidays? You'll get compassionate leave, surely."

"Yeah, I'll ring them and sort it out. Thanks for everything Catriona," I say, but realising that this is too impersonal a thing to say, I quickly add, "You were very good to me...don't know what I'd have done without you!"

"Call me tomorrow... or any time," she says and I promise I will.

* * *

I took holidays as well as the compassionate leave. They were probably glad I was finally using up my days. I stayed in Dungarvan for over a week and would have stayed longer but for the intrusions: Kitty Kyne came in as usual every morning and was beginning to get on my nerves; Tommy called every day too but he never bothered me. The biggest strain was my mother because neither of us knew what to say to each other. I usually went out for a walk or to the shops when she was there.

The evenings were fine, just me and Nan, talking or not. Strangely I slept a lot. It was inevitable that Nan would talk about Rosie. She said there was a reason for everything, though we may not understand it at the time. I listened patiently, giving the illusion I was heeding her.

Catriona rang every day around five, wanting to know how my day went and telling me about hers. Life seemed to be going on as normal without me. Catriona kept asking when I was coming back. She said she missed me. I felt rather guilty that I wasn't missing her as much. However, every time she called, I felt I was being thrown a lifeline.

On my final evening I was restless and Nan was giving me those penetrating looks of hers. She looked tired and it worried me that my presence was putting a strain on her. "I think it's time for me to go home, Nan. I must get myself back on track."

"Of course, you must go home!" She smiled.

* * *

Rosie's pictures are the first heart ache and I quickly avert my eyes. Somehow, it seems a contradiction to let in the light but I open the curtains anyway. I clear out the fridge of the foods I'd bought for her, surprisingly with little emotion. Putting the stuff in the bin outside, I spot her ball at the end of the garden. I squelch across the soggy ground and stare down at its muddied colours. I leave it where it is, however, for fear something seismic might happen should I pick it up.

I gather books and toys for the charity shop and take down her pictures. I'm doing fine until I discover the bag from the hospital with Angie in it. I guess I should be crying but I feel as hollow as a peashooter, yet, I must have some remnant of a heart, because I can't throw the doll in the bin. A bolt of awareness strikes me cruelly: I should have put the doll in the coffin with her! No one, other than Tim, knew of its importance, and there was no one else to guide me!

When Catriona calls me, I explain what I'm doing and she seems lost for words. "I'm nearly finished here…will I call over?" I ask thinking a trip up to the flat would do me good.

"I'd prefer to go out if you don't mind."

"Do you want lunch?"

"Just something small."

"The Long Valley for a sandwich so," I say without thinking. The truth is I really don't want to meet anyone.

"Grand…I'll meet you there so," she agrees.

Catriona seems a little awkward when she greets me, and this gear shift saddens me. The routine of getting our sandwich and tea breaks the ice a bit. Her friend, Ann, who was sitting down the back passes out; they have a quick chat and Catriona looks more herself again.

I spend the next two weeks in Clifton Terrace. Catriona is concerned that I've taken to drinking wine most evenings. I joke that I'm on my holidays but she doesn't find it funny. I promise to stop when I'm back at work. Another problem for her, is that I don't want to go out, not even for a walk. I suggest that she should go out and not worry about me which she does on a few occasions.

* * *

I am now back in my own house. Catriona would be the last to admit that I was preventing her from doing what she would normally do. Returning to work was not as bad as anticipated. It was surprising how quickly I settled back into the routine. All the talk now is of Christmas and parties but thankfully I'm not expected to go to any of those.

My mother and grandmother are going to Paddy's for Christmas. I'm invited too, my mother's doing, no doubt. Nan would know better. Evelyn is going to a friend in Waterford - sensible woman.

Catriona is talking about spending Christmas with me, saying we don't have to make a big deal of it. I appreciate what she's trying to do, but I would rather she go home, knowing how important Christmas is to the family.

Catriona wasn't exactly overjoyed with her Christmas present: I bought a guitar, one that I thought she had her eye on. Catriona is quite independent when it comes to her music so I guess it was a bit presumptuous of me.

Having finally convinced her to go home, I drive her to Tower early Christmas Eve. When we arrive, she makes no attempt to get out but sits in silence for ages. When I ask what's wrong, she turns to me with tear-filled eyes and says, "I just hate to think of you alone in that house, Piers…are you sure you'll be alright? If you change your mind, come down tomorrow night…or anytime really…I'll call you later and…"

"Stop worrying about me, Catriona! I told you I'll be fine. Relax and enjoy your Christmas. I'll be thinking of you!" She leans over and kisses me so sweetly I find it hard to leave her.

Torrential rain Christmas morning. At least I don't need an excuse for not going out. The day is my own. I can do what I want! Michael Hartnett talked of his cold ability to close the door: sometimes it is the only way!

* * *

Ostensibly I'm doing okay, Catriona, however, knows otherwise. Our sex life is strained, we only have sex when she is persistent. I am trying, but it's hard to be like I was. Catriona sometimes appears uncomfortable around me but I am unable to do anything about it.

I am continuing to write but my poems have taken on a darker quality and I'm wondering who in hell would want to read them. I haven't been able to listen to music much but tonight I force myself. Eine Kleine Nachtmusik seeps into every fibre. A breath of life is in me still, a breath that says do not give in to mournfulness, to bitterness, to darkness. I think of my father. I will try harder. I will, I will!

I arrive at Clifton Terrace in an upbeat mood, loaded up with wine and food. I'm staying the weekend and have promised to do the cooking. Catriona is happy to see me so cheerful and seems to relax more. We tell each other about how our week went over a glass of wine. I ask her to play something for me while I'm cooking.

"What would you like?" she asks.

"How about one of your new songs..."

"Right," she says, eagerly fetching her guitar (her old guitar). She looks through her songbook and strums a few chords, before playing, 'Tearing it Down,' a song full of anger and angst; an odd choice seeing I'm trying my best to be cheerful. I smile over at her anyway and when it's over I ask her to play, 'Here comes the Moon'. There are lines in that song I wish I'd written myself.

My efforts to be cheerful pay a dividend because later in bed I am the one to initiate sex and it's the best sex we've had in months. Afterwards Catriona holds on to me like she's saving me from drowning.

Evelyn calls next morning to ask if she and a friend could stay this evening. She mentions something about a concert which I barely register. I tell her there's no problem staying but that I'm in Clifton Terrace until Monday. I'm about to tell her where to get the key when she asks if we could meet in the afternoon. Checking with Catriona, I suggest we meet in the Imperial Hotel café. Catriona is delighted that we're going into town and actually meeting someone.

Evelyn turns up on her own, however. She and Catriona hug and I get her usual broad smile. "This is a grand place...haven't been here before," Evelyn says looking around.

"You like Imperial charm, do you madam?" I joke and she laughs.

Evelyn gives me the news from home: Mam's blood pressure is high and she's not sleeping too well and Nan of course, is still quite frail. *She was fine when I was talking to her.*

Evelyn and Catriona chat away about shops and what not. Catriona is telling her where to shop for shoes. I'm just beginning to relax when Chris Donovan, of all people, passes in. *Bloody hell, you can go nowhere!* He turns into the bar & restaurant opposite and I take a sigh of relief, but low and behold here he is again. He sees Catriona, waves and quickly scans the café. I don't know why Donovan and Healy get my back up so much. Some might say I'm jealous of not being in their inner circle but believe me, I'm not.

Catriona of course goes out to the foyer to talk to him. Donovan is waving his hands in dramatic agitation, just like what Healy does. In the meantime, I tell Evelyn where the spare key is and feel compelled to say, "I don't want anyone in Rosie's room, Evelyn. You can have my room...there's a sofa bed in my work room for your friend...sure you know where it is."

"Don't worry. I won't go in there."

"It's mostly cleared out now anyway, I even got rid of her bed. Do you think that was extreme?"

"You do what you have to, Piers. Everyone copes in their own way." I look around then to see what's keeping Catriona. "Piers, I've been meaning to talk to you..."

"Poor Chris...he's up to high doh," Catriona says landing back. "He was to meet people here... he's been here twice already and there's no sign of them. They must have gone to the wrong place. Ger is waiting for him...they're going to Clonakilty... to De Barra's."

Poor Chris! Poor fucking Ger!

"What was that you were saying, Evelyn?"

"Ah...nothing, nothing."

"Where are ye off to tonight," Catriona enquires.

"Not sure yet!" Evelyn replies. *I thought she said something about a concert.* "I better be off," she says and Catriona gets up and hugs her again.

"How about a walk around Town?" Catriona suggests outside the Imperial.

"No! Not in the mood for that...how about a drive out the country?"

Catriona's face lights up and she holds my hand as we stride up the Mall.

* * *

The hawthorn blossoms that framed the fields for weeks have been blown away by recent high winds. Pockets of elderberry here and there the replacing blossom. Trees and verdant verges, daisies, dandelions, and buttercups, make a heavenly path on either side of the road. On the stretch of road that winds almost full circle, my eyes devour the landscape below like an overdue fix.

Tommy is heavily dragging his cigarette on the steps and barely looks up as I pass in. A few neighbours are with my mother in the sitting room and more talking quietly around the kitchen table. My mother catches my eye and signals me to go straight in.

There are candles lighting on each side of the Nan's bed. She is just like I saw her before, white hair against the white pillow. I bend down and kiss her cheek; an icy sensation clings to my lips, like she's holding on to me. Sitting by the bed, not thinking or feeling anything in particular, a multitude of images of my grandmother sail across my memory.

Paddy startles me shaking my shoulder rather roughly. "I'd like some time alone with my mother now," he says with the pecking order of importance: he is the man; I am the boy again.

"Paddy thought you'd never come out," my mother says.

"I wasn't in there that long!" I say and my mother smiles whimsically.

"She went peacefully, Piers, just as it should be. Annie Power was a good woman," Kitty Kyne affirms. Kitty and I talk a while, but two people are smoking in the room and I'm annoyed at their cheek. However, it's Kitty who stands up saying she needs some fresh air. Kitty returns shortly after to tell my mother that Evelyn is outside talking to Tommy.

"She should come in!" Mam says crossly.

Tommy and Evelyn have always been close, more like father and daughter; you'd think my mother would be happy about that. I go out myself then for a breath of fresh air and pass Evelyn on her way in. "I'll see you in a while," I say and she nods. I walk to the end of the street with a refreshing breeze in my face. The thought of entering the house again depresses me.

My mother turns away indifferent when Evelyn tells her we are going out for a while. Unusually, Evelyn seems put out at my mother's reaction. "Don't mind your mother at the moment," Tommy says, "she's upset...sure, everyone's upset. Where are ye off to?"

"Oh, anywhere," Evelyn says, "getting a bit crowded in there...I won't be too long."

"Right! I better get back in and give Mary a hand."

I was surprised Evelyn was as eager to leave as me. Walking over Devonshire Bridge she brings me up to speed: Mam is disappointed that Frank's not coming, he's too ill to travel but Garvin will be there. Vincent Power, a distant relative and fine tenor, will be singing at the funeral mass.

"How was that organised so quickly?"

"Tommy! Vincent said he was only too happy to fulfil his promise to Annie...they were always joking about it, seemingly."

"That's good...Nan liked Vincent!"

Barely seated in a café in the square, Evelyn looks at me with an excited gleam, "You'll never guess who else is coming, Piers."

"Who?"

"Ivor."

"My God! Who got in touch with him?"

"Me!" She says, her eyebrows raised to heaven. "It's funny the way things fall into place...I only found out recently where he was. My friend Jean happened to mention me to her brother. The name rang a bell. He said he knew an Ivor Cantwell when he lived in London... said he had some business out in Lewisham. Well, Piers, I just googled...and voila, Cantwell Landscape Gardening. I was going to email but I thought ringing him would be better. I left a message and he got back to me! Isn't it great? I told him we all missed him. He was delighted I wanted to see him, but he said I'd have to come over there. I told him about you...about everything... I hope you don't mind."

"Why would I mind, Evelyn?"

"He was quite taken aback...I had to check if he was still there. He asked for your address. I gave him your phone number too, but he said he'd rather write. I rang him yesterday to tell him about Nan. He's flying into Cork Tomorrow. I'm going to collect him!" I understand she's excited about Ivor, but she is too exhilarated now for my liking, after all our grandmother has just died.

* * *

The window is open. Someone is playing a flute. Does Moira play the flute? The playing stops and I hear a male voice saying, "It's not working. It's no bloody good...not with that keyboard." Catriona is saying something in the background but I can't make it out. I look up to the window after pressing the bell, expecting her to put her head out but she doesn't. I'm wondering if I should go away and leave them to it, when Catriona opens the door with a cross face.

"Piers! I thought you were in Dungarvan."

"The house was crowded ...they'll hardly notice I'm gone! I'll go down tomorrow."

"Why didn't you use your key?"

"You have company," I smile, pointing up to the open window. She laughs at the idea that they could be heard. I suggest calling over later but she insists on me coming up.

A young man is scanning a music sheet on a stand and tapping his fingers on the flute as we enter. "Piers, this is Jake," Catriona says, and Jake reluctantly turns his head and nods. "I'm not staying long...sorry to disturb you." Jake barely acknowledges me and returns to the score.

"Are you going out home?" Catriona enquires.

"I am!"

"I'll talk to you in a while," she says, furtively grimacing and darting her eyes toward Jake.

"Let's take it from here," she says pointing to the score.

"There's no point...I'm going back to the school!" Jake says emphatically, wiping the flute with a cloth and placing it like a baby in the soft bed of its case.

"Okay! We need a break anyhow... I'll follow you down..."

"Whatever!" Jake retorts, taking the music sheet from the stand and heading out the door without even a goodbye.

"I'm sorry…I guess that was on my account."

Catriona only laughs and goes to the window and says, "Would ya look at him." I look down to see Jake stomping away, his brown locks flowing.

"Maybe he's right about the piano though!"

"You heard that?"

"Yeah…he was rather loud."

"He's nearly as bad as Moira! He's all keyed up, pardon the pun. It's bedlam below… everyone scrambling for space and instruments. It's just our luck… we could do with the new school now!" Catriona says sighing deeply. "It was his idea to come here, ya know…I was fine where I was. He didn't even give it a chance. I knew he'd be like this!"

"I didn't help matters…I shouldn't have called."

"Ah, it made no difference, he was already frustrated. He listens to too many CD's…he wants perfection all the time. We could have sorted out his timings, at least! It would have worked if he tried to adjust, tried to imagine… that's what's wrong with them…they can't seem to do that! When I play this piece, I listen to the other parts in my head before I come in: strings; flute; oboes; bassoons; horns; trumpets. Jake thinks only of his part. He's blaming my keyboard, but he'll be the same inside, the piano won't make any difference." Catriona then looks at her watch. "He'll be lucky if gets a piano now anyway," she adds, shaking her head.

The score of Mozart's piano concerto in d minor is on the keyboard stand. I particularly like this concerto, Mozart's first in a minor key. "This concerto reminds me a little of the d minor section in Eine Kleine Nachtmusik," I say to take her mind of Jake.

"Yeah, I suppose," she says absently and I wonder if I've got things mixed up.

"Play a bit for me!"

"We were only practicing this little section," she says, adjusting the sheet in front of her and sitting quite still for a minute or two. I now understand perfectly what she's doing. A modest entrance of the piano at first. I'm quite familiar with this part. Catriona's playing is fine but Jake was right about the keyboard; one can't get a proper feel for the music. I know now that Catriona has a unique awareness for her subject and probably cares more about the actual music than the exams.

A cool breeze blows as I walk along the riverbank. Birds are besting each other in the greenery: they should be giving me delight but if I give rein to good emotions, god knows what would follow. I changed my mind about going to the removal. Tomorrow morning will be time enough to go down. It would be nice to stay with Catriona tonight but I could tell she was stressed even though she tried not to show it. She has been wonderful to me despite all the pressure.

I remain outdoors until the light fades to tire myself out. A man passes with a dog so huge it reminds me of a timber wolf. I miss Claire – she hasn't been in touch for ages.

Catriona rings and is surprised I'm not in Dungarvan and asks if I'm at home.

"No, I'm out the Lee Fields."

"You love going out there!" She laughs. "Do you want to come over later?"

"It's sweet of you, love, but I'd only be disturbing you."

"I'll go to the funeral with you…I can always…"

"You don't have the time Catriona! I'll be fine."

"Well, I want to come with you."

"Are you sure?"

"Yes."

"Right so…I'll pick you up around ten."

Apart from once telling Catriona I had a brother in England, I've never spoken of him until now. "You must be excited about seeing him," Catriona says.

"Yes, I'm looking forward to seeing him. Evelyn's over the moon… she missed him more than anybody, I think."

"Did something happen? I mean that no one heard from him in so long."

"He and my mother never got on. He hightailed it after the Leaving Cert." How can I explain the inherent fractures in our family? I don't think she would understand.

"Will they be annoyed about yesterday," she asks after a while.

"I suppose! But I don't care! Nan knows...knew... I wasn't in to all that praying. It's just as well I wasn't there anyway."

"Why do you say that?"

"I don't think I'd have handled it! You know what, I think we should go straight to the church."

"It's too early for that!"

"We'll have a coffee somewhere.

Still early, Catriona and I wander around the graveyard. I point out all the Organs and tell her of Nan's devotion to Little Nellie.

"Where's her grave?"

"Oh, she's buried in Cork...Sunday's Well...I think."

"Oh right!" She says disinterested. I have no idea why I'm doing this because I have absolutely no interest either. It's like Nan's stuff is in a loop in my head.

There are many people already in the church before us. We take our seats four rows back. Tommy and Joan, Paddy and Greta are in the front row with other members of the family. Evelyn slides in beside Catriona and me and it is only then I see him! My god, he's a mature man! I still had a lanky teenager in my mind's eye. My mother unlinks her arm from his and they join the others in front. There is no need to tell Catriona who he is.

There is only a short distance out to the grave, even so, the bearers change over, no shortage of volunteers. I guess people are wondering why I'm not under the coffin. It's strange but I feel no connection whatsoever to that stupid varnished box.

Some family members are crying but Kitty Kyne is outdoing the lot of them. More prayers and holy water. A light shower rains down and someone says, "Tears for the dead."

I stay behind the throng, away from the hand shaking. Tommy puts his arm around my mother who seems quite upset. Ivor is being greeted by various people and is presently shaking hands with Ellen Penrose, a neighbour from where we used to live. His eyes search across the crowd and eventually find me: he smiles in that brotherly way I remember. I am instantly sorry I didn't go to the house.

Catriona and I skirt along the back of the crowd and head straight for the hotel. We're the first to arrive and are greeted by Con McCarthy who commiserates with me, saying my grandmother will be greatly missed, that there's not many of her kind left. He was sorry for my own tragic loss; he couldn't attend the funeral himself but his niece went. I thank him sincerely for his condolences. When I introduce Catriona, Con, suddenly awkward, says an indifferent hello and scurries off. I'm annoyed at his rudeness and wonder who has been in his ear!

Ivor strides purposefully across the room and when I stand up to greet him, he hugs me with such force I nearly fall over. He discomposedly wipes tears from his eyes. It's so good to see him, but I wish it could have been under different circumstances.

"Evelyn told me about your recent tragedy...I'm so sorry!" He says squeezing my hand. I introduce Catriona and he sits down beside her. Soon Evelyn and Garvin join us; I haven't seen our cousin since he was a teenager; he's Frank's youngest son; everyone says he's the image of Billy Power. The relations get talking and I'm happy to be left alone for a while. Right now, I would like to go over to Nan and give her all the news.

Liam and Angela are up at the counter and I go and buy them a drink. "It's great to see Ivor again! He's turned out to be a fine-looking fella," Angela says looking over at him. "He's probably a charmer, like somebody I know," she adds smirking at me.

"He's looking well alright!" Liam concurs. "He's around for a week, I believe!" This is news to me of course but I don't let on.

"Who's the lovely girl, Piers," Angela brazenly asks, "she looks very young."

Liam raises his eyes to heaven. It doesn't seem to bother him that Angela has always been especially interested in my affairs; but then, he doesn't know of the many times his wife has made a play for me; even on her wedding day, she tried to kiss me.

"She's a friend," I say to keep her guessing.

"She was down before...wasn't she," Angela quizzes. *So, it was you gossiping to Con.* From that moment, I direct all my conversation to Liam.

'There's no sign of Evelyn when I join the others, I thought she'd be stuck like glue to Ivor.

"Evelyn? She's gone to meet Jean…she won't be long," Ivor informs me. "I used to know her brother, that's how Evelyn traced me," he says.

I ask if anyone wants a drink; Ivor says he's fine with coffee and Garvin declines also and leaves us to talk to his cousin, Shane. Catriona doesn't answer at all but follows me up to the bar wanting to know why I'm drinking.

"If you have another drink, you won't be able to drive home," she reminds me. I order a pint anyway and she goes off in a huff.

Paul Ellis joins me at the bar and we start talking about fishing, of all things. "There's nothing doing in this business anymore, Piers… no competing with the big boats. Even the lads from Dunmore East I used to go out with have packed it in. We were sold down river a long time ago…and by our bloody own!" Paul laughs then at his seriousness. "I'm selling the boat anyhow! I've a job lined up in the meat plant. Siobhan's delighted. The conversation changes when Paul spots Tictack, one of our local characters. "Look, he's scoffing the sandwiches," Paul says highly amused.

"Nan would be pleased, she had great time for old Tictack."

"He never misses a do…weddings, funerals, it's all the one to him! And he's the best dressed man in Dungarvan with the charity shops," Paul laughs. "Listen, I'll head away … sorry about your grandmother, she was a great old skin altogether," he says.

I feel sorry for Paul, fishing was his life. I can't imagine him working in a meat plant, he was always such an outdoor guy. He probably won't stick it.

I'm glad Paul had the sense not to mention Rosie. But even thinking of her fleetingly brings a heavy weight which I try to unload. The only reality for me at this moment is Catriona, whom I glance at from time to time, like a sailor dropping anchor. I don't need to turn around because I can see her in the mirror. She's talking mostly to Ivor and it fires a little jealousy. He is of course younger and fitter and better looking. Guilt overtakes jealousy, however, knowing I should be down there with her.

Lost in my thoughts, Catriona comes suddenly by my side to tell me she is leaving.

"You don't have to go now…can't you relax, love."

"Don't *love* me...I need to go home," she says angrily. "You're getting drunk... I don't like you when you're drunk."

"Firstly, I'm not drunk! And secondly, I didn't ask you to come... and from what I see, you were happier over there with my brother."

"Cop yourself on, for god's sake," she says exasperated.

"I'm right though! Aren't I?"

"That shit won't work with me, Cantwell!" She says saucily. "You're the one who should be talking to him...he's your brother! A brother you haven't seen in ..."

"Well, that's my business...isn't it?"

"You know, you're right!" She says turning on her heels.

I can't drive her now anyway. She can stay in Nan's with me; I'll get her back early in the morning.

People's voices become a distorted drone and I experience a sensation of going deep down into myself and locking myself in. It's like I'm in some strange dream remembering bizarre events: Nan is showing a group of girls how to do the cat's paw, not the fisherman's knot, but a girl thing, with different coloured wool. I want to join in but I'm afraid of being called a sissy. They tap four tacks into an empty spool: a woollen thread is put through the hole and around the tacks. It's a kind of knitting. A colourful snakelike thing comes through the hole. One girl is winding her finished snake around in a circular pattern on the ground. The younger ones are in awe. Angela bloody Burke is one of them! Why in the name of God, am I remembering that?

My heart jumps when Evelyn puts her hand on my shoulder. "Do you want a lift out to Mam's," she asks.

"No! I'm staying in Nan's."

"Oh, right!" she says, looking surprised. "I'm going home. I think you should go home too."

"I'm going right this minute."

"Good!" she says kissing me on the cheek and I throw my arms around her.

"I love you, Evelyn," I say surprising myself. She looks bemused.

I look around then for Catriona but there's no sign of her. Evelyn tells me she left earlier with Ivor. Her phone is off; she probable forgot to turn it back on after the church. I guess she went to Mam's with Ivor.

I jiggle the key in the lock and give the customary push to the door but perhaps a little too forcibly because Paddy confronts me bull-headed in the hall.

"We weren't expecting you here," he scowls.

"I always stay here. I was always welcome in this house. Nan's not cold in her grave yet!"

"Enough of that stupid talk! You're full of drink…go to bed," he says with a stern face on him. "And go easy, Garvin's above asleep." *Asleep! At this hour? It's only a little after ten.* "I'm in my mother's room," he calls after me, meaning the main bedroom upstairs.

"And where's Garvin,"

"The front bedroom," he says, then shakes his head at my incredulous reaction.

I hurl a string of expletives at Garvin as I head into the back room. *Why the hell did he have to take my room? He'd better not touch anything.*

Screeching gulls wake me! I believe it to be early morning but on looking out, there is such a hub of activity to suggest otherwise. I hear no sounds from below and when I get up the house is empty. The curtains in Nan's room are open, cigarette smoke clings to the air and dust motes dance about in the streaming sunbeam. Dust and death! Is there any particle of her still lingering?

"I wasn't being disrespectful yesterday, Nan, you do know that." I say to the empty bed and almost expect a reply. I imagine her somewhere smiling wistfully. Almost lost in that somewhere, I hear the familiar push of the door, and voices: Paddy, my mother and Tommy!

"Piers, are you up yet?" Paddy shouts up the stairs in his big man tone. I come out and stand behind him.

"How's the head lad," Tommy enquires, and Paddy turns around surprised.

"I'm fine … didn't have much to drink really."

"That's a matter of opinion, Paddy butts in, "you were drinking all day."

Fuck you! I may have been in the pub but I wasn't drinking much!

My mother is pertinently silent and looks away when I catch her eye. "What time are you going, Paddy," she asks.

"Soon, Mary…must check in…just to make sure." Paddy has a plant hire business out in Lemybrien. He can't let things run without him even for one day! That's why I'm surprised he stayed here at all.

"Have a bite to eat before you go…there's plenty food in the house. Will you have something, Piers," she is obliged to ask me.

"I will…whatever is going," I answer agreeably.

"You're in the bad books there," Tommy whispers when Mam goes to the kitchen.

"Because I didn't carry the coffin?"

"God no!" Tommy says. "No…sure everyone understood that! It's because you treated your lass so badly. Ivor told us she went back on the bus."

"A bloody disgrace!" Paddy interjects, "If I knew, I'd have got someone to drive her. What must she think of us? Ivor at least had the decency to walk her to the bus stop."

I had been trying to block it out! Paddy has made sure though! Yesterday begins to unfold and I'm foundering!

Unsurprisingly, Catriona is refusing to communicate. I decide not to contact her till the exams are over. Besides, a little time apart will probably ease the tension. I send her a card, Serpents 1 by Klimt and write: I'm sorry, Catriona. My behaviour indefensible! Piers. When I hear nothing back, I send another, Caravaggio's Repentant Magdalene: I'm sorry! Thinking of you every minute. Hope exams went well! Love Piers.

* * *

Looking down on Patrick Street from a coffee shop in Merchant Quay, I'm hoping to see Catriona who often takes this route home on a Friday. Finally, I spot her coming along with a man and a woman. They stop in conversation opposite Father Mathew. Catriona then heads across the street to Patrick's Bridge; the others cross the street towards Mangan's Clock.

It occurred to me earlier that I could let myself into the flat and wait for her but I'm now glad I didn't do that. Even my plan to catch her on the way home doesn't seem such a good idea now either.

I go through the motions of cooking dinner even though I'm not hungry and I'm so restless I can't eat anyway. My call to Toby goes to voicemail. Barry isn't picking up either. My nerves are stretched from waiting for a response. Against my better judgement I drive over to the flat with another card, Rousseau's Tropical Storm with a Tiger: *I am that tiger! Please forgive me, Piers.* I push it through the letterbox, conquering my urge to ring the bell.

I'm not long back home when my phone rings and my heart sinks when it's not her. I don't recognise the number but answer anyway.

"Hello Piers. Hope you don't mind me calling."

"I'm glad you called, Ivor."

"I just wanted to know how you are."

"I'm okay! Are you still in Dungarvan?"

"No, back to the grind. Evelyn tells me you're not quite yourself lately. Is there anything I can do, Piers? Would you like to come over…for a break?"

"Ivor, I'm sorry, I just couldn't handle things the day of the funeral. I …"

"No need to explain! Anyway, do you think you might come over?"

"I've a lot on at the moment."

"I'd love to see you, Piers. You're welcome anytime, you don't need an invitation.

He's being so kind; I don't deserve it." "I'm glad I went home. I missed you all so much… my own fault, I know. I was dreading facing everyone…I had this awful scenario built up. Apart from Evelyn, I didn't think I'd be welcome. Mam was glad to see me, I think. She cried when I was leaving. Mam's worried about you, Piers." I say nothing to that and he continues, "Evelyn is coming over…I'm looking forward to that…she's bringing her friend."

"Her friend?"

"Jean."

Ivor changes the subject then telling me about his few days in Dungarvan, how he and Garvin drove up the mountains. "I'd forgotten how beautiful home was! I won't keep you, Piers. Think about coming over."

"I will! And thanks for the call."

I feel ashamed, I haven't seen my brother for years and when he turns up, I ignore him. Why couldn't I have been more forthcoming? I should have said something kind. He didn't mention Catriona which was nice of him.

Feeling less restless but still needing a distraction, I head into town. The Corner House is lively: The Lynch Mob are playing down the back. Standing behind people at the bar, the barman catches my eye and points to the Guinness tap and I nod appreciatively.

I barely have the pint to my lips when someone puts a hand on my shoulder. "Hello there, handsome," Claire Riley says beaming up at me.

"Hey! When did you blow in?"

"Back a week... I'm in New York these days."

"How long are you home for?"

"Depends," she says shrugging her shoulders. "I'm sitting over there... grab that stool." Claire looks different: hair dyed black, make up paler, many silver rings.

"You look like a Goth Claire," I joke.

"Ah, you know us poets, we love the melancholy allure!"

"How's New York?"

"It's great! How can I describe it...well it's just so alive! Things are possible there...they take you seriously...not like here. You'd love it! And there's a guy, Piers...he's a lot of the reason I'm there!" I keep a poker face. Claire's not great at relationships; I should know, I consoled her through enough broken hearts. She starts to say something but checks herself. I know what's coming, I know the look by now. "I heard about Helen and Rosie...I'm very sorry, Piers," she says reaching for my hand. "You've been through hell, haven't you?"

"I'm alright, Claire...getting there." Claire looks into my eyes and squeezes my hand.

"Where is everyone? I hardly know anyone," she says looking around.

"Is that so!" I laugh, having already spotted at least two people.

"Well, no one I want to talk to, that is," she says throwing an eye at an ex-boyfriend and giggling naughtily.

"But you found me! And I haven't been in here for ages."

"I sure did, honey bunch," she says lifting my chin with her open hand.

"You're getting very American," I laugh.

"Ah, they'd say, honeybun…like in South Pacific. Remember?" Claire and I watched the remake with Glen Close and Harry Connaught Junior in her flat the night I stayed over. She's trying to read me now but I sing dumb. "Are you writing at all," she asks then.

"Not much!"

"Don't worry Pet, it's understandable. It comes in waves anyway. It's either nothing at all or writing like mad." She's being sweet, and I appreciate it. Drama, she tells me is her new passion and that she's hoping to stage a play in the CAT. "Have you ever thought about it, Piers?... they're always looking for radio plays." I shrug my shoulders. "Piers, you could easily do a play!"

"I don't think so…I certainly couldn't write one in ten days."

"Ten days!" she says, her eyes wide. "Nobody could write a play in ten days."

"Lorca said, if you can't write a play in ten days, there must be something wrong with it."

"Why are you so hard on yourself…forget about what others say. Do your own thing is my motto."

"I know! That's why I like you." We talk a little more, but I can't keep up the momentum - she's too energetic and firing too many questions. "Look Claire, I'm going to head off, I'm rather tired. We'll catch up another night."

"Ok, pet. Listen, give me a call…I'm around for at least two more weeks." She hugs and kisses me in her usual flamboyant manner before battling her way down the back to hear Ricky.

Another time, I'd have been thrilled to meet Claire; I really like her and what's more, she's always interesting. It was a bit mean not staying till closing time, especially since I haven't seen her in so long. Claire was the first woman who talked to me in any real kind of way. I guess I learned a lot about women from her. I remember the steely look she gave me when I once said that a lot had changed for women in Irish society. "Not as much as we'd like to think, Piers! Look how I have had to work twice as hard as you! How many times have I been passed over? God knows where I'd be if I didn't have a hard neck." I reminded her how hard it was for me too. "But I'm from Cork!" She joked, almost pushing me off the chair. Claire complained that even though we were both poets, there would always be a distinction made because of gender. I accused her of being paranoid, but I added genuinely, that I thought her the better poet.

I wonder if Catriona got my last card. I fear it could still be lying in the hall. Thinking of her, however, brings on a wave of anxiety and for my sanity, I try to put her out of my mind. Strangely, I start remembering how it used to be with Claire: no strings, she had insisted; she fancied me that's all. I must admit, the sex was great, but it was a whirlwind that hit me and was gone. I soon discovered that Miss Riley was as needy as the rest of us, despite what she professed. I pulled back emotionally: Claire was too unpredictable and a little too conniving and sometimes even a little self-destructive.

Here in my bed, in my secret world, where things don't have to end, I nurture my aching cock and fuck Claire Riley the way I used to. It seems to me that we are all swimming in a giant whirlpool but some of us are better at keeping from the centre.

"Echo! Echo!" Ivor and Garvin are shouting down the Colligan Valley. Nan is calling their names - they are giggling. Ring-a-ring-a-rosy, pocket full of posies, atishoo, atishoo, they all fall down dead. I start to cry and hide behind a rowan tree with a trunk so thin, it's a wonder they can't see me. Nan finds me - "Don't be silly, Piers, go and play." I don't want to play! I need to go home to my mother - she's on her bed weeping.

I wake in beads of sweat to my phone ringing. "Hello!" I utter, clearing my throat.

"It's not like you to be in bed at this hour!"

"Catriona!" I exclaim, smartening up.

"Late night?"

"No! Just didn't sleep well." *Think fast Cantwell. Don't blow this!* "What time is it?"

"Nearly half ten."

"Jesus, really? I had a restless night…I was thinking of you."

"I got your cards."

"Catriona, what can I say, there's no excuse! I don't know what's happening

– 134 –

to me. I know sorry doesn't cut it this time but I...."

"It was the tiger that got me. How could I leave him out in the storm?"

"Are you at home? Will I call over?"

"I am at home but I don't want to be cooped up here."

"You could come here!"

"I don't want to be cooped up there either."

"Do you want to meet in town?" There is such a long silence, I begin to worry.

"You know, Piers, there's a lot I want! For one, I don't want to be stuck inside all the time with you not wanting to go out…"

"We could go somewhere…I'm off till Tuesday," I suggest but she doesn't answer. "I'm coming over."

All my suggestions are shot down. Dublin is rejected - too expensive. She stiffens when I say money isn't a problem. She doesn't see the point of driving all the way to Dublin but I bring her around in the end. At first the places we try are booked up and it seems to be giving her a reason to back out, but I hit lucky with the last place and book for two nights.

* * *

Catriona is delighted with the hotel's old-world charm and our room is lovely looking out on Molesworth Street. Catriona's imagination is fired by a leaflet she picked up in reception: before it was a hotel, it was The Queens Institute for the Training and Employment of Educated Women, started by a Mrs Anne Jellicoe, a campaigning Quaker and some businessman, but she's only interested in Jellicoe.

We eat in an Italian restaurant in South Ann Street, followed by a drink in McDaid's pub. There is still an awkwardness between us so I tread carefully on every subject. I'm afraid to ask about her exams. We don't stay long in McDaid's as she wants to try other places; we avoid Bruxelles across the street, too packed and too noisy. We try Grogan's on South William Street, crowded too but luckily, we get seats right inside the door of the bar when people are leaving. I like that people are talking to each other in a normal tone; no loud music and no sign of a television. Catriona is not very talkative, just sitting there taking things in. I get the feeling it's not her kind of place but when I suggest going somewhere else, she says we're fine where we are.

Back at the hotel, I'm surprised that she brings up the exams herself: she was asked to play a few phrases of Brahms concerto No 2 in B-flat Major, a very short piece from Rachmaninoff's Piano Concerto no 2, C minor, and another short piece from Beethoven's "Emperor" concerto; she was given plenty of time to read over the music. Talking about music seems to be lifting her mood. "I had to wing Beethoven, though," she laughs. "It must have been in my head from listening to Moira." The theory wasn't too bad, she said; the questions on Brahms were difficult but all in all she was happy with everything. She said if she doesn't do well this year, it won't be her fault.

I take a sigh of relief being all too aware that I had been no help at all! I reflect for some moments on what Moira said about her last exam and hope that Catriona is not smoothing over the situation for the sake of it.

Seeing that the mood is better, I pluck up the courage to talk to her. "I know things have been difficult recently but I promise things will get better," I say, taking her hand but it only seems to irritate her. She removes her hand and shrugs her shoulders, enough of an indicator for me to put a lid on it.

In bed, however, she is tender and loving and I feel connected again but I am riddled with guilt for the way I treated her. She nestles into me and I think everything is okay now but then I hear her crying. "What's wrong," I ask in alarm.

"You! You're a right emotional blackmailer!"

"Blackmailer...what on earth do you mean?"

"That tiger... in the storm!"

Catriona is a little moody Sunday morning. She's not exactly a morning person, so I tread cautiously. She's in better form after breakfast and seems eager to get going. Stephens Green is first on her list because it's close by.

There is a hub of activity inside the gates of the Green. Further on, there are makeshift tables wires and cables. An official looking woman explains that they're making a film and apologises for the inconvenience. "We're closing off this route for an hour or two," she says. Then she smiles and says, "I'll let you cross the bridge now but you can't come back this way. Exit at the other end of the park."

Our next stop is the National Gallery. Usually, when I visit a gallery, I only select a few pictures to view. It's crazy wanting to see everything in one go. Catriona wanders around on her own, which suits me fine.

I was hoping to get up to the Hugh Lane because it's not open Mondays, but Catriona wants to see the Book of Kells. After Trinity, Catriona wants to go up to the Stephens Green Shopping Centre. I suggest she go on her own and she seems fine with that. I head to Waterstones on Dawson Street. I'm impressed that they have a café upstairs; it would be great if the one in Cork had a café like this.

I meet Catriona as arranged outside the shopping centre and apologise for not giving her money as I had intended.

"You've spent enough, Piers. I don't want any money."

"Did you see anything you liked?"

"No!" she says a bit tetchy. "I'd like to go back to the hotel now...I'm a bit tired."

"Are you sure you want me to come with you? If you're tired, I mean." I say with mock lasciviousness

"Jesus! You're incorrigible," she says linking my arm.

Neither of us had any desire to go out to pubs last evening. It was a good idea to stay in the hotel because we had a beautiful intimate evening. We had good food and delicious wine in a lovely atmosphere and we went to bed happy and relaxed.

Time has gone by so quickly! I need to be on the road at least by two o'clock, which doesn't leave us much time. After settling the bill, we walk along Grafton Street where there is a hive of activity. There are many buskers on the street which Catriona seems to be enjoying.

In Wexford Street we stop at a beautiful old jeweller shop. "Isn't that lovely," Catriona says admiring a chain. "Look at the way the silver and gold are intertwined."

"Would you like to have it?" I ask.

"No Piers...I'm just looking," she says, a little discomfited. I take her hand anyway and we go inside. What Catriona assumed was silver is in fact, white gold. She tugs at my sleeve when we are told the price, but I ignore her. "I'll take it, please," I tell the assistant.

Outside she thanks me but is embarrassed at how much it cost. Normally, I would banter, saying something like, money is for spending, but there is still a veiled tension, like an overtightened string that may snap if I put a foot wrong.

* * *

Being away was easy: we seemed to need outer distractions; now it's like we have never been away at all. Catriona accuses me of brooding and is dead set on dragging me out to every damn thing. Now that the exams are over, she doesn't need to go to Tower to practice as much and has more time on her hands.

I used to look forward to weekends, especially when I had Rosie. Now I feel there is no order, no purpose. I still can't get it into my head that I won't be going down to Nan anymore!

Catriona has gone home this weekend and I'm rather relieved. At least I won't feel obliged to go out anywhere; it's becoming a strain trying to please her all the time. I even suffered Ger Healy's company recently when she bumped into him in the pub. But despite my efforts, it's getting harder and harder to please her.

Saturday's sunshine has invigorated me somewhat; midday and I have household chores and shopping already done. I thought of going to the sea earlier but it would have evoked too many memories. I'm happier here in my arboreal seclusion drinking wine and browsing through Marconi's Cottage, a book I bought months ago but never opened. I don't know why I keep buying books. Tidying my bookshelves recently, I realised I'll probably never get to read all my books; the number of French books alone is ridiculous.

The doorbell is an unwelcome intrusion: whoever it is, I hope they'll go away. Someone selling something no doubt, or one of those young women with their so-called artwork. One of these days, I'm going to invite one in and ask her to do a drawing. Annoyingly the ringing persists and when I answer I'm surprised that it's Mr. Cotter and his dog, Maisie.

"We're not disturbing you, are we? We won't stay long… you're probably busy," Mr. Cotter says apologetically.

"Not at all! Come in! You're very welcome…I'm in the garden taking the sun."

I pour him a glass of carbonated melon juice because he's driving and I pour a glass of wine for myself. The juice was to keep me off the wine but I still bought wine! Mr. Cotter asks me for some water for Maisie. The poor old thing looks quite panned out with the heat.

"I'm glad I found you in! I wanted to call many times, but I thought you might need time to yourself. Loss is a terrible thing! It took me a long time to come around after my brother died."

"I'm sorry, I didn't know."

"Ah, no… that was many moons ago. A car crash too! Only twenty-six…I was twenty-two then. It never leaves you…the sense of loss, I mean," he says wistfully. "God, I shouldn't be saying that to you…it's hardly consoling."

"It's refreshing actually, I've had enough pussyfooting."

"And how are you at all," he asks, his kind eyes penetrating.

"I'm okay. Well, most days…some days can be quite black."

Mr. Cotter nods. "We must keep going… that's the secret," he says after some reflection.

"Yeah, keep going…that's the secret alright," I say a little facetiously and Mr. Cotter bursts out laughing making me laugh too. I'm about to tell him about my grandmother but think better of it, we shouldn't overload our friends. We sit in the sun talking about what's happening in the world: about Iraq and how America is pounding Afghanistan and what the consequences will be for the people and the environment.

"There must be no wildlife left at all in those mountains," he says, "and from what I read about depleted uranium, sure god knows what the damage will be…for a long time to come. It can't be right!"

"Sometimes, it's too horrific to think about! If you express concern for the environment and wildlife, you're accused of not caring about the people." I say without thinking.

"But can't they see it's all the same concern," Mr. Cotter says. "We are so interlinked; if the environment is damaged, humans are damaged! Oh dear, it's such a sad affair…and all those little children…to see people with their limbs gone…oh god, it's all so cruel. It doesn't bear thinking." Maisie, lying on her side fast asleep, makes a funny snorting sound. "Dogs don't have much to worry them," he says looking at her. His eyes stray from Maisie to the garden, "It's a tidy little garden," he says, "I never spent time in it, but I have photographs of my mother and her parents…down there by the bushes." He goes silent with a faraway look in his eyes. "Ah…I'd better be going," he says pushing himself up from the table. "Come on lazy!" he calls to Maisie. She lifts her head disgruntled but refuses to budge. I'm smiling because she probably thinks he said Maisie.

"Why don't you stay for a bit of lunch? It will only take a few minutes to rustle something up."

"Ah no thanks…I've taken up enough of your time…I just wanted to see how you were doing," he says. "Come on girl," he calls, heading inside and this time Maisie rolls over on to her legs and scrambles stiffly after him. Mr. Cotter lingers in the hallway looking at the bare walls, then turns to me with a sad expression and with a shake of his head goes on his way.

Usually, I don't like people coming unannounced but I make an exception for him. I wonder if I should have pressed him more to stay. I wonder if he's lonely. I don't know much about him other than snippets he gives me from time to time. But I do know that I like this intelligent, gentle, and kind man.

I put on Wagner when the sun goes down but I find it too emotionally demanding and choose Mozart's Symphony no 41 in C Major instead. Best to stick to major keys! However, there are moments when music itself, is too much for me.

* * *

Tim rang me about the accident insurance; he has the forms for me to sign. He reminded me that he asked me to call before. I apologised, making some excuse. I didn't ask how he was coping and he didn't ask me either. Rosie's inquest is on the 19th of July, a date I can't forget because it's a day after my birthday. Tim was surprised I hadn't been notified. It was difficult to put my mind to anything after the call. Feeling unusually exhausted I took to the bed but found it impossible to sleep. I fell asleep around three and woke up at seven from a horrible nightmare.

I called over to Tim bracing myself for what might arise. He made tea while I read over the papers. I signed the necessary and apologised again for the delay. I thanked him sincerely for his help and there being nothing further to talk about I took my leave.

* * *

Despite my efforts to be cheerful, Catriona keeps asking me what's wrong. When she asked what I'd like to do for my birthday, I told her I didn't want a fuss and that I didn't want to go out anywhere. "That's okay, I'll cook a nice meal for you, instead." I didn't want to put her to the trouble of cooking in her makeshift kitchen but she insisted. "It's no trouble…it's your birthday…I want to make of fuss of you," she said, smiling broadly.

The flat is stifling hot. Both windows are open wide and there is hardly a current of air. I'd been out earlier for the Sunday papers and it was hot then. She's cooking roast lamb; I thought she would have chosen something easier. I was going to suggest cooking in my place, but then I thought she might not see it as her effort. My attempts to help are more of a hindrance given the conditions. She seems happier when I sit by the window out of her way.

The drone of traffic below and the announcements in Kent station rise in the air and a heat haze shimmers before the buildings on the docks. The distant hills to the right appear vivid and peaceful, under the now cloudless sky. I always associate my birthdays with ominous skies, and thunder showers. If I were to check weather charts, I'm sure it could be verified. Nan called July, the heavy month because it was often hot and humid.

Like waking from a dream, I see Catriona standing before me with two glasses of wine. I hold both as she pulls a chair over. She kicks off her sandals and leans forward to take her glass.

"Phew, it's warm," she says, sweeping back strands of hair. Brazenly she places her foot on my crotch and smiles mischievously. My eyes are drawn to the creases in her armpits; I'd like to see feathery red there now; it's a pity she shaves. I caress her toes and sip my wine. Tomorrow keeps rearing its head and the fact that I haven't told her. If only I had mentioned it before now!

"Why are you looking at me like that?"

"Like what?"

"Like the way you're looking at me, Piers."

"I was just thinking."

"About what?" I shrug my shoulders. She removes her foot. "Okay, fine!" She says getting to her feet.

It was stupid not to have told her. Sometimes I'm under the illusion that if I leave a problem be, it will magically sort itself out but of course it never does. If only I'd learn to deal with situations as they arise. Looking around I discover Catriona is no longer in the room and I'm wondering if I've upset her, but she returns soon enough hiding something behind her back.

"Happy Birthday," she says placing a present on my lap. I unwrap it to find CDs of the complete works of Jacques Brel and an accompanying book, Tout Brel, with all the songs in French. It is a beautiful gift; I know it will give me hours of pleasure. It was so sweet of her to get it. Seeing how pleased I am, she kisses my cheek and takes off again fussing over the meat. I'm thinking, it won't cook any faster opening the oven like that!

Catriona pulls out the small table from the wall and spreads a white sheet and sets cutlery. I'm puzzled when I hear her going down the stairs and wonder what she's up to. She returns with a bluish pink hydrangea bloom, "I stole this from next door," she laughs and looks for something to put it into. She rinses out a soya sauce bottle and places it in the centre of the table and nods childlike, pleased with herself.

The wafting aroma of lamb and rosemary strangely reminds me of a Sunday with Helen and Josie. Josie was over for mothers-day. Helen was happy and witty; Rosie hung out of Josie most of the day. I remember Helen laughing and being happy.

Catriona, wiping her brow with a paper towel, looks flustered. I make her sit down with a glass of wine and she seems relieved. I take over then putting the food together and serving up.

Throughout, I try my best to be cheerful. Catriona evenly measures out the last of the wine and it melts my heart. She really is sweet. I compliment her cooking and she smiles, the kind of smile that always invites me to love her. This is a great effort from a woman whose cooking skills were limited to scrambled eggs on toast, cheese on toast or a fry up.

"I'll put on some music," she says, "What would you like?" I tell her to put on whatever she likes. She chooses Vivaldi's Four Seasons and I look through the papers. The headlines are too much about trouble and strife so I go straight for the supplements. Catriona too scans the headlines. "It's awful, Piers, what's happening over there...I don't understand why that country has to suffer for the Twin Towers."

"I know love, it's awful... try not to think about it now."

"You're right! I'm sorry, didn't want to spoil your day."

"You couldn't," I say, leaning over to kiss her.

"We could go for a walk later," she says, "I think it's cooler now..."

"It doesn't look promising," I reply, looking out at the gathering clouds, my mind on overdrive trying to work up the courage to tell her about tomorrow.

"Yeah! You're probably right," she says, "it does look thundery."

She relaxes with the music and I pretend to read the papers. I'm getting a headache from the tension. I must tell her! I put the papers aside. "Catriona," I say plucking up courage.

"Yeah," she says looking up.

"Rosie's inquest is tomorrow," I blurt out without any lead up, trying to sound casual. "I'll have to be up early."

"What?" Her look of astonishment unsettles me. "My god! You wait until today to tell me."

"I thought you knew..."

"How could I know, Piers, when you didn't tell me, for heaven's sake?"

I know I'm completely in the wrong and think hard on what to say. "I've burdened you enough lately without putting this on you."

"Is that the way you see it? I thought we were meant to share things. I thought I was being supportive," she says, her eyes cutting into me.

"You were supportive...I mean are...I just wanted to spare you this!"

After a long silence, she sits down beside and says, "You don't have to face

– 143 –

this alone, Piers, I'll come with you?"

"That's kind of you, love, but there's no need... Evelyn will be there and Tim, of course." She is trying to remain composed but then her lower lip begins to quiver.

"You don't want me there! Just like you didn't want me at your grandmother's funeral... I can't fucking believe this!" She says rushing from the room.

I remain sitting, almost frozen, wishing I could feel something, wishing I could cry. I muster enough energy to clear the table and do the washing up. I wrap the remaining meat in foil to cool for the fridge. I wait a long while for her to come back. In the end, I knock on the bedroom door but there's no answer. I knock again and call her name. I refrain from opening the door: it's clear she doesn't want to speak to me.

I take a sheet of paper from my bag and write her a note:

Dearest Darling,

> *Thank you for a wonderful day. The meal was great and much appreciated. Tout Brel is an inspirational gift which I will cherish - you never cease to amaze me. As regards the inquest, I only learned of the date quite recently. Evelyn just happened to ring around that time and volunteered to come with me. I didn't ask her! It was as if I were being swept along by events. I guess I didn't tell you because I didn't want to think about it myself. Please forgive me. My head is all over the place. I'll call you tomorrow.*

> *I love you! Don't give up on me.*

> > > *Piers.*

* * *

Heretofore, all I knew was that Rosie died in a car crash; a truck had careered into them; the Polish driver was arrested for dangerous driving. I listened to various reports, most of which were over my head. I grasped snippets of information from a Doctor Harrison's testimony: the child was dead on arrival to CUH; there were no marks on her body; he concluded head trauma. He said with small children the brain could be seriously affected without outward manifest signs. The judge asked him what the post-mortem had shown in this regard and he said it showed a slight contusion on the left side of the brain. Doubt arose when another doctor said that such slight bruising was unlikely to have caused death. More questions and summing up: the child, Rose Kearns, died of a brain injury due to a car accident. The judge expressed sympathy for the families involved and said that the inquest had most likely caused unnecessary stress. Then it was over.

I welcomed the refreshing breeze as Evelyn and I waited for Tim outside the court. Tim came out looking quite pale. Evelyn asked if he would like to join us for something to eat but he said he had to get back to the office. Evelyn hugged him warmly and for a minute he was tearful but soon regained his composure and shook hands with me. As he walked away up the quay, I thought of how different our lives were and how there was nothing now to connect us.

Over lunch Evelyn enquired after Catriona. When I told her how things stood, she berated me for taking Catriona for granted. She was right, of course, but knowing and doing are different things: translating thoughts and feelings into actions is a complex reality. I veered the conversation away from Catriona and we talked about everything and anything except Rosie.

"I'm going over to see Ivor…in two weeks." She said cheerfully. I wondered how she kept it to herself for so long.

"Oh, that will be nice for you," I said, happy that Ivor was back her life.

* * *

Catriona is packing stuff into bags, next time I call to the flat. Various boxes are already piled in the corner.

"Catriona, what's going on?" I exclaim.

"I'm moving back home," she says matter-of-factly.

"What? And when where you going to tell me?"

"I'm telling you now!" She says flatly.

"But why back home? If it's about the flat, you could move in with me."

"No!" She says without the slightest hesitation.

"Why not?"

"Well, that's a question and a half!"

"Look, Catriona, I told you things will get better...these last months have..."

"No, Piers, things are not getting better, they're getting worse if anything. I don't know what to do anymore! You are in some dark place and I can't reach you. Your daughter died, Piers, not you. You don't relate to me... your head is always somewhere else. It's like I need to apologise for being anyway cheerful. Why do you want to be with me at all?"

"The last thing I want is to make you unhappy...you must believe that!" I say, fully aware of the misery I've caused.

"Maybe so, Piers, but it doesn't change anything...it's just not working."

How can she be so blasé! How can she make it sound so final? Dark thoughts come flooding and I suddenly feel resentful. "How come you never said you loved me, Catriona... was it that hard to say?"

"Saying something is easy!" She sniggers. "Doing something and meaning it is another. Actions are louder than words. But you prefer to dwell on words. Yeah, you love words! You knew I cared for you; god knows I tried against the odds."

"I didn't think you'd be one for clichés... and what do you mean against the odds."

"I mean you're such a strong personality. It was like I had no will of my own, always giving in to you. My concerns were always second. Were you even aware I had any?

"I always considered your feelings, I ..."

"The night you told me you loved me... it was like because you finally admitted that to yourself, I was to be assimilated into your world..."

"Are you sure that's the word you want, love."

"There you go again, words, words...well, taken over then, or whatever you bloody want to call it."

"That's ridiculous! You know that's not true. Anyway, you are the most independent woman I know."

"Except into yours and Rosie's world of course…" she says absently, ignoring my remarks.

"What?"

"I wasn't brought into that though, was I? You excluded me from everything to do with that child. It was like I wasn't good enough to be around her. Even when she died, I wasn't to be part of anything to do with her…"

"Catriona, that's not true!" I protest vehemently. "Look, I should have told you more about Rosie but…"

"Well, ain't that the truth!" She says cynically. "And my friends, what about them? You hate Ger and Chris…you barely tolerate Joe…what did they ever do to you? And Ann, you never asked a thing about her, never wanted to meet her."

"You never talked much about her yourself."

"Yes, I did! She's my best friend… you just never listened."

"I'm sorry, I didn't know she meant that much to you. And by the way, l like Joe Collins!

And I have nothing against Chris Donovan other than he kowtows to Healy all the time. Now Healy, well what can I say, you'll find out some day what he's really like."

"You don't even know him."

"Oh, but I do! He's a prick!" She looks at me now exasperated. "We all can't like the same people now can we," I add to ease the tension.

"And Moira, you never made an effort…always curt."

"Jesus, I can't win here, can I? You complain about her often enough… she's always criticising you and…"

"Only because she cares about me. There's a lot you don't know about her. I could never tell you. Any time I tried to, you put me off."

"I can't imagine you being put off by anything," I say derisively because she's beginning to bug me now.

"The evening you drove her to Tower …I tried to tell you! Remember? You were indignant at what she said. That's what Moira does…she says everything out…she can't help it! She only echoes what Daddy and Mammy say anyway. I wanted to tell you about her many times…god knows, I needed to tell someone," she says, showing a vulnerability which surprises me. My instinct is to embrace her, but she starts picking things up and putting them down again in agitation. "I tried to tell you when we came back from Henchey's … but you were more interested in sex."

How can she believe that? After all this time, she should know me better! But my god, I remember now, I did thwart her! How can I explain now that it was for far different reasons? And anyway, what about Moira?

"What's the matter, Cantwell… can't take confrontation?"

"What about Moira?" I finally ask.

"There's no point now, Piers," she says sighing. "Things haven't worked out for us. I'm not saying it's all your fault…you had enormous things to deal with…we …"

"Please tell me about Moira."

"Why now, for god's sake?"

"Because I need to know." She looks at me with that same tension on her brow like that night we went to Henchy's. Why did I make such assumptions?

"Moira! Where do I start?" she says sitting down beside me.

"Anywhere you like." I say giving her forearm a little squeeze.

"Moira isn't like everyone else, Piers. To explain I would have to go back to when she was a child," she says as if looking for a way out.

"Start there so."

"Moira never spoke a single word until she was five and a half… and that was after extensive speech therapy. Mammy thought she was deaf at first. A friend of Daddy's recommended a doctor in Dublin…an American." She stops suddenly looking frustrated. "It's hard to put a whole history into one conversation Piers. There's so much!"

Just give me the gist of it."

"That doctor said Moira had a rare condition… you'd think I'd remember what it was called… but it was a long time ago and anyway I don't think of Moira like that anymore. He said her vocal function needed to be kick started…it was like part of the brain was asleep and had to be woken up. My mother was relieved there was an explanation at last. She and Daddy did everything he advised and along with a speech therapist, Moira learnt to talk.

Her first word was piano! Imagine that being your first word. The therapist did the usual words, daddy, mammy, duck, ball, but it was Daddy who got through to her in the end. He'd sit her on his knee at the piano and press her fingers on the keys, saying piano over and over. He read to her every night, pointing out objects and colours. Blue was her second word."

"Good words to start with," I say and she manages a smile.

"That was only part of the problem though…she picked up fine with that. She was bright enough at school. She liked Miss Higgins… she had her for the last two years in primary. Mammy never talks about that time. Daddy often tells me things; he's very protective of Moira, as you may have noticed." She says looking for my reaction. "She didn't cope well when she went in to secondary… different rooms, different teachers. It was a hard time for everyone, seemingly. My mother was sent for one time… Moira was screaming and disrupting everything…and it was all because a teacher promised to look at their music projects on that day. Moira was probably the only one who remembered. The teacher said the projects would have to wait till the following term. I forgot to tell you… Moira could play the piano reasonably well from the age of eleven; her project was on Chopin - every detail of his life up to his death in Majorca. She played his music nonstop. I don't know if you ever noticed, but I never play or listen to Chopin!"

"Yeah…It's strange that… it reminds me of the grandmother in, Blackwater Lightship…she wished she could turn her house around because she was tired of looking at the sea. Sorry go on. What happened after, at the school?"

"They brought her to a specialist here in Cork. Moira had lots of tests. Mam worried about that…she was only thirteen then. I think she lied about what the tests were for. The doctor said Moira was on the autism spectrum but he didn't think she was a serious case. My parents explained her condition to the principal, Mr. Cunningham. Dad said he was great. Most of the teachers were fond of Moira, as I said, she was bright! Ye teachers like the bright students don't ye?" I don't know if she's being facetious or not, but I smile anyway.

"I was about eight when I found out. We used to spend the summers down in Myrtleville. I asked Mam why Moira never came swimming with us or played tennis. I knew she could swim… Daddy taught her. Mam explained how Moira was different, but that I wasn't to tell people. It became a kind of family loyalty, if you know what I mean," she says, looking at me searchingly. "That's how we know Joe. His family rented a house up the way from us. Moira related to Joe somehow. I suppose because he was so persistent. He kept asking her to go swimming… he never minded when she said no…you know Joe, he's easy going. Then one day she just went along with him. My mother was thrilled. You see, you have to try very hard with Moira.

"If I'd only known…"

"Well, I did try to tell you!" She says with a cynical shrug. "Remember the night in the Shelbourne bar, the night you were so horrible. Joe told me he'd met Moira that week and she was very agitated about something and he couldn't calm her down. I was very worried. I intended to talk to you after… but you know how that evening turned out. But then again, I wonder if I would have. You never thought there was anything wrong with her, did you?"

"No! I just thought she disliked me."

"That's exactly the point. People don't see her as different and I don't want them to either."

"And Joe, does he know about her?"

"No one ever told him. But he knows…he must! He's used to her."

A wave of regret hits like a tsunami: I thought Moira had been favoured over Catriona. I was resentful! I was wrong about so many things! I, who had always prided myself for being intuitive. When it came to it, I saw fuck all: the woman I love needed to talk to me and carried burdens I knew nothing about. "Don't feel you're betraying anyone by telling me… I won't tell anyone."

"I know that…I trust you," She smiles and I feel a glimmer of hope.

"Do you really want to move back home, Catriona?"

"I don't know," she sighs, putting her hands to her face. "I've given up the flat now!"

"Think about moving in with me. We could give it another try."

"No, I can't do that," she says starting to cry. I try to put my arm around her but she pulls away. "Don't Piers, don't make this any harder for me."

"I don't want to make things difficult…but I can't leave things like this. Think about it at least."

"I'm moving back home Piers!" she says with a pained expression.

"Okay…but it doesn't have to be permanent. Please think about it!"

She gets up and looks out the window for some time, then turns to me and asks if I'd mind bringing some things home for her in a few days.

"Yeah, sure! Anytime you want!" I reply but inside I'm in turmoil.

"How about Thursday evening?"

"Okay…I'll call about seven," I say moving towards the door, hoping against hope that she'll come and touch me.

* * *

Boxes are out on the landing along with three full plastic sacks. My footsteps echo as I walk across the room. The only thing left is the keyboard which I take out and put beside the boxes. Catriona fetches a few items from the bedroom and puts them in her shoulder bag. There is no echo in the bedroom because of the carpet and furniture. The only difference is there are no clothes in the wardrobe and the bed is stripped. I remember the first time she watched me from that bed.

It takes us two trips to bring the stuff down. I put down the back seat and fit in the boxes. I put the plastic bags at each side of the keyboard to keep it steady and push things down as much as possible so I can see out. Catriona runs up the steps to close the door and I achingly watch as the evening sun highlights her hair, reminding me of that day in Slievereagh. This is the last time I'll see her come down these steps or be inside the flat again! There is too much finality! This is more than I can bear! Catriona Lynch is moving away and I, like a fool, am assisting her!

Scenes unfold cinematic like as if all this is happening to someone else: familiar fields, trees and houses are on an alien landscape. My sense of myself has sunk down somewhere inside and is refusing to surface. Even my thoughts seem to be coming from somewhere other than my head.

In the clear blue sky, a large soap bubble moon seems to be falling to earth as we climb the Kerry Road and when we turn off for the house, I feel the moon too is deserting me.

"Would you like me to call you, in a day or two," I ask but she shakes her head and we sit again in strained silence. She turns to me eventually with moist eyes and says, "Piers, what I said the other night about you wanting to take me over...I didn't mean it the way it sounded...I only meant that I was finding it hard to be me...it was because I loved you so much... it wasn't your fault. I shouldn't have let that happen!"

What irony! The woman waits until she is leaving to tell me she loved me! What can I say? I grab her arm as she is about to open the door and pull her to me. She doesn't resist my hungry kiss. I release her quickly and get out to open the boot. When she struggles with the keyboard, I tell her to leave it. She takes the plastic bags instead. I follow and place it carefully against the wall. Jack whizzes in on his bike and is roped in to help with the rest. I get back into the car leaving them to it. Catriona comes over and I roll down the window. "Thanks very much, Piers," is all she says. I hold her eyes for a painful moment before driving away.

On the way home I convince myself that she just needs time to sort things out. l will wait until she misses me.

* * *

Toby raves about Cordoba and Seville; he could have gone to an opera in Granada but passed it up because he was too tired. What is he trying to prove? He isn't even interested in Opera! The subject of Cordoba arose a few months back when we were talking about the dancer, Joaquin Cortes, who was born and raised there. I expressed a wish to see that part of Spain. He showed no interest at all then.

Toby asks about Catriona and I tell him she's fine. He suggests we meet for lunch the following Tuesday but I tell him I can't because I'm meeting Diarmuid, who has been quite ill recently and I can't let him down. "We'll go for a drink some evening so," he says. I don't know why I feel so much resentment, he hasn't done anything to me; he is free to go where he likes.

I can't concentrate on anything because Catriona is my head all the time. Days have turned to weeks and she's not answering my calls. I got drunk the other evening and rang the house. Her mother called her to the phone, but discovering I was drunk Catriona refused to talk to me; I called her a hard-hearted bitch. Next day I rang to apologise but she didn't pick up. Harry told me she was gone out when I rang the house. I rang again the next day and it was Mae who answered.

"Catriona is not here! We're not expecting her back today. I would appreciate it, if you stopped calling, it only upsets her. I understand things have been difficult for you, Piers, and I'm sorry, but if you care anything for my daughter, you'll leave her alone."

"But I do care! That's why I'm calling."

"Catriona doesn't want you calling, Piers. Don't call here anymore!"

* * *

I'm in the same routine. My existence is like a blue note sustained; sometimes the progression breaks or is intruded upon and I'm hurtled further into a mist of melancholy and disconnectedness. I ponder the futility of my life. We are born, we live, and we die, with a lot of loss in between. Is it all about loss? Verdi must have thought so: everyone dies in, 'The Force of Destiny'. Seemingly, he had to tone it down for people's sensibilities. We must not speak too much of death! We are given the promise of an afterlife so we can endure the immutable fact that we are all going to die, that everything in our universe will end.

My recent collection has not been well received. Sometimes to get at anything real we must strip away the veneer, the happy façade. If that appears gloomy to some people, so be it. There will always be those who want a comfortable context. The title poem, Crying Landscape, was singled out as the best poem, others were considered gloomy and obscure. I guess the turbidity of the language caused difficulty. I had dredged the depths of my grief for words to formulate a structure that would express my sorrow because the language heretofore seemed inadequate: it was like I put all the words I found into a big still and whatever came out, I used to construct a new one. It is true, some poems were more complex than before, a necessary complexity I believed at the time. Obviously, I failed! I must have got lost somewhere between complexity and obscurity. Perhaps it wasn't language that was inadequate after all, but my skill as a poet.

I included two poems about Catriona. Originally it was just one upbeat love poem but when she accused me of trying to take her over, I rewrote it. Jack didn't want to include them, saying they were out of place in the collection and in his opinion, unfinished. I should have listened.

Sea Kiss

The wind flamed your hair like a bellows
Waves swirled effervescing round your feet
As you stood shivering at the edge of the cold sea
But I took your hand and pulled you in

And with stifled breath we waded in
Until the water reached up to our waists
Then raising our arms over our heads, we dived
Like dolphins into the Celtic Sea.

And running out like children, laughing,
I kissed your ocean quivering mouth
Touched your sea slippery skin and dreamed
In the salt-drop universe of your thighs.

Nebula Hypothesis

It could have been a forever
The way we were that summer
So close so finetuned in understanding
When we were hungry for the rhythm of the world
And looked to the stars for answers
And we kept the light of the stars in our minds
For what seemed like timeless moments
When we held each other safe from the troubles of our time.
But like the breaking up of nebulae

I lost my equilibrium when sorrows came
I descended into darkness and drifted far away
Yet, all the while I was holding on to you
With the imagined right of heaven.

The poems that some people consider to be my best, are often the ones I believe have failed me the most, not expressing the initial spark-thoughts that inspired them. Constructing a language for spark-thoughts and impressions is the challenge. I've been working on a poem about Caravaggio's, The Taking of Christ and it has changed so much from my first response, I hardly recognise it! When I first saw the picture in the National Gallery, I was amazed that an artist could encapsulate so much in one picture: the unfolding drama of human frailty, power, betrayal and of course, the vultures who feed on other people's misfortune, all masterfully painted with oil on canvas. I was captivated by the beauty of it all: the soldiers in their pink satin pants; the light burnishing their black helmets, the illuminated face of Christ. Maybe someday I will write another that will do it justice.

* * *

Jack calls to remind me of Daniel Gilmore's book launch on Sunday. I try to worm out of it, saying I have something important to do, but he's having none of it, driving home that a similar effort was made for my first collection and that Gilmore needs my support. He is so persuasive I hear myself promising to be at Tig Fili at eight.

"Oh, by the way, Piers, I haven't had a chance to look at those stories," Jack says.

"What stories?"

"The children's stories you sent."

"Oh, I sent them by mistake…were they in with a poetry folder?"

"I can't remember. I thought it was odd alright," he laughs.

"Just delete them."

"Listen, Piers, eight o'clock. Don't let me down," Jack strongly reminds me.

On Sunday afternoon, I drive down to Diarmuid's with a bottle of whisky. He is rallying health wise, but he is as cranky as hell lately. I have books for him too which I hope will cheer him up.

I bang on the back door, the usual entrance and Diarmuid shouts out for me to come in. I make my way in past a clutter of rubbish bags and muddy boots. He seems happy to see me and happier still to see the whisky, which he opens straight away. Unfortunately, I can't join him. I tell him about Gilmore's launch, but he knows all about it.

"Ah the new kid on the block. Pretty good by all accounts. Pick us up a copy, will you, I'll judge for myself."

The place is a mess with yellowed papers and clothes strewn everywhere and he has no fire going. I can't understand how he lives like this, he's not short of money, anything but as far as I can gather. "Sit down will you," he orders and I sit on an old wooden chair rather than the greasy looking armchair.

His mood mellows with the whisky. I ask about his painting. He says he's not doing much because he's working on an epic poem, about the warring Sumerian Gods.

"It's driving me bloody crazy, Piers," he says. "I think I'm trying to include too much, if you know what I mean." I know exactly what he means, there is so much information coming to light on that first great civilisation. We have talked on the subject many times. I wrote a few small pieces myself.

"Yes, that can be a problem all right."

"I think I might have to change it...just talk about one God."

"I'm sure you'll do an excellent job whichever way you go," I say encouragingly. He just looks at me and laughs. I thought then he might mention my book but he doesn't and I don't bring it up either.

"Anything else strange from the outside world? I'll have to get myself back on track, Piers," he says wearily and I rather feel sorry for him.

"You should take better care of yourself, Diarmuid. Sitting around in the cold isn't good. Would you like me to set a fire for you before I go?"

"Ah, there's no point now...I'll be going into bed in a while. I'll have a few more drops of this and I'll be right," he says, holding up his glass. "Oh, by the way, that book I promised you…it's over there," he says pointing to the shelf of books.

Before leaving, I tell him Catriona and I are going through a rough patch and that we haven't seen much of each other lately. He nods with that wiseman face he usually puts on for other people and it annoys me. I let it go, for now, because I haven't the time to confront him, besides, he still doesn't look too well.

Jack pounces the minute I arrive. "Jesus, Piers, I thought you weren't coming at all. You missed the actual launch."

"I told you I had something to do, Jack and *I* told you I'd be here…"

"Yeah, but you're unpredictable these days, Piers," he says. I just shrug my shoulders.

"Come on, let's get the introductions over with," he says, taking my arm.

Gilmore looks so young and full of enthusiasm. I rather like him and find him quite interesting. One of his poems was inspired by the film, Il Postino, and we talk for a while about Pablo Neruda and about his political influence. This leads to a conversation about films. He tells me he likes David Lynch, but we find common ground with Kieslowski. Daniel is well up on Japanese films. I tell him I liked Akira Kurosawa's, Dreams, but that I'm not au-fait with Japanese directors generally.

"Kurosawa was eighty, you know, when he directed dreams. It was different to his other work," Daniel informs. "I think it was based on dreams he had himself."

"As I said, I don't know much about him. It's an area for me to explore."

Daniel then asks about my work, but I tell him it's all about his tonight. We agree to meet for coffee one morning soon. I buy two books and he is shy about signing them. Jack hauls Daniel away then to meet other people and as I'm looking through the book, I hear Chris Donovan talking to somebody and where Donovan is, Healy usually is. What I don't expect, however, is Catriona, who is standing beside Healy at the other side of the room. I queue up for a glass of wine to contemplate what I'm going to say to her. Healy suddenly beside me says hello with forced civility.

Catriona has an expression of surprise as I walk towards her. Surely, she would have expected to see me here. "Hello! Great to see you. How've you been? You're looking well!" I ask trying to steady myself. She ignores the compliment and starts to babble about the changes in Tig Fili. "What did you think of my book," I eventually ask.

"I haven't read it!" She states coldly and for a minute, I don't believe her, but she was never one to lie. Healy returns in the meantime with a drink for her and hovers around; I'm waiting for him to go away but he stays put. Jack comes for me then to meet somebody.

Later, I find her alone again and ask if we can talk. "There's nothing to talk about," she says, looking about her.

"Nothing? Surely after everything we could at least talk. I only want to ..."

"Stop Piers...there's nothing to talk about!"

"Everything okay, Catriona?" Healy butts in. *Fuck you Healy - why wouldn't it be okay!*

"Fine, Ger!" She replies but when she looks at him, I detect a flash of intimacy in their exchange that cuts me like a razor blade. Healy then places his hand on her back and leads her away.

I go through the motions of talking to people, doing my best not to look. Eventually, when I can resist no longer, they are nowhere to be seen. Donovan is still here! I was right! In turmoil I make for the door and walk calmly at first down the passageway because I can still be seen from inside. Once outside, I run Russian roulette across MacCurtain Street.

Toby's phone goes to voicemail. I leave a message. He calls back an hour later and we arrange to meet in the Long Valley tomorrow.

Toby arrives with some colleagues but thankfully they go down the back to the large round table. He's barely seated when I blurt out, "I think Catriona is going out with Ger Healy. I can't believe she'd do this to me, Toby, Healy of all people!"

Toby sighs deeply and says, "If it were someone else, Piers, you'd be in the same state."

"But fucking Healy! Oh god, the thought of him touching her ...I just can't bear it, Toby."

"Keep it down, Piers," he says, furtively glancing around. He goes to order a sandwich and calls back to know if I want anything. I don't answer him. He's all smiles to the girl behind the counter. Does he even care what I'm going through?

"Maybe I got it wrong...maybe he was just fawning on her...just like something he'd do to wind me up!" I say to Toby the minute he sits down. Toby averts his eyes uncharacteristically and sighs. "You know something... don't you," I ask and his eyes meet mine. "If you know something, out with it for god's sake."

"She's been going out with Healy for months, Piers," he reveals finally.

"Months!" I say rather loudly and get an admonishing glare. "Why didn't you tell me?" I say lowering my voice.

"Ye broke up, Piers! Deal with it, for Christ's sake!"

"Is she doing this to punish me?"

"Don't be silly...why would she want to punish you?"

"Give me your phone...she won't answer mine..."

"She won't talk to you, Piers..."

"Can I have it or not?" Toby hands it over reluctantly and I rush outside.

"Hi," she answers cheerily.

"It's Piers."

"Oh, hello," she says more subdued.

"Why didn't you talk to me last night? You could have told me you were with him. I had to hear it from someone else...do you know how hurtful that is?"

"I'm sorry you feel that way, Piers...but really, I don't owe you any explanations. We split up ages ago."

"Ages ago! I was giving you space! Were you seeing him before...is that why you finished with me?"

"You know that's not true..."

"I don't know what's true anymore! Didn't take you long though! If you cared anything at all for me... or for yourself for that matter, you wouldn't have gone running to him..."

"I don't go running to anyone! Anyway, it's not for you to say what I do!

I'm hanging up now!"

"Catriona, please don't cut me off … talk to me please…you owe me that much…"

"I don't owe you anything! When I needed to talk to you, Piers, you didn't want to know…"

"But we were beginning to talk…you told me about Moira… and there's so much I …"

"That was different, I wanted you to know that! I'm going now!"

"You are doing this to get back at me, aren't you?" I say but she's already hung up.

"Fucking bitch," I roar to the air and turn around to the amused faces of the customers outside the Valley and the café next door. I feel like telling them to fuck off too.

Toby is putting his coat on. I know he has plenty of time yet, his colleagues are still down the back. When I hand him back his phone, he throws a look as much as to say, I told you so.

Part Two

I'M IN A strange room; the blue bedspread and the fact I'm wearing pyjamas suggests I'm in a hospital. Instinctively I touch my face: no bandages or cuts; my arms and legs seem fine too. I try to remember how I got here - fragments filter like a fading dream but when I try to make sense of them, my head feels tight and heavy. I scramble feebly from the bed and open a door to a tiny bathroom where I urgently urinate. I come out and look out the window and all I see is a big dirty extractor fan at the back of the building opposite and four large refuse bins in the yard below. I return to the bed, strangely exhausted. I force myself up again when I hear voices and look outside. Three or four people are talking up the corridor; one of them looks in my direction and within minutes a nurse enters pushing a trolley with files and medicines.

"Ah, we're awake, are we? How are we feeling? Roll up the sleeve there and I'll take the blood pressure."

"Why am I here? When did I get here?"

"You arrived Sunday night," she answers, ignoring the first question. "Were you on the tear? You wouldn't believe how many people end up here on account of the drink… or the other stuff," she adds grinning.

I have no recollection of being drunk! Maybe I fell or something and hit my head.

"We have a quiet one, here!" She remarks while writing on a chart and hanging it on the end of the bed. "The doctor will be along soon." She hands me a glass of water and two tablets with her hand poised for the return of the glass. Amazingly I swallow the tablets.

"I couldn't find my clothes," I say in the hope she might produce them.

"You won't need clothes…not for the moment anyway, love."

"I don't like being called, love," I tell her and I hear her muttering under her breath as he leaves. The chart may as well be hieroglyphics and I get back on the bed and punch the pillows. Trying to remember things only makes me anxious and I end up with a throbbing headache. I lie down trying not to think but suddenly feel very sleepy.

I think I'm in a dream when I see a gorgeous-looking woman standing over me. Her straight fair hair is cut to her jaw line and a delicate scent exudes from her body. She pulls up a chair and her white coat falls to the side and her skirt rides up a little when she sits down. I can't help noticing her shapely legs.

"I'm Doctor Kavanagh," she informs me. I quickly swing my legs over the side of the bed while she looks through notes held by a bulldog clip. She raises her eyes and fires a string of questions: what's my name, what month is it, who is the president. You'd think I had Alzheimer's or something! But I'm glad she didn't ask me what day it was.

"Could I have my clothes," I manage to ask.

"We'll get to your clothes later." I'm about to protest when she asks, "How are you feeling?"

"Alright!"

"No headache or nausea then?"

"Well, yes… it gets worse when I try to remember things…the headache I mean."

She nods in some secret affirmation, rises to her feet and leaves as quickly as she came. I'm annoyed I didn't ask more questions. Later, not sure how much later, a muscular black guy in a white coat looks in on me. I ask if he is a doctor.

"No, I am a nurse…my name is Tony," he replies.

"What day is it… and what's the time?"

"It is Tuesday… and… twelve thirty…almost." He has a deep resonant voice. "Dinner will be soon," he says with a smile. He leaves quickly too, perhaps to avoid further questions. I came Sunday. My god, what happened to Monday?

I hear someone singing a Phil Collins song outside the door and then a chubby dark-haired woman, in a blue overall comes in with the dinner trolley.

"Chicken and ham pie today…hope you're hungry," she beams. "I'm Lily by the way! And what would your name be?"

"Piers!"

"Ah, as in the famous Pádraig."

"No," it's Piers," I say spelling it out for her. "My surname is Cantwell."

"I haven't heard that name before," she says putting my dinner on the overbed table.

"There are a lot of us about! Can you tell me where I am, Lily?"

"You're in Maelruain's, love," she says patting my shoulder. "Enjoy your dinner!"

"Thanks Lily." Thank god, I'm not far from home. If only I had my clothes.

The same nurse from this morning comes with more tablets but this time I ask what they're for. "They're prescribed...they're on your chart," she says as if that explains everything.

"Yes, obviously, but what are they for?"

"You'll have to ask the doctor that," she says impatiently. "By the way, you're down for art therapy on Thursday morning. The room is down the corridor to the left but don't worry, someone will take you down on the morning."

"I'm not planning on being here Thursday."

"I'm just telling you what I was told..."

"What would I want with fucking art therapy, I'm a poet, for Christ's sake." Nursie feigns being shocked. "And I want my clothes!" I shout after her.

I see no one in the evening and I'm feeling quite alone. I wish I had my phone. Have people a right to take your phone away? Then again, who would I ring? I try to relax but my head is buzzing and I'm so restless, I don't think I'll get any sleep. However, after a while I can't keep my eyes open.

Evelyn visits me Wednesday evening but instead of greeting her normally, I demand to know who is responsible for my being here.

"Nobody but yourself!" Evelyn states in such a firm tone, it takes the wind out of my sails. She apologises for not getting in last evening...something about work. I barely hear what she's saying because I'm talking.

"You have to get my clothes," I say after a litany of protest, "and they took my phone."

"Your phone is at home, Piers. I can't get your clothes, not yet!"

"What do you mean, not yet? They can't keep me here. I'm not sick!"

"That's just it, Piers…you are sick…talk to…"

"I can't believe you're not on my side, Evelyn."

"Piers, if only you knew how much I am on your side," she says putting her hand to her forehead.

I jabber on about Nurse Bitch and the art therapy. Even if I tried to stop talking now, I don't think I could!

"You always find one person you don't like… it's the same at work… some patients love you and others hate you. As for the therapy, Doctor Kavanagh said she was going to talk to you …she thinks …"

"Hospital policy…that's all that is! You of all people should know that. It's always the same with you Evelyn, anything for a quiet life." I expect a reaction but get none. *What is going on in that head of hers?* "I won't stay here, Evelyn!"

"That's up to you. You need help… take it or leave it."

Why is she saying I need help? Have I done something awful? And even if I have, what is art therapy going to fucking do for me. When I start laughing at the split infinitive, Evelyn looks at me with suspicion. I forget what I'm saying. What did I want to ask? "You could just drop me home…I wouldn't even need a dressing gown." Evelyn sinks back into her chair wearily. *Why isn't she answering me?*

"You know, Piers, it wasn't easy getting here this evening; I only finished my shift at 5 o'clock. When I came Monday, you were sedated…and…"

"You were here Monday!" I exclaim.

"Yes… and…"

"Look I just need to get home, Evelyn, there is something very urgent I need to do." She just looks at me blankly. "I won't stay in this horrible place another minute!"

"Relax there for a minute, Piers, I won't be long," she says rushing out. I lie back on the pillows but I'm beginning to feel very weird: my scalp is itchy; my fingers feel fatter against my nails. In fact, my whole skin is in revolt! Even my crotch feels like it's on fire. I keep wiping my mouth as if I'm dribbling but there's nothing there.

Maybe I drove Evelyn away. It serves me right if she's gone. I'm scared now because my heart is racing. Evelyn comes back, however, and I'm relieved.

"I'm sorry Evelyn, I'm sorry," I say struggling out of bed with the intention of hugging her.

"What are you sorry for?" She says backing away.

"I thought no one cared I was here. It's not your fault...I just can't understand what's happening to me."

"I know! It'll be alright! Try and relax now. Here...I brought you something to drink and something to read. Only magazines, I'm afraid." She smiles and places the magazines on the bed. "I'll be in to see you as soon as I can. The nurse says you need to rest now... try and get some sleep." I go to hug her but she moves away. However, at the door she smiles and blows me a kiss.

* * *

I now have clothes. No one came for me on Thursday. In fact, I'm being left to my own devises quite a bit. I've given up trying to read the magazines because my head is so muzzy. My body feels stiff and achy. I should move around more but every time I leave the room, someone miraculously appears in the corridor. I don't like being watched.

Lying on the bed, I see a damp patch on the ceiling that I hadn't noticed before. The shape of the stain distracts me. Someone once wrote that Leonardo De Vinci looked for inspiration from stains on walls and ceilings. Now I know otherwise, Leonardo was greatly interested in ancient artifacts and cave paintings, why people have to lie is beyond me. I'm not looking for inspiration but if I concentrate on external things like this, I can avoid thinking of - well other things.

I sit up like an intruded-upon teenager when I become aware of Doctor Kavanagh in the room. She pulls over a chair, like the last time, and fixes her eyes on me. I try not to let her silence faze me. "Have you any questions Mr. Cantwell?" She asks at length.

I should be asking questions. Why didn't I ask Evelyn? If I ask the wrong questions now it might make things worse. The questions themselves are probably analysed.

"You don't have much to say! You do understand why you are here, don't you?" I look at her bewildered. "Don't you want to get better?" She says, raising an eyebrow.

Her easy assertiveness gets the better of me and I find myself answering, "Well…the truth is, I don't think I'm ill! Not like you people think anyway."

"You weren't in good shape when I first saw you!"

"How could you tell…you only spoke to me for a few minutes?"

A fleeting smile crosses her face. "If you are referring to Tuesday, that was not the first time I saw you!" *Is she trying to trick me?* "Do you remember anything about the night you were admitted?"

"No! The nurse assumed I was drunk!"

"No…you had no alcohol in your system!"

"How did I get here?"

"By ambulance. You were heavily sedated. I'll try to give you as full a picture as I can. If you remember anything, please tell me. There was a disturbance… you were arrested!"

"Arrested?"

"Yes, for disrupting traffic on Anglesea Street. According to one witness, you were creating quite a disturbance, running all over the place and shouting at motorists…something about changes coming and that people better be prepared, or something to that effect. You could have been killed or caused a serious accident."

"I'm sorry…there must be some mistake, I would never say anything like that. I'm not a bloody evangelist!"

"You were arrested for being drunk and disorderly…"

"But you just said I wasn't drunk."

"The arresting garda thought you were! Luckily Sergeant Ahearn was on duty, he thought you looked familiar and started talking to you. He said you were shivering…you had only a light sweater on. You kept insisting you had to go somewhere…ah… Clifden, I think it was," she says consulting her notes for the first time.

"Clifton! But she no longer lives there … why would I be going there?"

"Who no longer lives there?" She asks all interest. I don't answer. "You told the Sergeant you hadn't been drinking that you were at home all afternoon. He believed you. When you gave him your address, it confirmed you were the person he thought you were. Seemingly, you walk past that station quite often. He gave you tea and drove you home himself. When he got there, he discovered you had no keys... you told him your neighbour had a spare key."

I never go out without my keys. And why wasn't I wearing a jacket?

Dr Kavanagh consults the notes again. "The neighbour told him you were a lovely man and that you never caused an ounce of trouble since the day you moved in. She also told him you'd been through a great deal." *I can't not believe her, an ounce of trouble, that's exactly what Margaret would say.* "She volunteered to stay with you until a member of your family came."

"But I was home then...how did I end up here?"

"Yes! But a lot happened in between. Your neighbour had trouble keeping you there because you kept saying you had to get out. Your sister, Evelyn, arrived first... she had only to come from Youghal." *What was Evelyn doing in Youghal?* "It took your mother longer to get there." I react at the mention of my mother. "Is something coming back to you?" I shake my head. "Now to the interesting part. Evelyn said you were nervously looking around the room and started talking about spirals and DNA and about walls caving in. Evelyn managed to calm you and suggested you go lie down because you seemed exhausted. You didn't go to bed but Evelyn said you closed your eyes for a long time but she wasn't sure if you were actually asleep."

"I still don't understand how I ended up here!" I say quite frustrated.

"When your mother arrived, you screamed at her to get out, saying she had no authority in your house. Is something coming back to you?" She asks, noting my reaction again.

I put my fingers to my temples and shake my head as if that would prise out some memory.

"No! I'm sorry I can't...surely I would remember something about all this...I'm sorry...I..."

"We can continue with this another time, if you wish," she suggests.

"No, I need to know." Doctor Kavanagh looks at me steadily. "It gets worse, doesn't it?"

I'm afraid so!" She says gravely.

"How much more can there be?"

"You physically attacked your mother and your sister got hurt trying to intervene."

"Jesus! This can't be right! There's no way I'd …believe me, I'm not a violent person."

"You had your mother by the throat, Piers."

I have never been violent to anyone before. How can this be happening?

"Now to Doctor Murphy's report. He's your GP…is that correct?"

"Yes."

"Doctor Murphy was shocked at how volatile you were and at the condition of your sister; admittedly, she told him her injury was an accident. However, after hearing about the assault on your mother, and the incident on Anglesea Street, he considered you a danger to yourself and to others. And here you are! I thought it best to give you a few days to get your bearings before we talked."

"Evelyn never said a word! How did I hurt her?"

"You caught her with your elbow and made her nose bleed, and when she pulled you off your mother, you knocked her over and she hurt her side. She was bruised but nothing was broken, fortunately… she was more shaken than anything! She could have been seriously hurt and your mother too…you are quite a big man!"

My whole body goes cold and I begin to shake; tears that refuse to be checked cloud my eyes. Doctor Kavanagh offers me a tissue and sits patiently until I steady myself. "Take a little walk with me," she says. I feel too shaken to object.

We pass through a little office with a computer and lots of files and now we are going through a long room with tables; a metal shutter is pulled down at the end; It looks like a canteen. Stopping at a window, I can see the Lee flowing quietly by in the fading light; the ghostlike trees along its banks seem naked and vulnerable.

"Why do you stay in your room all the time? Why don't you use the communal room?"

"I like being on my own."

"You should walk around, if only for the exercise." We seemed to have walked full circle and are now back at my room. "I'll be back in a minute," she says, ushering me into the room. She's back before I can think. "Take these... they'll help you sleep." I swallow the tablets like an obedient child, and she says, "Things will get better, trust me."

Oh, those words - hadn't I said them to someone before. I feel so lost, so ineffectual.

Tony finds me standing at the end of my bed staring into space; he fetches pyjamas but when I see them, I tell him to throw them away. He looks confused. I tell my sister put other ones in the locker. He lays out the new pyjamas on the bed but I make no attempt to undress. He then comes and pulls up my sweater telling me to lift my arms. Then he sits me down and takes off my shoes and socks. I manage to stand up and take my trousers off and he waits till I put on the pyjamas, then guides me to the bathroom and waits outside for me.

* * *

I tell Kavanagh all I can remember about that Sunday: I was listening to a piece of music - it upset me for some reason. I can't remember which piece of music it was and the more I try, the more anxious I become.

"Don't worry, Piers, it will come back to you in time."

"I am trying to remember!"

"I know! Tell me about your family... you had a daughter..."

"My wife and daughter were killed... I mean my girlfriend... my ex-girlfriend... in a car crash."

"You called her your wife!"

"A slip of the tongue is no fault of the mind," I retort glibly and for the first time, she seems annoyed. "Helen wanted to be my wife and for a time I suppose she was. She was more than a girlfriend if you know what I mean. It was only when Helen's mother died, I discovered how mean I'd been to her. She accused me of not talking to her about anything significant. It's true! I never talked to her about anything...my work especially."

"Your work?"

"My writing."

"Ah yes, Nurse told me you were a poet." Doctor Kavanagh laughs at my reaction. "You don't like Nurse Brennan much, do you?"

"She's judgemental."

"She has a difficult job! There are many different personalities here, people who are ill, like you, Piers. She works long hours and I'm not the only doctor she has to report to. Did you ever think that perhaps you are not the easiest person to deal with?" She smiles at my indignant expression. "I hear you don't want art therapy. I don't recommend it for everyone...I thought it would help in your case..."

"I have my own ways of expressing myself!"

"I'm sure you do, but you might be surprised how it can help."

"Painting! I'd need another life! I'm on the receiving end of paintings." Dr Kavanagh looks a little impatient and seems about to say something but I continue babbling on about paintings. "I knew a guy who spent his scholarship money learning about paints for two years. Imagine two years doing that! You see there is so much to be learnt about everything."

Doctor Kavanagh interrupts me. "That's true indeed, but art therapy is not employed here to make artists. Where are we going here, Piers? What are we learning? What do we need to learn? You are ill, and I need to know why!" *Illness, fucking illness!!* "I guess I'll have to wait for an answer to that question." When she's gone, I recite lines by T.S. Eliot:

> "...And when I am formulated, sprawling on a pin,
> When I am pinned and wriggling on the wall,
> Then how should I begin
> To spit out all the butt-ends of my days and ways?"

* * *

Declan Harmon, wearing a brightly coloured woollen jumper and his hair tied in a ponytail, is endeavouring to talk to me about the art sessions. Ostensibly I'm listening but I couldn't care less: the quicker I'm out of here the better. "Whatever happens in the group is confidential!" He says and qualifies it with,

"What happens in the group stays in the group!"

"I do understand what confidential means," I fire back at him but he only smiles.

At my first session everyone introduces themselves. A young woman distributes paper and brushes; her horrible pink tracksuit emphasises her bulk. A guy called Johnny comes around with water in large paper cups. Declan says we can paint anything we want. Some are asking for a theme and Declan suggests, Spring. *Wouldn't winter be more relevant?* I muse a while on winter landscapes and feel a sudden ache: I really must get out of here!

The guy next to me has painted yellow flowers: could they possibly be daffodils? I swirl a few yellow and green shapes on paper for appearances sake. I don't have the patience to wait for any feedback, however, and slip out discreetly. But out in the corridor, I see big Tony and a nurse watching me.

Doctor Kavanagh seems pleased about the art therapy. She gets little out of me, however. "Declan is primarily a psychologist," she informs me. "He studied art as a hobby but then got interested in art therapy." As if sensing my indifference, she says, "Did you know Piers, according to a recent study, poets are thirty times more likely to suffer a depressive illness and twenty times more likely to be sectioned."

"Now who came up with that!"

"It's an academic study!"

"Poets are people…some people get sick…so A = B, I suppose. How clever."

"You have had a psychotic episode!"

I jolt at the word psychotic. "Anyone who knows me will tell you I was just stressed! It's because of my mother, isn't it? If you only knew, she's the one who should be in here!"

* * *

I haven't seen Kavanagh for a while, I must have pissed her off. I'm feeling low because I realise that if I left here today, I wouldn't know what to do. The biggest fear is being alone in the house, but I don't know why that is. I'm ashamed of what I've become, it's like all my molecules got jumbled around and will never again be in the right order. I used never swear or be rude to people; I was easy to get along with; and I was never violent.

Next therapy session, I say good morning to Declan and the others, intimating my improved sociability. Declan, however, only eyes me with suspicion. Strangely, I had expected him to be pleased, but why the hell should he!

Vince gives out the water, no sign of Johnny. The same young woman hands out the sheets of paper; she looks better in a shirt and jeans. Across the room a woman is talking to herself in the gravelliest voice I've ever heard in a woman. Nobody takes any notice of her, least of all Declan.

My enthusiasm wanes pondering on what to paint. I begin by drawing circles one of which becomes the outline of a face. I make straight for orange to paint hair. It's too orange and I try to tone it down, but now it's too brown. I'm already frustrated! I draw eyes and think I've captured something but my effort to improve them makes them hideous. I scrunch up the sheet and start over - the hair is okay, but the eyes are even more monstrous. I can't draw! I can't paint! Why the fuck am I doing this? I try to put her out of my mind but all I can see is her face. She was beautiful through and through. I will never meet anyone like her again! Why did I drive her away? Why was I such a bloody fool? Raw emotion spews from my gut. I stab violently at my hand with the brush handle but it's too blunt. I continue to stab anyway. I deserve to be punished. Not satisfied, I scratch at my face until I draw blood. An unearthly howl startles me and I'm horrified to find that it's coming from me.

"Easy Piers…easy now…it's okay," Declan says holding my arms. Big Tony is lifting me on to a chair and strapping me in. A lad standing by the door is like a figure from 'The Scream' as I'm wheeled out. In the room, I'm being held down. Something sharp jabs my thigh.

* * *

Judging from the shadows on the walls, it must be afternoon. I sit up to get out of bed but I fall back on the pillow with a head the weight of iron. Why is this happening to me after everything – did I do something awful in a previous life?

Nurse Brennan is now hovering over me taking my temperature and checking my blood pressure. She helps me to sit up placing the pillows behind me. My throat feels restricted, but I don't need to ask for a drink because she's already holding water to my mouth.

"You missed dinner…I could organise a cuppa for you and a slice of toast maybe," she says kindly. "You'll be getting your tea in an hour or so. I'll tell them to give you something extra."

"Thank you…a cup of tea would be great."

* * *

I haven't spoken to anyone since my episode of which I remember every damn detail. All I feel now is embarrassment.

"I can only help if you talk to me, Piers," Kavanagh says when she eventually comes to see me. "No more diversions like lectures on art," she adds raising her brows.

"The truth is, I know nothing about art…the making of it I mean," I say apologetically, remembering the spiel I gave her.

Doctor Kavanagh produces my crumpled sketch and says in a serious tone, "I want to know about this, Piers!" Thankfully, she puts it away, sparing me further embarrassment. "Who were you painting?"

"Just a woman I know!" Her name shapes in my mind.

"Was that the person you were going to see that Sunday evening…"

"Yes! She had a flat in Clifton Terrace, off Summer Hill. I don't know why I was going there… she doesn't live there anymore."

"The mind is strange territory, if only we knew a lot of things." I like when people admit they don't know everything and I'm more inclined to tell her about Catriona. Doctor Kavanagh, however, goes in quite a different direction - probing - asking about Rosie. She switches from one subject to another, never giving me time to arm myself.

"A parent shouldn't have to bury a child," I say looking away.

"When you were admitted you kept saying, everything is changing, what exactly did you mean by that?

– 173 –

"Catriona was the one who worried about the way the world was going."

"Is that the woman you were going to see?"

"Yes! She said people were under the illusion that the world was progressing. She used to get upset about things...like the invasion of Iraq and the way Palestinians are treated and of course the way our own country is going. She'd laugh if she heard me ... she used to accuse me of being apolitical. I see things differently now though. The world is a scary place... it's become almost like a shadow of the real thing. I don't know...maybe the world was always like that."

"How do you mean, a shadow of the real thing?"

"Oh, you know, consumerist veneer. Even food... we're supposed to be happy with packaged organic stuff that tastes like shit and costs a fortune. We're fooling ourselves, there's no organic, the soil is fucked. Sorry, I didn't mean to swear." Kavanagh gives a friendly smile and off I go again. "We've become like that character... in that film... the guy gets his hand cut off... he's given a plastic one... or is it gold? Anyway, he's thrilled with the fake hand. I see Celtic Tiger Ireland as the fake hand!"

Kavanagh's expression changes making it clear she's not going to be drawn into politics. I expect her to ask more about Catriona but surprisingly, she stands up and advises me to get some rest. *Why couldn't I remember the name of the film. Was it even a film? Am I losing my mind completely?*

Days later, an orderly puts his head in to tell me I have a visitor, a woman. I specifically told Evelyn I didn't want anyone near me. I hope to god it's not my mother or Aunt Joan. I tell the orderly that I don't want anyone up here. "Come on down so!" he laughs.

She looks quite solemn sitting on a grey plastic chair against the wall. She is the last person I would have expected to see. Her face brightens when she sees me and my heart begins to race in trepidation. When she kisses my cheek, her scent is enough for me to crumble; I steady myself and guide her into the adjacent room where we sit at a table. Luckily, there is no one else around.

"Well, are you not talking to me?" She begins with the familiar use of the negative. In an odd way I feel I've been given a safety net.

"I'm just surprised. How did you know I was here?"

"Oh, you know this town, Piers... they know what you had for breakfast."

"So, the word is out... that should make some people happy." She knows to whom I'm referring.

"There were rumours... you were arrested for being drunk and disorderly... now, I believed that might be true. Another was you were done for drugs." She laughs then at the idea. Her laughter draws me. She senses it and averts her eyes. After a few moments, she says, "Actually, Evelyn told me! I bumped into her outside Loafers and we got talking. I don't think anybody else knows."

"Ger will make sure though, won't he?"

"I won't tell him," she assures me. *So, she's still with him!* "Besides, I promised Evelyn to keep it to myself."

Running my hand over my thick stubble, I suddenly become self-conscious. I haven't shaved. I didn't want anyone standing over me. I'm sorry now! I drum my fingers on the table and my knee is jerking up and down; I don't remember doing that before.

"How are you?" She asks placing her hand over mine.

"Oh, coming on I suppose," I manage. "Now, did we ever think the like of this would be happening, eh?" I say trying to sound upbeat, while discreetly removing my hand.

"Things will get better, Piers...I know they will," she says earnestly.

Things will get better – the same old mantra! "I hope so! I'm sorry, I don't mean to sound negative... they will...I'm getting there." She smiles encouragingly, her eyes wide and lovely as ever. "But I won't have you, though!" I add with a shake in my voice. *Jesus! why did I say that?*

"That's all in the past now, Piers," she says matter-of-factly. It's only when she turns her head to the side, I see how thin her face is, indeed, how much thinner she is overall. And her hair, how did I not notice immediately, it's a deeper red, straighter and shorter.

"What have you done to your hair?" I exclaim suddenly.

"Oh, I felt like a change," she says, flicking her hair with forced nonchalance. I don't believe her! And why is she looking away all the time?

"Did he ask you to do that?"

"Don't be silly, Piers," she snaps.

I knew her overt sensuality, her independence, would be too much for preponderant Healy. I knew he'd try and mould her! Suddenly I get a prick of conscience, hadn't I accused her of luring me like a siren at the graveside, albeit mentally. Perhaps I would have tried to change her too. No! I will give myself that, it was only a fleeting emotion in stark circumstances.

"Piers, are you alright?" She asks touching my arm.

"Yeah…I'm okay!"

"We would have parted eventually, despite everything," she says gaining my attention again. "We were too intense about everything. Besides, when you most needed someone, I wasn't the one."

"That's not true! I needed you desperately! I just couldn't communicate how I felt. I was inadequate!" I can see that her defences are weakening a little. "We were happy a lot of the time, weren't we?"

"Don't Piers, there's no point going over old ground now."

"It was all my fault… I let things fall apart…when Nan died I …"

"Look, as I said, there's no point. I came to see you because I care about you. I don't want to get back with you! Things are different now!" Her lower lip slightly quivers, I guess this is proving much harder than she imagined. "We are still the same people, Piers…it's only circumstances that have changed… we should be able to remember the good things and move on. I want you to be well! I know you can be well," she says with tears in her eyes. "You have to get yourself out of here, Piers."

Oh, god, I could drown right now in those moist eyes. "How come you're so forgiving? I don't deserve it," I say fighting to keep back the tears. "You are a good person. I never meant to hurt you…you know that." I wipe the escaping tears with my sleeve and recover enough to say, "Your hair…the colour…your own colour…is beautiful. You don't need to change anything about yourself…don't let anyone tell you otherwise." I may have hit a nerve because she now seems subdued. Where is my feisty Catriona?

At the door, she reaches up and kisses my cheek. How can she be so close to me, yet a universe away? I yearn to hold her in my arms but I know I can't. With an unbearable ache, I recall twice before following her with my eyes till she was out of sight.

Back in my room, my mind is full of her, I go over every word every nuance. Strange how I feel happy and sad at the same time! I end up exhausted but when I close my eyes all I see is her face.

When Evelyn next visits, she acts all defensive "I'm sorry Piers, I had no choice…I couldn't lie to her."

"I'm not complaining, Evelyn, I'm glad she came! She wants me to get well."

"Of course, she does, Piers, we all do, Ivor, Tommy, everybody! Mam is upset that you don't want to see her." I shrug my shoulders. "It hasn't been easy for her. There's a lot you don't know!"

"Like what?"

"I'll tell you when you're stronger."

* * *

I try to convince Kavanagh that I'm well enough to go home. "I'm glad to hear that, Piers! That day is not too far off," she says smiling. "But we have a little more ground to cover first," she adds and my heart sinks. "What are you thinking about, Piers?"

"Nothing!" I say shrugging my shoulders. *How long must I put up with all this?*

"I'd recommend you go home today if I thought you were better. If you really want to get well, we will have to dig a little deeper!" Kavanagh surprises me then by telling me to call her Liz and while I am chewing on that, she fires a question about my relationship with my grandmother. "You depended on your grandmother a great deal, I think."

"I suppose! Nan was always there…like the air or the sky. When she died, the frangible threads that held me together seemed to dissolve."

"Did you grieve for her? Did you cry at her funeral?" *Who is feeding her all this?*

"No!"

"Why?"

"I guess I was afraid!"

"Did you cry for Helen and Rosie?"

"I cried at the hospital when I was told they were dead."

"Why were you afraid to cry for your grandmother?"

"I don't know!" *I must be careful! If I say too much about Nan or Rosie, I'll never get out of here!*

"What did you mean when you said your mother is the one who should be in here?"

"I don't remember saying that!" She nods affirming I did. She's confusing me! First Nan then Helen and Rosie and now my mother. A silence stretches tight between us. I feel I'm being tied in knots.

"Perhaps you'd like to talk about your father instead," she suggests.

I'm about to talk about my father when a whirlwind of emotion overcomes me and I start telling her about John Dineen and Alan Foley, about the day they hammered me after school. "Dineen was always picking on me. One day he grabbed my school bag and ripped off the stickers …Nan gave them to me for my birthday. I was so mad, I dived at him… but he was too big for me. He punched me in the chest and winded me…I fell and hurt my arm. Foley kicked me while I was down, the coward that he was. Dineen caught me by the throat and said he knew all about my crazy fucking mother…he said everyone knew she went to a psychiatrist.

"I punched him on the nose and made it bleed. I called him a liar and hit him again as he was getting up. I thought then he was going to do me, but he scuttled off. He still had the nerve to shout back, 'Your mother's a fucking loony.'

"When I went home my mother said I shouldn't be fighting. But when she heard it was John Dineen, she lost it." I stop for a breath as if reliving the whole thing. I relate then how my mother beat me and about all the trouble I caused. "I was only defending her against liars like Dineen." I suddenly become aware that I've been talking with the mindset of a nine-year old. Kavanagh seems to be waiting for me to continue but I feel too ridiculous to go on. Why did all that come flooding out anyway? "If my grandmother were alive, I don't think I'd be in here…I could always talk to her," I say absently.

"Did you talk to your grandmother about Dineen or ask what he could have meant?"

"No! Anyway, I didn't believe him!"

"But deep down you think there might be something to it."

"No, I don't."

"Why else would you say your mother should be in here?"

"I don't know! Evelyn says there's a lot I don't know about my mother. She wants to tell me something when I'm stronger."

"Do you think you're strong enough now, Piers?"

"I don't know! I never like talking about my mother."

* * *

I went down to the communal room this morning because I was restless and fed up being alone in my room. Conversations stopped and heads turned as I entered. A television blared but no one seemed to be watching. Two guys were playing cards, others sat around tables with paper cups. The guy by the dispensing machine stared as if I had just landed from Mars. I picked a paper from the rack and sat down. Those at the next table barely acknowledged me when I said good morning. My presence seemed to be making them uncomfortable but I didn't care. I stayed and read the paper through and even did the crossword for pig-headedness. And here I am alone again in my room!

No sign of Evelyn this evening. I can't remember if she said she was coming or not. I feel ashamed for being so insecure. I start to read Edmund White's biography of Genet, that I asked Evelyn to get from home but a few sentences in, I give up. All I read are papers and magazines and even those I flick through without any retention. This worries me, what if I can't ever get back to my books and my writing. If that happens, I'll kill myself!

Evelyn's arrival quickly dispels these dark thoughts. "Hi," she says kissing my cheek. "It took me ages to get here… some hold up… an accident I think," she says dropping into the chair.

"I hope to be out of here soon, Evelyn… it's hard on you, I know."

"Don't worry about me, Piers. I want to come to see you. Did Doctor Kavanagh say you can go home soon?"

"Not exactly. It's up to me now!"

"You look better! I see an improvement…oh, I see you're reading Genet."

"Trying to Evelyn. I just can't seem to focus…"

"Well, that's understandable…I did think it a heavy tome for you right now. But you would have it."

"It's only upsetting me. You might take it away with you."

"Are you sure?"

"Quite sure! You said you had something to tell me… about Mam."

"Yeah, but I don't want to set you back or anything. Maybe I should run it by the doctor first!"

"I'm a grown man, Evelyn, I can take whatever it is!"

"It's not a pleasant story…I found it most distressing, Piers…it's …"

"Just tell me, Evelyn."

"Promise me you'll never say a word to anyone!"

"My, you have me curious now," I laugh.

"I mean it, Piers!"

"Okay, I promise."

"At Nan's funeral I overheard a conversation between Mam and Tommy. Mam was full of regret for not telling Nan something. What she actually said was, 'I should have told her Tom; all these years I wanted to tell her about that bastard…to explained what changed me!' When I heard her saying, 'what changed me' I was intrigued. Tommy told her she should leave all that behind, that it was years ago. Mam said it might be years to him, but it was like yesterday to her. Tommy said what she needed was a stiff drink and went off to get her one. People came to condole with her then, so I heard no more! It was the heartfelt way she was talking, Piers…I never heard her talk like that."

"Well, you obviously found out something."

"I told Tommy what I heard and asked him out straight what it was about. He was furious. You should have heard him, Piers…he called me, a sleeveen for listening."

"That's a new one for the books…usually you can do no wrong in his eyes."

"Is that right!" Evelyn says slightly amused. "Anyway, I wanted to know why Mam was always so sad, why she was so harsh when we were small. He sprang to her defence of course, saying she was ill then and that I should learn to forgive and that whatever confidences he shared with his sister were none of my bloody business. I said that if my father were alive, I'd be asking him. He said he was sure our father would feel the same way, children had no right to know everything about their parents! When I said I thought my mother disliked me and I couldn't really talk to her about anything, it seemed to hit a nerve. He was shocked that I could think that! He said Mam loved all her children. I thought that was the end of it but he said then he was going to tell me something but I must never breathe a word of it to anyone and that Mam must never know.

Piers, he made me swear." Evelyn looks at me anxiously.

"Don't worry Evelyn, whatever it is I can handle it!"

"Well, you know Mam sang in the choir and all that. She was in a drama group too which I never knew! Did you know that?" I shake my head, not wanting to interrupt her train of thought. "Tommy said Mam was a ray of sunshine then but all that changed when she met a fellow called Jamie Dineen. Dineen never had a shilling even though he was supposed to have a car business in Waterford. Tommy said he was quick to spend our mother's money, letting on he had no cash on him and could she lend him a few bob till he got to the bank!" Evelyn stops suddenly, "What's the matter Piers? Am I going into too much detail? Oh god... you're not ready for all this..."

Dineen!!! I only recently uttered that name! And now! "No...I'm alright...go on...I was just remembering something!"

"Are you sure?"

"Yes!"

"Nobody liked him seemingly, but somehow he inveigled his way into Mam's affections. After a while, people noticed how nervous she was whenever Dineen was around. Dineen used to accuse her of trying to get off with all the guys but treating him like a leper. Tommy believes Dineen was aware of our father's interest...Dad was in the choir too as you know. Anyway, realising what a control freak he was, Mam tried to get rid of him but he kept turning up everywhere she went. Tommy said he'd be called a stalker now. One night she agreed to meet with him to make it clear she wanted nothing more to do with him. Dineen said they should talk somewhere other than the pub because people were listening. Tommy said that was her big mistake!

"He drove down to the strand and was all nice at first saying he loved her and didn't want to lose her, but he turned nasty when she held tough. He said he was sick of her convent school act. Tommy said he couldn't repeat the vicious things he said. Mam got so frightened she ran away." Evelyn stops and looks visibly upset.

"What is it? What's wrong, Evelyn?"

"She didn't get away, Piers! That bastard raped her!" *How can this horror story be about our mother?* Evelyn gets up and hugs me, saying, "I knew it would be too much for you... I find this difficult myself..."

"You shouldn't have to bear this on your own," I say hugging her. "I know it's hard but I need to know."

Evelyn sits back wearily on the chair and for a minute I think she's going to fall apart on me, but she looks up and says, "Even after all that, the fucker had the nerve to say he loved her, as if nothing had happened. When she refused to let him drive her home, he said there'd be no point telling anyone because he'd make sure the whole town knew she was a slut.

"He got married after to a chemist from Fermoy, a lovely woman by all accounts, but within two years she ran away, taking her child with her." Evelyn studies me to measure the effect.

"What happened?" Did she report him?"

"No! Tommy said her big fear was that she might be pregnant. She wasn't anyway. Evelyn laughs then, "Were you worried there for a minute, Piers?"

"The thought never crossed my mind."

"No, you're too much a Cantwell!" She says laughing again.

"Don't get side-tracked, Evelyn."

"Tommy said she was never the same after. People weren't stupid - they knew it had something to with your man. Anyway, she went to Doctor Kelly for something to help her sleep. He noticed how jittery she was and amazingly got the whole story out of her. He recommended she talk to his friend, George Moran. She was reluctant when she heard he was a psychiatrist, but Kelly convinced her it was only a bit of counselling. After a few visits, Moran advised her to confide in someone she trusted. That was Tommy!

"His reaction, of course, was to go after Dineen, but Moran had her well prepared for that. Mam's biggest regret was not being able to tell Nan. That's what they were talking about the day of the funeral."

"My God, Evelyn, I can't believe you got him to tell you all that, and in such detail!"

"Believe me, it was hard work! I kept probing. Poor Tommy! You got the short version; Tommy was more colourful calling Dineen all the names under the sun. Tommy said he should have ignored our mother and beat the daylights out of him. Only for promising not to tell anyone, he and Paddy would have sorted him out. Tommy said it was just as well Frank was in England because if he found out, there would have been a murder in Dungarvan."

"I never saw that side of Tommy. It's funny how we view them, isn't it... they have lives totally separate from us." Evelyn sighs and looks at me then and says, "In the normal run of things, we shouldn't know any of this! I probably crossed a line here, Piers. In one way, it helps me to understand but in another, I feel guilty knowing."

"Yes, I feel the same. Why didn't you tell me about this, before?"

"You had enough on your plate. You don't talk to me much anyway."

I never once considered what it was like for Evelyn, how alone she must have been, especially when Ivor left. Other than Tommy, she had no one else to talk to.

"Maybe, I should have waited till you were stronger," Evelyn says because I've gone quiet.

"No, I was just thinking... I should have been a better brother, Evelyn. I've been a selfish bastard!"

"No, you're not," she says kissing my cheek.

"I'm sorry you got hurt, Evelyn, I would never intentionally hurt you!"

"I know! It was my own fault for swinging out of you... you were only trying to shake me off. I pity anyone that ever takes you on in a fight," she adds to lighten things.

"I still can't remember anything..."

"Don't worry... the doctor says it'll come back to you. When your mind is ready, I suppose." She laughs then. "Listen to me...you'd think I was a psychologist!"

Evelyn has always been kind and supportive. It will be a lucky man that gets her.

"Piers, I haven't told you the most interesting part of the story yet, the part that affected our lives so much. I think we'll leave that till another time… you look quite worn out."

"Christ! You mean there's more! How much more can there be?"

"Believe me, there's more!"

"You can't stop now, Evelyn."

"Are you sure?"

"Yes! If you're not too tired that is."

"Friends coaxed Mam back to the choir. She and Dad became good friends, but they didn't get together for over a year. Tommy thinks Dad was slow to ask her out because he was so much older. They got married and were happy according to Tommy and when you came along, they were thrilled. But wouldn't you know, after I was born, she had postnatal depression," Evelyn says light heartedly but becomes serious again. "The problem was Dad knew about what happened to her."

"I suppose it's only natural she'd tell him!"

"Natural? I think that would be a hard thing to tell your husband! No, she never told him. Tommy didn't know the ins and outs of how Mam found out that he knew but it put a real strain on the marriage."

"Well, if she didn't tell him, how did he find out?"

"Kelly!"

"What! So much for patient confidentiality!"

"I couldn't believe Tommy defended him. He said Jim Kelly and Dad were the best of friends, as if that made it okay and that Kelly was always good to our family! I tried to make him see what it must have been like for her.

"Over the years Mam suffered bouts of depression. Of course, she never trusted doctors again. Dad took care of her most of the time. The rest you know! Do you remember how he used to take us out all the time, to give her time to herself?"

I can't go there now…I can't!

"The one thing Tommy stressed was that they loved each other deeply.

When she was well, Dad was a happy man. Tommy said he would do anything for her but unfortunately it took its toll of him in the end. It's all so sad, Piers," Evelyn says beginning to crack a little.

In my head, I always had the monopoly on my father and now I am made aware that he was Evelyn's father too. My life seems to be piecing together like a jigsaw. Telling Kavanagh about Dineen and now the mystery solved.

"He should never have said anything," I state bitterly.

"That's easy for us to say. God knows how it came out… they loved each other after all. But I can understand how she felt, Piers. She had put the bad stuff behind, had a happy marriage and suddenly it was stained with that bastard's dirty fingerprints."

"At least we were born out of love! I don't know about Ivor."

"How can you say that after everything I've told you! Things might have got a bit rocky, but she never stopped loving him. I'm certain of that!"

How can she be so sure? I don't remember any loving exchanges between them.

"You know, I could jump into your bed and go to sleep I'm so tired."

"Have you work tomorrow?"

"Yes, but I'm not on till six."

"Stay in my place again. I have a huge collection of old movies…maybe a nice weepy to cheer you up."

"That's an idea," she laughs.

"Thanks for looking after me, Evelyn," I say hugging her, recalling how panicked I was before she arrived.

"Things can only get better for us," she says and I really want to believe her.

* * *

Toby Holland enters the room like a whirlwind. He's had some altercation downstairs, insisting he was family. They let him up! He's in his bank uniform: suit, coat, and polished shoes. He has been trying to contact me for ages, he says, he even called out to the house. (I think he may have heard the gossip, but he doesn't say). "Only for Evelyn answering the phone the other night I wouldn't know anything. Why didn't you call me?"

"I don't have a phone…don't know where it is!"

"What the hell are you doing in here, Cantwell? This place is not for you! Look man, I know you've been through hell but believe me you don't want to go down this road. They'll work on you till you fragment. What are they giving you?" He's appalled I haven't a clue. "And how are they affecting you?"

"Well, I get drowsy and sometimes my speech is slow...other times I can't shut up at all! The thing that worries me is I can't read anything...well concentrate I mean."

"Fuck it! You think you're getting help here, but those tablets will mess with your head. Any substance that alters your brain chemistry can't be good and for what it's worth I happen to like your brain. You're just grieving, man... you just need to talk to someone."

"That's just it, Toby, I couldn't talk to anyone."

"You can always talk to me," he says earnestly, not realising how bad I really got.

"I seem to be grieving for a long time Toby, it's two years since ..."

"That's just it, you suspended your grief. Look I don't know what happened to you and how you ended up here but believe me there are other ways, Piers." Toby runs his fingers though his hair, uncharacteristically agitated. "Anyone I ever knew who went down this road didn't end up too good."

"And who would they be exactly?" I ask, thinking he just invented them for the sake of it. He goes so quiet I can almost see the wheels turning in his head.

"My brother, David, for one. You should see him now, all nervy and subdued... and that was the bloody medication...I know it was! First, he blew up like a balloon...he was always a fit bloke. He's completely obsessed with his weight now. And he has this head twitch thing that my father says will never go away."

I had never seen such angst on Toby's face. Strange how I never heard about his brother before.

"Look I'm not here to talk about him...I know you, Cantwell... you don't belong in here. You are a poet... people like you look the world square in the face. You're braver than anyone I know... you know about life ...you don't belong in here!"

People like me! If he only knew, I know nothing about life. Nothing! Nothing! "I believe Kavanagh is helping me, Toby, she…"

"O.K. that may be so! But the medication, Piers, that's what I'm worried about. You taking that medication is like capitulation to me…you can get well without all that. I believe in you, man."

He is saying much the same as Catriona; I'm so affected, I can hardly speak. He believes in me! Catriona believes in me! Why can't I believe in me? "I don't want to be here, Toby, I'm trying …I want to go home."

"Good…let's go from here then," he says standing up. "I've got to run… took an early lunch break. I'll be in this evening," he says. Toby is just about to go when he sees Liz standing in the doorway. She lingers a moment, smiles in at me but goes away. "Who was that?" Toby asks stressing each word, his eye having taken her measure like a camera shutter.

"My doctor… Elizabeth Kavanagh."

"Well fuck me! I can see why you're in no hurry, man."

I'm laughing…really laughing! It feels good!

Kavanagh is curious about my visitor and is amused when I tell what Toby said about me wanting to stay here.

"You are very fond of him, aren't you?" She smiles.

"We've been friends for a long time."

* * *

Doctor Kavanagh and I have covered a lot of ground and I'm more inclined now to confide in her. I told her about my heart racing when I'm stressed, to such a degree that I often think I'm getting a heart attack. I told her I had an ECG in my late twenties which showed slight arrhythmia. Having listened to how I felt other than the rapid heartbeat, she thought it most likely I suffer panic attacks. She said I should breathe slowly and remind myself that it is a panic attack and that it will pass. She also said my medication would help with anxiety. But she still advised a medical check-up.

I related what Evelyn told me about my mother but in much less detail. I talked a little about my relationship with my mother and my grandmother. However, she kept probing about Rosie and that made me uncomfortable, but I'm getting better at hiding things. I had to be careful too talking about Catriona because much of what happened between us was linked to Rosie. I tried my best to be honest otherwise. Out of the blue, she asked if I blamed my mother for my father's death. I was dumbfounded! Did she think that because I attacked my mother? She didn't wait for an answer, however, and left me to ponder.

With all my talk, I'm nervous about going home. Kavanagh assured me that I'm more than ready but if I have any difficulties, I can attend as an outpatient. I asked about the tablets and about how long I would have to take them. She insisted I stay on my medication for now saying I was on a reduced dosage on two tablets anyway. I didn't push it because I wanted to appear cooperative.

* * *

I'm functioning now with a semblance of normality. I wouldn't have coped only for Evelyn and Toby. My mother too has been supportive. I found out that it was she who organized and paid for my private room in the hospital. I was so self-absorbed at the time I didn't even question why I had a private room. She also organised the payment of my rent. I thought it was okay to use Rosie's insurance money to pay her back. She was reluctant to take the money but I insisted. She seemed a bit emotional when I told her I appreciated everything she did for me. However, I couldn't find a way to apologise or talk about what happened.

I am weaning myself off the medication with Toby's help. It is important for me to be able to feel, even if it is only sadness. Because of Toby, I now know quite a lot about drugs and mental health. It's a disturbing area that I can't dwell too much on as I'm trying to get myself better. Overall, I count myself lucky that Liz Kavanagh was my doctor.

Liz said everything can't be fixed overnight, that it takes time and effort and that sometimes fixing one thing often challenges another. Even though I've learnt to recognise what causes me to be sad, the sadness has not gone away, it lingers like a shadow, but at least I'm not as fearful as I used to be.

Christmas time again. Did my shopping with little pressure - a cashmere sweater for Evelyn which I know she'll like. I thought of getting Toby something but that would be strange territory for us. He'd probably think I was losing it. For Mam, I got a boxset of Inspector Morse; she likes the programme but has missed many of the episodes. My neighbour Margaret likes the character, Morse, too. Perhaps it's the limp, the vulnerability. It was like that with Wagner and Weber. Weber used to call to the Wagner's house every midday after his exhausting rehearsals. It was Weber's limp that endeared him to the young Richard, who ran to greet him coming up the avenue. Is it the imperfection that draws us?

Sleet stings my face as I step out into Patrick Street. Traffic taillights reflected in the wet street is reminiscent of Kieslowski. How strange the variety of images stored in our little heads - file after file: I'm walking the mean streets of New York with Henry Mancini music in my head; I'm some old timer going to the English Market or down the Coal Quay for holly in a bygone age. I'm Patrick Galvin's mad woman…I'm…I'm… Piers Cantwell!

Mangan's clock stands anachronistically on the new-look Patrick Street, with its quirky streetlights. It reminds me somewhat of Berlin's Checkpoint Charlie. I noticed that the Echo Boy is demoted from its more prominent position. The City Library is to be overhauled I hear. I rather like its old-world charm, the quietness, and the pleasant staff. The music section is a gem! I don't mind change if it's for something better but if we have something good and functional, why change? Of course, it could be something to do with the structure of the building.

I consider going to the Corner House for a pint but decide not to risk it. The blue Christmas lights are a reminder - she could be in town right now. It would kill me if I saw them!

In a coffee shop, in Oliver Plunkett Street, an elderly man is sitting next to me eating soup and a roll. He's wearing jeans and black shoes; there's something not quite right about jeans on an old person. He looks hard up but at least the staff are friendly to him. We both look out at people bustling by. A young lad in a white hoodie is kissing a girl on the corner of Prince's Street, oblivious to the rest of the world. The elderly man is smiling out at them.

I have always felt a close connection with this town, but now it's like she has aborted me and is breathing freer without me. I can't isolate myself. I won't! A sign over Budget Travel catches my eye – Simple, Simple, Simple. Yes, I suppose the only option is to leave.

In Pembroke Street, I see the old city library as just another bastardised shop front, its doorway used for a window. I saw it romantically of course when I was in love. How can two people who have loved each other end up so estranged? If she saw me now, would she pretend not to see me? I don't want to become bitter! Deep down I know she cares about me. 'Ne me quitte pas, ne me quitte pas…' how we laughed at the pathos: 'Laisse-moi devenir/ L'ombre de ton ombre/ L'ombre de ta main/ L'ombre de ton chien.' Would I become anyone's shadow? I can't mock it though, feeling it too much. Estranged? L'Étranger: 'Aujourd'hui, maman est morte. Ou peut-être hier. Je ne sais pas.' Meursault was the opposite though; his condemnation was for not feeling at all.

There was a time when I'd worry about my erratic thoughts, but now I'm just indulging in words and associations: estranged to L'Étranger. Brel and Camus…both associated with France, one a Belgian the other Algerian. I do it because I like doing it! 'To be or not to be…' simple enough words, but to have written them, Shakespeare must have been to, or imagined, some dark place. I wonder, if one has to reach rock bottom to fully understand, to see beyond what one normally sees.

I feel self-conscious now passing the Garda Station. We never know when we are being observed. Perhaps I should call in some day and thank the Sergeant? No, not a good idea, best to forget about it. It still frightens me to think I was out on that road disrupting traffic. I find it hard to believe it was me! At times like this I wish for the haven of my hospital room with Liz Kavanagh to talk to. I probably wouldn't be feeling so insecure if I were taking the medication. Toby warned me that I would have slumps like this. I was to ring him when I did. But I can't be babied for ever, I must weather this storm by myself!

* * *

Jack Wasserman is down in his summer house in Ballycotton and asked if I'd mind meeting him in The Bay View Hotel instead of his office. It suited me fine. Toby and I are looking forward to the cliff walk after the meeting.

Jack looks odd to me in his beige trousers, sandals, and cotton sweater. We shake hands and I'm about to banter with him but I get the feeling he's in a hurry. He heads to chairs by the window in the reception which I don't like because the receptionist will be able to hear everything we say.

"Now Piers, to business, and first things first," he says producing an envelope. "Money is always welcome," he grins. I glance at the reception desk but there is no one there now.

"But I got a cheque ...two months ago!"

"According to the books, you're owed this...I wouldn't argue, if I were you."

Wasserman's will continue to publish my work of course. I tell him I'm not exactly prolific right now, but he says he has every faith in me. He is being kind!

I know Jack since my teaching days, since the time he gave a talk on the making of a book to transition year students. The vice principal, a friend of Jacks, wanted them to produce a book on the history of the parish with emphasis on the school. Everyone involved had a great time, including me. It was by accident that I ended up working for Jack on and off over the years. I was editing my own work and got involved with other work because both their editors were out at the same time: one on maternity leave, the other due to an accident.

Jack says I'm a good editor and good with people. It was he suggested I go to London and has set up an interview for me with a contact of his. He wrote a great reference for me but it worried me when he wrote I had been working in Publishing for many years. It is true to a degree, but it was mainly on my own books and I have no qualifications in that area.

"You are more than capable of doing this work, Piers, just go for it. Get to know as many people in the business as you can," Jack advised.

Jack and I tie up a few loose ends and just when I think we are about done, he says, "Piers, I showed those stories to my friend, Edith, in Secret Gardens Press...they do children's books as you know...she's very interested!"

"I thought you got rid of them," I say, flabbergasted. But in an odd way, I'm happy that they still exist.

"No...I told you I'd look at them. I'm no judge of what will go in that area, of course."

"What do you want me to do?"

"Well, nothing really! I just need your permission to hand them over. Nothing might come of it! If they take them, Edith will want them for the Christmas market. She might want you to do a reading ..."

"That's out of the question, Jack. I think we'd better forget about them!"

"You wrote them for your daughter, Piers, it would be wrong to forget about them." Jack says untypically personal.

"That's just it, they were only for her!" *I would never have written them down only for Catriona*

"Well, all I can say is don't be so quick to let go of them."

"Would I have to be involved?"

"You could publish under a pseudonym...I could handle it from there. I can't tell you to think about it, Edith wants to know as soon as possible; actually, she wanted to know weeks ago."

Well...alright... if I don't have to be involved!"

"Right so," he says standing up and shaking hands. "Take care of yourself, Piers, and the best of luck in London. Keep in touch."

I find Toby sitting by the window looking out on the bay. "All done," he says looking up at me.

"Yeah, all finished."

Toby suggests having lunch here and I sit in beside him. Even fleetingly thinking of her has affected my mood. Intrusive sunlight streams through the windows highlighting myriad scratches on the laminated tables and dust particles eerily floating in the air; even the smudges on the empty glasses on the next table encroach like a dead zone.

"I need some air, Toby. Do you mind if we go outside?" I say, already on my feet.

"No bother," he says following me.

We sit at a table in the garden area in front of the hotel. Toby orders an open seafood sandwich and I order the same. A fresh breeze blows as we look out on the bay. I study Toby when he's not looking. I know his traits, the way he lifts his hair back with both hands, the way he wrinkles up his forehead when he's annoyed. He has been a lifesaver: I'd have given my notice too soon at work only for him; he even arranged for a colleague to buy my car.

Toby's eyes wander after two females who pass our table towards a flight of steps. "You can get down to the water that way, I think," he says, but I imagine his thoughts are on the long, tanned legs.

"Thanks for everything you've done for me, Toby… don't know what I'd have done without you, these last months." He shifts self-consciously, not used to me spelling things out, but I if I don't say things now, I may not get a chance again. "I still can't believe it all happened! I mean how I let myself fall apart like that! It's so embarrassing."

"You have nothing to be embarrassed about," he says vehemently, "I think you're great the way you got yourself back on track!"

There were many times over the years when I would have liked to confide in Toby about Rosie and consider if I should do so now. Maybe it would give him an opportunity too to talk about David. But where would I begin, it's far too complex to put into words; I can't even get my own head around it sometimes. But this may be my only chance. A line from Shakespeare comes warningly to my head: 'Give thy thoughts no tongue/Nor any unproportioned thought his act.'

"Piers! Where have you gone?" Toby asks, drawing me from my thoughts.

"Oh, just thinking…"

"About what? He probes, "You looked very serious."

"Well, Shakespeare actually!" I reply and Toby seems relieved. "He knew suffering…he lost his son, after all. That passage about Ophelia's death…he based it on Katharine Hamlet who drowned in the river Avon. Katharine was a friend of the Shakespeare family."

"I never heard that!" Toby says.

"Yeah, when I was reading Hamlet, I read it in the notes."

"It must be true so!" He laughs. "What's really bothering you, Piers?" He asks intuitively.

"You'll think I'm being morbid."

"Try me!"

"I was thinking of Rosie…about the eternal… or should I say, eternity. I don't believe in heaven, and all that crap about meeting your loved ones. I'm even more confused now having read, Zecharia Sitchin. Remember me telling you about the Anunnaki Gods who were reputed to have created us.

"Yeah. I must read him."

"You know that Clapton song, Tears in Heaven?"

"Yes."

"I don't have that consolation! I don't see Rosie as an eternal child. That idea is very weird. I don't know what she is now, a kind of energy perhaps, a part of something greater maybe. Sometimes I even wonder if she is at all."

"But we don't know! Perhaps there is a spirit world."

"You're a dark horse, Holland, didn't know you believed in such things."

"Well, if I'm a dark horse, Cantwell, you're Black Beauty!" He says grinning. "I believe in a lot of things, or should I say I believe more in the possibility of things. What intrigues me is why people all over the world believe much the same things."

"I was coming to terms with Rosie's death…well trying to…but then Nan died. You'd think I'd have been prepared for that, her being old."

"What about Helen?"

"Oh Toby, she was so happy at last. Arnold saw qualities in her that I never bothered to see… I treated her badly!"

"Ye weren't really suited, Piers… at least I always thought so. And I wasn't the only one."

"Actually, she said that herself…she said we'd have been mad to get married."

"There you go then."

"But it's not that simple! The bad things we do don't go away. Fuck that catholic confession shit, nothing is wiped away that easy…and it shouldn't! I think she knew I went with other women."

"Ah come on, you hardly fucked around, Piers…I know there was Claire."

"And Anna, the art history student, the one who pretended she was dying."

"Christ yeah! How could I forget that mad bitch? Didn't she own a gun? Sure, didn't you get rid of her fairly fast."

"But the point is, I shouldn't have been with her in the first place. What mattered most to Helen, as it turned out, was that I never talked to her… about anything significant, that is."

"That's a lot a guilt to be carrying, man; that thing with Claire and your wan… you and Helen were well and truly over then, for god's sake. Ye remained good friends, didn't ye? She even invited you to her wedding!"

"I know! I went through all that with Kavanagh. But the past haunts you, Toby! We both know Catriona was the main reason I didn't keep it together." I'm about to continue, but Toby's expression changes and he looks away. I must be over burdening him. It was Rosie I wanted to talk about anyway.

"You were a fool to lose her," he says with a bitter edge and starts fiddling with his spoon to avoid looking at me.

"Say what's on your mind, Toby." He sweeps back his hair from his face and looks at me squarely.

"If you weren't my friend, I would have made a play for Catriona myself… and what's more, I would have got her!"

"Gee! I knew you liked her … I had to keep my eye on you," I say joking.

"Oh Piers, you think you're so bloody clever," he says, uncharacteristically antagonistic, "like the night you went down Pembroke Street to get rid of me. I knew where she lived! You see I had my eye on Catriona Lynch long before you met her. Do you remember her asking if we'd met before, that I looked familiar? Well, Piers, I had met her before!"

"What! Why did you never say?"

"Catriona Lynch is not a woman you could easily forget," he continues, ignoring the question. "I used to walk behind her into town quite often… even going out of my way, sometimes. The first time I saw her she was carol singing in Daunt Square…they were collecting for some charity. I put a twenty in her collection box. We exchanged a few words…I wished her a happy Christmas. I thought she was lovely. It wasn't just her smile…she talked with her whole body and she was so good looking…in a natural way, I mean."

"And you never spoke to her after?"

"No!" He says looking a little vulnerable.

"That's not like you."

"I could hardly accost her on the street. She's not the kind of woman for the usual spiel."

"No, she's not!" *But it's not like you either not to pursue her. Maybe you were planning to.*

"I got you drunk on purpose with the rum!"

"Jesus! No wonder I felt so bad next day!"

"I didn't have a name, but when you described her, I knew exactly who you were talking about. I pressed you for more, but you were very secretive, to say the least! I kept filling your glass on the sly."

"Some friend you are, Holland," I say light-heartedly but his expression remains serious.

"And the way you treated her when things got difficult… I felt like beating the crap out of you at times. I met her on the street a few days after your grandmother's funeral. She was so upset. Every time she mentioned you, tears came to her eyes. Tears you didn't deserve!"

I have a horrible suspicion that Toby is not giving me the complete picture. But what more can there be? That day in the Long Valley he knew she wouldn't talk to me and he knew about Healy. I can understand Diarmuid knowing, being part of that scene, but how come Toby knew? And she answered so cheerily to his number. I know there are aspects of me that Toby never sees either, but I can't help feeling injured! I thought we were close, yet he never told me about David.

"Catriona loved you, though," Toby says interrupting my thoughts.

"Well, it's past tense now, Toby," I say trying to appear as if everything is normal. "I beat myself up for long enough, about her. I hated her for taking up with Healy. He could never stand the idea of her being with me; it was a rival thing. But he's not good for her, Toby, he wants so desperately to be king he won't have much room for anyone else."

"Don't be so melodramatic, Piers, it doesn't suit you!"

"You don't know him like I do…he's already trying to change her."

"In what way?" Toby asks with renewed interest.

Toby knows she came to see me in hospital but nothing else. I tell him about her weight loss and about her hair colour and how she couldn't look me the eye when I mentioned Healy. Toby's expression completely changes, I know now he hasn't seen her for some time.

"She'd hardly talk to you about Healy, now would she," he says recovering.

"True, but I know her. She was never timid."

Toby seems lost in thought. After a while he folds his arms, a sure sign he doesn't want to talk anymore. A silent barrier is suddenly erected. I get lost in my own thoughts then, my eyes straying to the coastline opposite. Youghal lies beyond the last visible headland: Fíorbhinn bheith ós a bánmhuir – we are running out of the water, our laughter stitched into air and waves.

* * *

Nothing is how it seems; nobody really knows anyone else. According to an old Tibetan text, we should regard all phenomena as dreams. Sometimes my life feels like a bad dream from which I will never wake, a life of loss and loneliness. And now, a paradigm shift with my friend.

We did not do the cliff walk. Toby seemed relieved when he dropped me home and for that matter so was I. I didn't have the guts to ask if he had slept with her. But then, what would be the point? If he had said no, would I have believed him?

Liz talked of emotional intelligence; I struggle now with what my mind is digging up. Was I wrong to say that the past never goes away? Can it not be put away - kept away? Toby has been my rock. He is my closest friend! I can't afford to lose him!

Being in a half empty house is weird. I open the bottle of red Evelyn left and listen to tinny music on Mr Cotter's kitchen transistor. One thing keeps surfacing: Catriona may not have run straight into Healy's arms after all.

I'm glad now I didn't confide in Toby about Rosie; I don't think he would have understood anyway. He doesn't view things as I do. Catriona, of course, is the person I should have trusted and if only I had, things would be different now. Rosie was the strangest baby; she rarely cried, always calm and easily pleased. She was about three when I started to notice things... perhaps even earlier. She used to ask such profound questions, things about the world and god. I can't recall specifically, only that it unnerved me at times. Rosie seemed to know things before anyone else; she knew Josie was going to die, without anyone telling her. There were so many odd things, some of which I have forgotten or suppressed. Nan knew! She tried to talk to me about it on many occasions. Helen knew - she must have - always so calm around Rosie. Why did we never talk about it?

I came close to telling Liz after an experience in art therapy. I'd been mixing white paint with a little brown when an image of Rosie's gleaming white hair manifested before me, reminding me of a day in the woods in Glanworth, an image that opened a door for me to finally admit, if only to myself, that my daughter was not like other children.

That day we came upon a tree that had been recently chopped down to about three feet from the ground. I was annoyed because it was a young tree. Barry made light of it, saying he had a fair idea who was responsible. He said the same fellow would cut the legs off the table while you were eating. As I was complaining to Barry, Rosie stooped down and began to sift the fresh sawdust through her fingers. I remember it now like a surreal painting: sunlight slanting fairylike through the trees; Rosie's hair gleaming white in the light; sawdust pouring through her fingers like an effulgent stream. Above all, I remember the sense of tranquillity I experienced as I looked down on her.

I believe I was meant to remember this vivid scene because the following spring, the year Rosie died, we were down again. Rosie and I went off up the woods, leaving Barry to his work. We were walking along a certain path when Rosie insisted on going another way. Halfway along that path, she sprinted ahead and stopped at the stump of the very same tree. A creeping sensation spread up the back of my neck in familiar trepidation: how could she remember exactly? I know I couldn't have found it so easily.

"Look Daddy…it's still growing," she said, pointing to its many shooting stems. "It's sticky, Daddy," she said touching one of the sappy buds and smelling her hands.

"That's what happens when a tree is dying, Rosie – it's kind of one last breath," I say but not explaining it very well.

– 198 –

"No Daddy," she contradicts, "it's a new life now!" When I told Barry, he said Rosie was right because deciduous trees can regenerate. He completely missed what I was trying to tell him. Sometimes other people make me question the way I see things. However, looking back now, I'm convinced Rosie was telling me something that day.

That same day I made her cry! She'd gone outside with Barry to see Charlie, a neighbour's donkey. When I went out, she was standing on a wire fence reaching out with something in her hand and Charlie was coming hotfoot towards her. Instinctively I rushed forward and grabbed her off the fence.

"I want to give Charlie the sausage," she bawled. I got her to throw it over to him but it fell into a clump of grass and he was oblivious. She cried and cried, the likes of which I'd never seen before. I tried to explain that Charlie could have bitten her fingers but she wasn't to be consoled. Inside, she nestled into my chest hiccoughing from all the crying making me feel like a criminal. Looking back, I wonder if it really was the donkey she was crying about.

* * *

Knowing what I do about my mother hasn't brought us any closer, but at least I don't view her now with such resentment. I blot out what happened to her, it's something a son should never know. I appreciate everything she has done for me; she is helping again by storing my books and records. All I could do yesterday was to say thanks. She said she didn't need thanks, that she was only too glad to be of help. I kissed her on the cheek as usual in farewell. There was no display of emotion; it would have been odd as we were never demonstrative. When a pattern is set, it's hard to break it.

This morning I visited the grave. It was a mistake! I felt alienated looking down on a rectangle in the ground and seeing Helen Arnold and her daughter Rose etched, below Josie's name into a too ornate headstone.

The rest of the day I spend visiting old haunts: the Honan Chapel to soak up Harry's colours and a nostalgic walk around the college grounds looking at the maple trees.

Back in town, I went to see the new School of Music on Union Quay. Crossing over Trinity Bridge I imagined I was boarding a great big ship. I thought the building's beautifully curved lines were appropriate for the quay. The interior didn't disappoint either. I met a guy I knew from my teaching days and we went into the café. Looking across at Moore's Hotel, I faltered a little thinking of all the times I dropped her off there.

The Old Cork Library has been given a face lift: the ugly paintwork is gone, and the owls and columns stand proudly on each side of an actual doorway. There's hope for the city yet!

Relaxing with a coffee under the canopy of sails, I'm thinking how Catriona used to worry about all the changes to the city. Perhaps it was the escalation of change that she most worried about. R & H Hall looms ugly down to my left and redevelopment suddenly seems appropriate.

Seagulls are screeching in some melee over something on the water; three red cranes dominate the skyline behind Free Fit Exhaust; men in yellow helmets are working on a new high-rise in the distance.

A brightly red-painted pub stands conspicuously across the river on the left: lots of windows on the upper level. When things are gone it's hard to remember what was there before. City Hall will still be there: hard to imagine that it was once destroyed by the Tans; the British had to pay for its restoration, a small recompense for what happened to the city. Down on Morrison's Island, the gothic spires of Holy Trinity needle the blue sky. Will I remember all these details when I'm living somewhere else? Or is this river carrying my quotidian experience away for ever out to sea.

Part Three

I HADN'T ENVISAGED how difficult things were going to be in London. I find the people strangely reserved. Cork was small and intimate and I had everything at my fingertips. On the upside, these difficulties provide a challenge and are helping me to focus on the present.

I now work for Wilson & Lyle. My title is Assistant Editor, but I am solely looking after three clients which is a challenge. Non-fiction seems to be where the money is: cookery books; health & fitness; history; biography. I haven't met anyone so far from poetry publishing houses but it's early days.

I am happy that Ivor and I are getting to know each other again and getting on well despite our different personalities. Before I took up my position at Wilson & Lyle, I worked for him cutting grass. Ivor calls grass his gold. He has three vans, two of which are on the go daily, carrying lawnmowers and other equipment; all three are needed in the spring when there's a lot of planting to be done. He says Autumn can be just as busy.

I mainly worked with a guy called Mike Weaver. Mike was great fun! His expressions and speech patterns fascinated me, lots of sexual innuendo, especially when other guys were around. Ivor laughed when I told him this. "That's nothing compared to the building sites," he said, "When I was a raw recruit, I looked like a beetroot most of the time...they had great fun teasing Irish Ivor. I was a right eejit, Piers. I'll never forget the first time...I was driving nails...and obviously using the wrong ones because they kept buckling on me. The gaffer made a show of me in front of everyone: 'if it had hair on it,' he said, 'you'd put it in quick enough!' It took me a while to toughen up."

Ivor lives quite a regimented existence and the house is very much his place and serves as his office as well. He used to have an office and a secretary called Elaine, but since he got the hang of computers and mobile phones, he has no need of one. He does all his own promotional advertising himself.

Elaine, however, still does his bookkeeping.

Ivor is a great believer in order and discipline; it keeps him on an even keel, and I have come to know how vital that is for him. Unfortunately, it is suffocating me! He doesn't even cook! The first week with him, I cooked a roast chicken dinner; he sat down politely and struggled to eat to oblige me. It turned out he had already eaten. He eats out all the time - even goes out for breakfast! He knows all the little cafes in the neighbourhood and beyond. All he seems to make is tea! He tells me to make myself at home and to cook whenever I want but I'm starting to eat out as well.

Drink was Ivor's initiation into the world of building sites: men were paid in the pub on a Friday night and of course many stayed on till closing time. Ivor got so bad with the drink, he ended up living rough. I remember his expression when I said, "For a guy who lived rough, you haven't done too badly…your own business and your own house."

"I fought hard to be where I am, Piers. I had nothing …you don't have a clue what it's like to have lost everything." I refrained from further enquiry because he seemed annoyed with me.

I was curious as to how he managed to go from being homeless to where he is now so I asked him another time when the mood was better. "It was a long road, Piers. Where do I begin? I wasn't long on the streets…and even then, I had a roof over my head at night. I hung with this guy, Rob… we used to sneak into a house every night…we had electricity and everything! Rob even knew the owners, as far as I can remember. I didn't see myself as homeless at all. It's called denial, by the way. I was lucky! People helped me…people like The Doc… he was some character! Liked a drink himself…but unlike me, he could keep things together. When he found out I was off the grid and living rough, he searched all my old haunts till he tracked me down. Irish Ivor, he used to call me, or sometimes, Irish Eyes! Doc was clever: he filled me with drink and took me home with him after the pubs closed. Next morning, I was up bright and early ready to slip out. I didn't want to meet his wife, you see," Ivor laughed, shaking his head with his eyes closed. "The Doc was a step ahead of me though, waiting at the end of the stairs, saying he wanted me to meet a friend of his. To be honest, Piers, I thought he was taking me for a drink and to meet someone about a job. Ah, but there was no drink! Before I knew where I was going, he was walking me into Kairos House, 110 Brixton Road. I'll never forget that day! I wasn't to know it then, but that day changed my life. He introduced me to John Lyons. I took to John...I suppose because he didn't come over all judgmental and he had a sense of humour. He and Doc had a great laugh remembering old times. After a long talk with John, he suggested I go to AA. It had never occurred to me to get help; I felt too far gone and worthless for that. I thought no one cared anyway...Gillian and Oliver were out of my life...there was no way back to them."

Gillian? Oliver? The names hung in the air.

"The Doc advised me to keep away from Robbie; he'd done a little homework on that, 'lowlife' as he called him. Well, it escalated from there. I dried out! Eventually that is...I fell by the wayside many times." Ivor looked to see how I was taking it all. "How easy it all sounds!" He said, taking a deep breath. "Believe me, it was far from easy ... if there's a hell, it can't be worse. To cut a long story short, I went to live in what they call a dry house. I met people far worse off...a little further along the road than me...it was a real eye opener. I was housed eventually by the Council...thanks to John and Social Services. People were good to me when they saw I was trying. I've been climbing Everest ever since." He stopped then, seemingly deep in thought. "Would they have been so welcoming if they knew all this at home, Piers?" He said deprecatingly.

"They would be more welcoming if anything, and proud. I'm proud of you, Ivor!"

Ivor smiled at me. That warm smile I always remember from when he was young. I remained silent then not knowing what else to say to him.

"Don't be afraid to ask, Piers," he shot at me with a mischievous eye.

"Gillian and Oliver...who are they, Ivor?"

"Oliver is my son!" He said, keeping his composure at my incredulousness. "Gillian remarried - doesn't want anything more to do with me. I don't blame her...I was a wild man then."

"But you're not the same person now," I encouraged.

"I was earning great money when I met her," he said with a snigger. "I was half cut when I asked her to marry me!... I was in a great hurry to have a family, you see. Oliver was born that first year! Things were okay while the money was coming in. The work was gruelling. She never showed any concern when I was flat exhausted. And she never stopped nagging about my dirty clothes. I think she cared more about her house than me. I could have lived with that, though, it was other things, nasty things, she said about the Irish. It was a shock to me how much she disliked the Irish. I couldn't fathom why she married me at all. I started to drink more then and missing out on good jobs... sometimes, I'd come home with nothing after a week's work...well never nothing, but a lot less than I should have had. Well, that's it... I'm not blaming anyone, Piers...I've learnt to accept responsibility for my behaviour...I drank too much...I let things fall apart."

"I suppose she thinks we're all drunks...that's the general impression over here...lonely, dispossessed and drunk." I was surprised to hear myself saying this as I had never given it any thought.

Ivor laughed. "I'm sure that was the case with previous generations...I never saw myself in that light. I was a global kinda guy...I was into music. Gillian and I went to hear lots of bands. After Oliver was born, we didn't do that as much."

"Does she know you're sober now?"

"No! She'd be impressed with the business...and the money I make. She never thought a drunken Paddy could rise to that." Ivor gave a little chuckle and said mischievously, "I never told her I had an extremely wealthy uncle in Kingston-on-Thames."

"And you never had any contact with Uncle Frank in all the years? He would have been only too willing to help you."

"I had low self-esteem, Piers. I burnt my bridges with family...I was very stupid."

"What about Oliver? You can't burn that bridge, Ivor."

"I did inadvertently, and you know when you burn a bridge there's no way back..."

"That's silly, you can build another one! You went home...you were part of the family again...and look what it meant to Mam and Evelyn." I felt stupid and presumptuous then, who was I to preach, I couldn't sort out my own life. Ivor was doing fine!

"It *was* good to be home! I hadn't realised how much I missed everyone," he said. "When I went up the mountains with Garvin, I finally felt at home… connected…if you know what I mean…"

"I do!"

"A visit home doesn't make up for everything, though."

"It's a start, Ivor, like coming here is a start for me."

"You're right, Piers. I'm sorry…I'm usually more positive but thinking about Oliver… well it's hard! I used to think he was better off without me when I was drinking, and the years just flitted by. He's twelve now, nearly thirteen!" It suddenly dawned that Rosie wasn't the first grandchild: Mam has a grandson; Evelyn has a nephew.

Ivor began talking about Rosie then: how he felt sorry that he had never seen her. "You should talk about her. Evelyn said you were a great father! Cherish your good memories, Piers, God knows, we have enough bad ones. The last time I saw my son, the only thing on my mind was the next drink…I was watching the clock to bring him home." I began to imagine what Rosie would be like now, but quickly realised there was nothing to be gained from what would have been.

Ivor took a fit of laughing when he heard I was looking for a place and was nervous about telling him. It turned out that he likes his own space and copes better on his own.

"I knew you wouldn't last long with me," he laughed. "I was probably inhibiting you from taking a drink and being yourself, generally."

"No, you weren't. I'm like you, I like my own space …and drink, well it's not an issue for me."

"You're lucky," he said. If he only knew how drunk I was at Rosie's funeral.

* * *

Sometimes, I think we are all destined to be alone. *'Chacun de nous est très loin!'* We are like the stars in, *'La Voie Lactée,'* seemingly together but millions of miles apart in reality. Edgar Allan Poe must have known this too when he wrote *"Alone."*

Even though Ivor and I are close now, I never tell him when I'm depressed; he treats me with kid gloves as it is. He has taken on the role of elder brother and sometimes I feel undermined. I haven't told him that I stopped taking my medication. As I said, Ivor leads quite a regimented life, going to AA meetings once a month and meeting regularly with John Lyons. I don't think he'd understand where I'm coming from.

Lately, Ivor is talking a lot about our father, I'm interested in what he remembers and engage with him on a surface level but I am not prepared to share my secret world, my treasure store, with him.

I now live in a rented apartment off the Kings Road. It's quite small and on the expensive side, but Ivor says for London it's not a bad deal. It's handy for work and I can get down to Ivor easily enough. The upper apartments have balconies which I would have liked but I do have access to a pleasant little yard that has shrubs planted along the walls.

Londoners constantly complain about public transport; about the government not delivering on the promised underground rail link from Paddington to Stratford and seemingly the stations are to have no escalators. For me, however, who has waited unduly on many occasions for buses at home, the transport here is great!

Ivor offered me money which put me in an awkward spot. I assured him I was okay financially. I wanted to tell him then that Nan left me 20,000 euro but I didn't want to hurt his feelings. I also have money that was put by for holidays that were only dreamed about and money from the sale of my car. Rosie's insurance money is in a separate account and apart from paying my mother back, it remains untouched. Somehow, I feel it's money I shouldn't have.

I'm the only grandchild Nan left money to. No doubt Paddy is resentful: he always thought Nan spoiled me. To be honest I never knew she had that kind of money. According to my mother, Nan was shrewd and that it was her money that bought my grandfather's fishing trawler. The trawler was much sought after locally when Billy retired; none of his sons were interested so people assumed he'd be glad of the money. Nan, however, had other ideas: it was leased to a friend's nephew until he bought his own boat, then it was sold on to a young man in Baltimore. My grandfather was left a little embarrassed for letting the boat go out of the community. Mam remembers the arguments over it and Nan saying that there was no room for sentiment when it came to money matters.

Nan left the house to my mother and I was glad; she never liked the bungalow. Initially, I hoped she wouldn't make too many changes but then I realised the house will never be to me what it was.

* * *

I dissuaded Toby from seeing me off when I moved to London. He didn't know what the reason was of course. It took me a while to get over what I was mentally accusing him of. However, we have kept in contact. He talked sometimes about coming over but I didn't think he would, so I was surprised when he asked if he could come this weekend. I wasn't long home when Toby arrived earlier than expected. "Hello," he said dropping his bag and giving me a warm hug.

"I thought it would take you longer to get here..."

"I took a taxi! Didn't want to be walking around looking for your place." As I walked behind him, I noticed he had put on weight and his hair was shorter. "Oh, this is a grand place," he said looking around. "I expected a dog box the way you were going on."

"I suppose I got used to the space in Ivor's house. He completely renovated the place. A friend helped him and got all the materials at trade price for him."

"It's great you have your brother here!"

"Yeah, it is nice. Come on, I'll show you your room."

"Is this the main bedroom?" Toby asked, testing out the bed.

"No, that would be mine next door!" I laughed.

"This is a great size! Some apartments in Cork are like boxes ...slapped up during the Celtic Tiger."

Toby got settled in while I fried up our steaks and opened the wine. When he came out, I asked him to cut some bread and bring over the salad.

"Thanks man, this is great!" He said tucking in. After dinner we just sat around talking and catching up. He hadn't much news of interest other than saying he heard Diarmuid Ó Buachalla was ill.

I assumed Toby would know London well but he said he never got time to look around when he was over on business. I confessed I didn't know London well either, outside of my own area and Lewisham. "We'll have to be tourists tomorrow so," he laughed.

Toby was highly amused at how impervious to distraction the guards outside Buckingham Palace were. He made a show of me reciting Spike Milligan's, 'Soldier Freddy' to them. I dragged him away for fear we'd be arrested.

He was impressed with the Gherkin. "It reminds me of Gaudi," I said. When I stepped carelessly off the pavement a little further down the street, Toby yanked me back by the collar saying I'd end up like Gaudi, if I wasn't careful. Gaudi, he informed me was killed by a tram in 1926.

Toby liked the Millennium Bridge too but I couldn't make up my mind. Was the design suggesting we live in a high-tech sophisticated society? I wasn't convinced. I kept my views to myself because Toby is always accusing me of being too conservative. When I suggested going to an art gallery, Toby made such a face all I could do was laugh.

"I spend a lot of time in them," I told him.

"What's new, Cantwell!" He laughed.

For Toby's sake we used the underground most of the morning, but I began to feel nauseous and claustrophobic with the odoriferous sulphurous air. Toby assumed I'd know where to go for lunch and I had to remind him what I said last night. I know the cafés in my own locality but that's about it. We walked along for another while and came across a nice pub restaurant. It was quite busy but we opted to wait, enjoying a beer in the meantime. It was worth the wait because the food was great.

Back at the flat Toby complained when I had no music to play. I told him to put on the radio and he grumbled, saying it was alright.

"My stuff is still in Dungarvan. I must sort that out."

"When Piers, in your next life," he confronted.

Later in the evening, we went to a pub and after that on to a nightclub. I went for his sake but ended up enjoying myself. I drank and danced and felt exhilarated, an exhilaration that expunged the residue of my recent depression. Toby called me over to meet Ruby and her friend, Kelly. Kelly was all over him even as he was talking to me. Kelly had keys to a friend's apartment nearby and Toby was hugely surprised that I was up for the idea.

The apartment was quite plush to my surprise. Toby and I sat down on an expensive looking sofa while Kelly liberally poured vodka; I was thinking its owner might not be too happy. After a second drink, Kelly whispered something in Toby's ear and they left the room. Ruby then came over and sat beside me grinning and after a few minutes took my hand and led me to a bedroom.

"Must go to the bathroom…won't be long, love," Ruby said disappearing. I took my wallet from my jacket to get a condom. I began to worry then that I might get rolled, so I put the wallet into the back pocket of my trousers which I folded and placed under my shirt and shoes. I had no intention of falling asleep in any case.

Ruby finally appeared with a glazed look in her eyes. She took off her clothes and danced about shaking her breasts at me. She was surely on something! She made me come; apart from the excitement and release, I felt little emotion. She showed no sign of crashing and talked incessantly. The only thing that interested me was the mangling of her own language. I stayed for a discretionary length of time before I made a move.

"Must go Ruby…work in the morning."

"On bleedin Sunday?"

"Yes, I'm on call today."

"You a doctor or some'it?

"Yes."

"I thought Toby said yous was a writer."

"I am…in my spare time."

I texted Toby: going now – will leave key where I showed you.

Toby was snug in bed the following morning when I looked in. I was considering bringing him a coffee when he came into the kitchen bright and cheery. "How did ya get on with Ruby Roo?" He grinned.

"Okay!" I laughed. "She was lovely… wired to the moon, though."

"That makes two of them. Kelly thought we looked the type to have a few lines. I told her alcohol was my only vice but she didn't believe me. She was great gas though...very funny. She's a wardrobe supervisor so she gets to meet a lot of actors...can't remember what theatre."

"Ruby didn't tell me much."

"I better get dressed," Toby said going off, taking his coffee with him.

"This is great, Piers. I'll come here again," he said when I placed a fry in front of him. I expected him to talk more about last night but not another word. In fact, he said little other than to tell me his flight to Dublin was at five.

"You're flying to Dublin? I asked surprised.

"Yes! Haven't seen the family for a while."

When I offered to see him to the airport, he said, practicable as ever, that it would be a waste of time and money. He promised to come over again soon. "You're welcome to stay with me if you'd like to come home anytime."

"Thanks, but that's not on the cards for me, not now anyway."

"Okay. But you know where I am."

"Thanks."

"You're doing great, Piers...better than I expected," he said, standing at the front door. "Going out with women an'all," he laughed.

"I have you to thank...I mean, blame, for that."

He hugged me in farewell and when he let me go, I detected a slight unease in his clear blue eyes, a look that haunted me for the rest of the day. I should have asked him how he was. I should have asked about David. Sometimes I get so caught up in myself, I don't see how it is for others. There was so much I wanted to ask him, but there is a barrier still, one of my own making, I suppose. I wondered if the whole Ruby and Kelly thing was a kind of laying-aside ritual: that Catriona Lynch is well and truly in the past for both of us.

Romantic love! Why do we go off the rails over one woman? Surely it is in our nature to relate to more than just one person! Given the right conditions, anybody can grow to love anyone.

Toby said I was doing well. I am to a degree. I could have told him about the long nights when darkness envelops me, nights when I feel alone and afraid; afraid that someday I could walk out the door and lose myself.

Toby said once (in jest) that poets don't get depressed but suffer melancholy for the sake of it. I wonder now, though, if melancholy is a true component of my personality.

* * *

My boss, Terry Lyle, assumed I would attend the Christmas party. I took this as an indication that I was expected to attend. I'm not looking forward to the Christmas festivity, feigned or otherwise, but I decided not to lose any sleep over it. I got up this morning before daylight, donned my boots and took a taxi to Hyde Park. There had been a light fall of snow overnight and I thought the park would be nice. It was not how I imagined. It was cold, not a crisp cold but a seep-into-your-bones dampness. The stars I'd hoped to see were obscured; trees were shadows yet and birds were few, but I could hear out of sight water birds honking and hooting. I realised I was not the only one about when I saw footprints snaking the slushy paths. As I neared the Serpentine, voices echoed eerily and through the rising brume I saw men swimming, the sight of which made me feel colder still. I watched them in awe for some minutes, wondering how healthy it was to swim there.

When morning light spread across the sky, I left the park and walked along streets, different now in the early hours. I was glad to find a small café on a side street where I had a delicious coffee and a croissant with butter and jam. The young man who served me wore reindeer antlers and a lit-up dickey bow and didn't appear fully awake.

At the next table, a woman was consoling another woman who seemed quite upset. I closed my ears to the conversation as best I could. When she began to cry, the young man looked down disapprovingly. This was supposed to be a time of Christmas cheer. I was disconcerted then, thinking that it could be me there crying in an instant.

The Christmas party went off quite well. I had a great laugh with Carl from the printers. Everyone, in high spirits after drinks, wanted to go to the night club at the other side of the hotel. Terry Lyle had already left so I thought this was a good time to give the rest of them the slip, what we at home call, an Irish Goodbye.

* * *

Ivor is organising a Christmas dinner for the homeless and has been ringing me constantly even though I assured him I'll be all his on Christmas Eve. He has no faith in me at all, it seems. I'm recruited to do the cooking, along with two other volunteers. Their regular cook is in hospital, unfortunately. I suppose that's why Ivor is so wound up.

Ivor arrived at my place at 7.30 on the morning. I'd just made coffee so he had to wait for me but he paced around like a lion in a cage. "Sit down, Ivor, you're making me nervous. We have plenty of time!"

"I *would* like to get there early…I want everything to go right. These people have been good to me and I want to do a good job," he said.

"Everything will be fine!" I told him and he sat down reluctantly.

We arrived at the community hall in Catford in no time at all as the traffic was light but I guess that's why Ivor wanted to come early. He introduced me to a bleary-eyed young woman called Susan and quickly took off, his shoes clip-clopping across the empty hall. Susan looked at me blankly when I asked advice on where to start. "I don't know," she said shrugging her shoulders. "I'm only here to help decorate the place!"

Ivor soon returned with the helpers, Alan and Jimmy, and steered us into the kitchen, where four large raw turkeys begged for attention. I wondered how many people were expected. There were four hams also but thank goodness they were already cooked and boned. Jimmy told me all the food had been donated by local businesses. After a quick assessment, I suggested we plan out how we were going to tackle things. Alan sensibly had already turned on the two ovens. Jimmy asked if we were doing roast potatoes and Alan dived on him. "No way! You couldn't reheat them…they'd be horrible!" he snapped. Alan suggested cooking the potatoes and reheating them in the morning but on thinking it over, we agreed it would be just as easy boiling the potatoes in the morning as reheating them.

Ivor came into the kitchen with a pile of boxes and looked anxiously in our direction. Curiosity got the better of him and he came over asking us if everything was okay. "Yeah…everything's fine, Ivor," Jimmy answered but

Ivor looked worried. I was about to explain that planning is half the battle, but he took off again suddenly.

Fifty people were expected, according to Alan but some may not turn up. Alan and Jimmy started peeling potatoes. I put the giblets into a large pot with onions and thyme to make stock for gravy. We worked out the time per pound for the turkeys and gave extra time to ensure they were well cooked. There was no stuffing (thank god) so we filled the cavities with herbs, seeing that we had so much. We had a bit of banter while peeling the potatoes; I talked about a film, where Laurel and Hardy were thrown in the brig and given a mountain of potatoes to peel. Neither had seen it, but it lightened the mood and Alan started calling Jimmy Ollie. Jimmy then told us about Boo, who was expected for the dinner: Boo sleeps every night in the boiler house of a well-known hotel – highly secret of course. After a few weeks going in there, he woke up one morning to two men standing over him. He jumped up all apologetic trying to come up with his best excuse, when one of the guys said, "We're not security, mate, we're here to service the boiler. We haven't seen you…know what I mean!" Two years later, Boo is still a guest of the hotel and is on first name terms with the lads from the gas company. Jimmy laughed saying that Boo is now an expert on boilers.

Three o'clock we took out the turkeys and put in the other two. We let the cooked ones cool on foil trays and covered them with tinfoil and tea cloths. I asked what would happen if more than fifty turned up; what if the word got around.

"That won't happen…they get tickets!" Alan explained. Seemingly the shelter had been giving out tickets for the past three weeks.

"I suppose if anyone came without a ticket, they'd hardly be turned away," I innocently remarked.

"And where would we put um," Jimmy said, looking at me as if I were stupid. "If they knew they could that…I dunno what would happen…they know the bleedin score…there's other places they can go."

We took a break then and went down the road for something to eat. I was about to turn in to the nearest pub when I noticed Alan giving Jimmy an odd look. "We'll go to the caff on the corner," Alan said decisively.

There was no sign of Ivor when we returned but his team were decorating the hall and lining up tables. In the kitchen I noticed the rubbish bags had been taken away. We filled another with carrot peels shortly after. Frozen peas were the second vegetable and I sent Jimmy to find out where they were. I had already looked in the freezer compartment earlier but only found ice cream. The main section of the fridge was full of fruit salad and cartons of cream, custard, and milk. I worried about the hams! Alan assured me they'd be fine as there was no heat on out in the hall and it would be as cold as any fridge during the night. Jimmy found the peas in the chest freezer in the storeroom, so everything was set for the morning. By the time we had the washing up done and everything prepared it was nearly ten o'clock!

Ivor was pleased with the way things went. It was nice to see him more relaxed. I stayed in his place and we both had an early night. He was up like a lark again the following morning and anxious for road, but I insisted on making tea and toast, (he only had instant coffee).

We reached the shelter at eight thirty. Alan arrived at nine and started slicing the hams and I started on the turkeys. At ten o'clock there was still no sign of Jimmy. Alan was furious! I told him not to mind, that all the hard work was done. At least I thought so at the time.

"You can't even rely on reformed alcoholics," he laughed. I just smiled not sure if Alan was a reformed alcoholic too.

The potatoes were on the boil in three large pots. We planned to cook the carrots and frozen peas as near to the time as possible. I set to making the gravy: there was such a large quantity, I worried how it would turn out. I'd never cooked for more than five or six people in my life! I looked for cornflour to thicken it, but there wasn't any. Alan produced packets of Bisto and laughed heartily at my reaction "I guess you ain't a Bisto kid then, Piersy mate."

I thickened the gravy with some flour Alan found in the storeroom. It was still on the thin side, but I left well enough alone. "This will be token gravy, Alan," I laughed but he ignored me.

Finally, we put the trays of ham and turkey in the ovens to heat. People were expected at around twelve but to our surprise they began arriving shortly after eleven! Come to think of it, why wouldn't they! Each table was decorated with a centre piece of holly and ivy and the cutlery was wrapped in a red serviette. A shiny banner on the wall said, Merry Christmas and an ugly giant Santa stood in the corner.

Alan went outside for a smoke and I took a breather. There was a much higher ratio of men to women in the hall and the ages ranged from quite old to very young. A group in the centre of the room started singing, Rudolf the Red Nose Reindeer while pointing to each other's noses. Lots of laughter.

Alan, calmer after his smoke, set to mashing potatoes with me but it proved difficult in the large pots. In the end, we took out small amounts and mashed them in a bowl and smaller pots with seasoning and butter. "Christ, these will be soup!" Alan roared looking at the third pot. "We better strain them straight away." Alan took out the more solid ones and strained off the rest. We mashed them and dried them off a bit in the oven. When the carrots were ready, we put on the peas. Alan cursed Jimmy again when he saw we hadn't heated the plates. I wondered where all the plates came from but didn't ask. Ten minutes past twelve and everything was ready to go. We heated plates in the oven and used the microwave for some too. Ivor helped us plate up the food while other volunteers took them out. I was pleased that the gravy had thickened a little. When everyone finally had food! Alan and I were fit to drop. Ivor told us to make up plates for ourselves and the other volunteers came in turn for theirs. Alan, Ivor and I were heading to the volunteers' table when somebody shouted, "Hey mates…we got no stuffing," and the room erupted with laughter. I ate my Christmas dinner to the noisy banter of the biggest group of strangers I have ever been among.

Ivor's team took care of dessert: apple tart with cream or custard. Slices of Christmas cake and boxes of biscuits were put out and big kettles of tea were doing the rounds. Ivor had already told me how much they all loved the hot tea!

When all the guests had left, Alan and I faced into the kitchen to tackle the mess! This time, however, we had lots of help.

I spent Christmas night under my brother's roof again, exhausted but content. Ivor planned to go down to the hall on Boxing Day to make sure it was left clean and tidy. He had already left when I got up. I sought out my favourite café near my flat and was delighted it was open. I smiled thinking that everywhere would probably be shut in Cork on Stephen's Day.

Lots of messages on my mobile and on the answering machine. Toby wanted to know if I was alright! I rang him immediately explaining what I was doing. He took a fit of laughing at me doing the Good Samaritan. "I'm glad you kept busy, man. I thought you might find Christmas a bit lonely."

"No, it was a great Christmas, thanks to Ivor and the down and outs of South East London! I suppose you put your feet up listening to music."

"Of course! Why change a good thing." Toby laughed. He never makes a big deal of Christmas.

I rang Evelyn next. She was worried when neither of us picked up. When I explained, she was happy; all she cared about was that I spent Christmas with Ivor.

Happy and relaxed, I poured myself a drink and turned on the radio: someone was talking about the album, Changing Horses, by The Incredible String Band. I listened to the various tracks being discussed and various lyrics quoted. Then I heard the lines from, 'Creation,' the last of which turned me inside out: it was like an echo of, Sea Kiss. I could almost taste the salt drops on her thighs. Even the word Amethyst, sent a shiver down my spine. What were the odds? Memories came flooding: the blue velvet dress; the amethyst pendant; the blue Christmas lights on Patrick Street; our passionate kiss on the Kerry Road, a moment in time when I was whole and hopeful!

* * *

Every word ever uttered, every thought formulated, are suspended in the ether somewhere. On N'oublie Rien: what is uncomfortable is just ignored, but everything is remembered in the end, like that Christmas Eve when I wandered around the streets of Cork, playing word associations; words that unconsciously searched out the mind's recesses. In bed that that evening I remembered everything: it was a Sunday morning like any other. I was in reasonably good form, in so far as I wasn't torturing myself about her. On Friday evening, determined not to brood, I had gone out in torrential rain and returned drenched to the skin but exhilarated. I planned to go out Sunday morning too no matter what the weather was like.

The sky was a strange yellow glow and an east wind whipped around the house. I drove out to the Straight Road, parked up and went for a long walk. The Lee flowed by indifferent; birds were few and there was no one about. At first, I found solace in the stark environs, but when I could no longer endure the cold, I scurried back to the car and returned home.

I lit a fire and thought of Rosie as I put up the fireguard. After breakfast I did some chores. The day progressed with humdrum monotony; I read a few articles in Saturday's paper and watched some brain-watering TV. I went outside for coal. Winter's rationed light was fading and clouds were gathering. I averted my eyes from the bushes but in my mind's eye I saw the ball; I saw her.

I thought of calling Toby but changed my mind. Resolute in my solitude, I put on Wagner's Tristan & Isolde. I listened to the dissonant chords that poignantly expressed feelings of loss and regret but at every passionate rise and fall, every frenzied rush of notes, emotions were dredged that were better left imbedded; even the very first chord of the Prelude had unnerved me. Yet, I was compelled by its fervour. Like Tristan, I too had destroyed something beautiful.

The same disturbing passion with Siegfried and Brünnhilde, there was no escape. I jumped up and turned off the music, but it was too late! Something weird was happening in my head; it was like a convergence of every emotion and sensation ever experienced. To say my mind snapped would not quite explain what happened, I just seemed to be transported to a different dimension, where familiar objects looked vibrant and strange; then suddenly I was looking at everything through a red haze. I blinked and blinked but the haze was still there. I closed my eyes to rid whatever it was but when I opened them, I saw spirals, white spirals, one rotating clockwise the other anticlockwise. I shut my eyes again but when I opened them, the spirals were still moving around the room. When they began to whirl violently towards me, I fled from the house.

I walked out into the middle of Anglesea street because I saw no danger.

To me the world had altered, nothing was the same. I remembered too what I had been saying - I wasn't evangelising! I knew that couldn't possibly be true. I was reciting, Sailing to Byzantium, by Yeats. The strange experiences in the house had made me think of his cones and gyres. I was on the third verse when a fireman tried to pull me off the road (the fire station is next to the police station). Upset by the interruption, I tried to continue; the last verse was even more important to me, but by then a Garda had my other arm. It might have been helpful, had I remembered all this in the hospital; but then again, what difference would it have made, it happened to me. No doubt, it would have been suggested that I imagined the whole thing. For me, it was a real experience, even though I have never been able to interpret the phenomena. I wonder if having a breakdown, or being ill is just some kind of transition, or awakening.

* * *

Ivor rang me all excited, "Guess what? Evelyn and Jean are finally coming." When Evelyn couldn't come the last time, he had been disappointed. "They're coming to me, but I was wondering if you could put them up for a day or two, seeing you're nearer to everything."

"Yeah, no problem," I said, not quite understanding what the everything was. I nearly scalded myself with my coffee at what he said next:

"What does Mam think about them? Does she even know they're lesbians?"

"I don't know," I said, trying to steady myself and thanking god he couldn't see me!

"Surely, she must have an inkling at this stage," he said.

"You wouldn't know with her...she'd never let on," I said forcing a laugh.

"When are they coming? I must give the place a good clean!"

"Probably the end of January, early February."

I stood there afterwards feeling a right fool. Poor Evelyn! I remember now, she wanted to tell me something that day in the Imperial Hotel, and didn't Catriona say she met her outside Loafers pub. How could I have been so blind?

At work the other day, a guy was talking about New Year's resolutions. I told him I never make any. I believe we continue doing the same things no matter how much we want to change. I'm beginning to understand what Liz meant about emotional intelligence. She said I could educate myself and be as clever as I wished but without emotional maturity, I would always be in trouble. She made me see, at the time, that emotionally I was still that fourteen-year-old boy distraught in his bedroom. I learnt that my grandmother was the cornerstone, with whom I felt safe, yet, even with her I blocked out anything she had to say about Rosie. I wanted to see Rosie as my little daughter not some prescient angel or guiding spirit.

To most people I was shut off, especially with my mother, sometimes with good reason. I feel ashamed about Evelyn! Deep down I knew she was having problems. I remind myself that I was ill then and couldn't even sort out my own life.

Liz asked one time if I'd written any poems about Rosie and was surprised that I hadn't. I wanted so much to talk to her about Rosie then. I'd like to think she would have understood but I couldn't take the chance. She may well have considered me delusional and I could have been dragged deeper into the whole mental health system and may not have fared too well.

I would like to think that I am wiser now and understand a lot more about myself. I am determined never to speak to anyone about Rosie. I believe there are some things in life that we must keep to ourselves! Not everything needs to be talked about!

* * *

London has been good in so far as I have been able to carve out a living but deep down, I see it merely as a stepping-stone. Publishing, though interesting, is not really for me. I want to write but I'm finding it hard and the poems I do manage to write are of little substance. I yearn for the landscape that nourished me, a landscape that was part of me. Maybe I'm using this as an excuse. Maybe I'm still an emotional cripple! All the analysis in the hospital seems to have chocked my creativity! Have I even improved emotionally?

I invited Terry Lyle and his wife, Andrea, to dinner with the intention of being up front about how I was thinking. I cooked a simple beef casserole and boiled potatoes and got two nice bottles of red and a lemon tart for dessert. When I took Andrea's lush black coat, I told her it was so soft, I could give it a hug. She frowned but then laughed when her husband said, "I'm glad it gives some satisfaction…you should have seen the price tag."

"Take no notice of that skinflint, Piers," Andrea said pushing him ahead as I followed behind in her subtle fragrant trail.

Terry hadn't been to my apartment before and looked around with an observant eye. I could guess what he was thinking, apart from the sparse furniture, it is rather dreary. My only possessions are books and they are mostly in my bedroom, stacked against the wall, not yet on shelves.

Andrea was impressed with my culinary skill and thought I made the tart myself. I told her I like to cook but I don't bother much just for myself.

"Oh my, we will have to remedy that…why a good-looking guy like you. Terry, we have to get Piers a woman!"

"He's had plenty of opportunities, from what I hear," Terry said taking a rise.

"Oh really…do tell…"

"Can't! Tales out of school and all that… besides, he might tell you things about me."

"Oh, I see!" Andrea said, feigning indignation.

I told them then about the time I cooked for Ivor and how he tried to eat a dinner to please me.

"He sounds nice!" Andrea said. "At least he considered your feelings."

"We Irish are a little more direct, Andrea. I would have just said, no thanks I'm not hungry…or I'll have some tomorrow."

"Yes! We know how direct you can be, Piers," Terry quipped.

I felt this was my cue, "Speaking of being direct, Terry, I do have something to tell you."

"Oh!" He said looking at me earnestly. "Out with it then!"

"I've been doing a lot of thinking lately… about the direction I'm taking…"

"You want to leave," Andrea said perceptively.

"You do?" Terry asked astounded.

"Yes! Well, no! Not immediately. I didn't want to spring anything on you down the line." Terry sighed deeply and looked at Andrea.

"Well dear, he is being honest with you!"

"What are you planning…have you another job?"

"Terry, I just told you…it's something I'm thinking about… I want to get back to writing more. I'm not thinking about another job."

"But you have been writing…what about those articles and book reviews you've been doing …you earn money from them…why can't you do both?"

"Oh! You're a writer, I didn't know," Andrea said. I just nodded, not wanting to be led on a tangent.

"I'm finding it hard to write here…I feel disconnected, somehow. I like London, but I don't think it's really for me. I need rivers and wilderness…I can't explain it…I just do…I'm a culchie at heart."

"A what?" Andrea enquired.

"Oh! It's and Irish expression…a rustic…a country person." I answered feeling a bit ridiculous.

"Hardly that, Piers!" Andrea smiled.

"Well, if that's what you need why don't you go into the country more… go up north…go to Wales or something…visit Scotland for Christ's sake… you don't have to quit your job," Terry said earnestly.

"It's not as simple as that, Terry," Andrea said, "they would only be little breaks…I think what Piers is talking about is a way of life." Andrea's insight surprised me and I could have conversed easily with her but I didn't want to let my guard down. Terry Lyle was my boss!

"What timeframe are we talking about…when exactly are you planning to leave?" Terry asked in his head of the company voice.

I was just about to answer when Andrea interjected, "He already told you… he's not going to leave you in the lurch!"

"I need to know these things well in advance."

"I'll stay as long as you want…till you get someone suitable… someone you're happy with. I just wanted to tell you in good time."

"I think that's very fair!" Andrea said looking from me to her husband.

"Yes…I suppose." Terry conceded. Andrea leaned over and patted his forearm. He remained silent for some time before looking at me and grinning.

"By the way, Piers, have you not noticed that big river flowing through London?"

"I have, Terry…I have!" I said and we all laughed.

Andrea brought up the subject of books and mentioned her favourites. She confessed to not having read much in recent years, but that she read quite a lot when she was younger. Terry, I noticed wasn't partaking in the conversation, so I asked him what he liked.

"Everything! I am in the business of publishing books after all," he said, affronted at being asked at all!

"That's different, darling…he wants to know what you personally like to read."

"History and biographies mainly but I like Clancy and le Carré…action kind of books and I like Patrick O'Brien," he said, lightening up a little. It was all about authors for a while until Andrea changed the subject to music. I have no idea why I suddenly felt uneasy and I was sure she noticed.

"What kind of music do you like?" she asked regardless.

"Oh everything…anything from Mozart to Frank Sinatra." I said a little glibly.

A smile crossed Andrea's face and she turned to her husband and said, "That reminds me, Terry, did you organise the tickets for Caroline?"

While they were talking, I cleared away some dishes; when I returned, I asked if they'd like more wine but they both declined. Terry was driving and Andrea said they should be going, anyway. It was only when they were leaving, I saw the bottle of wine they had brought on the counter next to the microwave. I'm sure it would have been far superior to what I gave them.

* * *

Evelyn and Jean stayed with Ivor for three days. I got the impression Jean was happy to stay in Lewisham despite it being so far out. They did come to me however, as arranged, but I think that was down to Evelyn. They went out together the two evenings on their own. Jean hung around Evelyn like a mother hen most of the time, so it was hard to get Evelyn alone. I caught Jean observing me from time to time when she thought I was unaware.

Ivor called to tell me he has booked dinner for us on Saturday night and that he will drive them to the airport on Sunday. He seemed quite excited about us all going out together.

I had a few drinks with Carl on Friday night so I slept a little later Saturday morning. I was woken by hushed voices and movement around the place. I wandered into the kitchen to find Jean and Evelyn, both in pyjamas. Evelyn was bending down to the cupboards when Jean ran her hand down Evelyn's arse and between her legs. I was jolted awake! I know it was silly of me, but up to then I just saw them as two women. Suddenly, with this unequivocal sexual act, I was made aware that they were very much lovers.

"Good morning...how are the heads?" I said opening the fridge, pretending I hadn't seen anything. Evelyn seemed a little flustered, but Jean stood there triumphant. I wondered had she done it deliberately for my benefit.

"What are you making Evelyn?" I asked regaining my equilibrium.

"Ah! Not too sure...scrambled eggs..."

"Would you like me to do the breakfast?"

"Right so," she said with no hesitation. Evelyn is not exactly domesticated; she wants everything instantly and usually ends up burning something.

"Scrambled eggs, tomatoes and mushrooms...is that okay with you Jean," I asked.

"Yeah...sounds grand. I'll have a quick shower so," she said.

I couldn't help thinking of Evelyn then in terms of her sexuality. When she was with Brian, I never entertained the idea of sex. Well, one doesn't with a sister. Evelyn was sitting cross legged on a kitchen stool, her dark wavy hair falling over her face; even pyjamas couldn't restrain her shapely body. I was thinking any man would go wild for her! I could see what Jean sees in her but what did Evelyn see in Jean? Jean is stocky, hard featured with short hair and well, let's say, I wouldn't find her attractive.

Jean wanted to go to a Boots so I gave her directions to the nearest one, which is within walking distance. I thought this was my chance to talk to Evelyn. However, when Jean was ready to go, she said, "Come on Eve...let's go." I hated her calling Evelyn, Eve!

"I'd like Evelyn to stay, Jean ...I want to talk to her about something!" I said expecting a reaction.

"Right so...see ye later," she said and gave Evelyn a peck on the cheek.

I began by telling Evelyn how sorry I was for everything and asked her to forgive a very foolish brother for not paying attention. She said I was being too hard on myself. All she cared about was that I was doing well. She cracks up laughing when I tell her how I nearly scalded myself when Ivor asked if Mam knew she was a lesbian.

"I pretended I knew...please don't tell him, Evelyn."

"I won't say a word! Ivor assumes everyone knows! He's out of Waterford too long, I think."

"Did you tell him when he was home?"

"No, he just asked out straight if Jean was my girlfriend. It was quite refreshing really."

"Does Mam know?"

"Yes, I told her. At first, I thought I'd made a mistake 'cos she went so quiet. But then I saw the smile and knew I'd done the right thing. There was I thinking she'd be horrified...just goes to show how wrong you can be about things. She's not as tetchy with me now...do you remember what she was like? Mind you, she can still be difficult at times. If only everyone was the same... it's not easy being a lesbian in Waterford. I've told no one at work...but then again why should I...it's no one's business but mine."

"I haven't told anyone either that I'm a heterosexual," I said making her laugh. "But seriously, are you happy with Jean?"

"Yes, of course I am, silly... Jean is solid...she'd do anything for me."

"But how do you know she's the one ...I mean..."

"Don't worry Piers," Evelyn laughs, "I'm not some naïve tenderfoot...I've had other girlfriends."

"Oh right!" I said feeling foolish. "I just want you to be happy. I may be a bit slow on the uptake, but I'm always here for you...you know that don't you?"

"I do!" She said giving me a tight hug. "Things have taken a turn for the better for us at last...haven't they?"

I closed my eyes wishing it were true! While I had the chance, I thought I should tell her about Ivor. "Evelyn has Ivor told you anything about himself…about all his years over here?"

"Not much! Why? Is there something to know? There is, isn't there?" She said searchingly.

"I just thought he might have talked to you."

"Things were pretty hectic when he was home. Why?"

"He hasn't had an easy time of it, Evelyn. I don't know how to help him …he sees me as the one with the crutch."

"I don't understand, Piers. He's doing alright, isn't he…"

"Better than you know. Look, you'll understand when I tell you!" I then related Ivor's struggle with the drink and where it led him. But when I told her he had been married and has a son, she was speechless. "He's twelve now! Mam has a grandson… you and I have a nephew."

"My god! Why didn't he tell me? But where is his boy?"

"Oh, Evelyn he was so happy to see you and the family and to be home…I think he was too ashamed to say anything."

"My god, what are we to do?"

"He just needs a push, Evelyn."

"I don't think I'm ready for any more surprises in this family," she said wearily, caging her face with her fingers. "What other skeletons are in the cupboard?"

"Come on now… this is a good thing…he just needs to re-establish contact that's all!"

"Yeah…but it's such a shock."

"Gillian is married now to a Julian Preece. I know where they live, Evelyn! I called half the Preeces in the greater London area. It's only a stone's throw from Uncle Frank as it turns out. Well, that's a bit of an exaggeration…they live in Surbiton."

"Have you been to Frank's?"

"No, he probably wouldn't know me…he hasn't seen me since Dad's funeral. No doubt Paddy gave him the lowdown on me."

"What lowdown? You have nothing to be ashamed of, Piers!"

"Paddy has never liked me."

"You worry too much about what he thinks. Nobody takes any notice of holy-up-his-arse!" I roared laughing at her apt description.

"Anyway, what do you think... should I tell him? Do you think he'd see it as interfering?"

"Tell him! I'll talk to him too!"

"No, you can't! Ivor told me in confidence. I told you because I don't want any more secrets between us, but you mustn't tell anyone else."

"I understand, Piers. I won't say anything, I promise."

Saturday evening, we went to a restaurant on Regent Street for dinner. It had a lovely atmosphere and we were all pleased with the food. Ivor looked much younger, all spruced up. He seemed comfortable in female company. I wondered why he hadn't a girlfriend. But then again maybe he has one somewhere.

Jean seemed more friendly and I tried my best too. However, there was still an awkwardness and we found little to talk about. She was much more at ease with Ivor, laughing and joking. I was surprised at how witty she was.

All in all, things went well. It was pleasant spending time with Ivor and Evelyn. I have learnt not to take things for granted. These are the moments that make up my life.

* * *

Ivor looked all worried when I said I wanted to talk to him. "It's nothing bad...I was just thinking about Oliver and..."

"What about him?" He asked impatiently.

"I know it's none of my business but...ah...I know where he's living."

"How do you know that?" He said studying me.

"I phoned nearly every bloody Preece in the book... pretended I was doing a survey for a telephone company. I finally spoke to a Gillian Preece."

"You should have asked me!" Ivor said with a whimsical air.

"I thought you didn't know where they were."

"I'm sorry if I gave you that impression."

"But you said Gillian didn't want anything to do with you!"

"Yes! But I never said I had no contact. Gillian has my address and number if she needs to contact me. I do support my son, Piers…at least financially."

"Ivor, I'm sorry! I shouldn't have interfered. It was presumptuous of me. And who am I to advise you… I can't even sort my own life out."

"It's okay, Piers. You were only trying to help," he said putting his arm around me. "You were the one I was able to talk to …that's important to me."

* * *

I got a notification of a parcel for collection at a post depot in Putney. I brought the docket to work and got one of our couriers to collect it. I explained it was a personal thing and gave him a tip. He went off whistling, probably thinking I was nuts. The parcel was from Jack – three books and a letter.

Dear Piers,

> *Secret Garden did a great job - used one of their own illustrators. Edith pulled off a little miracle. She's delighted they are still moving off the shelves. She wants to know if you have any more and if you would be interested in doing a series for The Lost Fox. I told her I thought it unlikely! No mention of money yet! As you can imagine there were many costs involved.*

> *Glad things worked out for you with Terry Lyle. He's a good guy, he'll see you right. Business steady here; doing another book for Gilmore - better than the first one. Where are the poems? Don't keep me waiting too long!*

> *Take care Piers. Regards to Terry & Andrea.*

I put the package on the table when I got home. Even though I was eager to look at the books I was a little nervous. I confronted myself for being ridiculous and bravely opened the package: Peter Cantrell, pseudonym; great illustrations; good quality all round. Catriona was the only person who could connect me to the stories but I thought it unlikely she'd come across them. I had visualised the stories in one book but this was a much better idea. I remembered then going through Tim's book that Christmas, but these books were truly Rosie's. I went through each one, turning each page as if I were showing it to her. When I finished looking at them there came an onslaught of grief that I was not prepared for and I cried a torrent of tears. I don't know for how long I was there, or even if I had dozed off from exhaustion but when I opened my eyes the room began to recede before my eyes and I was drifting and drifting down a foggy tunnel. Suddenly I began to rise through clouds, up and up to the stratosphere and beyond. Below the blue earth was turning and the heavens were full of stars.

I came to an abrupt stop in a dark void, alone and frightened, separated from everything familiar. I felt a tightness in my chest and was about to panic when suddenly I was surrounded by a ring of bright light. Adjusting my eyes to the light, I saw that the ring was composed of crystals; I'd seen quartz crystals in an exhibition once, but these were enormous and more brilliant than I could ever have imagined. The crystals began to vibrate and a wave of colours streamed through them as if they were dancing. My mind was an overload of wonder. The crystals then emitted a heavenly music, rather like notes of the highest register of an organ. I heard a child's laughter mingled with the sound of tinkling bells. Rosie suddenly appeared before me, smiling at me the way she used to. When the supernal sounds diminished, Rosie ran towards the crystals, laughing. Desperately I tried to follow her but I felt a sudden weight on my chest and a powerful force pushing me down. A voice, like a human male voice, said, "Come back now!"

The room was filled with a pale silver light which within seconds changed to a beautiful blue. A strange stillness permeated the air and I felt a tingle on my skin. An aura of tranquillity enveloped me and I saw Rosie, like that day in the woods: her hair gleaming in the slanted sunbeams, white sawdust streaming through her fingers. I tried to speak, tried to tell her that I missed her but I had no voice. Her smiling eyes held mine in the longest gaze, then she waved and evanesced in the shafts of light.

Part Four

AFTER MY BREAKDOWN, I worried that I would never be able to write as well as before. Currently I am writing profusely and I believe some of my work is even better than before. This is a subjective view of course and I guess only time will tell. I have salvaged some older poems, especially the one about my father that gave me so much trouble. Out of that initial poem, I wrote three new ones and I'm happy that they captured everything I wanted to say. Terry would laugh to know I've written about the Thames – well a prose piece. I have also written a series of haikus: themes of water, moon, sun and stars. They seemed to have come magically out of the ether.

I look back at my last collection in horror! What a farrago! If only I'd weathered the storm a little longer, I would have been more objective. I can't help thinking of Wagner having to sit through the performance of his New Overture with agonised embarrassment: the audience went into hysterics at his enthusiasm to bring out the 'Mystic Meaning' of the orchestra: he had added a fifth beat after every fourth bar, announced by a dramatic blow of the kettle drum. Afterwards he said, "The laughter had gone and they looked as if they had been through some terrible nightmare." Saint-Saëns said there were three divided categories of Wagnerites, the third being the sane who having studied Wagner's works had no illusions about their defects yet found in them many beauties. I don't know what category I'm in; I don't have a musical background or experience, but I feel the emotion and see the beauty.

Thinking of Saint-Saëns, I read somewhere that he destroyed a lot of his music, believing it wasn't good enough. I guess Ó Buachalla was right about the endeavours for perfection.

* * *

I suppose it was to be expected that Terry and Andrea would invite me to their home. Apart from being a writer, Andrea knew little about me. I was a little apprehensive knowing how formidable and probing she can be. Besides, I wanted to keep my relationship with Terry strictly professional.

Their large house in Chiswick was exquisitely decorated, with many fine paintings in the hallway alone. We sat down to a lovely meal in a stylish dining room, again with many paintings but the atmosphere was homely and relaxed. Andrea enquired about my writing and expressed a wish to read my poems sometime. I told her I was writing again and had just completed a series of haikus.

"Oh wonderful! You must show them to me."

"I'll copy them for you…they're not in book form yet."

"Writing *again*, Piers…were you suffering from writers block or something?"

"Of sorts…writing comes in waves, either writing like mad or nothing at all," I reply, suddenly remembering what Claire said.

"Was it the move here do you think? You mentioned you missed a rural landscape."

"Yes, I suppose that was partly it."

"Partly?" She probed. Women are such inquisitive creatures!

The rest of the evening went smoothly enough, Terry was in good humour and talked a lot, mainly about current affairs which suited me fine.

I was invited again shortly afterwards which really surprised me. I thought of making some excuse but in the end, I thought it was easier just to go. However, on that occasion, I wasn't guarded enough unfortunately. Andrea talked openly about her own background: her father was a coffee importer, retired now; her mother worked for Spink & Son, also retired; her elder sister Johanna is married in Salzburg and her younger sister Jodi is a lecturer on Art History in San Francisco.

I talked a little about Ivor and his line of business and how I worked for him when I first came to London. Andrea was amused at the idea of me cutting grass but sounded in no way disparaging. She said she would have liked having a brother. She talked then of Johanna and her two little boys, happily recounting her last visit. She asked if my sister had any children and when I told her Evelyn was a lesbian, it didn't knock a feather out of her.

"That doesn't mean she won't have children at some stage!' She said and smiled at my surprise. "I'd like to have children," she said absently.

When I said, "Maybe you will yet," Andrea glanced like a startled deer towards the doorway. After a few minutes, she settled back in her chair and looked at me in a silent communication. I don't know how it happened, but I found myself telling her about Rosie and Helen.

"You know I knew there was something," she said nodding as if finally solving a riddle. "What a tragedy! But my word, you should have told us." It was my turn then to be alarmed! What might she ask next? She didn't ask anything further, however but sat sombrely for ages without saying a word. Then roused by a sound from outside, she blinked in rapid succession and rising from her chair went to the drinks cabinet. "What's your pleasure, darling?" She called exuberantly to Terry who had just entered the room.

Weeks later, Terry was driving me out to Chiswick again. "Oh! I meant to tell you," he said, grinning, "Andrea has invited a friend…for your benefit, I should imagine."

"Jesus," I exclaimed quite forgetting myself. Terry laughed at me but I wasn't amused at all.

"Silly me…silly me," Andrea was saying as we entered the kitchen. "I forgot to put this in the oven," she said holding a pie. "We'll just have to skip dessert," she said nonplussed. "Come and have a drink, Piers. I want you to meet someone.

Caroline Stevens, attractive and stylishly dressed, smiled as she shook my hand. She had a nice smile. She seemed quite at home with Terry and Andrea but was quite reserved and said little throughout the evening, especially to me. From observing her, I didn't think she was in on Andrea's little scheme. Left together later in the evening, I impulsively asked if she'd like to meet up during the week. "Yes, that would be nice," she said. "I'm free Monday evening."

Later, I wondered if I asked her out just to gratify Andrea.

I thought going for a drink was the simplest option. It was a strained evening to say the least; Caroline made little effort to engage with me on any subject, just nodding impassively from time to time to what I was saying. I thought it strange that she agreed to come out with me at all. We exchanged phone numbers but I had no intention of calling and felt sure she wouldn't either.

As it happened, I bumped into her on Kensington High Street a fortnight later. It was like she was a different person, open and friendly. She was on her way to meet a friend and asked me to come along. I didn't want to intrude but she insisted, saying her friend would love to meet someone new. It occurred to me, on the way, that Caroline may have been gratifying Andrea also.

Caroline introduced me to Madeleine Thierry, a rather small boyish looking French woman. She and Caroline exchanged so much information, I got the impression they hadn't seen each other in a while, but it was only a little over a week, as it turned out. Madeleine's English was quite good. She had an intelligent and lively face and used her hands expressively as she spoke. Caroline was delighted to hear I spoke French. I told her I used to teach French and had been to France on a few occasions. I told her I read French well enough but that my conversational French was a bit rusty now. We switched to French, for the fun of it for a while but Caroline reverted to English again for Madeleine's benefit. I said goodbye to them outside the café and went off to buy shoes, which brought me to the area in the first place.

Andrea came into the office with Terry the following Wednesday. I was surprised as I'd never seen her in the office before. "You are full of surprises, Mr. Cantwell," she said, coming over and dropping her oversized handbag on my desk.

"How so?" I asked, uneasy as to why she called me Mr. Cantwell.

"We are quite the linguist it seems...I heard about your encounter with Madeleine. You never told me you were a teacher! You must be the most reticent person I have ever met!"

"That was a long time back, Andrea, I didn't think to mention it..."

"I thought we were friends, Piers... friends tell each other things," she said annoyed.

"Didn't I mention it in my CV?" I said, looking around seeking Terry's help but he was engrossed in some papers he was just handed and turned into his office. Why was Andrea so concerned anyway? Was it because Caroline knew something about me before she did? I expected Andrea to follow Terry but instead she sat on the edge of my desk with one leg on the ground, exposing an inner thigh. A waft of her delicate perfume reached my nostrils as she leaned towards me.

"If you're free Saturday, I'd like you to come to lunch," she said all smiles.

"Andrea, it's my turn to invite you two," I said recovering.

"Oh, don't be silly, it's just lunch. I want you to meet someone."

"Who?" I asked suspiciously.

"Why Madeleine of course!"

"You're not trying to matchmake are you," I asked tetchily.

"No, Piers, I wouldn't dream of it," she laughed, "Caroline said Madeline would like to meet you again and from what I hear, you two hit it off! Besides, we like your company."

I agreed, mainly so she'd leave me alone; I was uncomfortable talking about personal things in the office.

I arrived in Chiswick a little early around 12.30. "You're punctual," Andrea said opening the door. "I thought you were coming down with Caroline and Madeleine?"

"I told Caroline I was getting a lift...my brother drove me."

"You should have invited him in."

"He was in a rush. Ivor is always too busy!" I laughed.

"Not too busy to drive his brother somewhere though," she smiled. "Terry won't be joining us," she dropped casually, as I followed her in. "He's away on business." I assumed it to be personal business because I would have heard otherwise. In the kitchen, she put the final touches to the food. "It's only quiche and salad," she said half apologising. "Homemade though," she boasted. "Would you like a drink? I'm having a white wine," she said taking a bottle from the fridge. "I can drink what I like today, Caroline will drive if we go out," she laughed. "And, I won't have Terry looking over my shoulder," she added. At that moment, I felt awkward being in the house without Terry present.

"I'll have an orange juice," I replied, having spotted the carton in the fridge.

I was determined to keep my guard up on this occasion.

"Oh god! don't tell me you're going to be boring," she said.

"Okay, I'll have wine so… I wouldn't want to be boring,"

"Maybe you'd like a whisky or a gin instead."

"No wine is fine, thanks."

"Let's sit in the garden while the sun is shining," she said, bringing the bottle with her.

"You have a beautiful garden, Andrea…such a selection of shrubs and…"

"Nothing to do with me, Piers. All down to Terry. He loves his garden," she said putting her glass and the bottle on the ornate white garden table. She filled her glass again and topped up mine. She reminded me of the poems I promised her.

"I forgot, Andrea. I've been a bit busy. I can email them or print them out for you…"

"Okay…whatever," she said. I sipped my wine and Andrea said nothing further which I thought strange. I was never so glad when Caroline and Madeleine arrived.

Throughout lunch, I did my best among three females. Andrea now seemed in better spirits and I relaxed somewhat. When Andrea and Caroline were chatting in the kitchen, Madeleine and I went out to the garden. We were walking around admiring the beautiful flowers and shrubs, none of which I recognised, when Andrea breezed out, suggesting we take a trip to Richmond Park. Caroline following her out, caught my eye and grinned wryly. I took this as a hint that Andrea was a bit tipsy.

I'd been to Richmond Park once before: the river boat goes right up there. Only for Madeleine's wanting to see the wild deer, I would have made an excuse and gone home. As it turned out, I was glad I went. Unfortunately, we saw no deer, only their droppings, which I pointed out to Madeleine to prove there were in fact deer. She was in no way disappointed as there are lots of wild deer near where she lives. When we caught up with the others, Andrea, complained that we were dawdling too much and seemed out of sorts again.

Once over the threshold of her home, however, Andrea became again the charming hostess and invited us to stay for dinner. "It will have to be an order in, of course," she laughed. I had plans to meet Mike Weaver for a drink so I couldn't stay, besides, three women, all afternoon, was quite enough! I thanked Andrea for a wonderful afternoon, and she kissed me on the cheek in farewell. Caroline, even though she was staying, offered to drive me but I insisted on getting the train.

Terry was his usual self on Monday morning but there was no mention of Saturday. I wondered then if he even knew I had been there. We saw little of each other the rest of day both preoccupied with our own work.

Days went by and Madeleine hadn't called. After all, it was she who asked for my number. She did call eventually saying she couldn't get time off. "You could have phoned!" I said, irked at her seeming indifference.

"I am foolish! I lose your number!"

"But you just rang me, Madeleine!" I said, thinking she was making excuses.

"Yes," she laughed, "I get it from Caroline."

I mellowed then and we arranged to meet. We went to the cinema, her suggestion, and afterwards we went for a walk. I discovered she had a sense of humour and was very direct, something I wasn't used to. When I asked if she'd like to come back to my place, she said, "Pour la nuit ou peut-être un café?"

"Peut-être pour les deux!" I replied.

"Non," she laughed, "je plaisante...je dois travailler demain, malheureusement!"

Madeleine stopped to look at one of Rosie's pictures. Carl had them framed for me: the larger ones were backed with board and covered in glass. He made a collage of the smaller ones in a rustic frame which suited them.

"Oh, how beautiful...une peinture d'enfant ne c'est pas?"

"Yes," I said moving away. Madeleine went along to the next one and said, "I like very much the freedom of the child...the movement...the...how you say?"

I didn't say, not wanting to talk about Rosie right then. "Would you like a drink, Madeleine? I have whisky or wine."

"I would like a whisky, please," she said coming over. "Oh, whisky irlandais...good."

Madeleine told me then about the Nantes exchange project which involved people from the tourist industry. She was here with catering staff and hotel managers and two chefs. She didn't like the chefs! It was the only category she could join. It was through obstinacy and the efforts of the local Mayor that she got on the project because technically St, Denis D'Anjou was not on the list. She had submitted plans to the tourist board to convert her grandmother's old farmhouse into a guest house; her plan to farm the land and produce organic food was a big plus. She took a fit of laughing telling me she neglected to tell the Mayor that she had no money to develop the property with its many outhouses and had yet to negotiate with the bank. She was laughing so much she made me laugh. The financial aspect didn't ruffle her one iota; her dream was the focus. I admired that.

I readily gave my opinions on organic farming to which she simply said, "The land is like a person... if you abuse, it will give little! If you are good... eh... it will nourish!"

I expressed the view that nothing is truly organic anymore because of the overproduction of the soil and the cross fertilisation of GM foods. I ranted about how strawberries and other fruits were grown without soil in tubes with water and chemicals. "But we must attempt our...our very best...that is everything we must do!" She said a little weary of my arguments.

She seemed happier when I talked about Ireland, describing the Cork and Waterford Landscape. She talked about her home and the old farmhouse on the banks of the river Sarthe. She missed the long walks with her dog, Sylevebarbe, whom she named after Treebeard in Lord of The Rings because he was grey and gangly.

It was getting late so she had to go. Saturday mornings were especially busy; she was out of favour already for taking one Saturday off. I understood then that she had gone to a lot of trouble to meet me. I kissed her while we waited for her taxi and even though she responded warmly, it felt odd. She said it would be more convenient for her to call me. "Don't lose the number so," I joked as she got in the taxi; my number was already in her phone so it was a silly thing to say.

I had another drink wondering what the bloody hell I was playing at. I really didn't need more complications in my life. However, I went to bed content - a contentment that lasted until Monday!

Monday, I got the push! Terry had found a replacement! In fact, two people, Simon Harmon, to take over my work and Paula Davis, to take the load off him, and deal with things generally. He was giving me a month's notice but gave me the option of two if necessary. He delivered all this in a detached manner.

"You could have told me before now, Terry. And a month's notice! I deserve better than that, surely."

"I've been more than fair, Piers. You told me months ago you were going to leave. I need staff that are one hundred per cent committed!" He said firmly. Even though he sprung it on me, I had to agree with him. However, he didn't leave it there. "This is a business...I'm not running a do-gooder-halfway house!" The first thing I thought was that he had heard about my breakdown. But where would he have heard it? Jack would not have said anything, I'm certain of that.

"What do you mean by that, Terry?" I asked trying to contain myself. "I worked my ass off for this company. I earned my salary!"

"I didn't mean anything by that, Piers...I..."

"Well why say it then...do you think by keeping me on these last months was some big favour..."

"No! I just meant that when it comes to business, we can't let our personal feelings interfere...that's all..."

"Yes, I agree, but you could have told me you were interviewing. Why be so secretive?" I left his office then before he could reply. I sat at my desk, unable to concentrate. I turned off my computer, answered a few calls and left shortly afterwards. Mulling over the situation I thought yes, he had a perfect right - he had a company to run. I'd told him months ago where I stood and I thought he would do the same in return. I was deluding myself to think there was any real friendship between us.

By the end of the month, I had cleared out my desk and inducted Simon Harmon to the best of my ability: I especially drew attention to details that perhaps another individual might not have bothered to do. I was thinking more of the clients.

Terry suggested a farewell drink in the office but I declined: it would only have prolonged our mutual discomfort. I did however have a drink with Carl. He had a good laugh when I told him I'd given my notice months ago. "What's all the bloody fuss about so?" He asked having heard a lot of rumours.

"There's no fuss on my part, Carl," I laughed and we clinked glasses.

Convincing Ivor was harder. He worried about how I was going to survive. I assured him I was okay: I had my weekly column with a popular newspaper and I wrote regularly for a monthly magazine. I had also received a cheque from Secret Garden Press, through Jack of course. It was more than I expected given the breakdown of the costs involved. I had to tell him then about the money Nan left me. He laughed to hear I was afraid to tell him in case he felt rejected.

"I was the one who did all the rejecting!" he said.

"Anyway, I can always cut grass if the going gets tough," I joked.

* * *

Madeleine called eventually. I hadn't been sure if I wanted her to or not but there were times when I did - perhaps that was an ego thing. Yet, I was happy to hear from her and we arranged to go out for dinner.

Madeleine is older than she looks, going on thirty-three. I had guessed around twenty-six, twenty-seven. We had a very enjoyable evening; it was like we had known each other for ages. She already heard about me leaving Lyle's and thought I would be upset. She laughed when I told her the whole story.

Madeleine talked a lot about Caroline, who is the coordinator of the London/Nantes project and speaks fluent French and German. Caroline has been especially good to Madeleine ever since she found out the chefs were giving her a hard time. It was obvious Madeleine likes her very much.

"I went out with Caroline once," I said, feeling obliged to mention it.

"Yes, I know. Caroline said you are nice but a little...euh... strange!"

"Strange...in what way strange? I was on my best behaviour...she hardly said a word!"

"She talks very little to men," Madeleine said.

"Is she a lesbian?"

"Non!" Madeleine laughed. "She likes men, okay...but she is...ah, *safe?*"

"Cautious?"

"Yes, cautious! Someone was very bad with her one time."

We sheltered from a downpour in the doorway of the restaurant until the taxi came. Even getting from the doorway to the taxi, we got rather wet. At the apartment, I searched for one of my t-shirts for her and as she dried her hair, I poured us some whisky. Madeleine likes Irish whisky.

I talked a little about my writing because she asked and she talked mostly about her family. After running out of things to say, I leaned across and kissed her. Her arms went around my neck. It felt awkward, but I wanted to give it a try. I froze however, when her hand went inside my shirt. It seemed too familiar! I got up with the pretence of wanting some music, wondering why I was so put out. I tuned on the radio, explaining that all my CD's and records were in Ireland. Madeleine asked why I didn't bring my music with me.

"Maybe, when I'm settled, I will get them."

"That is making your life into the future..."

"Putting on hold..."

"Yes, thank you, putting on hold... you must use technology, non... perhaps to buy un iPod."

"You are not the first person to tell me that," I said bringing the whisky bottle over.

Madeleine placed her hand over her glass, but I topped up my own. "There is something wrong," she quizzed when I remained standing.

"No!"

"Come sit beside me," she invited. I didn't sit, however, but pulled her up and kissed her. Her arms went around my neck; her lips were warm and inviting.

"Are you going to stay, Madeline," I found myself asking.

I got under the covers and patted the space beside me. She took off my t-shirt and unfastened a flesh-coloured bra to reveal small pert breasts; her thighs were lean but muscular; her bottom round and firm: she didn't seem boyish to me at all at that moment. Having folded her clothes, she got in beside me. Her warm body pressed against mine and my penis hardened to her touch. It felt right when I kissed her, but when I closed my eyes, other eyes, hazel eyes, were staring back at me. I quickly dispelled the images but it was too late, I was limp, and there was nothing I could do about it.

"I'm sorry Madeleine…I can't do this," I said embarrassed. I got out of bed and went outside. This had never happened to me before. I liked this woman! Why couldn't I? I had no fucking problem with Ruby.

Madeleine didn't follow me which gave me time to pull myself together. I returned to the bedroom feeling embarrassed. She was lying back on the pillows with my t-shirt back on.

"You are okay?" She asked, putting her hand on my shoulder as I sat on the side of the bed.

"I'm sorry Madeleine…I don't know what came over me…you are a lovely woman…it's me…I just…"

"Andrea told me about your woman and child in the accident! Don't worry about the sex," she said throwing back the covers and nimbly getting out. I didn't want her to go but I had humiliated her enough. I had my head in my hands when I felt her fingers through my hair.

"I thought you were leaving," I said looking up.

"Je reste! Unless you wish me to leave."

"No, I'd like you to stay…if you think you can put up with me!"

"Put up… qu'est-ce que tu dis?"

"Come to bed and I'll explain," I smiled. She held me for a long time in silence and it was comforting. "Madeleine, there are a few things you need to know about me!"

She put two fingers to my lips and said, "You can tell me when you must… relax now!"

I did relax, so much so, I opened up to Madeleine Thierry like a river overflowing its banks: I told her about my grandmother, my suppressed grief for Rosie, and my breakdown. How much she understood I'm not entirely sure as I spoke only English. Naturally, I didn't talk about Catriona. Madeleine stroked my head but remained holding me in silence. Relating these events quite exhausted me, and I drifted off to sleep.

I woke early and felt happy that this woman was beside me. I lay there admiring her clear olive skin, and then, seized by a demanding erection, woke her by kissing her slender neck.

* * *

If somebody had told me a year ago that I'd be going out with a small boyish looking French woman, I'd have laughed in their face. The parts of me that I thought were closed off for ever are beginning to unlock. Madeleine is a formidable woman who confronts me when I'm arrogant or judgemental and deals candidly and humorously with my quirky inclinations. Unlike Terry Lyle, Madeleine accuses me of not being direct! Perhaps the French are more direct but I refuse to denigrate my own, we Irish are not so much two-faced as complex.

When I arrive at Ivor's, I curb my exuberance in case he thinks I'm slipping. Ivor makes tea - the ritual always amuses me. I'm talking away about this and that when I notice he's not saying much. "You're very quiet today, Ivor!" I say eventually.

"Sorry, Piers…I'm a little distracted. I've been doing a lot of thinking lately and I've decided to go home."

"When are you going," I ask.

"In a few weeks. Thought you might come with me. It won't cost you anything…I'll be taking the ferry!"

"Now is not a good time for me," I say, sparing him my reasons for not wanting to go home. "Besides, I've met someone."

"Oh! Tell me!"

After telling him about Madeleine, I'm reminded of what she said about putting my life on hold. "If you're taking the car, you might bring back some things…records and CDs mainly."

"Yeah, no problem."

"I'll give you a list of what I want. You'll find them easily enough… all the boxes are labelled.

"Maybe I should take the van," he quips. "Are you sure you won't come with me?" He grins. "I need to fix things with Mam, Piers, I gave her a hard time!"

"Well, that went both ways…she was never the easiest…"

"She wasn't the worst either, Piers! You should hear the horror stories in AA. I think she was harder on you though!"

"Well, no use dwelling on it now," I say, suddenly realising that I don't want to run her down anymore.

"Sorry…don't mean to rake things up."

"You're not…I've put all that behind me."

Ivor drinks his tea looking rather pensive. Then he looks at me and says, "I'm going to tell her about Oliver!"

"Oh! Right."

"Don't you think that's a good idea?"

"Yes… but…"

"But what, Piers?"

"Well, it might be better to establish contact first… she might be upset… that you don't see him, I mean."

"I have seen him, Piers!"

"That's great, Ivor!"

"I told Gillian I was thinking of writing to him. She thought it was a good idea… he's been asking questions seemingly. I wrote a short letter saying who I was and that I'd like to meet him."

"And?"

"We met! We went for a burger. He was very shy…it was a bit awkward. I told him a little about myself, and what I did for a living. I told him about you living here now and that he had an aunt and a grandmother in Ireland. He told me nothing about himself. Then it was over! His stepdad came to collect him."

"But it's a start, Ivor."

"The good thing is, he wants to see me again."

I think now of what Evelyn said about things finally going right for us and I hope to god it's true.

* * *

Jack called, all excited: two TV companies are interested in the Tibby Titmouse story and The Lost Fox specifically. "The English Company is offering more money...I'd go with them, if I were you," Jack advised. I was less enthusiastic, however; when I agreed to publish the stories, I thought that would be the end of the matter, I never envisaged any further financial rewards.

"I'll think about it!" I said, feeling a bit put out.

"What's there to think about?" Jack said annoyed. "That money would free you to concentrate on your writing. You can't sit on this one, Piers. Get back to me...sooner than later!"

I considered the matter carefully and even though I felt guilty about further gain from Rosie's stories, I had to admit Jack had a point. I took his advice and went with the English Company.

Ivor was delighted when I told him; he'd been worrying about me. I think Ivor is a worrier full stop. "When did you start writing children's stories, Piers," he asked.

"I don't Ivor! They were stories I wrote...I mean they were stories I used to tell Rosie. It all happened by accident. Catriona got me to print them up one time and they were sent to Jack by mistake.

"It's a sign, Piers!"

"A sign of what, Ivor?" I asked

"A sign that the stories were meant to be...that everything will be okay!'

* * *

Since leaving Wilson & Lyle, I've never been as busy! I've taken on another weekly column, book and poetry reviews mainly. Madeleine calls this work, 'Un travail alimentaire.'

Madeleine stayed with me for a few weeks when the London/Nantes project finished but is now back in France. Ivor didn't get to meet her but I assured him he'd meet her soon.

Rosie's and Helen's anniversary didn't cause me the anguish it used to. I marked the day in my own special way, including my grandmother although she died in May. Nan gave great credence to Samhain.

Out of the blue, Andrea called asking if she could call around. I was uncomfortable at the idea of her coming to the apartment, so I suggested we meet at the 'The Coffee Spoon' in Earls Court instead. Andrea breezed in, looking fabulous as always in her well-cut clothes. She seemed in good spirits, hugging and calling me darling. However, the mask was soon to fall.

"I'm truly sorry about the way Terry treated you, Piers…"

"Water under the bridge now, Andrea. I had given him my notice, remember!"

"Yes, but you don't understand, Piers… he acted that way because he was jealous of you."

"Of me? What had he to be jealous about?"

"Me!" She said, ignoring my astonishment. "Terry knew we talked about things…he was furious I told you about wanting children. Apart from my sisters, I never spoke about it to anyone. You see, Piers, Terry is the one who can't have children. He wouldn't believe that I hadn't told you that."

"So why are you telling me now, Andrea? What has any of this got to do with me?" I asked feeling irked.

"He was afraid I'd leave him… leave him for you, that is."

"What gave him that idea?" I said but then I suddenly remembered the lunch. "Was it because I was at the house that Saturday when he was away?"

"No, Piers, that had nothing to do with it." Andrea bent her head and sighed, then lifting her eyes, she continued, "It's complicated. I'm not getting any younger! Adoption was never an option. Terry is too chauvinistic! The Lyle heritage and all that. He feared we'd be stuck with a dullard, or worse, a psychopath. He doesn't buy the nurture versus nature viewpoint. He believes genetic compatibility is important… he says we don't understand the complexity of our brains. Oh, enough of this…I'm only trying to explain why he acted so unfairly to you. Terry can be difficult if he feels crossed. He was ruthless with the Wilsons, you know…forced them out completely."

Carl had mentioned something about the takeover not being too harmonious. Anyway, it had nothing to do with me now and I didn't want to be dragged into anything. "You shouldn't worry about me, Andrea, I'm doing fine!"

"Well, I'm not really...I just needed someone to talk to. You see, I'm planning on leaving him!"

"It can't be that bad, surely, Andrea. You love him, don't you? Maybe things will work out!"

"I do...I mean I did! But I've come to know that Terry Lyle doesn't care a farthing how I feel. He thinks by buying me expensive gifts I'll be satisfied... at least he thought that before I met you."

"Don't be rash, Andrea...he might come around about adoption."

"Well, that's just it...I've given up on that idea. I'm going to have my own children and we'll see how he likes that."

"Have you met someone?"

Andrea laughed hysterically, and then burst into tears. I glanced around at the other customers but then remembered myself in the Long Valley. I handed her a serviette but she continued to wipe away the tears with her fingertips. "First things first, darling... first I have to leave him!" She said half laughing, half crying. I thought this woman had everything, now here she was, as vulnerable as the rest of us.

"Andrea, if you need to talk, I'm willing to listen...any time."

"I knew I could count on you, Piers," she smiled. She pulled herself together somewhat then. I asked if she'd like another coffee or perhaps something to eat.

"No thank you, Piers. I must leave shortly...have a few things to do." She looked at me then with a worried expression and said, "That Saturday we had lunch...I felt so bad... I knew what he was up to. I told him to be upfront with you. You know he accused me of caring more about you than about him. I was going to tell you! I was a coward really."

"It wasn't your place to tell me, Andrea. Terry had every right..."

"Yeah! Terry and his rights!"

To change the subject, I told her I was planning on going to France but she already knew: women tell each other quite a lot it seems.

"I'm going to Salzburg for Christmas...on my own."

"Salzburg...at least you'll have Mozart there," I said to encourage her.

"Yes, you're right! I'll ask Johanna to book something," she said cheering up.

I walked her to her car where she kissed me on the cheek before sliding her lithe body onto the plush leather seat.

"You know where to find me!" I said closing the car door. "Take your time…don't do anything rash!"

She rolled down the window and said, "I knew you were a sweet one," and blew me a kiss.

* * *

Shadows that have haunted me for so long are beginning to disappear. To my family however, I will always be the vulnerable one, the one who has had a breakdown. Things I do and say are somehow made lesser - even with Evelyn. Ivor cares deeply for me, I know, but he acts now like an older brother. I am aware that I am flawed, perhaps may always be so, with moods that swing from high ecstatic to low melancholy; but like Pandora, I have something to hold on to, despite the negative bird on my shoulder that says hope can be a dangerous thing. That vestige of hope, however, lies outside my family. I believe Toby Holland sees me as he always has and I hope that Claire Riley would too. I don't know about Ó Buachalla – there has been no communication. Perhaps our relationship was more a meeting of minds than a friendship.

One never knows what people may enter our lives and effect change, Madeleine Thierry sees me for what I am now, the *before* is only what I reveal. Madeleine is happy in her skin, (one of her own expressions). She is tough and yet so gentle. Most importantly, she is not perturbed by my shaky past and has tapped into an aspect of me I never knew existed: a light heartedness that draws on a capacity to laugh at myself.

Madeleine says she misses me! We talk regularly on the phone and write letters to improve her English and my French. She provides such details about her mother, Marylene, father Antoin, and brother, Daniel, I feel I already know them. From her descriptions, I visualize her walks along the River Sarthe and in the woods with faithful Sylevebarbe.

* * *

Vladimir Ashkenazy's Mozart Piano Concerto is playing on my new turntable that can convert my vinyl to computer, USB or MP3. I am improving but still need only look at the cover of Mario Escudero for an onslaught of chest-tightening emotion! Music is interwoven with so many aspects of my life.

Madeleine asked why I don't listen more to Wagner seeing that I profess to liking him so much, but how can I explain. Madeleine never listens to Wagner: she's a little influenced by the negative aspects much espoused by the French: they don't forget Meyerbeer. I explained to her that even though Wagner was influenced by Meyerbeer, they had quite different ideas on music and especially opera. Wagner blamed Meyerbeer for the failure of his opera, Rienzi, in Berlin. Wagner disliked Meyerbeer because he made no effort to help him when he and Minna were practically starving in Paris. It had nothing to do with him being Jewish. Madeleine thinks I'm blinkered. The most stupid thing Wagner ever did, in my opinion, was write that pamphlet on Jewish music.

It is not important that Madeleine and I have different tastes. She is all for Berlioz, Bizet, Fauré, Ravel and so on: funny how self-promoting the French are! However, I'm delighted she has introduced me to artists like Jean Ferrat, Serge Reggieni and George Brassens. She knows I like Brel but I never listen to him when she is around.

Madeleine once asked why I don't listen to new recordings or contemporary music. It was a good question. I guess I was stuck emotionally too with music – with my father's collection. It was always the piece of music rather than the player that mattered: unfair to the artists I know! Catriona too often asked if I'd heard of such and such a singer or musician, but the questions never sank in.

I am aware that I'm thinking of Catriona and Madeleine at the same time - Nan would be proud of me; she'd be happy too that I remember her now without falling to pieces. Thinking of Nan brings other things to mind and for once I allow myself to be homesick: I miss the Waterford landscape; the lilting Cork accents; the new Echo Boys from far flung places; the City Library. I miss my sandwich in the Long Valley; I miss the Corner House; but most of all, I miss the River Lee like a severed arm.

The philosophy of living in the moment I find hard to grasp. My life experiences are woven into the fabric of memory, and the paths, thorny or otherwise, that I have taken have led me to be what I am. The fragrance of a flower or the humming of a bee can evoke powerful memories for me and I draw on those memories for my work. I guess the key is not to dwell too much on the past.

Consciously I try not to think of her: images and thoughts are quickly dispelled; she exists in a veiled recess somewhere in my brain. Dreams, however, escape such regulation and every now and then I am reminded of when I first made love to her on that Saturday afternoon, of our swim in Youghal, of her hair like fire in the sunlight and of the night she came to me on her birthday.

About the Author

Mary Jane Butler lives in Midleton Co. Cork. Her poems have been published in various anthologies. She has had two stories published in the Cork Library and Arts Service Bealtaine Short Story Competition in 2006 and 2007. She was selected to be part of the Sense of Ireland Literary tour to Nantes, France in 1996 and had poems published in the associated French Literary Journal, Signes no 20 Special Issue on Ireland.

Lightning Source UK Ltd.
Milton Keynes UK
UKHW010806160921
390678UK00006B/835